Sophie

You may need to consider this an early Birthday present! Hope you enjoy it?!

Love Always,

Neil x

Chapter One

Above them the sky was still a dull, turbulent grey despite the sudden summer storm having delivered most of its payload over the previous few hours. It had been torrential, tropical almost in its intensity, leaving the street around them slick with unlikely sediment, grit and refuse. Though somewhat cleaner due to it's dousing, the South London street still looked unkempt and neglected.

Tris held his face up to smell the air hoping that he could clear his nose of the stench in which they sat, whilst trying at the same time not to draw any attention to them from the dozens of policemen gathered at the other end of the street.

Tris's companion looked at him quizzically as he once more tried to find a comfortable position in which to continue their vigil. The last hour had flown by with the arrival of the police and the ensuing chaos which inevitably results from too many people not knowing what they're supposed to do, but the many hours they'd hidden there prior to that were beginning to weigh heavily on them. Such a long period of in-action followed by such explosive violence had left them both drained.

As they huddled down amidst the filth, they could both hear the latest in a long series of sirens approaching the site of their most recent encounter with death.

'Sirens! Always sirens! What is it with sirens and these people?'

'Garf, shhh!'

*

Inside the Jag there was an intense silence engineered by two men concentrating hard on what they were doing. One was driving with the appearance of practised ease, despite the fact it had taken a lot of training and experience to be able to drive safely at such high speeds in an urban environment. The other was occupied in clearing his mind in an attempt to attain the calm and clarity necessary to confront the crime scene awaiting him. Both were comfortable with such silences...after all, they were both professionals.

The unmarked police Jaguar drew up to the curb with a screech as the driver broke hard, pulling up behind a very new, shiny silver Mercedes Benz which had obviously been parked in a hurry, if the way it was caught up against the curb was anything to go by. Looking out of the passenger side window Stands could see little past all the blue uniforms crowding around the front of an old derelict cinema.

The older of the two men puffed out his cheeks. 'This is supposed to be a low-key response. What the hell are all these uniforms doing here?'

'Sorry Sir, but we weren't the first to receive the call.'

Outside the car, Metropolitan Police Constables were milling around outside the front doors of the decrepit remains of the old Odeon Cinema on Forrester Street. Having secured a perimeter around the building, and with no further orders they were standing around looking like a flock of lost sheep.

Leaning out of the passenger side window Stands called the nearest police officer over. 'Who's in charge here?'

The constable ducked down in order to study the two men in the car briefly before answering. The man at the wheel looked to be mid to late thirties, but in good shape by the looks of it, and good looking in a serious kind of way.

Whilst the older man sat in the seat looking up at him had the impatient authority of a man used to getting his own way. Looking at the car again before he answered the young constable swallowed nervously before glancing over at the driver and back again.

'I'm not sure Sir. Sorry Sir, but can I see some ID.'

Both the men in the car reached inside jacket pockets and withdrew standard police issue ID wallets and flipped them open for the constable to see. 'I'm D.I. Stands, and this is D.S. Waves.'

The constable blinked, then smiled.

Stands knew exactly where this was going. He hadn't given it any thought when he'd interviewed the Sergeant, and it wasn't until he'd become aware of the quiet grins and guarded chuckles that he'd realised what his colleagues were finding so amusing. Stands and Waves. Well it couldn't be helped, so he'd dealt with it in the same way ever since. Though right now it really wasn't helping him keep his focus.

'Before you even think about commenting on our names think very carefully about who you're talking to constable.' The Inspectors tone brooked no room for a humorous response.

'No Sir, I mean yes Sir.' Gulped the young constable. 'It would appear you're the ranking officer Detective Inspector.'

Looking around Stands could see quite a crowd of gawkers and curious bystanders building up on the pavement behind the line of policemen, craning their necks trying to see what was going on.

'In that case, tell me what the hell's going on here. This is supposed to be a crime scene, get all those constables away from the building and make sure no one contaminates the area, and for gods sake get a few of the men to move all those people away. Take names and contact details, statements where necessary and disperse the rest.'

Turning to the driver Stands raised his eyebrows in resignation to the vagaries of low ranking stupidity. 'Waves, can you please try and take control of the situation here before I have to get out of this bloody car and start screaming at people.'

'Yes Sir!' Sergeant Waves could tell by his boss's face that he wasn't joking and hid his smile as he pushed open the drivers side door.

'And Daniel...'

'Yes Sir?'

'This could be serious. Remember procedure. Get the SOCO and forensic boys down here pronto!'

'Yes Sir.' Getting out of the car, Waves once again thanked his lucky stars that he was in a position where he could avoid taking the blame for the inadequacies of the average boy in blue.

*

He'd watched the arrival of the unmarked police car with interest, and was well aware of the way the Met was structured. The arrival of SCD Officers always put an interesting spin on any response the police had to events that he and his companion were involved with. The Specialist Crime Directorate had far reaching authority, and a way of dealing with things that was far too efficient for Tris's liking.

The end of the street was crammed with police cars. Lights flashing, doors slamming, and men running backwards and forwards with no obvious intent. From their vantage point down the street towards the tube station the two hidden observers were quietly taking bets as to whether anyone up the road had a clue as to what was really going on, let alone as to what had actually happened inside the abandoned cinema.

'Tris, do you think we should perhaps be making ourselves scarce?'

'Patience Garf, I just want to see what they're up to, and possibly find out who's in charge.'

Just as Stands and Waves had walked inside the main doors of the cinema the Inspector was once again accosted by a young constable wanting to know what to do.

'Right now young man you can make sure that no one else asks me any more stupid questions. Now get everyone out of here and keep a perimeter of men around the building. Make sure no one but the crime scene technicians get in or out without my say so.'

'Yes Sir! Right away Sir!' With that the constable hurried off with an appearance of purpose which would hopefully hold sway amidst the general air of confusion.

'Waves, please, for the love of Christ, can you sort these amateurs out while I take a look at the crime scene. It's bad enough working on second hand information without having to explain the job to these jokers.'

Waves looked down at the floor briefly before squaring his shoulders and striding towards the door through which they'd just come.

'Oh, and Waves!'

'Yes Sir?'

'Can you find out who found the bodies and reported it in.'

Stands followed his subordinate with his eyes for a second before he too looked at the floor. Sighing he straightened his back, and with a resigned shrug walked decisively forward into the dim interior of the old building.

Inside there wasn't much left that could distinguish the buildings use other than its rather obvious layout. This was partially due to the state of the roof; a succession of irregular holes let in glimpses of ragged grey clouds which were slowly breaking up, but still succeeding in obscuring the blue sky above. Luckily the rain had stopped hours before, but that still meant that the Inspector was left hopping from side to side of the aisle left by the old, rotting velvet covered seats in an attempt to avoid the greasy looking puddles which had formed in the main aisle of the cinema.

It really was an old one, the kind where you bought your ticket from a booth facing the street and then walked in to the huge space containing the only screen the cinema possessed. Stands could remember coming to such places himself when he was a kid, paying for the Saturday matinee and being thrilled by the cartoons or whatever else was showing before the main feature started.

Stands had a vague idea of what he might be about to confront, and so took some little comfort from these recollections of those halcyon days of his youth. If only he could go back right now, rather than face what he was all too afraid he was about to see.

The holes in the ceiling, though letting in the elements, weren't big enough to admit enough light for the cinema to live in anything but a state of perpetual gloom. Looking ahead all he could see in the shadows around the base of the raised stage area, supporting what was left of the cinema's screen, were heaps and mounds that suggested something unceremoniously dumped on the ground. Stands had seen more than his fair share of dead bodies in his time and was familiar with the visual disorientation that often accompanied the viewing of things which men really were never meant to see, so he steeled himself as he picked his way closer to what was looking more and more like the site of a battle, rather than your standard multiple homicide. Stopping before he started stepping in blood, Stands squatted down to get a closer look at the nearest victim, briefly raising a hand to his mouth and nose as his proximity brought with it the metallic scent of blood mixed with the inevitably delightful mix of scents released by a body's insides being exposed to the outside.

The blood which had pooled around the body had a marbled look to it where the slowly congealing fluid didn't want to mix with the water that saturated most of the floor. The man's organs which had been exposed to the air had begun to take on the grey look of death, the lustre of life having diminished as the blood settled in the body and the elements started to get to work on braking down what was in the end just more dead organic matter, leaving the exposed flesh paler than it would have appeared in life

The man lying blindly looking up at the sky through the holes in the ceiling, wore an expensive looking suit, and an expression of pain and surprise, as did the other men who's faces he could see; obviously they had shared the same fate. The blood splattering and the gaping wounds in the victims all looked to be consistent with slash wounds inflicted using what must have been a long knife or even, Stands imagined, some kind of short sword. He reached down and gently lifted the dead man's arm. It moved easily, rigor mortis hadn't set in yet, so they must have met their end within the last few hours.

He stood slowly, surveying the scene as he rose slowly from his crouch, as he did he tried not to stare at the pink and grey bloody loops of intestines lying beside the corpse next to him. Looking away he noticed a large, cone shaped pile of ash amidst the bodies. The ash was a red brown at the base where it had soaked up some of the blood on which it had been piled. As he continued to stand he caught the glint of something partially hidden within the ash. He paused as he stooped over to get a closer look. It appeared to be some kind of misshapen, metal ring, but it didn't look like it was gold or silver, it was tarnished and soot blackened.

'*Strange.*' Thought Stands as he stood and surveyed the other bodies. Then he spotted the tip of a blade of some kind partially hidden beneath the body next to him. Looking around he spotted another, though it wasn't a knife exactly, more of a dagger in shape and length, and by the look of it the blade was clean, as was the one beneath the victim next to him. Stands stepped back and circled the area looking for more weapons.

He spotted five in all, and all but one appeared to

be unused. Stands unconsciously scratched his head. Four men had died brutally, each of them cut to ribbons by some kind of bladed weapon, but the only weapons that were present didn't appear to be the ones responsible for the wounds. The anonymous tipster had said there were six dead bodies inside the building, he could only see four, unless they were hidden somewhere else in the building. This was getting weirder by the minute. Five daggers, four dead bodies and a pile of ash with what looked like a ring in it. He just hoped the forensic team could make some sense of all this, otherwise he was going to have one hell of a time writing this one up.

It was then that he noticed something else. The body nearest the raised area upon which the old cinema screen had stood was in a heap and looked to be lying on top of something else. He stepped carefully around the area, edging his way towards the corpse. As he got closer Stands couldn't prevent a low groan escaping his throat when he saw a small, pale hand sticking out from beneath the man's body.

*

Outside Waves was just about in control of the situation. For some reason the severity of the initial report had brought in every available constable who didn't have anything better to do. Too many Indians and no chiefs had made the situation confused and initially hard to control. But now the perimeter had been set with police tapes, and all those constables who weren't actively involved with the scene had been sent packing with an admonition not to start gossiping about what may or may not of happened within the dilapidated old building.

Turning sharply at the sound of the doors swinging behind him, Waves was shocked to see the expression on the Inspector's face. He had become used to his mentors stoic façade revealing little about his personal feelings towards any case they had handled in the last two years of working together, but the pale look on Stands' face could not be interpreted in any other way than utter revulsion at what he'd obviously seen inside.

Looking around he spotted a constable leaning against a patrol car, his body language leaving the Sergeant in no doubt that he had nothing better to do.

'Constable! Yes you! Go and find the Inspector something to drink. Preferably water.'

'Right away Sir?'

'Yes, right now!'

He turned back to where he could see his boss standing absolutely rigid in the middle of the pavement outside the cinema's front doors. As Waves walked over Stands looked up and watched his subordinate approach, his expression slowly softening to a look of profound sadness.

'Sir, I've found out the order of events leading up to our arrival. An anonymous call was placed to the local station from a phone booth just down the street.'

They both looked round in the direction of the phone booth. It was about twenty metres away on the other side of the road and had been wrapped with Police tape and a small cordon put around it to stop anyone from contaminating any remaining evidence.

'The operator says that the caller wanted us to know that there were six dead bodies in the old Odeon Cinema on Forrester Street. The caller didn't identify himself, but was male, and well spoken, not a local lad, and anywhere between the ages of twenty-five and forty.'

'The operator got all that just from his voice?'

'She said he had a very distinctive way of speaking, quite cultured sounding, though the depth of his voice suggested maturity, and well…'

'What?'

'She said his voice was far too sexy to be very old.'

'And over forty is very old is it?'

Waves raised his eyebrows in appreciation of the Inspectors implication. He himself was on the cusp of forty, and he had a fair idea that Stands was somewhere in his mid to late fifties.

'Anyway, the operator got on to dispatch to get one of the cars in the area to get here A.S.A.P. to check it out. As it happens it was a mixed unit who picked up the call and turned up first. They parked up and reported that there was no sign of anyone or any disturbance, and no one obviously hanging around the building, just the abandoned Mercedes. Control told them to go in and take a look around, but to be on their guard and call in for back-up if they found anything.'

Just then a constable came over and handed the Inspector a small bottle of water. Stands nodded his thanks as Waves continued.

'They went in expecting to find nothing, hoax calls made by bored pranksters are apparently quite common in this area. Anyway, they did find something.'

Waves hitched a thumb over his shoulder. 'The WPC is in the back of one of the patrol cars over there waiting to be taken to the hospital for treatment for shock, and the PC who was with her is still pretty shaken up too.

I had trouble getting what little information I did out of him. He couldn't tell me exactly what they'd found, or how many bodies there were.'

'No, to be honest Waves, I doubt either of them had any real idea what they were looking at… not with all the shadows, the general lack of light, and with there being so much blood everywhere.'

'Do I really need to see this? If not I'll just send the SOCO team and the forensic pathologist in when they get here, which should be any minute.'

Stands visibly straightened as he looked Waves in the eye. 'Sorry Daniel, but I am going to need you to see this. It's a bad one… and I need you to get a feel for the scene, walk around it, get some first impressions. You won't be able to see what I need you to see just by looking at the photos.'

'Yes Sir.'

'You're not going to like it, but you'll understand what I mean when you see it. Go in with the Scene Of Crime Officers and I'll give you a little time to draw some of your own conclusions. Then I'll come in and we'll walk through it together…see if we can make some sense of this madness. In the mean time has anyone found any witnesses? Anyone around the area hear anything, or see anybody going in or coming out? Perhaps someone can tell us who owns the Mercedes? Does it belong to the victims inside?'

'Traffic division are looking into it, but with the time it's taking for them to get back to me I suspect the plates are stolen, which would tie in with the fact that someone's scorched the V.I.N. off. The spot where it should be by the corner of the windscreen appears to have been melted. Though to be honest I can't understand why the owner hasn't reported it missing. A CL Coupé like that's worth around a hundred grand new, and if it's not stolen what the hell is it doing here? It's a little conspicuous to say the least, and no one would just abandon a thing of beauty like that.'

'You'd be surprised Waves.' Stands said darkly.

'Yes Sir. Anyway, it's looking more and more likely that the car is involved in this somehow.'

'Agreed. What about the phone booth? Anyone been seen using it?' 'The constables have been asking all the bystanders if they've seen anything, but nothing so far. They seem to have been attracted by all the flashing lights. I've had the phone booth sealed until it can be swept for evidence. You never know, our mystery caller may have left some fingerprints or something.'

'Good. What about those two tramps over there, have they been questioned?'

Waves looked round to follow where Inspector Stands was pointing, towards what at first looked like just

13

another heap of black rubbish bags thrown against the side of a wall not twenty feet away from the phone booth on the other side of the street, but as Waves looked closer he began to make out the outline of what looked like two figures, huddled amidst the rubbish.

'Sorry, I hadn't spotted them, and I doubt anyone else has either, you've got sharp eyes Sir.'

'Well, don't just stand there man, go and question them. They may well have seen who used the phone if nothing else.'

Turning towards the duo Waves looked around before walking towards them. He caught the eye of one of the constables standing next to a patrol car and beckoned him over. The young constable trotted over. 'Just follow me, I want you to take notes while I question those two over there.' As he said it he pointed towards the two figures huddled amongst the pile of black bin bags.

'Who Sir?'

'Just follow me and don't interrupt. I'll do the talking, just take down the pertinent information.'

As he got closer Waves could see that it was almost definitely two men. Both were wearing dark hooded tops with the hoods up obscuring their faces. These tops were in turn worn underneath what looked like long leather coats, though the state of them left their origins a little murky; it was hard to tell with the rubbish bags piled around them. When he and the constable were merely metres away from them Waves began to detect the offensive odour of rancid rubbish. How long the bags had been there he couldn't tell, but they'd definitely been there long enough for whatever was inside them to start to rot.

Waves halted when he got to the edge of the pile of bags. 'Right you two, out of there! Get up! I want to talk to you.'

Both the men carefully got to their feet and waded through the rubbish bags to stand in front of Waves and the young constable stood next to him. Waves was a little surprised by the unlikely pair that stood before him. They were both soaking wet and must have been out when the storm had hit. Waves wondered idly, as he always did when confronted by the fringes of society, how people managed to live in such a way. Shaking his head he dispelled such trivial thoughts from his mind and concentrated on the two figures before him.

The one on the right was roughly six foot and slim built, with shaggy dark brown hair framing a face that could almost be described as pretty, though pretty as a concept didn't do justice to the almost aristocratic features marred only by the faintest hint of stubble around the jaw.

The other...well the other one was a different storey entirely. He was obviously older, but an exact age was difficult to guess when so little could be seen of his face. Long muddy brown hair spilled out from the confines of the dirty hood drawn up over his head, this together with a bushy beard the same colour as his hair meant that other than a strikingly large nose and dark brown eyes, everything else could only be guessed at.

However, the most obvious difference between the two was that the man with the beard could not have been more than five foot tall, with what could only be described as a heavy build.

'So where should I start with you two then?' Waves looked them both up and down with a frown. 'How long have you been hiding in there?'

The impassive expressions on both their faces didn't change as they exchanged an unreadable look before the taller of the two spoke up. 'We weren't hiding Sir, and we've not been here long, at least I don't think so. We don't have a watch between us Sir. We just sat down to have a rest and watch the show.'

'The show?'

'Well, begging your pardon Sir, but we don't often see this much action on the streets.'

Waves studied the tall young man before him. His voice suggested very little in the way of regional affiliation, and though his vocabulary was common sounding and deferential, almost to the point of taking the piss, his bearing was straight, proud even.

Waves frowned. 'Where are you two from, are you dossing around here?'

The shorter of the two piped up. 'We're not dossers Sir, just passing through. Always on the move we are. Not ones to spend too long in any one place if you get my meaning Sir!'

The voice was in contrast to that of his friend. Deep and gravely, the sort of voice that lends itself to movie trailer voice-overs, and sounded like its owner should be suffering from terminal lung cancer from the excessive number of cigarettes needed to sustain such deep tones.

'No, frankly I don't get your meaning. What are your names?'

'Tristan Sir,' said the tall one, and then gestured to his right, 'and this is my good friend Garfield.'

'Last names as well please.'

'Tristan Forest, Sir.'

'Garfield Stone, Sir.'

'And where do you both live? On the streets I presume.'

'Absolutely Sir…free spirits. Wandering the world free of all care and burden Sir.'

Waves glanced at the constable next to him and raised his eyebrows.

'OK, all I want to know from you two jokers is whether you've seen anything strange around here today? Anyone going in or out of the old cinema over there, or anyone using that phone booth in the last hour?'

Tristan and Garfield once again exchanged a brief look that was unreadable to Waves. Tristan then looked at Waves and then at the constable next to him and back.

'No Sir, we haven't seen anyone, or anything which we'd consider strange.'

'How about that car over there, the expensive looking Merc, did you see who left it there?'

They both shook their heads whilst boldly meeting his gaze. For some reason Waves found their stares disconcerting, enough so that he had no idea whether they were telling the truth or not, which was an unusual experience for him.

'OK then, but be on your way, I don't want to see you two loitering around here any longer. You understand me?'

Both Tristan and Garfield nodded once in unison. Strangely this action seemed almost dignified to Waves and brought to mind images of Japanese people bowing to each other in films. Shaking his head Waves turned to go, the young constable followed suit and strode off ahead of Waves towards the relative safety of his fellow police officers.

'Begging your pardon Sir!'

Waves looked round to see that the taller of the two had taken a step towards him as he'd moved away.

'What do you want?'

'Sorry Sir, but the older gentleman stood on his own by the cinema doors over there. Is he the man in charge?'

Waves looked back to where Inspector Stands was stood talking quietly on his mobile phone. Probably telling the SCD Assistant Commissioner the situation thought Waves as he turned back to the taller of the two tramps.

'Yes. That's Detective Inspector Stands. Why do you want to know?'

'No reason, just curious Sir.' And with that the unlikely pair about faced in unison, and strolled off down the street away from all the excitement.

Waves liked to think that he was a good judge of character, and a fair assessor of men. He had to be, it was part of the job, but all he could do was stand there, metaphorically scratching his head as he watched the two tramps disappear around the corner.

*

As they walked away they could both feel the Sergeants eyes on their backs. Neither wanted to give the man the satisfaction of looking back, though they were both itching to see the expression on his face, but it was time to get out of there and take stock of all that had happened. They were still wet through and stiff from sitting still for so long, but they'd rectify that when they got to where they were going. Besides, such minor discomforts were negligible compared to the endless catalogue of injuries they had both sustained over the years.

Once they were safely around the corner Garf looked round at his friend and grinned. 'Do you think we over did it Tris?'

Tris smiled back. 'I don't think so. The trick is not to give anyone any reason to think that you might be lying. Besides, neither of us did see anything that *we* would consider strange; Satanists, instantaneous human combustion and virgin sacrifices are all in a days work for us.'

Garf laughed ruefully, a noise that rumbled deep in his chest, and could easily be confused with the sound of faulty industrial machinery. 'True…but I'll never stop wishing that it wasn't.'

*

Just as Waves was about to tell the Inspector about the two strange tramps a couple of large white police vans appeared from around the corner and came to a halt in front of the police barriers outside the cinema. The drivers showed their ID to the constables blocking their path, who then waved them through the barriers so that they could pull up beside the doors to the building.

'About time they got here...you were about to say something Waves?'

'It doesn't matter Sir. I'd best go and let the SOCO and forensic teams know what the situation is, and I s'pose I'd better escort them in and take a look for myself. You'll be along shortly Sir?'

'Yes...and remember what I said. Don't concentrate too much on the bodies, we can examine them in photographs, and up close and personal in the morgue. Just try to get a feel for the scene itself...the situation, and try and have a good look around before they get the incident lamps up. Part of what I want you to see is what you can't see.'

Waves tilted his head slightly in silent query as he regarded his boss.

'Remember, whatever happened in there was violent, lethal…and very quick!'

*

It was around half an hour later that Waves emerged from the dim interior of the cinema. He opened the cinema doors and blinked in the light before looking around distractedly for his mentor.

Stands had been chain smoking whilst Waves had been studying the crime scene with the SOCO techs.
During this time Dr Watkin, the Chief Forensic Pathologist, had turned up and had been ushered into the building by Stands, as he puffed away on a Marlboro. Now, as he stood studying his obviously disturbed subordinate, he wished, once again, that he didn't have to share this kind of horror with others. Even though this was the case, he often had difficulty admitting to himself that this was the very reason that he was still single.

Stands dropped the smoking cigarette butt and

ground it resolutely underfoot before walking over to where Waves was still looking a little pale.

'So?'

'Not much to say Sir. I think I need a minute to try and process all that…' Gesturing back towards the cinema he didn't bother finishing his sentence. They both knew too well what the Sergeant had recently had to examine at close quarters.

'To be honest Sir, I'm kinda glad that most of the murders we deal with involve guns. They're a lot less messy!'

In a rare moment of empathy Stands reached out and placed his hand on the Sergeant's shoulder, squeezing it gently. 'I know what you mean Daniel.'

Lowering his arm Stands sighed. 'Well, lets go and have another look, and then maybe you can explain to me what the hell happened in there.'

*

About an hour later, after some rather queasy moments for both them, they were still none the wiser. However, the forensics team assured Stands that by the time the blood splatters had been mapped, the bodies thoroughly examined, and the mysterious pile of ash had been analysed they'd have a much better picture of what had happened.

Stands, shook his head ruefully. 'If they think they're going to understand this mess just like that, then they're sadly mistaken. This is an odd one. I'm going to get some fresh air.'

'Yes Sir, I'll be right behind you after I've had a quick word with Dr Watkin.'

*

Stands was outside waiting patiently when Waves came striding out looking a little more confident, but also a little bemused.

'Do they need me in there? Or can we head back and make a start on our initial report?'

'It's fine, Dr Watkin said they'd gather all the forensic evidence as soon as they've finished documenting the scene...which could take the rest of the day if you ask me. Once they're done here they'll head back, and then start the autopsies tomorrow. Dr Watkin asked if you'd want to attend?'

'We'd better, considering how little we know, and if we're there we can make sure nothing gets missed.'

Waves straightened his back, standing taller. 'Do you mind if I comment Sir?'

Stands raised his eyebrows quizzically. 'Sure, just make it relevant.'

'Well, I'm not sure what it is really, I don't know if you noticed, but the Doctor seemed almost excited by the time he'd finished a cursory examination of the scene. He then called someone on his mobile phone and...well, from what I overheard it sounded like he was describing the crime scene. Problem is I couldn't make out who he was talking to. It just seemed a little odd.'

The Inspector frowned and turned away from Waves with a thoughtful expression on his face. Who could the Chief Pathologist be calling with delicate information like that? Another Department, another Agency?

'Thanks, and no I didn't. I was a little preoccupied in there.' Stands turned away for a moment, his expression distant as he gave the matter some thought. 'I think this case could possibly get a bit complicated...politically, if you get my drift. It's our case at the moment, but I have a feeling that we may have to fight to keep hold of this one.'

Stands looked intently at Waves. 'Question is, do we want to keep hold of this one?'

Waves chuckled quietly. 'I've seen that look on

your face too many times. Besides, it happened on our patch, and I'd sure as hell like to know what happened in there.'

Smiling broadly Stands nodded. 'Stay alert and keep your ears open, feel free to comment whenever you feel the need... but don't trust anyone you don't already trust, OK'

With that Stands strode over to their unmarked car and waited for Waves, who regarded his boss's back before striding after him to the passenger side of the car. He unlocked and opened the door before walking round to the driver's door to get in himself.

Before swinging into the passenger seat Stands took a last quick look back at the cinema, his brow deeply furrowed by the lines of a frown that he wore far too often.

Chapter Two

Since leaving their smelly hiding place on Forrester Street Tris and Garf had covered a lot of distance, even though they'd doubled back more than once just to be sure they weren't being followed. It was easy for them to navigate London on foot, having lived there for so long. Having said that they were, more often than not, still amazed by how quickly it changed it's appearance, especially since the last war.

Walking down a small side street somewhere north of the river, the two friends made sure there was no one around before ducking down a filthy side alley thick with old rubbish and littered with the remains of antique shopping trolleys. Occasionally the pair would find more junk to fill what little space there was left just to deter others from using it, not that it really went anywhere. About a third of the way down a low arch on the right hand side held a small, very secure looking door made of dark, ancient wood bound with iron. If anyone had bothered to fight their way through the debris strewn alley they might have thought the door seemed somewhat out of place, especially in modern London. Strangely enough the door was in fact centuries older than the wall in which it was situated, or any of the buildings around it.

As soon as Garf got to the door he pulled a delicate iron key from inside his coat and inserted it into an almost invisible key hole set only a couple of feet above the ground. With a smooth twist the mechanism released more than just the physical lock. The door swung open easily, not a horror film creak in sight, testifying to the door being frequently used and well maintained.

Behind the door was an almost unnatural darkness that was undiminished by what little light there was in the alley.

Without a backward glance they both stooped and

walked through the opening, seemingly sucked in by the darkness inside the doorway. The door then closed itself behind them with a resolute click.

The two emerged moments later into the cellar of an old boarding house the doorway from the debris littered alley led into. They entered the room through a doorway the twin of the one through which they had first stepped. After waiting for the momentary disorientation always associated with stepping through such portals to pass, they then made their way quietly up the stairs leading to the reception area at the front of the boarding house.

Behind an old hotel style reception desk sat a purple tinged octogenarian. Shrouded in an old purple cardigan and purple rinsed hair it was difficult to distinguish her from the old purple flock wallpaper behind her. As they both emerged from the doorway beneath the stairs leading to the cellar the old woman gave no more sign of alarm than to smile broadly at the pair. A smile that was warmly and gratefully returned. Gladys had given them the all clear.

Without a word they slipped up the stairs and headed for the top floor where the stairs ended in a plain white door. It was as modern looking as the small door they had entered through earlier was ancient. Tris having reached the top of the stairs first, due to longer legs, put his hand flat against a blank glass panel next to the door. The panel activated at his touch, a green bar of light moved down and then back up the glass plate. There was a moment's silence, a soft whirring noise and then a dull clunk as thick steel bolts retracted back into the steel door frame, the door then swung slowly inwards. Garf, having caught up, passed his friend and stepped through the door. This door also closed by itself after Tris had entered, though it was merely powered by terrestrial hydraulics, and automatically locked itself behind them.

The white steel door led into what constituted the entire top floor of the building. Apart from two bedrooms, a bathroom, and a kitchen, all of which were small and functional, the entire space was open plan. The main room was painted entirely white creating an atmosphere akin to an art gallery. Down lighters strategically spaced around the ceiling created an even light, which was enhanced minimally by the light coming in through steel meshed glass windows. Standing still in the centre of this space the duo could just about discern the hum coming from the electrified mesh within all the windows. Finally the two old friends looked at each other and smiled.

Garf snorted and slapped Tris on the back. 'If I don't get in a bath soon I'm going to choke on my own stink.'

With that the smaller of the two hopped towards the bathroom door whilst removing the beggars clothes they'd been wearing to disguise themselves, discarding them on the floor as he went. Tris looked over in amusement as the diminutive figure huffed and puffed his way to the bathroom and then noisily closed the bathroom door behind him.

Despite his apparent youth, Tris was often given over to mental reflection and inner examination, a fact which had always made his more scholarly endeavours, such as his study of meditation, that much easier. And after the day he'd had he really felt the need to relax without thinking about anything. He found it a simple task to slip into the kind of mental meditative state that masters of the art took their whole lives perfecting. He paid no mind to the thought that it had actually taken him the equivalent of a human lifetime to perfect it. Such thoughts and comparisons were considered unworthy of contemplation by a race so long lived.

As his mind relaxed and withdrew to its centre, his eyes took in everything around him equally, from the motes of dust spinning lazily through the air currents created by the spot lights above, to the many ancient artefacts and the more modern furniture which occupied the room. The space was unique despite its often-vaunted aesthetic ideal, if for no other reason than many of the objects and works of art dotted around the room would not have been recognised or easily valued by any art expert or historian.

*

So it was that Garf found him, over half an hour later, still stood motionless in the centre of the room. His posture suggested both extreme relaxation, and an odd alertness that defied the very slow rhythm of his chest, as he breathed at an unnaturally slow rate that would have alarmed most doctors.

Having enjoyed his bath, and finally feeling relaxed for the first time in days, Garf was feeling in a playful mood, when he saw Tris standing in the same spot as when he'd left him he couldn't help himself. Naked, but for a fluffy white towel, he eased himself onto the balls of his feet and leapt at his friends back with every intention of giving him a good beating.

As soon as Garf was airborne Tris seemed to disappear as he went from immobility to full flight in the space of a heartbeat. Seizing Garf's wrist in mid air, Tris twisted his body and sent his friend flying safely into one of their overstuffed sofas, rather than the wall where his trajectory would have terminated without Tris there to interrupt it. Despite being virtually upside down with his face sandwiched between two cushions Garf still managed to laugh heartily as he pulled himself slowly free.

'One day I'm going to catch you out!'

'Never Garf, you possess all the stealth of an elephant. The day you sneak up on me is the day I cut my own ears off!'

'It still amazes me how you manage to do that. I was sure when I leapt that you weren't in your body…I thought I could tell.'

'Now that's not altogether true Garf, but I was

projecting. The trick is to leave a little bit of yourself as a caretaker, just to make sure everything's still OK when you get back from your wanderings.'

'I still don't understand how your race does that. Telepathy is one thing, but pushing yourself out like that…I'm not so sure you weren't just waiting for me.'

'Just face it Garfan, my *old* friend, you're never going to catch me out like that.'

The look on Garf's face was darkening by the second.

'And don't you dare sulk because of it. Our skills are different, we are different races after all, we compliment each other.'

With that Garfan smiled ruefully. 'That we do Tristellis, that we do.'

Leaving Garf now sitting on the edge of the sofa, Tris walked slowly over to the bathroom door in order to start his transformation from dirty beggar to wealthy man about town. With his hand on the doorframe Tris looked back at Garf. 'I think we should talk to Elarris, we need to go and see the Elders.' He smiled and then went in to the bathroom and closed the door behind him.

Garfan shook his head slowly, and muttered under his breath. 'That boy is going to be the death of me.'

*

Around an hour later, it was two rather different looking gentlemen who exited the boarding house, through the front door this time, and set off towards Regents Park at a brisk walk. Despite Garfan's lack of stature he looked extremely dapper in a bespoke Saville Row suit, dark charcoal grey wool, double vented, but still casual looking due to its comfortable cut, and an accompanying black silk shirt. Even Garfan's hair and beard were immaculate and neatly coiffed.

Meanwhile the more fashionable Tristellis was sporting a dark brown pinstripe Paul Smith suit, finished with a casual cream shirt and Prada boots. His shaggy hair was brushed back behind his ears, which appeared the same as anyone else's, one of the advantages of being a half human hybrid, an advantage that Tris had resented in his youth, but now thought of as a godsend, and though pure bloods were occasionally prone to such snobbery, none would dare insult Tristellis to his face.

A casual observer would never have been able to guess how the pair had looked only a couple of hours previously. Nor would they have guessed at the weaponry the pair routinely managed to carry undetected under such urbane apparel, the rest of their street gear stowed safely in the stylish brown leather holdalls they were both carrying.

*

At about the same time that D.I. Stands was leaving the crime scene the two friends were just approaching their London home. Now that they were wearing their normal clothes you wouldn't have looked at them twice, unless it was to admire their obviously expensive attire, and the grace with which they both strode down the street.

During the somewhat circuitous journey they always had to make in their transition from one identity to another, the two of them had spoken little. Both lost in their own thoughts, both compulsively, though they would both have denied it, replaying the recent confrontation with the enemy. A battle that had been as startling as it had been sudden and unexpected.

In approaching the turn into St Marks Square, they both became more alert despite the fact that they had been residents in the area for the past one hundred and eighty years, since it had first been built in fact. The pair were always on guard at this point, until they were sure that they hadn't been followed and that their home was safe. They continued up the street until they reached the house, perceptibly slowing as they entered the driveway.

Walking slowly they surveyed the exterior of the house before going up the front steps to the impressive front door. On opening it they both waited for a moment before stepping slowly inside. After so many years of training and innumerable battles in the continuous war they waged, their homecoming ritual had become instinctive. Each of them having his specific task, each following a path which took neither of them far enough away from the other that should the worst happen they could not instantly leap to the others aid. If they'd had guns they would have looked very similar to a pair of FBI agents sweeping a property for felons. Though if this had been the case the FBI agents would probably have considered them to be the bad guys.

*

They found nothing untoward, and as the pair slowly relaxed, so did the atmosphere of the house. When they had first entered the air had been palpably tense, watchful, aware even.

This sense of watchfulness continued even as it seemed to relax around them, as though the building was in fact a big dog, ever alert, but passive when the masters were home. Having deactivated all the alarms and checked the computerised system activation log for activity, they could, at last, relax.

The house could so easily have been a mausoleum. The huge Regency property was within spitting distance of London Zoo and had more rooms than the pair needed, or used, but as they had overseen the design of the building, and also its construction, it meant that they had been able to make some rather extraordinary modifications to the original design. This left them with an utterly unique property holding a number of surprises for the unwary burglar. The full extent of these surprises could only be determined by a very sharp-eyed surveyor, and one of those hadn't been near the building since it was in the process of being built. Though over the last one hundred and eighty years since its completion there had been a number of burglars, one of whom had even made it out alive, though he did leave without his sanity.

The exterior was unremarkable in its similarity to every other large Regency town house in the area. White pillars holding up the stucco porch, one that could easily shelter a dozen people, this being just the first period feature designed to make any guest feel small, and possibly poor by comparison. The front doors themselves were deceptive and also unique, looking much like all the others in the street, which were all black painted wood with large etched, frosted panes of glass giving light, but no view into the interior.

Only these doors were not wood, but bullet resistant high tensile steel, with cleverly disguised bullet resistant glass, each pane a laminated two centimetres thick. A reasonably recent addition since such technology had only just become privately available.

It was an investment Tristellis was rather pleased with, the doors were so well balanced that they swung easily on their hinges at the slightest push, but would resist all but a shaped charge or a direct hit by a mortar shell.

Inside the front doors were the main stairs. There were two other staircases, one of which was the servant's staircase, and a hidden third staircase, which was a result of one of their many special modifications. The building was in fact teeming with odd doors that didn't open and blank looking bits of wall that did. All of which was hidden behind the façade of a normal Regency town house in one of the more affluent areas of London. Though their neighbours were aware that the house had belonged to the wealthy Forest family for almost two centuries, none knew that the same family member had been in residence all that time.

Tris had last decorated in the early nineties. The walls were all either soft off-white shades or, like the main bathroom which was a tasteful Clarin's green, various putty colours designed to draw attention to the architectural details and the many works of art hanging on the walls. Moving through the house you could see that much of the interior was furnished with the original pieces that Tristellis and Garfan had chosen when they had first moved into their newly completed home, and was thus worth quite literally a fortune, despite the fact it was all well used.

This didn't mean that they hadn't moved with the times and embraced the changing styles of the decades. In fact the whole house was an eclectic mix of original pieces from all the years through which they had lived there. Regency had given over to Edwardian, Edwardian to Victorian, Victorian to Art Nouveau, to Art Deco and onward.

For example, in the lounge a piece by Chippendale was complimented by a piece by Macintosh, and another by Eileen Grey. In the study there were Eames loungers and Victorian bureaus.

The same eclectic vision had influenced their choices in art, Pre-Raphaelite bumped shoulders with Sisley and Cezanne, whilst Warhol fought it out with Banksy in the main lounge. Any antiques dealer, designer furniture freak or art collector would have given their right arm to have wandered through this labyrinth of treasures, did they but know it was there.

But for all this love of art and design, which Tristellis was mostly responsible for, the two of them invariably spent most of their time together in the basement kitchen, probably the most modern, utilitarian room in the house. Having been the centre point for servant's activities in all the other Regency houses, here it

31

was on the same scale, a massive open-plan room with a flagstone floor. But for all its size it was definitely the most cosy and comfortable room in the house.

Around the walls were a number of overstuffed sofas and arm chairs, whilst a huge scrub-top farmhouse style table with old, mismatched wooden dining chairs dominated the centre of the room, though for most of the time it was unrecognisable under an accumulation of abandoned daily papers, mugs, plates and bowls. Despite owning a dishwasher Tristellis and Garfan had never mastered the art of using crockery, running it quickly under a tap and then putting it straight into the dishwasher in order to avoid such debris piling up.

It was to a table in just this state that they retired, drained by the battle earlier that day, and the ducking and diving required to get them back to the house without being followed. Tris reached the bottom of the stairs leading into the kitchen and stopped, exhausted he held on to the banister as Garfan came down behind him.

'Tris, move your butt! Sit down and let me put the kettle on.' He gripped his friend's arm and steered him to a chair at the head of the table. 'Now, what's it to be? Tea or coffee?'

Tris had sunk into the chair with quiet relief. Now, not having to worry about sustaining any vestige of alertness, he just looked at Garf blankly.

Garfan snorted and smiled. 'Coffee it is then. You need to get a grip Tris. We need to talk about what happened today, and right now you're fit for little more than your bed.'

Not wanting his old friend and sparing partner to get the upper hand Tris pulled himself up in his chair and rubbed his face. 'I'm fine. I'm just a little tired, it's not just the action earlier, but contacting Elarris on top of that really took it out of me…and if you're going to make coffee, for the love of God, don't use that instant shit. I want real coffee.'

Garfan put the kettle down and grumbled as he put

down the jar he'd just retrieved from the work surface.Looking round at Tris he scowled as he looked up at the wall mounted cupboards.

'If you want real coffee, you're going to have to get the espresso pot down. You know damn well I can't reach it up there, and I'm not climbing up there on a chair for your amusement!'

Tris laughed and hauled himself out of his chair. 'We can't have you tarnishing your dignity just for me now can we.' He reached up and opened the cupboard just as the kettle came to a boil and started to whistle on the gas hob.

Garfan hustled over to the hob and turned off the gas before pushing the kettle on to one of the back rings. 'We won't be needing this then. Here, give me that and sit down before you fall down.'

He took the aluminium espresso pot from his friend's visibly shaking hand and gently pushed him back down into the chair he'd only just vacated. 'You need more than just coffee. Food is what you need, and we have just the thing, one of my patented all day breakfasts will sort you out a treat.'

Tris grinned his thanks and slumped once more into the chair as Garfan busied himself in making coffee and creating the sort of grease laden, artery withering all day breakfast that one can only find in the greatest greasy spoons in the land.

*

Half an hour later Tris was looking somewhat restored having had two cups of strong coffee. His countenance visibly brightened as a massive white plate laden with eggs, bacon, sausages, black pudding, fried bread and mushrooms, and a glistening heap of baked beans was placed before him. Tris smiled as Garfan sat opposite him with a plate piled even higher with food.

'You're never going to lose weight like that!'

Garf gave him a disdainful look and blew a raspberry. 'You need fattening up my boy, as for me…I'm in fine fettle, besides I'm hungry. Now eat up before it gets cold. Then we'll talk.'

Any kind of verbal sparing was quickly replaced by the kind of intense silence only ever experienced whilst eating. The scrape of knife on plate, the sound of coffee mug being replaced on table, lips smacking and the general background noises of food being truly appreciated, despite its lack of gourmet styling or pretension, were the only sounds to be heard as the pair wolfed down the meal Garfan had so lovingly prepared.

In a lot less time than it took to cook, Tristellis leant back in his chair and wiped the back of his hand across his mouth. With a deeply contented sigh he put down the now empty coffee mug which he'd been holding in his other hand and looked over at Garfan who was still engaged in making the mountain of food which had occupied his plate disappear.

He could tell without looking that Tris was watching him with an indulgent smile on his face. Choosing to ignore his friend's sometimes irritating, laconic superciliousness, he concentrated on his plate.

Having known each other for over four hundred years had understandably led to the pair being able to read each other like a book, so Tris didn't push his luck by trying to goad his old friend any further, but instead slowly pushed back his chair and busied himself with making more coffee, leaving Garfan to finish his meal in peace.

Chapter Three

'Right then,' Garfan said as he pushed his empty plate away and leant back contentedly in his chair. 'Now that I feel more like myself, lets discuss exactly what the hell happened out there today.'

As he'd been speaking Tris was just finishing loading the dishwasher. He smiled and handed Tris his plate. 'Thanks.'

'My pleasure Sir. Would Sir like a cup of tea to sup whilst we try and fathom the mysteries of the ancients?'

'I believe I would Jeeves, thank you.'

The pair of them often indulged in such mindless banter as a prelude to tackling those subjects which neither of them took any real pleasure in.

Putting the last plate in the dishwasher Tris flicked the door up with his foot to close it and put the kettle back on the hob. 'So?'

Garfan was stroking his beard thoughtfully. 'Well it all happened too damn fast didn't it. Lets try and look at this logically. There's obviously much more to these people than we first imagined.' Garf followed Tris with his eyes as his friend began to pace backwards and forwards as the kettle started to boil.

'OK…so we knew that someone was using the old cinema as a meeting point. Stumbled across them in fact when we'd actually been tracking something else.'

'Yeah, that's one of the things that's worrying me. We felt that presence and homed in on it, then conveniently got side tracked by those guys at the cinema. What was it we were tracking? We still don't know, though whoever or whatever it was is pretty damn powerful, it'd have to be to draw our attention all the way from this side of the river.'

'Yes I know, but lets stick to what we know for

sure. We tracked whatever it was to South London. Then we lost it when we sensed something weird nearer to us. I think I know what we were drawn to now, but lets move on. We got nearer to the old cinema, and it became pretty obvious that something was in there.'

'Garf, we both felt it, and to me it felt weird, but not so unlike others we've come across. You agreed with me at the time, remember?'

'You're right, but lets carry on shall we. So we hang around the cinema, and eventually five men come out, get into that expensive silver Mercedes, and that's when we lost them.'

Garfan looked up. 'Stop pacing will you, it's getting on my nerves. Sit down. It wasn't our fault we lost them. How the hell were we supposed to track them with no transport. It doesn't matter though. We knew they'd be back. Whenever freaks find somewhere where they feel reasonably safe to indulge their vices they always make the most of it until something happens to make them move on. Anyway, at that point we had the perfect opportunity to check out the building knowing that they weren't around, and lo and behold there's traces of candles and the scuffed remains of chalk drawings on the raised area at the back of the main room. Classic indicators of something dodgy going on.'

'We've encountered enough Satanists in our time to know damn well that's what they were, or at least appeared to be. Ever since that damn 'Satanic Bible' was published it's become even easier to identify them, even organised groups like those stupid fuckers in 'The Order of Nine Angels' aren't intelligent enough to ever consider doing things differently in order to not be so easily identifiable. They're as bad as Scientologists, both of them taken in by carnies. Why is it faith of any sort fails to give insight, it seems to just leave humans blind to the greater truths.'

Garfan cut in, 'Lets not get into a philosophical debate right now. We both know they're wrong. The thing is I'm beginning to think that we're wrong on that count as well as a few other things as well. But like I said we'll come back to that. So we know they'll be back and we stake the place out. The things we have to do!'

Tris laughed. 'You're getting too used to your creature comforts Garf…you're getting soft.'

'I don't remember you particularly enjoying sleeping rough for two days. Garbage sacks aren't the most comfortable of beds at the best of times. To be honest I'm surprised my sense of smell still works at all. Anyway, so we wait for them to come back in order to find out exactly who the hell they are so that we can decide how to play it, when they turn up again in the same car they disappeared in the first time. Only now they've got some young girl with them who doesn't look as though she's just along for the ride. How old do you think she was?'

Tris shook his head, his eyes closing briefly with regret. 'Difficult to tell, she can't have been more than seven or eight though.'

'OK, so there we are watching them go in, and we both know damn well that something rather repulsive is about to go down, so we have to act. Only we don't know a damn thing about these people, at least one of them is not what he appears to be. In that close proximity even I could feel it, it always leaves a nasty taste in the back of my mouth when I get that close to madness.'

'After all these years it still surprises me that you haven't hardened to this stuff. We deal with so much of this shit all the time, how can you stand to be so sensitive still?'

Garfan shrugged. 'Just because we have to do this doesn't mean that I have to like it, and so many times it's just humans being human, choosing to perpetrate the same old evil madness. They have all the choices, and so often they throw away everything that could make them great in pursuit of self-gratification. It will always sicken me Tris...when it ceases to I'll retire.'

'OK, I get your point, and I do agree with you. It's

just sometimes I think I'd go mad if I didn't shut my mind to it sometimes.'

'Your problem is that you're even more sensitive to it all than I am. So where were we?'

'About to charge in without knowing what we were letting ourselves in for.'

'Thanks, yes, knowing we had to get in there, but hesitating due to lack of intelligence.'

Tris raised an eyebrow at his terminology. 'And that's when we both felt the little girl die.' Tris closed his eyes as he said this, remembering the way he had felt the girls life force dissipate into the ether with no warning. He shook his head wearily, opening his eyes when he felt Garfan's hand on his.

'There was nothing we could have done to save her, it was so abrupt. We were both expecting to have at least ten minutes to play with while they conducted one of their stupid, pointless little psycho-dramas. The sick ones always like to draw it out, delay the finale as long as possible. It's no fun otherwise.'

'You're right, but it just came as such a shock. I felt her slip away, one minute she's being walked into that old shit hole, the next she's dead.'

'Then you just sprint in there with no warning. You were very nearly on your own there. Next time you do that I might just leave you to it.'

Garfan was serious, Tris could tell by the look on his face, the tightening of the muscles around his eyes, that he wasn't joking.

'I'm sorry Garf. I couldn't just stand there and let them get away with it. The only consolation I have is that it was quick, they didn't have the time to make her suffer in any way.'

'Its just the shock of it happening like that that threw me when I'd just convinced myself we had time to get into position and save her. I lost it, I'm sorry.'

Patting his hand Garf smiled. 'It's OK, I felt exactly the same, only you managed to move faster than I did.'

Tris grinned his thanks. 'So, I go belting in there, and it was almost as though they'd been expecting us. One of them was abusing the little girls dead body, and the others were drawn around them in a circle, only they were all facing out, and looking extremely alert.'

'Which is when I almost crashed into the back of you!'

'Yeah, almost…lucky for you I move fast, otherwise we might have been in trouble if we'd both ended up in a heap on the floor.'

'OK smart arse…so, we run into them and cut them down, which is when *it* happened.'

'Yeah, what the fuck was that. We've killed a thousand monsters and assorted nightmares, but that one went up like a fucking Roman Candle as soon as I cut him. It wasn't even a killing stroke, at least it wouldn't have been for any kind of normal creature. It was lucky for me he was the last, if he'd been the first I'd have been left wide open. It took me a moment to be able to move after it happened, I didn't know what the hell was going on'

Garfan was once again looking thoughtful, and as if unable to think without doing it, he was once again stroking his beard. Tris could see that he was mulling something over, he'd already said he had an idea as to what had happened, so Tris got up from the table to make tea. More coffee would be pointless. They'd definitely had enough of a caffeine boost.

He was pouring the kettle when Garfan cleared his throat with a distinctive sound a little like shifting rubble.

'I don't know what you're going to think of this, but looking at it logically I can only think of one explanation for what happened, it's pretty improbable, and I don't think you're going to like it.'

Tris poured milk into the teacups and carried them over to the table, placing one in front of Garfan before sitting and placing the other before himself. 'Well, I hate to admit it once more, but you're the logical one, I can never seem to make those connections the way you can.'

Garfan couldn't help but laugh out loud at the humble look on his friends face. He knew he was the thinker of the pair. Tris would always be the impetuous one, the doer, the lover, the fighter. Whilst he was the plodder, the rock on which his oldest friend often leant.

'OK. Here goes. I think we were set up. I think you're right to worry about whatever it was that drew us there in the first place, because whatever it was put us off the scent by placing those four men and that demon, or whatever he was, there to distract us. That was not a group of Satanists, that's just what they wanted us to think. You're right about being able to spot one a mile off, anyone who knows about such groups knows exactly what they do, they made it look as though they were cultists just to keep our attention on that building, knowing that if we thought they were Satanists we'd assume they'd be back. I should have noticed at the time that it was a little too perfect, it didn't click at the time that they'd actually used Aramaic in some of their scribblings.'

Garfan paused for a moment, his mind working faster than his mouth. 'Then when they did come back with the little girl it was a trap. That's why they killed her so quickly, in order to force our hand and not give us the opportunity to think it through. They wanted us to come straight in at them.'

'I still don't know who the hell they were, but I think they honestly thought they had a shot at taking us. They knew who we were and what it is that we do. They were there to kill us, and when it went sour that *thing* knew we'd try and get information out of him, so he sacrificed himself in order to keep us in the dark.'

He was trying to read Tris's expression as he finished what he was saying.

Tris started nodding. 'You're right, there was no surprise on their faces when we ran in there, and usually the sight of us charging in like that would be enough to surprise the Devil, but they were expecting us, not just anyone, but us. Shit! Who the fuck were they? How could they have known about us?'

'Well, if we follow the same dubious logic, then I would have to say that whatever we were tracking felt us and identified us. The sooner we talk to Elarris the happier I'm going to be. We're not going to be safe until we get to the bottom of this.'

It was Tris's turn to laugh. 'You've got me feeling like Dr Watson, but you're right. No matter how improbable the answer, if that's where the evidence leads then that's the most likely answer. We'll leave first thing tomorrow, though I think we're safe enough here for now. We kicked their arses after all. I'll go and call Avis, get them to deliver a car first thing…and after that I'm going out for a drink, I need to clear my head.'

'Tris, I don't think that's a good idea, we really have no idea what we're up against.'

'You worry too much, I'll be fine, but if it makes you feel any better I'll give Martin a ring. If I'm with him you know I won't get into any trouble.'

'What, just because he's more sensible than you? He may well be…but he's only human.'

'Yes, but he's one of us. He's fought side by side with us. Other than you and Garanth, there's no one I'd trust more at my back.'

'OK, just mind you do watch your back. If anything untoward happens I'll kick your arse myself.'

Garfan turned away as Tris took the stairs two at a time. He'd never approved of Tris's philandering. The Twentieth Century had seen it get steadily worse, culminating in the absolute excesses of the Sixties and Seventies. Then in the last decade something had happened to make things worse, and though that situation had come to a head, he wasn't convinced that Tris was over the worst of it.

He'd spoken to him about it, and could understand what drove him to seek momentary comfort where he could. It was just a shame that Tris refused to confront the personal demons that drove him to do it in the first place.

He looked up at the stairs when Tris's voice floated down from the entrance hall above.

'The car will be here at 8.30 tomorrow morning!'

*

Tris was on his way out the front door of the house in St Marks Square, when Daniel Waves was just about ready to sit down with a freshly microwaved curry, a can of beer, and the news just starting on the television.

The room in which he sat was comfortable though spartan. There was very little in the room that would reveal much about the man that called it home. He'd rented the bijou one bedroom flat years ago and had never got around to moving anywhere else. After all, what was the point. He'd been involved with, and had done things that had permanently changed the way he looked at the world and his place in it. Things that had revealed to him just how transient life really is, so why waste time trying to accumulate possessions that he couldn't take with him anyway. The other three rooms in the flat were just as sparse, though the contents of the kitchen would suggest that whoever did live there knew how to cook, as well as how to reheat ready meals.

Half an hour later the Chicken Dansak still lay untouched, unlike the now empty can of beer, another fast approaching the same state clutched tightly in Daniels hand. Leaning back heavily into the sofa, he was silent as the reporter on screen was finishing up his piece on the murders at the Cinema on Forrester Street with the usual conjecture about the abilities of the Met, and the freedom of information act. *What bollocks* thought Waves as he waved his now empty can of beer at the screen. What do you know?

'Nothing,' shouted Waves as he threw the can at the TV. He was all too well aware that he and his boss, and numerous others in different agencies, dealt with all kinds of shit that the greater public would never know about, for the simple reason that society as a whole just couldn't handle it.

Surging up from the sofa, he looked around for his mobile phone and swore in disgust before he made for the phone on the table next to the front door of his little flat. I've got to tell the boss about this.

*

The moment the phone started ringing Stands knew who would be on the other end of the line. Waves was only predictable in his thoroughness, he'd no doubt just been watching the very same news story that Stands himself had just finished digesting. Stands let it ring as his eyes roved idly around him, his mind continuing to analyse what had just been reported on the news.

As soon as the reporter had started to wind up the piece Stands had tuned out, his gaze falling on the well stocked book shelves either side of the fireplace. As his mind sifted through the news report his eyes moved to the mantelpiece, he wondered idly how much longer it would be before the print above the fireplace would need re-framing.

The slightly soot stained, heat damaged frame was beginning to come apart at the corners, it looked as though all the damned were trying to make a break from the Heronimous Bosch print trapped inside it.

Stands glanced at the ringing phone. The report had been worryingly accurate, but most troubling were the details that no one except those who had studied the crime scene first hand could know about. The forensic guys were renowned for their professionalism, they had to be…

although. What was it Waves had mentioned about the medical examiner? Finally irritated enough to take action, Stands picked the receiver up from the small table beside his armchair.

'Stands here.'

'Sorry to disturb you at home Sir, but I just thought you should know that the incident at the cinema has just been featured at some length on the national news. I don't know how it happened, but they seem to have gotten on to this one rather fast Sir.'

'Good evening Waves, it's lovely to hear from you.'

Waves could detect the sarcasm and the implied rebuke in his boss's voice. 'Sorry. Good evening Sir. I'm afraid I was a little too preoccupied with the news to pay attention to such pleasantries.'

Waves sometimes wondered why he was such a stickler for these things. He knew damn well that Stands himself held very little regard as a rule for such meaningless social banter.

'Daniel, such social pleasantries help grease the wheels which allow us to do our jobs that much easier. You should always try and remember the proper form. If you can keep your head at all times and remember to practice such small talk you'll be surprised by the rewards it can deliver.'

'Hmm…I'll try Sir. Anyway, as I was saying, I don't know where they got their information from, but it was more than just the normal speculation based on hearsay or a colourful press release, they were rather accurate.'

'Yes, I know. I watched it too. But don't fret, if the source of the information is on the inside it's doubtful that whoever it was contacted the media directly, in which case the leak should be easier to trace, the more people involved the easier it is. No, what's worrying me is they might have received the information from somewhere other than within the force, and if so then where? The perpetrators? Somehow I don't think so, I doubt whoever it was would really want the publicity. But if not them, then the only other link would be with the victims, but if that were the case how could anyone know what happened? Unless someone got out alive, someone who could answer a lot of questions. What do you think Waves, do you think we've got a survivor out there?'

'To be honest Sir, having seen what happened in there my gut tells me no one got out apart from whoever did it. They seemed to be very thorough.'

'Just what I was thinking. The only problem being that we're left with even more questions, and a possible mole in our midst.'

Waves waited, he could tell that there was more to come, but he didn't want to interfere with the Inspector's train of thought.

'Well Waves, the only way forward is to follow the facts and the evidence. We're going to have to wait awhile before we can start getting creative with this one. Good night Waves, I'll see you at the morgue in the morning.' And with that Stands put the phone down.

*

Waves was perplexed, Stands though obviously irritated by the interruption had seemed very relaxed about it all, as though he knew, or guessed at more than he was letting on. But usually he and the Inspector were very open in sharing information on a case. They had both experienced incidences where the smallest change in perspective had suddenly inspired breaks that had then led to arrests and satisfying conclusions. They both knew that something as simple as a different point of view could often blow a case wide open.

'Hmm…what's going on?' It was all becoming

45

increasingly complicated. With these frustrated thoughts chasing each other through his mind Daniel decided that at this point the only answer was another drink. Only this time he reached for the whisky.

*

Tris met Martin in the 'Albany' on Great Portland Street, a large, rather trendy watering hole that catered to the local after-office, and pre-club drinkers. The décor was subdued, greys and putty tones, with the music pitched at a level that if you wanted to talk you could.

It had taken him about twenty minutes to get there, whilst Martin had to come across the river from St. Johns Hill, a journey which had involved an overland train and five stops on the Bakerloo line to get to Regent's Park. Unusually it had only taken him around forty minutes to reach the bar where he and Tris had arranged to meet. It still amazed Martin how un-empathic a nominal telepath could be, often completely blind to the consequences of what he expected other people to go through for him. A failing which Tris's friends could only endure.

On entering the bar Martin almost instinctively knew where Tris would be despite the fact that he couldn't immediately see him.

In Martin's mind Tris's location shone out like a blip on a radar screen. Smiling Martin wound his way through the crowd to the bar.

Just as he was ordering a pint of lager he suddenly had the impression that he'd forgotten something, he was gripped by that odd nagging feeling, the kind that could, if you let it, consume you, leaving you unable to think about anything else. A moment later he clicked his fingers and when his pint was placed before him Martin apologised and added a large Gin and Tonic to his order. As the Barman turned away from him he wondered whether Tris was feeling OK, he would never normally use his abilities in such a prosaic fashion.

With the two drinks in hand Martin pushed his way through the crowd of be-suited men and women and other after work drinkers towards the corner where Tris was sat.

Tris looked up and frowned as Martin put his drink down in front of him. 'You took your time didn't you?'

Martin just grinned and sat down, took a long pull on his pint, wiped his mouth with the back of his hand and stuck his tongue out at Tris.

'You cheeky fucker! You're lucky I'm here at all. I did have plans for tonight before you phoned me so abruptly earlier.'

'You didn't have to meet me, you could have gone out with your other little friends.'

Martin's pint was halfway to his lips when he heard this. He scowled as he answered, 'Petulant brat! How can you say that? You know my first allegiance will always be to you and Garfan. Besides after I talked to you I phoned Garfan on his mobile to find out what was going on, and he asked me to meet you. So here I am. Now if you want me to piss off then I will, but if this is just about you having a bad day, which I know damn well it is, then you can stop taking it out on me. Right!'

Tris sat very still, his eyes narrowed as he looked intently at his human friend. Reaching up, he ran a hand through his hair and visibly relaxed.

'Yeah. Sorry man. Thanks for coming.'

Martin was quietly relieved and smiled gently at Tris. 'It's OK. Now drink up, we've got some catching up to do. I haven't seen you or Garfan for ages, so get that down your neck and I'll get some more in.'

*

47

An hour or so later they each had three empty glasses sat in front of them, and both of them were grinning like idiots having only just stopped laughing hysterically at a story Martin had just told Tris concerning one of his friends. Martin was still wiping moisture from his eyes as he got up.

'Lets go on somewhere else when I get back from the loo, OK?'

Tris nodded as Martin turned and made his way over to the door to the toilets. He looked around and breathed in the atmosphere. The music in the bar had gradually got louder as the clientèle had slowly got more voluble. This is what he had needed, this was why he loved spending time with Martin. Humans were so much more straight forward, with so little time to live they couldn't help but be so much more direct in their dealings with each other. It was this immediacy that drew him to these places, to the people, to the girls.

There was no way a female elemental would ever sleep with you before she'd got to know you over a couple of years or so, whilst some human women would open their legs after literally a couple of hours. Not that Tris was a sexual predator, it was just that his vocation put him in no position to spend much time with his own people. Besides which, he had now spent so much time with humans that he often behaved more like a human than an elemental.

As Martin emerged from out of the crowd around their table Tris looked up into Martin's hazel eyes. Suddenly he was transported back to the time he had first seen those eyes looking up into his own.

It had been years ago when Martin was little more than a child. It was a filthy night in a back street somewhere in central London. Tris and Garfan had been hot on the heels of a shape-shifter they'd been tracking for a few nights. On this night they'd just missed the opportunity to stop it from tearing a young woman's throat out and were close to bringing it down when it had disappeared down a dark alley which appeared to be a dead end.

Catching their breath the two friends looked at each other in the dark. Each was wearing tramps clothes underneath their old leather coats. Suits and smart casual clothes were fine for everyday life, but in back streets strewn with filth you became much less obvious if you looked like you belonged there. Besides, you could stash so many more weapons under a big leather coat than you could under a well tailored jacket.

Tris signalled silently to Garf that he should go down one side of the alley while he took the other. Nodding Garfan stepped back into the shadows and all but disappeared. Tris did the same and crept along the wall, mind and ears straining for anything ahead of them.

All he could feel was a vague presence towards the end of the alley. Getting nearer Tris felt the hairs on the back of his neck begin to rise as a low, threatening growl came from somewhere ahead.

Elementals are normally blessed with better night vision than their human cousins, but the clouds were low, and the rain was unrelenting.
Both he and Garfan were soaked to the skin, and the alley had virtually no light cast into it from the street. Tris was beginning to think that this was a really bad idea, when he heard what sounded like a child cry out in fear, the sound coming from mere feet in front of him. Not thinking of himself Tris threw himself forward, narrowly escaping the same fate as the unfortunate young woman they had failed to save earlier.

He rolled as he hit the ground, coming up into a crouch with his daggers held defensively before him, only to find Garfan standing in front of him, a grim look on his face, and his hand axe and dagger pinning the naked body of a young woman to the wall. Garfan's sides were heaving, rain running in torrents from the end of his beard, the blood splattered on his face mingling pinkly *with the rain.*

Tris was just about to lower his guard when he felt, rather than heard a presence virtually next to him. Huddled in a doorway beside him he could just make out a lumpy shape, one that looked to be shivering. Looking closer he could just make out the outline of a young face peering from beneath a baggy hood.

Garfan looked down. 'OK boy, you have nothing to fear from us. There'll be no more blood shed tonight young human.'

With that the boy, as he indeed was, pulled back his hood, and Tris saw clearly the hazel eyes he was looking into now, so many years latter. So much happened in those years, starting with Martin's martial training, which had finally led to him being based in London as one of their fund managers, and as occasional backup when he and Garfan felt they needed it.

Martin stood looking down at Tris, concern etched into the lines around his eyes. 'Are you OK Tris? Looked like I lost you there for a minute.'

Tris smiled his lop sided smile. 'Sorry, just thinking about the past.'

'Yeah…anything specific?'

He grinned. 'Yeah, I was just remembering how Garfan and I stumbled over some young wretch who had just come very close to being eaten by a werewolf.'

Martin smiled ruefully and slipped his leather jacket off the back of his chair. 'I seem to remember it was *me* that saved you from getting *your* throat ripped out.'

Tris stood up and picked up his coat. 'Ungrateful child, lets get out of here. Lets go to a club, I feel like dancing.'

'Me too. Though what you have to remember is that I will *always* be a child to you.'

Tris just snorted, slapped Martin on the back and started making his way towards the door.

Chapter Four

High up in an exclusive, modern block in Canary Wharf, a group of figures were relaxing around a huge wall mounted Plasma Screen TV, which was currently showing a recording of the news broadcast that Stands and Waves had both watched earlier.

The room was minimal to the extent of severity, bare white walls were textured to reduce the blankness of the space, at least that's what the casual observer may have thought. A more in depth examination by someone more learned in the esoteric arts may have come away from the examination with the sneaking suspicion that there may be more to the almost hidden designs on the walls than initially met the eye.

The floor was of highly polished hard wood parquet, which reflected the image on the television screen to create rather odd lighting effects on the occupants of the room. Each member of the group was sat in old leather armchairs equally spaced from the next with side tables next to them. Each table displayed evidence of the vices of the user. On one was a champagne flute, an ashtray full of cigarette stubs, and a small mirror displaying a small heap of white powder. The next held a cut glass tumbler holding a generous measure of amber liquid, next to which was an ashtray holding the still smoking length of a huge Monte Cristo cigar. Next was a steaming cup of rich black espresso, a glass of water and a brandy glass holding a caramel coloured liquid. The last table next to the most deeply shadowed member of the entourage stood seemingly empty, though when viewed out of the corner of the eye there did appear to be something there, though what it might be was another question entirely.

Behind this chair stood a tall, silent figure. The being's face was relaxed, passive, though etched with an obvious arrogance that did little to endear him to the occupants of the other chairs in the room. Having said this, each man in the room knew that to cross him would mean instant death. The little they knew about him only fuelled their private speculations further, though the physical resemblance between him and the being in the chair before him were striking; even though they all knew that it was not a direct familial resemblance. They both had slightly up-swept and pointed ears which were obvious on the standing figure, his long black hair held back in a pony-tail which only served to accentuate the alien quality of his ears. Other than that he appeared completely human, all be it an exceptionally tall and physically powerful looking human.

During the broadcast there were various snorts, coughs, and muffled laughs from the figures as they sat back in their chairs viewing the huge screen in front of them. At the end of the feature on the cinema killings the silent, shadowy figure sat at the end gestured idly with his hand towards the television that instantly became silent as it continued to show the rest of the local news from earlier that evening. The others looked towards their master with mixed expressions ranging from drug-induced glassiness to suspicion and awe.

'*Well gentlemen, it would seem that I cannot trust you to do as you are told. This use of an innocent was novel, but as I would have predicted, had you shared your ill-conceived plan with me, it was ultimately doomed to failure. In the process you have also lost me a valuable lieutenant, one who could never be replaced by any of your puny race. If we weren't harried on every side by the threat of betrayal from within I would not overlook this carelessness so readily.*'

The indistinct figure slumped back into its seat.

'*However the betrayers are still protected by their faithful guardians, who continue to protect this kingdom despite the fact that they receive no thanks for it. I would not have let this happen had it not been necessary to illustrate to you all what they are capable of. The Brothers you sent were some of your best, yet still they failed. Therefore we must use everything at our disposal to rid ourselves of these pests. The various agencies with which many of you have links can help us in this. The more information we can gather on these meddlers the easier it will be to dispose of them, and all their kind...eventually.'*

The men were silent as they let these words settle around them. The speakers voice was such that it always took a little while for the listeners to adjust themselves to the sensation of the simultaneous thoughts that accompanied the spoken words. Having meanings and images arrive full-blown in the mind from an external source was always a little disconcerting to say the least.

Many who had had the misfortune to come into direct contact with this being had gone quickly mad when confronted by such brutal telepathy, their minds virtually scrambled by the forced, almost physical intrusion into the most private areas of their lives and experiences, leaving the recipients little more than vegetables. To use such an ability as a weapon was considered by the few who possessed it as a sacrilege, though the casual way in which this creature reamed human minds could hardly be considered a conscious act. It was more like the act of a butterfly hunter pinning his specimens to a board. There was no conscious act of abuse, just the casual disdain which any higher creature might display towards an inferior species.

The three men sat around this being took what comfort they could from the individual powers they wielded in the more prosaic, everyday world of men. As far as they knew they were worth more to their master alive than dead.

After all, how would a being so obviously inhuman operate in the real world without human agents to make his plans reality. Besides, the risks they took were worth the immense power and wealth they had gained. They were now more powerful than kings, in each arena in which they had specialised they were famous, infamous even, but outside of these specialised circles they were virtually unknown, giving them an anonymity which had proven to be more valuable than a hundred bodyguards.

They could do anything, indulge any whim, the more depraved the better. In many ways these mere men were bigger monsters than their non-human master. They weren't aware that exposure to such power had, over time, corrupted them so completely.

He and his race had been twisted by hatred and envy over millennia, leaving them with what they saw as no choice at all but to hate, torture and corrupt. A sad state for a race who had been, at the beginning, so bright, vibrant and alive. So much knowledge had been lost through the ages, and all the many feuds had become ingrained in the very nature of each of their races.

After a silence, which was on the verge of becoming embarrassing, only one of the men present had the courage to suggest any new course of action in the face of their most recent defeat.

'My lord, would not now be a good time to send assassins after these guardians. They must be fatigued, and therefore vulnerable. They can have no idea of what is really going on. If we were to track them down now we may gain the advantage.'

Looking around the semi-circle of seats at the speaker their master smiled in a rather unpleasant way.

'It is good to see that at least one of you hasn't completely lost his wits to the lazy vices you humans seem so fond of. Yes, this is so, which is why I have already arranged for our recently departed to be stolen back before they can be properly identified.

The fallen members of our Brotherhood will be brought to me, and I will send them out against our foe once more. Let these foolish heroes try and defeat them again, I'm sure they'll find the already dead that much more difficult to dispatch.'

*

Tris and Martin had ended up getting a cab to Brixton. Martin had reservations, but Tris was still feeling edgy and needed to get it out of his system. Martin often privately thought that his friend was some kind of masochist, hell bent on punishing himself for some unfathomable reason.

So now Martin found himself in the 'Fridge' surrounded by wannabe gangsters and various other human flotsam and jetsam, and Tris seemed to be having a high old time. At this point in the evening, having already imbibed enough to feel relaxed despite the hostility all around him, Martin couldn't help but start to examine his friend's motivation for putting them in this situation.

Tris was surrounded by a group of three white girls who were lapping up all the champagne and attention he could give them. All three were no older than twenty three or four. Two brunettes and a blonde, each wearing tiny, shiny dresses which left very little to the imagination, and enough make-up to ice a cake. Martin watched them for a moment, he could see groups of very large black men looking at them, and it was pretty obvious they were pissed off, but they weren't doing anything about it. Even these thugs could sense something about this cuckoo in their midst, something that gave them pause. Martin turned his attention back to his friend, only to find Tris studying him intently.

Putting down his glass Tris moved a little closer. 'Relax, there's no need to be so wary, we're safe here.'

'You could of fooled me. How can you not be aware that there are at least a dozen huge black guys in here who'd quite happily rip our heads off. Look around, this isn't our turf...it's theirs.'

Tris looked around and smirked. 'You worry too much Martin. It's a simple case of dog psychology. They can sense I'm the biggest dog in here, maybe even smell it

...maybe it's my pheromones. Relax, being an undisputed Alpha male has it's advantages, so while you're with me there's no danger. OK?'

'This may be your idea of good time, but if you ask me it's a little fucked up!'

He laughed and shook his head. 'Martin, have another drink and join in the conversation. Trust me, these girls are good to go.'

He winked and turned back to the girls who'd just emptied the last of the champagne into their own glasses. He looked back at Martin. 'Looks like we need another bottle!'

*

An hour or so later Martin finally managed to drag Tris out of the club with the three girls in tow. By now he and Tris had drunk enough to be more than just visibly relaxed, truth be told they were both a little drunk, he'd even managed to put aside his distaste for the whole situation and put some effort into chatting up the girls. Only problem was they couldn't seem to take their eyes off Tris.

Holding him back and letting the girls walk ahead Martin spoke quietly to Tris. 'Every time we go out this happens. Can't you just turn off the charm, the pheromones, or magic, or whatever it is? We both know you're not really that interested.'

'Why would I want to? These may be just fleeting engagements with rapidly wilting flowers, but such beauty as there is in the world should always be appreciated at its best.'

Martin chuckled sadly. 'Oh to be an immortal and hold such an Olympian view of life. I know we've talked about it a hundred times in the past, but you can't begrudge me my mortal failings of jealousy and envy.

Especially when it *is* my birthday!'

Tris stopped dead in his tracks and turned to Martin open mouthed.

'Why didn't you say so earlier? How could I forget…but it seems like only yesterday since your last birthday.'

'Yeah I know…and the seasons pass as if in a blur…yada yada yada! What really pisses me off is that in comparative terms I'm older than you. Only I'm twenty-nine, and you're five hundred.'

Tris shook his head. 'Five hundred! When I was fifty I never thought I'd reach a hundred, it seemed such a long way off, and so old at that age. I was still getting used to the idea of all my human friends getting older before my eyes.'

He looked over at Martin and grinned. 'What a party though, five hundred was a good one to celebrate.'

Martin laughed in unison. 'Yeah, we had quite a weekend. Though Garfan definitely out did us, he walked away smiling while you couldn't speak let alone walk, and it took me another week just to recover.'

'Well, earth elementals are renowned for their constitutions. Anyway, I know it pains you sometimes that you're not truly one of us, it pains me too. Whenever I care for one of your kind I have to watch you fade so fast. But never underestimate my regard for you my friend. We have fought together side by side. You are a brother, and we face the struggle together, ever since I found you on the streets. How long ago was that now?'

Martin though drunk managed to be serious, though a little verbose. 'Sixteen years ago, and yes brother, father, friend, as both you and Garfan are, the hope you have given me, an ideal worth fighting for, dying for, better yet worth living for, is something I can never repay. Something I will always owe.'

'Nonsense, you owe us nothing, you never have. You are kin, be it distant, yet still kin. Remember that always. Now, I take it you want me to let you have the blonde!'

'I thought you'd never catch on.'

'Very well my young apprentice, the force is strong with you…you shall have the blonde!'

Tris glanced back over his shoulder and frowned. 'Thanks man. Are you OK?'

Tris's face had darkened with concentration as a look of doubt slowly spread across his face. Looking around wildly at their location he suddenly came to a halt. The three girls ahead of them oblivious to anything going on behind them just carried on walking.

'We're not alone. Are you armed?'

'Always. Just as you taught me. What's wrong? Who's out there?'

Immediate danger had a suddenly sobering effect on both of them.

'I'm not sure, they don't feel like anything I've come across before. They're just shadows in my mind, all I can feel is a malevolence. But whoever they are they're closing in on us, three of them trying to surround us.'

'The girls, they're innocents, they don't deserve to get involved in this. You're still weakened by what happened this afternoon. Get them away now, I'll distract whoever, or whatever they are, and once you've got the girls well away from here you can come back and we'll take them on together.'

Tris shook his head. 'I can't let you, it's too risky, they're closing fast, and if you get trapped you won't have a chance.'

'Yeah, so no time, you'd better shift hadn't you. Anyway, we don't know who or what they are, I might be able to take them. Remember those vampires? Tris just go, take the girls while you still can. Save the innocent, isn't that why we fight, to protect the innocent! I took a vow, as did you, now go, fulfil it. Just make sure you find me!'

Martin grabbed Tris' forearm in a brief gesture of solidarity. 'Be swift, and come back fast!'

Tris squeezed his arm in turn. 'Run... fight only if

you have too, stay alive till I get back.'

As Tris said this Martin could feel the hair on the back of his neck rising, even he could feel their presence now. They were close, and it brought a bitter taste to his mouth as the evil drawing closer started to make its presence felt.

The girls had stopped some metres away when they'd realised their wealthy, handsome escorts were no longer following, and having heard some of the conversation, had been growing gradually more nervous, glancing around themselves at the dark walls and empty doorways in the narrow street around them.

Tris grabbed them by their hands and ushered them away from Martin who now stood rooted to the spot as he strained his senses in an attempt to target the approaching foe.

'Come on girls, we've got to get out of here, we've got some rather unpleasant enemies who seem to want a bit of a show down. We've got to get you out of here now!'

As they started to trot away down the street Martin distinctly heard one of the girls complaining. 'I should have known you guys were too good to be true. Why do I always end up with gangsters?'

Tris fled, dragging the terrified girls with him, leaving Martin alone amongst the puddles and rainbow hued oily remains of peckish party goers takeaways.

'Right then, what the fuck have I let myself in for?'

Glancing around Martin knew that they were even closer now, the bitter taste in his mouth worsening as the adrenaline swiftly rose within him. They were getting colder by the minute, and as he watched in disbelief the road around him very slowly released a mist that could in no way be natural. Too late…he knew it was too late to run now.

Slowly he slipped off his leather jacket. Despite the deepening cold he knew that it was vital in close quarters combat not to have anything that an enemy might be able to grab hold of in order to unsteady him. Reaching into the back of the jacket Martin swiftly withdrew the two daggers he carried concealed in padded panels in the back of the jacket. Throwing the jacket away he took a dagger in each hand and then took hold of his shirt and started tearing it from his torso. With this task complete he stood quietly, his muscular chest slowly expanding and contracting, his head down concentrating on his senses, now fully aware that he had no avenue of escape. Whoever they were they had surrounded him. They'd moved incredibly fast, obviously they had sensed Tris' retreat and moved in before he too could escape.

Martin lifted his head and glanced around him as three vague black shapes moved slowly into view. One slipping unnaturally down a wall like some huge spider, the other two appearing from around corners in such a synchronised way that an image of black clad ballerinas appeared in his mind. Shaking his head he could hardly believe he was here like this in the middle of a deserted London street, bare-chested and about to do battle with god knew what.

'Come on!' He shouted. 'Come on you vermin! Mortal I may be but I don't fear you. We've prevailed, only skulking maggots like you remain. Now reveal yourselves.'

As his shouts faded the three figures seemed to shudder, physically detaching themselves from the shadows around them.

As they drew nearer, tightening the ring around Martin, it became apparent that they were wearing dark hooded cloaks to hide themselves from the world.

The tension was beginning to get to him. 'So what are you...maggots, demons, monsters or men. Show me, enough of this hiding, let me see you before I butcher you.'

Inside Martin was quaking, for all his bravado he knew he didn't have much chance. Three normal men would probably not have been a problem, and in the company of Tristellis and Garfan he had killed many a creature of nightmare, but three such creatures alone were more than he could handle. He had to stall for time until Tris came back.

The three were closing fast whilst circling him. He knew he was open to attack from the rear, and, though his senses had been heightened by the Elders magic, and his martial training, the cold hatred that was being directed at him by these things left him tense and desperate to run.

'Show me god damn it! If I'm about to die at least reveal who's hand I'm about to die by.'

At last, as one of the creatures circled into view on his right, it spoke. A rasping, dry croak whispering from its hood. 'We have come for your blood mortal, we who were once as you.' And with that all three pulled back there hoods and shed the cloaks, dropping them at their feet in the puddles and the filth, leaving them horrifyingly naked.

Martin almost bit his tongue trying to stifle the scream that wanted to be released from his throat. At the first sight of the men before him, for that was what they had obviously once been, the word 'zombie' flashed into his mind, closely followed by ghoul and wraith. It's amazing how many of our nightmares and creatures of horror so closely resemble man, as though it were the little differences that made them all the more terrifying. In this case that was the literal truth.

Human they looked at first glance, but there was a bloated purpling to their skin, wounds that should have oozed blood just glistened blackly. They had once been men, but the sex organs had been removed, flapping empty skin all that remained of their genitalia. Their faces were barely recognizable as such, the empty sockets of their eyes making it even more difficult to find any humanity in their faces.

The faces managed to smile though, as the one who'd spoken before once more managed to articulate its hatred. 'Yes, we were once as you, but now we are your death. Fear is our master, and pain our pleasure.'

He could feel the panic rising, it was overpowering, the adrenaline which had all too recently made his heart pound and his body itch for action, now sapped his strength, leaving him feeling shaky and sick. Now it was just fear that flowed within him. In a flash of inspiration he slashed his own chest with the dagger he gripped so tightly in his right hand. The pain was sharp and harsh, but just what he needed to clear his mind of the numbing fear which had threatened to freeze him to the spot. The heat of the wound reminding him that he was still alive, for now.

'Fuck it! Come on, do it now!' With that Martin leapt forward in the direction Tris had taken, knowing that attack was the only way he could stay alive any longer. To stand still and listen was to die a slower, colder death.

Shouting incoherently he flew at the figure before him, hoping to somehow get past his tormentor and run. His daggers were raised and automatically wheeling in offensive patterns his mentors had drilled into him over the years, *Remember Martin, when all hope is gone rely on your instincts and your training, let the primal animal guide you. Become the berserker and you may just survive'*.

Swinging swiftly around in front of him the once human thing shrieked a challenge, and reading Martin's intention blocked his escape as the other two moved in from behind.

Chapter Five

Tris was running faster than he thought he'd ever run, back towards the centre of the anxiety blooming in his brain. His entire being strained towards what was going on ahead of him, passing shop windows, doorways and buildings at an Olympic speed. Then he heard it, the kind of scream that leaves others screaming, a sound that could leave a fragile mind shattered by unimaginable horror. At that moment he knew he was too late.

Tris skidded to a halt as he turned the final corner back to the source of the scream. In the shadows of the ill lit street he could just make out a huddled form lying amidst a slick puddle in the middle of the tarmac. He could sense nothing lurking in wait so moved determinedly towards what he knew must be Martin. As he closed the distance the black puddle around the body slowly expanded.

He'd witnessed death thousands of times, in a thousand different forms from violence to disease. When he was a youth in the Sixteenth Century he had witnessed first hand the virulence of the Black Death. Before he was born it had spread from Asia into Europe, killing millions as it went. In the Seventeenth Century it returned to England, and in 1666 Tris saw The Great Fire of London end the last major outbreak in the Kingdom. Tris had lived through it all.

Now there was one more battered and mutilated body on the ground before him, the body of a man he'd known only sixteen years, which seemed like the blink of an eye to him. But Martin had been a friend, a close friend and comrade in arms. Tris had met him on the streets of London a short time after he'd run away from home, a misfit, an outcast who didn't seem to fit, and Tris had instantly recognized why.

Martin had possessed latent elemental genes,

passed down from which of Martin's forebears they would never know. Over the ages the elementals had mated with humans more times than could be numbered. Tristellis himself was not a pure blood, one of the very reasons he had become what he was. Hybrid elementals were often physically stronger than their pure blood brethren. In fact there were many mortals walking the earth who had no idea of their unlikely heritage.

Having seen this in Martin, Tris and Garfan had taken him in and revealed his heritage to him, and so had begun Martin's training. Having discovered what he was, he wanted to help, the fight gave him a cause he could believe in, a calling that would give his life meaning. So they'd called upon the Elders to re-awaken what dormant genes he possessed so that he could tap into such gifts as his heredity could give, and had joined them in fighting the war against the enemies of the Kingdom.

Now that boy, who had become a good man, lay semi-naked and eviscerated in the middle of the street, his intestines coiled haphazardly beside him, his blood pooled around him like an oil slick. The closer he got the more detail became horrifyingly apparent. There was blood splatters everywhere. Small gobets of flesh accompanied the worst as though he had been flayed with hooks. What was left of his body was slick with blood and other bodily fluids.

Tris had to force himself to look closely at his friend, all that remained was cooling flesh with little left that could be recognized as the man he had been. His face was in taters, cruelly slashed and hanging off his skull, a gruesome parody of a funeral mask.

As Tris studied the body he couldn't help but notice that Martin's genitalia were conspicuously absent, the fabric of his trousers and the flesh around his groin torn as though the organ had literally been ripped from the body.

Tris felt numb as he knelt to take a last look at the remains of Martin's face. As he lifted Martin's head away from the road, his hair sticking to the blood pooled around him, a final sigh escaped his lips, an involuntary exclamation as his last breath escaped his lungs with the opening of his airways. Tris bit down on his lip to deny the flood of anger and grief that threatened to overwhelm him. Martin's hair clung to his hand in strands as he gently lay his dead comrades head back on the ground. His eyes were missing too, his beautiful hazel eyes ripped from his skull along with half of his face.

Kneeling next to the remains of what had once been his friend Tris covered his face with his hands, trying with all his force of will not to cry. With a deep shuddering breath Tris hauled himself to his feet, letting his hands drop to his sides where they involuntarily clenched into fists.

'You fought bravely my friend. I will make sure your name is remembered with honor. Forgive me for not disposing of your earthly remains as they should be.'

That said he looked around himself once more making sure he was still alone, then looked up at the stars and knuckled the tears he couldn't stop from his eyes. A moment later he turned and ran with all the speed he could still muster.

*

When Tris finally arrived back at St Marks Square he slowed his pace to a slow trot. The speed he'd been going had meant virtually no one saw him, such was the elementals ability to move quickly and unnoticed. Turning into their driveway he couldn't help but notice that most of the lights in the house were on. Garfan was awake.

As he closed the front door behind him he heard a heart felt sigh. 'What happened Tris? Where's Martin?'

He was sat on the bottom step of the stairs. 'I know somethings happened, I could sense your pain miles away.'

Tris could only stand there and look at him with tears welling in his eyes. 'He's dead Garf, they killed him…and it's all my fault.'

Garfan blinked rapidly and looked up towards the ceiling his jaw tightening as he tried vainly to hold back the tears. Suddenly he closed his eyes, his head falling forward and down as if suddenly too heavy for his neck to support it. All Tris could do was look on in anguish as his oldest friend silently wept for their fallen friend, his tears falling onto his beard and trickling down the long strands like water off a ducks back.

Tris leant back against the door and slowly slid down it till he was sat at its base, his legs bent up in front of him, his head in his hands. Finally able to give himself over to his grief, his shoulders shook with it as the tears started to soak the front of his shirt.

He tried to emulate his friend but had never mastered the art of keeping his grief quiet, especially when it was made so much worse by the huge burden of guilt he could feel almost physically weighing him down. As he watched Garfan he couldn't help but gulp, sniff and snort as clear snot dribbled from his nose in much the same way as the tears leaked from his eyes. He almost wished that his old friend would blame him, maybe even stand up and attack him, beat him senseless as he felt he deserved. Feeling a sudden stabbing pain in the vicinity of his hands he was almost thankful for the diversion as he held them up and unclenched his fists only to see a series of crescent shaped cuts in his palms where his fingernails had bitten into his flesh. The iniquity of these tiny wounds caused a fresh bout of hot tears to burst from Tris's eyes, his sobs becoming even more frantic.

Garfan meanwhile was using his head rather than dissolving into a hysterical wreck, he shook his head wearily and slowly wiped the tears from his cheeks, ignoring the wetness in his beard. He'd seen Tris like this on numerous occasions. Every time one of their human comrades died in battle Tris would blame himself, taking an almost masochistic stance, always thinking that he should have found some way to have stopped it from happening. Leaning his elbows on his knees, he clasped his hands together and studied Tris's face, at once incredibly sad, but also racked with misplaced guilt.

'Tris it's their fight too, every human should fight against evil. Many of them do in their own little ways, protesting against wars, fighting disease or corruption, and many die fighting these causes. Martin chose to fight with us in a more literal way...he knew the risks.'

He sighed as the tears continued to pour down Tris's face. 'Knowing Martin he died bravely, he was a good man, an honorable man, and one I'll sorely miss. But you've got to let it go Tris.'

Gasping he looked through his fingers at Garfan. 'But it's my fault he died. I left him there, I left him alone to fight those monsters, three of them.'

'Yes, and knowing him it was his idea for you to leave. Were there others there?'

'Three girls we'd met in a club. I'm such a fool, I should have made him get them away.'

Garfan shook his head fiercely. 'In which case it would be your corpse lying there now, not his. He knew you were depleted, somehow he might even have realized that you were the target. He saved your life.'

Tris looked at Garfan in disbelief. 'What do you mean?'

'For fucks sake Tris, think about it! You must have told him about what happened, and the conclusions we'd made. Don't dishonor him by crediting him with as little intelligence as you seem to have. He was a smart lad. They tried to surround you, right?'

Tris nodded.

'They weren't just tracking you, they were hunting you. Martin put two and two together instinctively and did what he thought was best, for which I will be forever grateful.' He shook his head wearily.

'Dolt you may sometimes be, but I couldn't carry on doing this without you.'

Tris wiped his eyes in an attempt to halt the flow of tears. 'Why did we choose this life Garf? We could have been Poets, Musicians, Craftsmen, Lore Keepers, Farmers even. Why did we choose this?'

Garfan could do little but shrug and raise his eyebrows in resignation. 'It chose us Tris. All callings have a way of taking their own. It's what we were born to do, and we do it better than anybody.'

He snorted. 'All those other pursuits, noble all, would never make you feel as alive as this. We both know it, and if you'd stop feeling sorry for yourself for a second you'd recognise that fact too. You're just tired and upset. You love the fight as much as I do. Go take a shower and get a grip, there have always been casualties, and there always will be. I know it sounds harsh Tris, but now more than ever we need to be focused. We don't have the time for grief.'

He got to his feet and walked slowly across the hallway towards Tristellis. Stopping at his feet, Garfan offered him a hand up. 'Come on, go get some sleep. Avis'll be delivering the car early, and I think we should take a detour to Avington. Lord Wessex may be able to help us with some of our more mundane enquiries. It's going to be a long day. Go sleep, and don't grieve for Martin, he'd be the first to tell you to snap out of it. Besides, he's at rest…so let him rest in peace.'

Tris looked up at his old friend thankfully, took his hand and pulled himself up. He smiled ruefully and gripped Garfan's shoulder briefly before slowly making his way up the stairs to his bedroom.

Meanwhile Garfan followed the figure with his eyes. Shaking his head as he went to the kitchen to make himself yet another cup of coffee to stop himself from falling asleep during his self imposed guard duty.

*

The phone ringing next to his head woke Stands with a start. Reaching out for the mobile handset on the beside table he couldn't help but notice the alarm clock standing next to the phone glowed greenly showing it was only 4.30am. Groaning he looked at the screen on the mobile before answering it. 'Make it good Daniel, you just woke me up!'

'Sorry Sir, I'm on my way round to pick you up.'

'What? It's only half four, what's so god damn important?'

'I don't know how else to tell you this...but the morgue where the bodies from the cinema were taken to this afternoon was broken into tonight. The night porter has been murdered, and three of our bodies are missing.'

Stands was unusually quiet on the end of the phone.

'I'll be there in around fifteen minutes. I'll brief you on what I know when I get there. The Assistant Commissioner is aware of the situation, and expects us to get to the bottom of this as quickly as possible. Sorry Sir, our case, our problem.'

All Waves could hear as the connection was severed was the start of a quiet expletive.

'Bollo...'

*

When Waves arrived the Inspector answered the door already dressed and clutching a mug of industrial strength coffee. 'Good morning Waves, coffee?'

Waves grinned. 'That would be good Sir, thanks.'

'Well come in and fill me in on whatever the hell has been going on.'

He closed the door behind him and followed the Inspector down the hallway to the kitchen. The gruff tone alone was enough to warn Waves that his boss was not in the best of moods, even without the scowl that looked like it was going to take some effort to remove from his mentors face.

'I'll keep it reasonably brief as I'm sure I haven't been given all the facts myself. What I do know is that the morgue where the bodies from the cinema were taken was visited by persons unknown at some time between midnight and two o'clock this morning. Security were making their usual rounds at three am, and found the body of the morgue's night porter some time later. The security guard called for backup from the other guards and searched the morgue. They found there was no one there, which is when they called the police. The officer who arrived at the scene had the good sense to call out the Senior Pathology Assistant, who upon arriving discovered the fact that there were three bodies missing, which he then identified as three of the adult male bodies from the old cinema on Forrester Street. That's when I was called Sir.'

Waves took a sip of his coffee and swallowed politely. He'd forgotten what terrible coffee the Inspector made. 'After I was initially called I was just getting dressed when the Assistant Commissioner called. He didn't say who'd called him, but he sounded none to happy about the situation and suggested I call you and get over there ASAP. That about brings us up to date.'

'Well Waves, rather than standing around here we'd better get going hadn't we.'

Daniel put down his coffee mug with some relief, and followed Stands to the front door. By the time he got there Stands was outside waiting by the car. As Daniel closed the Inspector's front door behind him he asked himself quietly, and not for the first time. 'Why the hell did I become a Copper?'

*

It was around 5.15am when Waves pulled up outside the Royal London Hospital, Whitechapel. Yet again there seemed to be constables everywhere.

Stands shook his head in disbelief. 'Waves aren't we supposed to be suffering from a shortage of manpower?'

'According to the latest reports you're right Sir.'

Stands detected the humour in his subordinates voice and decided against commenting any further. He resisted the urge to smile too, inwardly thanking his lucky stars that he'd had the good sense to have Waves assigned to him. Not only was he a good man, but he also seemed to share his sense of humour; a blessing for two men who had to work so closely in situations that many would find impossibly stressful.

Having at last got over his bad mood at being woken so early Stands finally smiled. 'OK, I'll wait for you inside and try and find out what's going on while you park the car.'

He got slowly out of the car, but before shutting the door he ducked his head back in. 'Don't be long, otherwise I may have to start shouting at people, and you know how the boys and girls hate being shouted at.'

That said, the Inspector shut the car door and sauntered over to the Hospitals main doors. Waves laughed quietly and put the car in first gear. 'One day I'll figure that man out!'

*

As Waves walked into the Hospital Lobby Stands looked over from where he was talking to a Police Sergeant who was holding some paperwork and looking

71

impatiently at his watch. Waves could tell that the Inspector wasn't happy just by the way he was standing despite the calm expression on his face.

'Sorry Sir, trying to find a space in the car park was a nightmare. There must be a rush in A & E.'

'Never mind that now, we need to get down to the morgue. The SOCO boys are already there with forensics. We need to have a look before they start moving things around.'

The Inspector turned back to the policeman he'd been talking to as Waves came in. 'OK, lead on Sergeant. Oh, and you may want to set up a perimeter of some kind in order to keep the press out.'

The Sergeant nodded, making notes as he turned away from the Inspector. 'If you'd care to follow me Sir, the morgue's this way.'

The Sergeant led them away from the main hustle and bustle of the Hospital, on a course that was slowly angling them down into the bowels of the building. As they walked the Inspector fired questions at the Sergeant.

'I'm assuming that whoever did this didn't enter the morgue through the main body of the hospital?'

The Sergeant looked a little confused. 'Sorry I'm not with you Sir.'

'What I mean to say is that the unknown subjects didn't follow the same route we are, in order to enter the morgue. The thing being that we've already passed at least two security camera's, and if they'd come this way their appearance would be well documented by now.'

'No Sir, they entered the morgue through the loading bay which abuts the morgue facility. There are cameras down there too, we've already checked the footage.'

'And?'

'Well, all that appears from the estimated time of the break-in is static. It covers a period of fifteen minutes, after which the recording returns to normal. We've talked to hospital security and they can't explain it. No one else has access to the equipment, or the digital tapes, and according to their technical guy there's nothing wrong with the cameras; I made him check them myself. Unfortunately the live feeds from these cameras aren't routinely monitored by hospital security, so they were unaware of the incident until one of them went down there on a regular sweep of the Hospital.'

'The recordings from the appropriate cameras don't show anything?'

'No Sir. One minute everything is fine, then the three cameras which would have shown any activity at all show static for exactly fifteen minutes, then return to normal. The only thing that is obviously different in the images is the fact that the night porter is sat in the same place, but it appears someone made a pretty good attempt at decapitating him.'

Waves winced. Stands looked over his shoulder at him and caught his pained expression, before turning back to the sergeant. 'Well thank you for your insight, just make sure that those tapes are properly tagged and given over to forensics for examination.'

Stands noticed a sign indicating they were going the right way to the morgue. 'How much further is it?'

'Just round this corner Sir.'

And there they were. Two constables were stood outside the doors to the morgue. As they approached Stands took out his ID. 'Thank you for the escort, but we can take it from here. You seem to have everything else in hand, just remember those tapes.'

'Yes Sir, as soon as I can I'll have them sent to you.' With that the sergeant about turned and walked back the way they'd come.

He held up his ID for the constables standing before the door, Waves did likewise as the Inspector pushed open the door to the morgue.

Inside the room was brightly lit by rows of overhead striplighting, providing a harsh, slightly greenish-yellow light. The room they'd stepped into was an anteroom to the autopsy suite which could be seen through a large internal picture window on the wall to their right. On the other side of the room from that were large double doors through which could be seen a loading area. Straight in front of them on the other wall was the entrance to the room holding the cold storage cabinets where all the cadavers were kept.

The main piece of furniture in the room was a large desk facing the door through which they'd just entered. The forensic team were busy enough not to take much notice of their entry, besides they all knew Stands from any number of other homicide scenes.

He was glancing around him when he noticed that Waves was transfixed by the body slumped in the chair behind the desk. The Sergeant who'd led them down there hadn't been exaggerating. The guys head was leant so far back on glistening red and pink strands of flesh that he was almost looking behind him at the entrance to the cold storage room. Stands could see blood splatters across the floor to the right of the body, and blood splatters all over the wall. Looking up he also saw that directly above the body there was blood, indicating that when the head had fallen back the pressure in the body had forced blood from the severed carotid arteries in the neck right up to the ceiling, about five feet above the body. This had also had the effect of raining blood down in a rough circle over and around the body to a distance of nearly four feet. There was literally blood everywhere.

He looked back at Waves who was shaking his head as he noticed the Inspectors look.

'I hate to say this, but it's going to be a pleasant surprise when somebody connected with all this turns up with gunshot wounds.'

Stands' snort of laughter managed to draw the attention of the crime scene technicians busy shooting video coverage of the scene, disapproval obvious on their faces.

Stands didn't even blink, and walked over to the

two men studying the body in front of them. They turned at his approach, one of them even smiled. 'Good morning Inspector, fancy seeing you here.

'Morning Marcus. So who was he?'

'Sam Goodwin, very reliable man, been here for years doing the night shift. Strange looking at him in this state, but hell I'm sure he'd rather it was me poking him about than someone he didn't know.'

Stands smiled as Marcus Benning, Senior Assistant to the Chief Forensic Pathologist, got on with his job. The Inspector had, over their short acquaintance, come to have a lot of respect for this unprepossessing young man. His down to earth attitude, and obvious respect for the bodies of those he dealt with made him much more approachable than his arrogant, taciturn boss.

'OK, so I know this is going to sound like a stupid question, but how did he die?'

Marcus laughed. 'Don't worry Inspector, that would only sound like a stupid question to a stupid person.'

The Assistant Forensic Pathologist frowned. 'Actually it's a very good question. There's absolutely no sign of a struggle, his hands and feet weren't bound in any way, and if you study his face the expression is one of shock and surprise. Whatever happened was so fast that Sam had no time to respond in any way, except to look surprised.'

Stands and Waves exchanged a long look. Both were thinking exactly the same thing, the M.O. was the same as at the cinema the previous day, extremely fast and extremely lethal.

'OK Marcus, what can you tell me?'

'Well apart from the mystery of how this happened, there is the mystery as to what the hell kind of weapon was used to do this. Whatever it was must have been at least a couple of feet long if the blood splatter patterns are anything to go on. If you look to your right you'll see what I mean, the way the blood splatter follows through to your right, eventually hitting the wall. It's characteristic of the swinging motion of the blade that did this. Not only that but I would guess that the blade was reasonably heavy to give the momentum required to take it right through the cervical vertebrae of the neck. The biggest problem I have with this is that the blade would have had to have been impossibly sharp.'

Waves spoke up. 'So what you're saying is we're looking for someone very fast and very strong who walks around wielding a razor sharp sword?'

'Well yes, my guess is it was some kind of sword, but when I say impossibly sharp the emphasis is on impossibly. Take a look at the wound, there's very little evidence of tissue tearing, the weapon sliced cleanly through muscle and cartilage. The only evidence there is of any kind of tearing caused by brute force is the indication of some bone chips around the edge of the second cervical vertebrae that was sliced almost completely in two. It should be virtually impossible to do that even if you had a three foot scalpel.'

Waves was shaking his head again. 'Is it just me, or does anyone else feel like they're taking part in some kind of 'Highlander' remake?'

Marcus and Stands chuckled quietly.

Marcus studied the two detectives. 'Funnily enough I've been thinking much the same thing since we walked into that old cinema yesterday afternoon. Something very weird is going on here. I think you guys have got your work cut out for you on this one.'

Stands nodded his agreement. 'All we can do is work the evidence until we get some kind of break. Until that time we need you to give us as much evidence, and as many educated guesses as you can. In the mean time is there anything else can you tell me about what happened here this evening?'

'Well the first thing I did after the constables let me in here, after having a cursory look at poor old Sam here, was to have a scoot round and see what was missing.'

'And what was missing?'

'Nothing. I checked everywhere, and there was nothing obvious missing, no equipment, no paperwork, as far as I'm aware. That's when I thought I may as well check the cold storage. That's when I found what had been taken. Come and have a look.'

The young forensic scientist led them over to the big double doors leading into the storage room. 'It's exactly as I found it. I've taken a look in the other refrigerated lockers to make sure all the others were there, but other than that and the SOCO boys videoing it all it's not been touched. I knew you'd want to have a look before anything could be disturbed.'

'Thanks Marcus, I just wish half our constables had your common sense.'

Marcus handed the pair some latex gloves like the ones he was already wearing. 'As soon as you've had a look I'll get them to come in and sweep for prints.'

As soon as Stands and Waves walked in the drop in temperature was pronounced. White puffs of vapour appeared in the air when they breathed out, the overall feeling, if it hadn't been for the location, would have been that of a very crisp winters morning.

Waves tried unsuccessfully to rub his hands together to warm them. 'So you came in here and found these individual refrigerator doors open, and these three trays empty, and the fourth telescoping tray half pulled out?'

'Yep, that about sums it up. There's seven doors open, one's empty, one holds the body of an elderly heart attack victim who was discovered three days after death, we did his post mortem yesterday just to establish cause of death. That one down there holds the body of that poor little girl. The three that are fully extended held three of the adult male bodies from the cinema, and the fourth is just there, as you can see for yourselves.'

Stands hadn't said a word. He was quietly looking

around to make sure he wasn't missing anything obvious. Waves could see the perplexed expression on his face, assuming he was thinking the same thing.

'This makes no sense to me, the obvious motive for this is to recover the bodies in order to sabotage identification of the corpses. So why the hell would they leave one behind?'

Waves looked at the Pathology Assistant. 'They weren't disturbed were they?'

'No, the first security knew about it must have been at least an hour after Sam was murdered. Plenty of time for them to escape with all the bodies. In fact one of your constables told me that the security footage from the cameras had a gap of fifteen minutes or so on them. Fifteen minutes would be plenty of time to open the fridges find what they wanted and get the hell out of dodge. Especially when you consider how quickly they must have dispatched Sam.'

Stands had been following the conversation whilst trying to get to grips with the fact that the obvious motive obviously wasn't the real motive.

He looked at Waves. 'OK, so the obvious motive is to prevent identification, but that theory falls apart when we've still got one corpse for identification, unless of course they know that the body won't be identified, but that's a long shot. Faces can always be tracked one way or another. So where does that leave us?'

Waves swapped a confused look with Marcus. 'Nowhere! No obvious motive.'

'Precisely, so lets start thinking about not so obvious motives.'

Stands turned and walked out of the cold room rubbing his hands together. 'Marcus, before this happened did you or one of your colleagues have the opportunity to put together preliminary reports on all the bodies from the cinema?'

'Yeah Kevin gave them the once over when they came in yesterday.' Looking over to where his colleague was still studying the corpse of the night porter. 'Hey Kevin, have you checked that your preliminary findings on the missing cadavers is still where you left it?'

The young man called Kevin looked up, shook his head and wandered out past the two constables outside and up the corridor to the pathology department's offices.

Marcus shrugged. 'He's reasonably new here, quite quiet, but a nice enough guy. Seems to know his stuff, though I think all this happening on our doorstep has freaked him out a little. To be honest its freaked me out a bit, I never thought this kind of thing would ever happen in the office as it were, especially not surrounded by the weirdness that this one seems to be generating.'

Waves nodded his agreement. 'I don't suppose you've got any coffee in your office?'

Marcus looked at Stands who was looking a little weary. 'Good idea, lets go and sit down, have a coffee and look at Kevin's reports.'

*

Being sat in a warm office with hot coffee in front of them seemed to revive all three of the men in Marcus's office. Kevin could see them from the corridor outside. He'd just delivered his preliminary reports on all the bodies from the cinema incident, but hadn't been invited to hang around. Feeling a little resentful at not being included, he went back to studying the corpse of a man he'd spoken to only the night before.

*

Stands took charge as soon as the young intern had left the office. 'I suggest we each look at all the reports,

79

and then we can discuss any similarities, or irregularities which may or may not be of any significance.'

Marcus was a little surprised. 'Isn't this something which you guys do amongst yourselves?'

Stands put down the coffee mug he'd been about to drink from. 'You don't mind do you Marcus? I'd appreciate your input.'

'Not at all, glad to be of help, though I don't know how much help I can be. You're the detectives.'

Waves smiled and picked up the first report that came to hand.

*

Three quarters of an hour later Marcus was still waiting for the two detectives to finish the reports they had in their hands.

Waves had of course scrutinised such material before, but the medical descriptions of these types of wounds were not the norm.
As he'd pointed out to his superior earlier, gunshot wounds were a lot less messy, and cause of death was that much simpler to describe. He threw down the last report on the table in front of him. 'Makes for grisly reading.'

Stands looked up from where he was absorbed by his own thoughts, the last report he'd just finished, folded closed in his lap. 'That may be so Waves, but there's a few things here which can help us.'

Marcus chipped in as he rose to his feet. 'I have to admit that despite the obvious connection made by the wounds received, the evidence leaves me with more questions than answers. More coffee anyone?'

The two detectives shook their heads. Waves turned in his seat to look at Stands. 'And you're referring to?'

'The ring that was left in that pile of ash at the

scene. It obviously has some significance, and the nature of its creation, being hand made should make it somewhat easier to trace. Besides which we were informed that there were six dead people in the cinema. We've only found five and that pile of ash.'

'You can't seriously be suggesting that the ash represents the remains of another victim?'

'Why not?'

'Well,' and here Waves glanced towards the Pathology Assistant, 'please correct me if I'm wrong Marcus, but as far as I'm aware such examples of human instantaneous combustion are extremely rare. Not only that, but when it does appear to happen there is always at least a small amount of human tissue left as evidence of the human origins of the ash. Then there is the damage caused by the fire and extreme heat needed to reduce human bones to ash. There would be scorch marks and evidence that the heat from the body incinerating itself had left in its immediate environs.'

Stands raised an eyebrow and looked towards Marcus.

'Well Inspector that sounded like a text book answer to me. I can check if you'd like, but as far as I'm aware Daniel's correct in every detail. Which from the evidence we're presented with would suggest that the ash is not a result of instantaneous human combustion, and if that ash had been a body how else would it have been reduced to a small pile of ash like that? No flamethrower or other weapon of that kind was used, no immediate evidence of an accelerant used. They'd be other evidence, scorch marks, burn damage, and there was nothing like that at the scene.'

Marcus shrugged. 'To be honest there's no point speculating further until we get the results back from the lab, then we'll know what the ash contains and we'll be able to make a more educated guess. At this stage I'd suggest that it was some kind of sacrifice for a fallen member. The pile of ash being representative of a dead

Satanist. You never know, it might actually be a dead Satanist's cremated remains. People like that are capable of anything.'

Waves nodded. 'I agree completely, and you yourself said we should follow the evidence, and that's what the evidence in this case would seem to be pointing to.'

Stands looked unconvinced. 'I don't know why, but it doesn't feel right to me, but as of now it looks like the most likely explanation. So we have evidence that the four victims were definitely linked in what would appear to be some kind of Satanist/Paedophile ring. The little girl, remains unidentified, which is a detail that's bothering me. No young girls have been reported missing that match this girls description.'

Stands sighed and shook his head and regarded the other two. 'I know this is unpleasant, but lets continue. According to young Kevin the girl's throat was cut from behind, and she was already dead before she was abused by one of the victims whose corpse is missing. The evidence for this being that there is very little bruising around the rectum, despite its dilated appearance, which would suggest that the abuse occurred post mortem'

The room was quiet, the two younger men subdued by the topic of conversation. He understood their discomfort. 'If it's of any help to you both, the animal that did that to her suffered as a result. Whoever executed these people caught him in the act and cut it off before he had a chance to…disengage. I took it out of her myself, I know it meant tampering with a crime scene, but it just didn't seem right to leave it sticking out of her like that.' Stands looked down, somehow embarrassed by the admission.

Waves raised his eyebrows but didn't comment, if it had been him he would have done exactly the same thing.

'Sounds like the fucker got what he deserved if you ask me, though obviously I'm completely impartial in this.'

Both the detectives smiled at Marcus's remark.

Waves couldn't help but comment. 'Until I saw what had happened here tonight I thought they might be vigilantes, good guys.'

Stands frowned at his subordinate. 'No matter whether I agree with you or not Daniel, I'd be grateful if you'd keep such opinions to yourself, understood?'

'Sorry Sir, I'll try to keep my own council in future.' Waves looked suitably chastised, so Stands continued.

'What other similarities did the missing bodies display?'

He looked at the other two who both managed to look blank. 'OK, all the bodies displayed similar wounds caused by edged weapons, daggers, knives, even some kind of small axe perhaps. So they all bled out, or died of trauma.' The others nodded.

'Apart from the one that's been left behind. According to Kevin the one that's left is the only corpse which displayed a classic cause of death stab wound, rather than just slashes. He also suggested that the victim was probably the last to die, the stab wound being the last wound inflicted on any of the four victims. He backs this up with evidence of blood from underneath the body, showing that significant amounts of blood had been shed by the other victims before the body dropped to the floor. He also goes on to suggest that from the positioning of the wound it would appear that the weapon used more than likely pierced the victims heart, unless the weapon had a disproportionately short blade.'

Waves and the Pathology Assistant were both frowning, obviously not comprehending what the Chief Inspector was getting at.

'The body that was left is the only one that suffered damage to the heart.'

Waves still didn't get it. 'Is that significant?'

Stands finally shrugged. 'I've got no idea, but it's the only thing that differentiates that body out there from the ones that were taken. It could mean nothing, or it could mean everything.'

He looked at Waves. 'The only thing I know for certain right now is that I'm hungry. Thank you for your time Marcus. We'll be in touch.'

Stands stood and shook the Pathology Assistants hand before going to the door. Waves nodded and followed his boss out the door.

Stands was waiting for him outside.

'What now boss?'

'Breakfast. Know any good greasy spoons round here?'

Chapter Six

Tris moaned quietly to himself when his alarm went off a few hours later. He reached over to the small table by the side of the bed and palmed the switch on top of the alarm clock. As he slumped back into the pillows memory rushed back into his alcohol abused brain, slowly filling his mind with the horror of what had happened last night. Martin was dead. Tris lay there, feeling very small in his king size bed, twitching with each new recollection. Finally he could stand the memories no longer and sought to shut them out in the heat and vapour of a scalding hot shower.

Pink, shiny, and feeling reckless, he emerged from his en-suite bathroom just in time to hear the front door bell. He looked out of his bedroom window down to the driveway below. Outside on the gravel was a shiny black Audi A3. He knew that Garfan would approve of his choice of cars, it was after all renowned to be a very safe model, with twin air-bags and ABS. It was just a shame that Garfan wouldn't be able to drive it.

'Tristan!' Garfan's bellow could probably have been heard half way down the street.

Tris dived into an old pair of jeans, grabbed a T-shirt and started cramming it on as he hot tailed it out of his room and down the stairs to the hallway. At the bottom of the stairs Garfan was waiting with the representative from Avis Prestige Cars. As was to be expected the young man was decked out in one of the company's rather fetching red jackets which Avis, for some unfathomable reason, felt would look good and reaffirm their company image.

Garfan saved his scowl for Tris's eyes only as he came bouncing down the stairs towards them. 'Good morning Tristan, good of you to join us. I hope I didn't inconvenience you by calling you down?'

The Avis Rep looked a little uncomfortable stood next to Garfan's diminutive figure. Tris just grinned in response and held out his hand for the clipboard the Rep was clutching to his chest. He looked at the Rep and read his ubiquitous name badge whilst filling in the details on the form. The Rep caught his look and smiled at Tris.

'No, no inconvenience Garfield old chum, though if you'd bother to learn to drive you wouldn't have to call on me to fill these things in now would you? You could have just filled it in yourself, and the lovely Chris here would have been able to give you the keys instead.'

Garfan's scowl deepened as the Avis Rep blushed in such a way that it was obviously not from innocent embarrassment.

Tris handed back the completed form. 'I'm so glad you have my details on file, it keeps this sort of paperwork to a minimum, which is such a blessing. I hate to waste time messing about. Wouldn't you agree Chris?'

By this point, with the rather short gentleman going red with anger next to him and this beautiful young man stood in front of him wearing nothing but an old T-shirt and very tight jeans which he'd failed to button all the way up, the Avis Rep was left sweating heavily.

'Thank you Sir, it's always a pleasure to make people happy.' With a cough Chris handed over the car keys and fled through the still open front door.

Tris had followed the young man's flight with his eyes, so he didn't see the back of Garfan's hand heading his way, but he felt it when it impacted at speed with his left cheek. Recoiling Tris clutched at his face.

'Christ, what the fuck was that for?'

'You know damn well what that was for. After last nights debacle, which you seem to have rather successfully put behind you, you stand there and toy with that poor boy. His sexuality may have been obvious, but that doesn't give you the right to lead him on. You know the effect you can have on humans. Look at you, you're even dressed like some cheap rent boy. Sometimes Tristellis I despair for you.'

That said Garfan stormed off towards the kitchen without a backwards glance. All Tris could do was stand their and hold his reddened cheek.

*

A little later, and more soberly dressed, Tris tiptoed down the stairs to the kitchen. Garfan didn't even bother to look up from where he was sat reading 'The Guardian' and finishing a bowl of cornflakes.

'What, no fry-up this morning Garf?'

Garfan threw the paper on the floor just as Tris reached the bottom of the stairs. 'Bollocks to this!'

He stood, forcing his chair to skid back and fall over with a clatter.

'After everything that's happened in the last twenty-four hours, if I have to come over there and beat the shit out of you in order for you to start taking things seriously, I fucking well will.'

Tris paled. He could see that Garfan was visibly shaking in an effort to control his anger. Not a good sign.

'Garf, I'm sorry OK. I don't know what came over me, I could feel the kids lust and I…'

'You what?'

He walked over and collapsed into a chair, 'I don't know. I'm sorry, I don't know what came over me. Things are so fucked up right now, I really need to sort my head out.'

Garfan pursed his lips and exhaled slowly. He shook his head and picked up the paper before righting the chair. Then he paused, looking at Tris, before sitting down slowly.

'OK Tris, lets just leave it for now.'

Tris looked relieved and nodded, cowed by Garfan's disapproval.

'I've been in touch with Lord Wessex, he knows we'll be arriving around lunch time, and Elarris already knows we're on our way. We should be safe on the road. All I can say is you better sort yourself out before we get to Northumberland, 'cos if you don't I won't be the only one ready to tear chunks out of your hide.'

Startled, Tris looked up guiltily. 'You wouldn't tell *him* about all this would you?'

'If you don't get your head together I won't have to…will I?'

Tris shook his head. 'No I s'pose not, he'd pick it out of my mind as if I it was playing on a TV screen embedded in my chest like some damn teletubby.'

'If I knew what the hell you were talking about I'd probably agree, however, the dialectic will have to wait. It's time we got out of here, *you've* got a lot of driving to do today!'

'What about breakfast? You've had some.'

'If you'd got up earlier you'd have had some too. No time now, you can grab something on the road…lets go. You know the route?'

'How many times? I could drive there in my sleep, M3 all the way, couldn't be simpler.'

*

Having found a local café that catered almost exclusively to London's delivery drivers, the two detectives had indulged in the kind of breakfast that Garfan would have approved of.

*

When they'd both finished, their empty plates

testament to their hunger, they sat back with their industrial sized mugs of tea and independently mulled over what they'd discovered at the morgue. At this point in the investigation there was little they could do but speculate until they received the scene of crime reports from both the cinema and the morgue incidents. With less forensic evidence to go on, due to the lack of bodies, the crime scene evidence might well be of even greater significance to the case.

So they could only wait until the Chief Forensic Pathologist turned up for work at his usual time. Hopefully Dr Watkin would be amenable to carrying out the post mortems on the two remaining corpses from the old cinema as soon as possible, as well as that of the unfortunate morgue attendant Sam Goodwin.

Stands was reasonably sure that they could rely on Marcus Benning to make the necessary arrangements and inform them of when they could go in and observe the first autopsy.

Marcus didn't keep them waiting, and called the Inspector as soon as his boss arrived. They could come in and observe in a couple of hours, after he had completed the initial routines that were essential in preparing to cut up a dead body.

*

Dr Watkin stood back against one of the few areas of bare wall in the autopsy suite as Marcus wheeled the body in from the cold room.

'Don't worry Detective Inspector, we've got all the basics, like weighing the body, done already, so you won't have to be here any longer than is strictly necessary.'

Waves looked a little uncomfortable as Marcus manhandled the body onto the autopsy table. He was actually a little surprised. The dead man had been physically fit and was at least six two in height, whilst Marcus was slight in comparison, but he seemed to move the body with ease. Once the body was in position on the slanted stainless steel table the Pathologists assistant placed what looked like a plastic brick underneath the body in the small of its back, causing the chest to protrude and the shoulders and neck to fall back, almost as though the body had taken a breath and puffed out its chest in pride.

Daniel had never liked attending post mortems, and luckily he wasn't often required to do so, this case was shaping up a little differently though. The body was still unidentified. No ID had been found on the body, no one resembling the corpse had been reported missing, and so far the fingerprints had come up blank. Stands seemed to be hoping that the body itself might supply some answers.

'Right then, thank you Marcus, I think we'll start by completing the external examination. Could you start the tape recorder for me.'

The assistant paced over to one of the trolleys next to the autopsy table and pressed the record button on a large digital voice recorder that was attached to a mike hanging from the ceiling above the body.

'Now then, we have an obviously physically fit, white male, six foot two and a quarter inches tall, one hundred and eighty pounds, and approximately thirty years old. His upper torso displays a diagonal cut from right hip up to left pectoral.'

The Doctor took a tape measure from the trolley next to him. 'The wound measures five hundred and seventy-three millimetres in length. The cut is deepest at the hip, gradually getting shallower as it rises up the torso. A second cut has been made to the throat, the wound is one hundred and nineteen millimetres long, deeper on the left hand side of the throat, becoming shallower as it travels across to the right hand side. The third and final wound is located in the chest between the fourth and fifth ribs down on the left hand side of the chest, it is twenty-five millimetres long and in shape resembles a squashed diamond. At this point I would almost definitely state that this finale wound is the cause of death, though the neck wound would definitely have resulted in death pretty swiftly, I won't know for sure until I open him up and have a look.'

Stands was looking impatient. 'I'm sorry Dr Watkin, but at this point how can you be so sure that the chest wound constitutes cause of death, when the much more obvious culprit would be the fact that someone had slashed the bastard's throat open?'

'Detective Inspector, just because something appears to be obviously true, does not necessarily make it so.'

'OK, how about the weapon that caused these wounds, what can you tell us about it?'

Dr Watkin looked up from the corpse to study Stands for a moment, before once more concentrating his attention on the corpse. The Doctor started fingering the wounds.

'I would say that the weapon was razor sharp, the edges of the wounds are very clear, little or no tearing, and the flesh beneath, blood vessels, etc. are cleanly sliced through. I would say it was a large knife of some kind, though the profile presented by the chest entry wound would suggest to me some kind of dagger, not a domestic knife.'

The Doctor started looking more closely at the skin of the rest of the body. 'Marcus could you turn him over so I can have a better look at his back.'

The assistant pulled the dead body over on its side then pushed the plastic block out of the way in order to slide it over so that it was now laying on its front. The pathologist continued his inspection of the body, then looked up at Stands.

'There are no other marks on the body, not

even any bruising of any kind. Just evidence of Livor Mortis where the body was laying on the floor.'

'Livor Mortis?'

'Yes Inspector, Livor Mortis or lividity, it's a settling of the blood after death. The heart stops pumping it around the body and the heavy red blood cells sink through the serum by action of gravity. If you look closely you can see which parts of the body were in contact with the ground. Those areas which aren't showing any of that slight purplish red discolouring are where the capillaries were compressed by contact with the ground.'

'Do you think that the lack of bruising is significant in some way Doctor?'

'Not really, but I'd say he was dead before he hit the floor. Turn him back over for me Marcus.'

Marcus once more shifted the body into position, replacing the block ready for the first incision in the chest, he then turned on a small faucet at the head of table designed to flush away any fluids released from the body.

Dr Watkin looked round at the two policemen, the expression on his face hidden by the green surgical mask he'd pulled up to cover the lower half of his face.

'So, lets take a look inside and see if this young man has any surprises for us.'

Waves couldn't help but look down and shuffle his feet as the Doctor picked up a scalpel and placed the tip of it against the body's sternum. The Doctor continued his commentary.

'First we make a Y-shaped incision. This reaches from the sternum down to the pubic bone. This is then joined by two incisions from the front of the shoulders to the original incision running down from the sternum.'

Daniel swallowed, took a deep breath and focused his attention on what the Doctor was doing. He was always amazed by the lack of bleeding, even though it had been explained to him that obviously a dead body has no blood pressure.

With the incisions made the Doctor put down the

scalpel for a moment, poked around with his fingers, then picked up the scalpel and started to use it to help peel the skin, muscle, and soft tissue off the chest wall.

Waves averted his attention to his superior as the Doctor proceeded to pull the flaps of flesh he'd created back to reveal the rib cage, breastbone and the abdominal cavity. The Inspector's face was blank, though Daniel was sure he could detect a certain tightening around the jaw. He found this tiny indication of distaste in his mentor strangely reassuring, lending him the fortitude to once more concentrate on what the Doctor was doing.

Thankfully the top most flap of skin and muscle tissue had been pulled right up over the body's face making the whole thing more bearably impersonal for Waves.

'It's now possible to see where the weapon pierced the rib cage and entered the organs beneath. From the position of it I'd say that the weapon entered the heart.'

Leaning closer he signalled for Marcus to step forward and take a look. 'What have we got here? What do you think Marcus?'

His assistant bent over the body's chest and examined the rib the Doctor had indicated. 'There does appear to be something there.'

Stands stepped forward closer to the table. 'What is it Doctor? What have you found?'

Looking up the he glanced at Stands. 'Patience Inspector. Marcus would you pass me that magnifying glass and the tweezers behind you.'

The atmosphere in the room had become noticeably tense as Dr Watkin hunched over the corpse's chest and used the tweezers to extract something caught in one of the ribs.

'Pass me a test tube.' The Doctor straightened and pushed the tweezers into the test tube and deposited something small and shiny. He held out the test tube to Stands.

'What do you think inspector? My guess is that

it's a splinter of metal from the weapon where the blade sliced into the bone of the lower rib.'

Stands gently took hold of the test tube and held it up to his face looking intently at its contents, then held it out for Waves to have a look at.

'I think you're right. How quickly can we get it analysed?'

The Doctor shrugged. 'We'll have to send it off to a specialist lab, have a metallurgist have a look at it. We could probably have some kind of result in a few days maybe.'

Waves looked at the tiny sliver of metal in the test tube. Maybe this could be the break they were looking for, though what such a small piece of metal could tell them was beyond him. He passed it to the pathologist's assistant who sealed the tube and put it aside out of the way.

'Well, lets continue shall we. Marcus pass me the bone cutter would you.'

His assistant passed the Doctor a shiny metal implement that looked remarkably like a pair of large curved pruning shears. Dr Watkin took them in hand and used them to cut the cartilages joining the ribs to the breastbone. This done he put down the bone cutter and sliced the last strings of cartilage holding the chest plate in position with a scalpel.

Waves found himself holding his breath as the Doctor pulled the chest plate away revealing the lungs and heart beneath. It was immediately apparent that he'd been right, the glistening red and grey heart displayed the same profile which had been displayed by the chest wound, the blade had pierced the heart almost dead centre.

The Doctor reached into the chest cavity and cut through the four main arteries anchoring the heart in place and lifted it out of the body leaving a disconcerting hole amidst all the other organs.

'Well there we have it gentlemen. Death was caused by the weapon entering the heart, the weapon went almost all the way through by the looks of it, instantly causing irreparable damage, halting blood flow, and causing almost instantaneous death.'

The Doctor, still holding the heart, pulled down the surgical mask with a bloody finger and smiled at his audience. Waves couldn't help but think that he looked curiously triumphant.

Stand's face was a picture of restrained anger. 'Thank you Doctor, we'll leave you to carry on, I don't think my colleague and I need to see any more.'

Stands then turned and walked quickly out of the room.

The triumphant look on the Doctors face faded as he looked round at Waves.

'Let us know when you've finished your reports on both bodies. We'll come over to your office to collect them. Maybe then you can share you're opinions on this case with us.'

Not wanting to be in the room any longer Waves too turned and walked quickly out of the autopsy suite, completely missing the concerned frown the Doctor displayed as his eyes followed the sergeants departure.

*

As Waves caught up with him the Inspector turned, angrily confronting his subordinate.

'Why is that man intentionally obstructing this investigation?'

Waves paused before answering. 'Well I know he wasn't very helpful Sir but...'

'But what Waves? Give me a bloody scalpel and I could have performed that autopsy.'

'Well he did get it right about the cause of death, there would have been no point stabbing the man through the heart if he was already dead.'

'Waves you appear to be missing the point. There

was no obvious bruising on the body. This can be accounted for by the subject being dead before the body hit the floor, just as the Doctor said.'

'So if the Doctor was right what have I missed?'

'Think about it Waves, three wounds inflicted one after the other, the second enough of a wound to kill and lay the subject out on the floor in a heartbeat, but yet a third wound, a stab to the chest precise enough to pierce between the ribs and through the heart. Have you any idea of the skill and speed required to inflict those wounds?'

'Maybe the assailant was just lucky?'

'Lucky!' Stands snorted. 'I would say that it's almost impossible to move that fast, with that much accuracy, and with enough strength to pierce a body that deeply. Have you ever stabbed someone Waves? We're talking well muscled flesh here, not candy floss.'

'So what are you suggesting Sir? Are we looking for some kind of superman, or are we just looking for some kind of psycho martial arts expert?'

'I don't know Waves, but all this use of blades where everyone else uses guns these days is beginning to look…well, for the want of a better word, weird.'

Waves smiled. 'I think that's the first time I've ever heard you refer to anything as weird Sir.'

Stands blew out hard through his nose and shook his head. 'The way this case is going it won't be the last time either.'

Chapter Seven

Just outside of Winchester, which had once been the great capital of Wessex, and at one point the entire kingdom, Tris turned off the M3 at junction 9 and took them back along the A31, and up towards Itchen Abbas, and Avington Park.

The Wessex family had been at Avington since the 10th Century, when it had been called Afintun, the land having been granted them by their kinsman, Alfred the Great, who unfathomably was remembered for having burnt some bread. An historical detail that doesn't include the fact that it happened whilst secretly consulting with one of the Tristellis's kin, luckily that little detail isn't known by human historians.

Finally driving up the long winding access road which led to the family quarters Tris once again felt saddened that the Wessex's had been put in a position where they had to open their home to commercial considerations. The Wessex family had always been friends of the elementals, in fact it had been Elarris who had convinced King Alfred to deed the land to the family in the first place.

The present Lord Wessex, David Wessex, still honoured the family's old allegiance, but wished for some kind of independence from the elementals patronage. Unfortunately pride was this man's sin of choice, and despite Tris's friendship with David's father, and his father before him, David was wary of him. Seemingly much more comfortable in Garfan's company, David still respected the old ways, but wished to deal with his allies on his own terms. Of course he knew why David felt the way he did, but his past indiscretion was such that he could never openly discuss it with the new Lord Wessex.

Garfan was all too well aware of the friction between his friend and Lord Wessex, he knew what it was that rankled the young Lord, but it was a situation that he was unwilling to intrude upon. Some things were best left to those immediately involved in them. Tris was on his own with that one.

Tris pulled up outside the entrance to the Wessex family's wing of the house. The gravel gleamed cleanly in the midday sun, the recent showers had done much to give an illusion of newness, not only lending the buildings façade a freshness which showed off the brick and stone wonderfully, but the surrounding trees also seemed to glow with life and an almost unnatural greenness.

The trip had been uneventful, just as Tris had said it would be, the route being such a direct one. As Garfan got out and stretched, enjoying the fresh air, he just hoped the journey to Bower would be so quick and easy.

Tris opened the drivers door and got out just as the big black front door of the East wing was opened from within. Revealed standing in the doorway was the ever smiling face of their old friend Arthur, the family retainer.

'Masters Garfield and Tristan, we've been expecting you. You're just in time for an aperitif before lunch. Shall I take the liberty of preparing your usuals?'

Tris laughed with obvious pleasure at the sight of their old friend. 'Arthur, as ever it is a delight to see you again, and a drink would be perfect, but you better make mine a small one, we've many more miles ahead of us and I'm afraid I must take my responsibilities as designated driver seriously.'

His far from subtle wink caused the old man's face to crease into an even bigger grin. As Tris passed the old man in the doorway he held the old man's shoulder, briefly squeezing it. 'It really is good to see you again old man. How long has it been?'

'Too long Tristellis.' He said quietly.

As Tris moved forward into the empty hallway within Arthur straightened and presented a much more dignified demeanour to the smaller figure of Garfan, before bowing deeply.

'Master, your visit is timely, I fear your wisdom is too long absent from this house.' Arthur unbent his ageing frame and looked at Garfan seriously. 'Lord and Lady Wessex are awaiting you both in the Drawing Room, but may I be so bold as to have a quiet word with you before you go in? Lady Wessex requested that I make some things known to you before you meet with them.'

Tris had halted at the tone of warning in the Butlers voice, and turned back to the still open front door. Looking past Arthur he caught Garfan's eye and raised an eyebrow questioningly.

He caught Tris's look and inwardly swore. This was all they needed.

*

Arthur led them quickly to an anteroom just down the corridor from the Family Drawing Room. Closing the door behind them the old Butler visibly relaxed.

'I don't know quite how to put this, but I'll give you all the information available to me. I apologise for such abruptness, but I must keep it brief. Lady Christine is adamant that Lord David be kept unaware of her meddling in this matter.'

Garfan and Tris exchanged resigned looks and prepared themselves for the worst.

'OK Arthur, spit it out. We're all friends here, and the sooner you tell us the sooner we can do something about this...whatever *this* may be.'

The Butler stood silently for a moment obviously collecting his thoughts.

'Well Sirs, it would appear that Lord David has once again been drawn into some foolish treasure hunt. You may recall how the last time he went off on one of these pointless adventures he almost died whilst diving off the coast of Peru looking for lost Inca gold stolen by the Spanish. Anyway, he and the same clique of would be adventurers seem to have gotten wind of some ancient treasure hidden away somewhere in what used to be Persia. To be more exact somewhere in the Zagros Mountains.'

Tris was looking impatient. 'Sorry Arthur, forgive my geographical ignorance, but Persia doesn't exist any more, and I thought the Middle East was mostly desert.'

Arthur glanced at Garfan who shrugged as an indication of his apologies for his friend's ignorance and motioned for him to continue.

'Master most of the Eastern area of the Middle East is desert, and quite inhospitable, but Iran is mostly mountainous. The Zagros Mountain range runs almost the entire length of the country.'

Tris's eyebrows rose as he looked from Arthur to Garfan and back.

'Iran, you must be joking! David's not seriously considering going into Iran with his little chums is he?'

Arthur nodded. 'It would seem that his friends have come into contact with some mysterious group with contacts out there who swear blind that should anyone have the gall to try it, they could find…well that's where the available information fails us. It would appear that Lord David refuses to reveal to Lady Christine exactly what it is they'd be going there to look for. I must admit that Lord David is being uncharacteristically reticent about further details. In fact he has not been behaving like himself for a while now. Lady Wessex and I are rather concerned that there is more to this than some idle adventuring, not to mention the all too obvious dangers of an expedition into the mountains of Iran, current political, social and religious problems aside.'

'Bollocks!' Tris leant back against the wall next to the door. 'If David's as serious about this as you suggest how are we going to be able to talk him out of it? He's pig headed at the best of times.'

Arthur's frown at this comment was not lost on Tris.

'I'm sorry Arthur, but you know what I mean. When he takes it into his head to go off on one of these little trips of his even Elarris would have trouble getting him to see sense.'

'It's funny you should say that, but Lord David was going to contact you if you hadn't beaten him to it. It seems that before going any further with this foolishness Lord David was hoping to approach your Elders for information concerning whatever it is that's apparently hidden away in those mountains.'

'What?' Garfan's exclamation was louder than he'd meant it to be. 'Look, we've been long enough as it is. We can't stay here any longer without arousing David's curiosity. We'd better get in there. If he needs information from our people then he's going to have to talk to us about this anyway. We'll deal with it then, when he brings the subject up himself.'

Arthur quickly opened the door for them. 'Masters, maybe a little dissembling is called for.'

*

Arthur opened the door and stepped into the Drawing Room ahead of Garfan and Tristellis. 'Lord and Lady Wessex...Masters Garfan and Tristellis, High Guardians of the Kingdom.'

As they entered Garfan couldn't help but notice the smile on the old man's face. Seldom did anyone bother to use their formal title, it seemed somehow unnecessary in this era, but Garfan did not miss the implied gravitas that Arthur was trying to lend them.

He was not the only one surprised by the manner in which the old Butler had presented them. Lord Wessex's eyebrows were virtually in his hairline, while his wife Lady Christine had diplomatically put a hand to her mouth to conceal her smile.

Arthur closed the door behind them and moved over to the sideboard to prepare drinks for their guests as the two friends moved to the centre of the room to greet their hosts.

Garfan was the first to bow to the couple before them. 'As ever it is a pleasure to see you both, Lord and Lady Wessex.'

The formal greeting complete he stepped forward and warmly shook Lord Wessex's hand. 'David, good to see you. I'm glad we could call on you like this, but I'm afraid that this is not just a social call, we were also hoping that you may be able to help us with something.'

David laughed a little too readily. 'Always straight to the point. Please don't give it another thought, my family owes both your races a debt which may never be repaid, so if there is anything I can do for you it will be my pleasure.'

Despite the warmth of the words Garfan couldn't help but interpret them differently. He released David's hand and stepped over to Lady Christine. Tris stepped into his place before Lord Wessex and offered his hand. The tightening around David's eyes and mouth, along with the slight hesitation in shaking his hand told him all he needed to know about the state of play between them, he was still unforgiven. Wordlessly they shook hands before Tris joined Garfan before Lady Christine.

Christine glanced at her husband as Tris took her hand and raised it to his lips.

'Christine you are as beautiful as ever.'

'Thank you Tristellis.' Pulling her hand away from his teasing kiss she turned away to retrieve her drink from the coffee table behind her.

The sharp pain which blossomed in Tris's side made him wince. The look on Garfan's face beside him left him in no doubt as to the origins of the elbow which had been jabbed so swiftly into his side. In timely fashion Arthur's hand appeared before him holding a small Vodka Martini, the other held a Campari and soda out to Garfan.

'Thank you Arthur, after spending all morning cooped up in a car with Tris I need this.'

Everyone but Tris laughed, releasing some of the tension which had been building in the room.

Tris smiled indulgently and blew a raspberry. 'Very funny!' He said before turning back to Arthur. 'Any chance you could show me the new plantings you were just telling us about Arthur, if there's time before lunch that is?'

Arthur looked towards Lord Wessex.

'Of course Arthur.'

David nodded to Tris. 'You'll be pleased that I took your advice with the planting, go see for yourself.'

Garfan smiled his thanks as Tris passed him on his way out of the room with Arthur.

*

Once the door had closed behind Tris and the Butler, Garfan placed his drink on the coffee table before him and sat down on one of the two rather chintzy sofas that faced each other in the centre of the room. Lord and Lady Wessex did the same, making themselves comfortable.

'So Garfan, what exactly can a mere mortal such as myself do for you?' Lord Wessex smiled in an effort to soften the all too obvious sarcasm in his words.

Garfan wasn't surprised, just continually disappointed by the young Lords attitude to himself and Tristellis.

'David, I know you're not truly comfortable with us, which is one of the reasons we seldom call, but we have a duty to your family, one which we will always honour.'

He let his words sink in before continuing.

'Anyway, as it happens we were hoping you could help us. We need some information which you might be able to use your friends and contacts to get for us.'

David raised his eyebrows. 'What kind of information?'

'Well, yesterday there was an incident in an old, disused cinema in South London, you may have heard something about it in the news.'

David and Christine looked at each other and smiled. Christine put down her drink and looked intently at Garfan.

'We saw it on the news last night, I said to David that I wouldn't be surprised if you two were mixed up in that somehow.' Christine frowned. 'That poor little girl. Personally I'm glad you killed those monsters!'

'Well for a change they weren't monsters...just men.'

David took Christine's hand and squeezed it. 'We know what you have to do Garfan, but Satanists are monsters, when men do those kinds of things they cease to be able to make any claims to humanity.'

Garfan nodded. 'The problem is they weren't Satanists.'

'What?'

Garfan could see that his hosts were puzzled. 'They were just posing as Satanists, it was just a ruse to draw our attention away from something else. What happened at the cinema was meant to be a trap…for us.'

David looked confused. 'Garfan, what are you saying? They knew about you and Tristellis?'

'Yes, somehow they knew, and they set up a trap using that little girl as bait. They thought they could...take us out.'

David shook his head. 'More fool them.'

He glanced at Christine before continuing. 'Garfan, you know that I don't always feel very comfortable with my family's relationship with…your people. I remember my grandfather trying to explain it to me when I was a boy, and I really didn't believe it until I got older and saw how you and Tristellis hadn't aged. My father told me stories of the things you, Tristellis and he did during the war. He told me how you'd both saved his life more than once during covert operations in Scandinavia.'

Garfan smiled, a far away look on his face. 'Your father was a very brave man. The Nazis were a bigger threat to the Kingdom than any rogue creatures we've ever had to deal with. We were honoured that your father took such risks getting us involved with the SIS.'

'Which is why, despite any personal feelings on my part, I honour my family's ancient alliance with you and your people.' David leant forward. 'So tell me what kind of information you need.'

'These men, whoever they were, weren't working alone. We need to find out who they were so we can hopefully find out who is behind this. Tris and I aren't safe until we get to the bottom of this. But the police are holding all the cards, we need to find out what they already know, and whatever they find out in the course of their investigation.'

David sat back and briefly looked up at the ceiling. 'Hmm, that's not going to be easy. There are still friends of my fathers who have links to both MI6 and MI5, and I have friends who have contacts in the police, but if I start asking questions there will be people wanting to know why.'

'I know you think we represent some kind of anarchic old guard which has no place in the modern world, and there are those within our own ranks that argue that we should withdraw ever further from the affairs of men, but please don't make the mistake of thinking that we don't understand the world we now live in. I'm fully aware of the risks you'd be taking in arousing the interest of the intelligence community, so please don't think that I ask this lightly.'

Garfan sighed, shaking his head. In the old days if he'd asked a favour of a human ally there would never have been any question of compliance. All involved understood that what they had to do was more important than the petty considerations of mere individuals.

'David, we have many human friends, but none are in as good a position to help us with this quickly. Besides, until we find out who or what is behind this, we could all be in danger. Do you think withdrawing yourself from us now would protect you from any reprisal aimed at us and our human allies?'

'Garfan I'm sorry, that's not what I meant, and I would never do that. You, Tristellis, and all the rest of your people represent proof of something more than the shallow reality the human race clings to so desperately, something that I personally will never understand. But I would never turn my back on you, I and all my forebears owe you too much for that to ever happen.' He looked wearied by the conversation. 'I just worry about putting my family in danger.'

Garfan laughed. 'And why should you ever worry about that. It saddens me that you still don't seem to understand that I, or Tris, or any of our kin, would gladly lay down our lives to protect you and your family. Your father must have told you that, we are here to protect the Kingdom, and the kingdom is it's people.'

'Without it being expressed it's difficult to credit, but...well, I'll do what I can.'

He paused and looked nervously at Christine. 'Would you excuse us darling, there is something I need to discuss with Garfan, something it is best you know as little about as possible.'

Christine's face hardened. 'As you wish.'

She stood and turned to go, but looked back at her husband coldly. 'I'll see what Tristellis thinks of our new trees, I'm sure we'll have much to talk about.'

And with that she swept from the room, closing the door noisily behind her.

David looked pained by his wife's outburst.

'I don't mean to pry David, but are things OK with you and Christine? I'd thought that things had improved since James's birth?'

David's rueful laugh was warning enough that things were not as they may appear.

'Garfan, whatever you say about being in touch with time, it never ceases to pass you by quicker than you think. James is seven now. Don't get me wrong, I love him and Christine dearly, but I don't know if we'll ever get past what almost happened between Christine and...Tristellis.'

He looked intently at Garfan. 'I'm sorry Garfan, but I don't think I'll ever be able to forgive Tristellis for being in love with my wife. I know nothing has ever happened between them, and I trust Christine implicitly, but his presence makes me uncomfortable. To be honest, if he were just a man I'd have beaten the living shit out of him and that would be that, but...'

'But he's not human.'

'No he's not…'

'David, the only comfort I can offer you is the knowledge that Tris suffers for it. Our races tend to mate for life, and the pain it causes him knowing that he can never be with her is more punishment than you could ever give.'

'You mate for life?'

'Yes, did you not know?'

He shook his head and laughed ruefully. 'My grandfather was the scholar of the family, and that piece of lore he failed to share with me. Thank you Garfan, it helps, though in a way it makes me pity him too. Hmmm, this was unexpected.'

David finished his drink in one long, slow draught. 'Anyway, that's not what I wanted to talk to you about. The thing is I'm glad you came as I was hoping to ask for your aid too.'

Garfan tried to look surprised. 'Really? If we can help you in any way you should know we will.'

'It concerns an expedition which some friends and I are organising.'

'Another of your adventures David? I thought becoming a father had cured you of your reckless streak. Besides, didn't you promise Christine that when James was born you'd leave all that Indiana Jones stuff behind you?'

David was not amused by Garfan's Hollywood comparison. 'I'm never reckless Garfan. I always take all the necessary precautions, I enjoy my life far too much to risk stupidly cutting it short. Anyway that, as I said, was over seven years ago now.'

'And now your feet are itching again. But reckless or not, you almost drowned on that last little adventure. Isn't one brush with death enough for you?'

'How can you have an adventure without at least a little danger?'

It was Garfan's turn to laugh. 'OK what is it we can help you with?'

David became serious once more. 'Some of my friends have come into contact with a group of people who have hinted at something hidden in an uninhabited part of Iran, an area in the Zagros mountains to be exact. A treasure which is beyond value. Now this group appear to be a rather odd bunch, and we don't seem to be able to find anything out about their background.

Not only that, but in the digging we have done we've come across some rather strange stories about the area where this so-called treasure is supposed to be hidden.'

'So what is it you want David, help with the expedition? Maybe a guide?'

'Nothing like that Garfan, we've got a group of ex-SAS mercenaries together to guide us and help with entry into and exit from Iran. They'll take care of us. What we really need is more information. As far as we can gather from our sources whatever is there has been there since before the crusades. What I was wondering was whether I could approach the Elders, my grandfather once told me that some of your people were involved in the crusades. I thought maybe they might know something that could be of use in preparing for whatever's out there.'

'Now you've got me worried. Who are this group you've become involved with?'

'I'm not involved with them Garfan, stop worrying. None of us are *involved*, we're just using them as a source of information. As to who they are, well they seem to want us to think that they're some kind of ancient secret society or something, they call themselves 'The Brotherhood'. To be honest I think my friends are having their legs pulled. Gullible foreigners being bled for some money and told some local myths in order to make some quick cash. We'll probably get out there and find an old goat farm or something.'

Garfan grinned. 'Lets hope so.'

David smiled too. 'Who knows, I'm on the edge of all this, but when the others asked me to do a little background research I agreed. Hey, if there's anything weird out there the Elders just might know something about it right?'

'We'll see. We're going up to see Elarris when we leave here. I'll ask him to contact you. When is this little expedition of yours happening anyway?'

'I'm taking Christine and James to France to visit Christine's Grandmother in a couple of days. I'm staying there for a few days, and then flying out to Ankara, to meet up with the rest of the expedition.'

'I don't mean to pry David, but how do you plan to get into Iran? I get the feeling that this is all somewhat covert.'

'Yeah I know, that's the main reason I don't want Christine to know any details. She'd worry too much. Anyway, we're planning to skirt Iran and Armenia, and slip into Azerbaijan where we'll meet up with friends of our SAS chaperone's to pick up the bulk of our equipment, including weapons, etc. From there we'll slip into Iran and hook up with guides from 'The Brotherhood' who'll lead us up into the Zagros Mountains. The whole area is under-populated, and as a result there's virtually no Iranian military or official presence there. We should be fine, besides which should we need it we've even got our own air support. I feel like James Bond, and if all we uncover is a big scam so what, it'll still be fun.'

Garfan shook his head good-naturedly and stood up. 'Your idea of fun is twisted David, but like I said I'll give Elarris and the other Elders the details and see if they can tell you anything. In the mean time I'm hungry, lets go see what's for lunch.'

David held out a cautionary hand to Garfan.

'Don't worry, I won't mention any of this to Christine.'

Stands and Waves were back in their office when Marcus Benning phoned from the Pathologist's offices at the hospital.

'Sergeant Waves, it's Marcus Benning from the…'

'Hi Marcus, please…just call me Daniel.'

'OK Daniel. I just wanted to let you know that we've finished the post mortems on the three bodies connected to your case. Dr Watkin is, at this very moment, writing up the preliminary reports on our findings, so that you'll have something to work with whilst waiting for the official reports.'

'How long is it likely to be before we get the final reports?'

'Well if bodies keep turning up like this it could be weeks.'

Daniel groaned.

'Look, the prelims should be ready for you in a couple of hours, and will include all the important stuff, so you will have something concrete to work with.'

Daniel sat back in his chair, the hand not holding the phone unconsciously going to his face and pushing his hair back off his forehead.

'Well that's good news…any surprises we should be aware of?'

'Not really, there is unfortunately very little useful forensic evidence available from the bodies themselves. Though I am looking forward to getting the results back from the metallurgist we sent that specimen to. I'm hoping it might give us some insight into the kind of weapons that were used.'

'That would be great, though I'm not really sure how a component breakdown of the composition of the metal is going to help?'

On the other end of the phone Marcus laughed. 'Well it could give us a clue as to where, when and how the weapon was made, it may also explain how it is possible for a blade with such a broad profile to be so impossibly sharp. Talking of which we've matched the wounds on the little girl to one of the knives found at the crime scene, the only one which displayed any traces of blood. The edges of the wounds show the characteristic tearing of the tissue around the edges of the wound consistent with the use of that blade. Which kind of rules out your mystery men as the girl's killers just as you suspected. There were fingerprints on the handle of the knife, but they don't match our remaining corpse, and unfortunately we didn't get a chance to print the others before they were stolen.'

'I take it there's no match on the database?'

'No...you don't sound surprised?'

'Well, generally speaking you have to catch someone doing something illegal before you can take their fingerprints. I get the feeling that these guys have been operating below our radar.' Daniel scratched his head.

'Anything else?'

'Well just a matter of elimination really. All the wounds inflicted on the group of men found at the scene were superficially examined and photographed. The wounds were the same as those on remaining body, all except for the stab wound that is. All showing that characteristic lack of tissue tearing around the edges of the wounds.'

'How about our unfortunate friend at the morgue?'

'Sam Goodwin, yes, well the single wound that he sustained shows the same lack of tissue tearing, which would suggest that it was your mystery men that did it.'

Daniel had been thinking about that whilst listening to the pathologist's findings. 'Or it could just mean that Mr Goodwin was killed using a similar weapon.'

'Yes, that could be the case, but it seems kind of unlikely.'

'Why? Didn't you suggest that the blade that very nearly decapitated Mr Goodwin was possibly around two feet long, like some kind of short sword?'

'Yes, and I suppose that seeing as none of the wounds on the bodies from the cinema could have been caused by a weapon that long then there is room for doubt, but what about the M.O?'

'I know the similarities do draw them together, but Sam Goodwin could have been murdered with another weapon, one we haven't encountered before.'

'Well the weapons used at the cinema were more than likely some kind of hatchet and a long dagger of some kind. Both very different weapons, but both inflicting wounds with very unusual signatures, the same signature as the weapon used at the morgue. Who knows what kind of weird arsenal they have at their disposal. I think you're clutching at straws to try and differentiate between these two incidents.'

'Maybe you're right Marcus. I'm beginning to feel like we're going around in circles on this one. I'll be sure to let Inspector Stands know about your findings, and we'll see you in a couple of hours when we pop in to pick up the prelim reports.'

'Actually you won't. I have to head out to another crime scene in North London as soon as I get off the phone. Doubt I'll be back in the office any time soon.'

Daniel winced. 'Not another slice and dice attack?'

'No, don't worry, this one is apparently your normal everyday murder, gunshot wounds and all. It wouldn't appear to be linked in any way with your case, but I'll let you know if I come across any evidence of Freddy Kruger, OK.'

'Very funny Marcus. Thanks for your help. Will Dr Watkin be there to give us the copies of the reports?'

'Yep, he'll be here. I'll warn him that you'll be coming. Good luck with the investigation Sergeant.'

'Thanks.' Daniel put the phone down and rubbed his face. Now he had something else to look forward too. Being in the same room as his boss and Dr Watkin.

Why can't people just get on with each other?

*

Some time later Daniel was again wondering why so called professionals couldn't just be a little more professional, when he happened to glance up and notice something above a large filing cabinet in the corner of the Chief Pathologists small office, a small plaque bearing an inscription in what could only be Latin, *Hic locus est ubi mors gaudet succurrere vitae*. Waves glanced sideways at Inspector Stands and noticed that he too was looking at the plaque.

Stands turned back to the Pathologist. 'Sorry, but that plaque in the corner, something about life and death. What does it say?'

Dr Watkin looked over at the cabinet and the plaque above it. 'Oh that, it's kind of a Pathologists motto. It says, *This is the place where death rejoices to teach those who live.*'

The doctor turned his head back to look at Inspector Stands and found him studying him with narrowed eyes.

'A little morbid don't you think Doctor?'

'Maybe you should take it a little less symbolically, and take it more literally Inspector. Every corpse we look at here gives us more information about how people live and die. You could almost say we worship science here, and the post mortem is our act of worship, the cadaver being the sacrifice.'

'I was under the impression that science was anti-religion?'

'Science has always been fostered by religion, whether it knew it or not. The search for understanding of God's creation is a noble pursuit, one which we practise here.'

'Sorry Doctor I was under the impression that this was a purely secular establishment, and proud to be so.'

The Doctor tilted his head slightly, his lips compressed in such a way that Stands was convinced he was holding back a retort.

Waves was beginning to get the distinct impression that he was witnessing a major personality clash here. Stands really didn't seem too taken with Dr Watkin, maybe they should just conclude this and get out of there.

'So, is there anything else you can tell us about the unidentified body which you haven't already told us during the autopsy?'

Dr Watkin's eyes slid away from the Inspector and focused on Waves.

'No, I'm afraid not Sergeant. The only information which we don't have at the moment is whether the fingerprints will come up with a match, or whether that small metal fragment will provide anything significant.
Other than that there's little else I can tell you I'm afraid, after all I'm not a detective.'

Stands snorted and rose from his chair. 'No, you're not…are you.'

With that Stands pushed open the door and walked out, Waves got up, struggling to keep up with the Inspector. As he got to the door Daniel looked back.

'Thank you for your co-operation Doctor, if we have any further questions we'll be in touch.'

Dr Watkin appeared understandably annoyed. 'Thank you Sergeant, I'd be grateful if it was you, rather than your boss that I have to deal with in future.'

Daniel forced a smile in response and then followed the sounds of Stands striding angrily down the corridor.

*

Back in Avington they were just finishing lunch when one of the mobile phones on the dining table nearest their host started to vibrate violently.

Lord Wessex picked it up and looked at the mobile phone's screen before pushing his chair back and standing. 'If you'll all excuse me, I'm afraid I need to take this call.' Turning to the door, David was just walking out the door as he answered the phone.

'Hello…'

Garfan put down his knife and fork and regarded Christine. She had remained very quiet throughout their lunch, obviously still smarting from being summarily dismissed by her husband. Garfan looked at the seat next to him where Tris was busy studying his empty plate. The tightness around his lips revealing his discomfort.

Glancing to his side, he looked at the ever present and stoic form of Arthur. Catching his eye he made a slight movement with his head, his eyes rolling towards Christine.

Arthur immediately stepped forward towards his mistress. 'May I clear your plate Lady Christine?'

Christine did her best to smile as she thanked Arthur. 'Thank you Arthur, and maybe some coffee, if our guests have time that is?'

Garfan glanced over at Tris, who shook his head imperceptibly. 'Thank you Christine, but we've got a long journey ahead of us. We should be going.'

Tris passed his plate to Arthur and, displaying an uncharacteristic awkwardness, pushed back his chair and stood.

'Thank you for lunch Christine.' The moistness in his eyes left little doubt to his inner feelings. 'It was good to see you and David again, I hope that next time we won't have to leave so abruptly.' And with that he brushed past Garfans chair and left the dining room, heading out towards the car.

Garfan sighed as he watched Tris's back disappear around the door. Looking round at Christine he found he wasn't the only one who had watched him leave with regret.

Christine noticed Garfan's eyes on her and smiled wanly. 'It would appear to be my lot in life that love has a tendency to walk away from me.'

Garfan shook his head emphatically. 'That's not true, and you know it. Besides, little James will never walk away from his mother. As to David…you needn't worry about him. When we talked in private earlier he told me everything, well I think he told me everything, about this little expedition of his, and to be honest it sounds like a wild goose chase to me. But he's set on going, and he's essentially a sensible man, he'll be careful, and it sounds as though they've thought it through pretty thoroughly. So I shouldn't worry. He'll be away for a few weeks, and when he gets back his lust for adventure will be satisfied.'

He smiled at Christine. 'At which point I'm sure he'll rediscover his love for you!'

She snorted at that, seeming sad once more as she looked down at the tablecloth and then balled her napkin in her hands. Looking up her eyes were moist, just as Tris's had been when he'd walked out of the room.

'Arthur, could you leave us for a moment.'

Arthur nodded and quietly left the room, carefully pulling the door closed behind him.

'Garfan, please look after Tris. I know how much it pains him to be here, it effects him more than you know.'

'I will Christine. I always do.'

*

As Garfan reached the front door he turned, suddenly aware that someone was behind him. 'Christ Arthur, please don't sneak up on me like that!'

'Sorry Master Garfan, though I'm sure that if your mind hadn't been elsewhere you would have heard me coming.
I just wanted to inform you that Lord Wessex was called away, and sends his apologies at not being able to say goodbye.'

'That was sudden. Do you know where he was going?'

'He wouldn't say, though he did look troubled.'

'In which case Arthur keep your eyes open, and look after Christine and James. If anything happens you know how to contact us?'

'Yes Master, though I'm sure there's nothing to worry about. Lord Wessex can look after himself.'

Garfan studied Arthur briefly. 'I hope so…'

Arthur closed the front door behind Garfan, and leant back against it, for once letting his fatigue take over for a moment. Looking up at the ceiling he shook his head sadly. 'I hope so too.'

*

Garfan crunched his way over the gravel drive towards the car. As he got nearer he could see Tris sat in the drivers seat looking blankly out of the windscreen, his mind obviously elsewhere. Before opening the passenger door Garfan took a moment to lean against the door, his arms folded in front of him on the roof of the car, his chin on his hands. Garfan closed his eyes and offered up a silent prayer to his ancestors.

Help me help those I love through these difficult times, and give me the strength not to judge them.

Garfan opened his eyes, unfolded his arms and opened the passenger door. Tris's head swung round as Garfan got in beside him, settling himself before pulling his seatbelt across his chest. Both sighed simultaneously, their heads turning to look at each other, both aware of the humour inherent in such small coincidences.

'Are you OK Tris?'

Tris's smile was only a little forced. 'I'll survive.'

He knew that was all the answer he was going to get right now. 'So, you know the route?'

Tris shook his head and laughed. 'Garf, we've got Sat Nav. We couldn't get lost if we tried.'

'The joys of modern technology,' said Garfan, whilst inside he was thinking how nice it would be to be able to get lost occasionally.

Chapter Eight

The atmosphere in the car was subdued. The black Audi was purring softly at a steady 80mph up the M40 in the middle lane. They'd already been travelling for over an hour and a half, already having passed Oxford before joining the M40 motorway going North.

Despite being in apparent control of the car it was obvious to Garfan that Tris's mind was elsewhere. Since first getting into the car and watching Avington house diminish behind them in the wing mirror, he'd not bothered to try and pierce the self-obsessed funk that seemed to surround his old friend like a cloud.

There was more than one reason for being wary of intruding on Tris's thoughts, not least of all being a great big dollop of good oldfashioned guilt. It had been apparent to Garfan for years that of all the places Tris could have lost his heart, it had actually happened at Avington.

Having known the present Lord Wessex all his life Garfan had been pleasantly surprised when David had first announced his engagement, and finally introduced his fiancée to his ageless benefactors. Christine had been just twenty-four at the time, and had already proved her commitment to David by helping him weather the loss of his father to a cancer that even the Elders healing powers could not defeat.

Despite never having been very close to his father David had been hit hard by the swift and merciless way in which the cancer had eaten away at his always robust father. The once powerful and resourceful man who had been the veteran of many covert operations against the Nazi's in the Second World War, had slowly become ill, and then had seemingly crumbled before his son's eyes. At the last even denying David any chance to say goodbye, as his father became completely incoherent just days before he suddenly died, leaving his son to become the latest in the long line of Lords of Wessex. In the background Christine had been there, nursing the son's mind as the fathers body was nursed by more professional carers.

Christine was the half-French daughter of a wealthy young French Débutante who'd had the dubious taste to fall in love with a talented, but ultimately unsuccessful English artist. When her father had committed suicide a year after his wife, Christine's mother, had died in a rather brutal and messy car crash, her mother's family had taken Christine in, her grandmother taking her to her bosom as some sort of consolation for the loss of a much loved daughter.

She had taken to France like a fish to water, and after finishing her indenture at the Sorbonne, Christine had returned to England, moving to London to act as an interpreter, having somehow managed to master Russian as well as her mother tongues of English and French. It was at a diplomatic party in London that David and Christine had first met, and from which moment David had known that he wanted to possess her.

So Christine was introduced to Garfield Stone, and Tristan Forest as old family friends. That had been ten years ago. In that time David and Christine had married, and their son James had been born. Also during this time Christine had learned the truth about Masters Forest and Stone. Unfortunately during that time David had become a more distant member of their marriage, and Tris had gradually fallen in love with a human woman who still loved her husband and who could never be his.

Garfan had watched all this develop before his eyes, an unwilling witness to the inevitable heartbreak his best, and oldest friend must eventually suffer.
He had watched Tris throwing himself from one meaningless sexual encounter to another in an attempt to block Christine from his mind. He had, at one point, even stooped to abusing any drug he could get hold of.

After one particularly humiliating, and painful

episode which had almost caused them both to be killed when confronting a coven of inexplicably successful blood suckers whilst Tris had been under the influence of a veritable cocktail of drugs and alcohol, Garfan had put his foot down, grounding Tris and nursing him off the uppers, downers, alcohol, and more exotic substances.

When he was finally physically healed, Garfan had decided that Tris should confront the cause of all this rather than just addressing the symptoms. This led to him convincing Tris to tell Christine the truth about how he felt about her. Of course Garfan knew that Christine would turn him down, and hoped that such an absolute rejection would leave Tris free to get on with his life. However, this assumption was based upon the premise that Christine would turn Tris down because she loved her husband.

Outside the car's windows the world was whizzing past as they sped up the M1 towards Rotherham. Garfan shook his head at this point in his ruminations. Just goes to show how wrong a wise old elemental can be.

Christine had not turned Tris down because of her love for her husband. Far from it, she had in turn fallen in love with Tristellis. Christine ended up turning him down for much more prosaic reasons; her son, James, and the fact that she knew it could never work. Tris would outlive her, and James, by hundreds of years. He would stay young, beautiful, and vigorous for centuries, whilst in mere decades she would age, die, and decay.

He had read it all wrong, leaving him looking in from the edge of an almost Shakespearian tragedy, completely powerless to change what he had put into motion.

Garfan silently observed his friend out of the corner of his eye.

Tris was intent on the road and his own thoughts. What he was thinking Garfan could guess at, but never appreciate, being all too aware that we only ever truly experience our own realities. The hard truth being that we are always alone inside the prisons of our own minds and bodies.

*

Stands hated this, more than anything he hated this aspect of the job he loved so much, being at his masters' beck and call. What made it even worse was that he had so many masters. It wasn't just the Commissioner who could call him in to account for himself. No, there were so many agencies, so many Top Brass. Civilians could never hope to understand the complexity of the web of individuals and groups responsible for sheltering them from the harsh realities of…well, reality.

So here they were, investigation well in hand, if a little slow in producing any solid conclusions, but it was under control. And just when he was getting into his stride, warming up and starting to get a sweat on…they go and pull this shit. It pissed him off to be pulled in like this, why couldn't they just let him get on with doing his job. It *really* pissed him off.

Waves sat quietly watching the Inspector slowly pacing around the office. Gradually this would result in Stands slowly speeding up until he was virtually bouncing off the walls. Waves could see it coming. He'd seen it all before, and it wasn't a pretty sight.

They'd been waiting outside the Commissioner's office for the last twenty minutes. His secretary had announced upon their arrival that they would have to wait until he was ready for them.

It had taken a lot of self-control for Stands not to ask why the Commissioner had requested their presence in the first place if he was not then going to see them when they arrived. Surely conventional logic would dictate that you would want to see someone when you had asked to see them. Now the secretary sat eyeing the inspector warily, as if he were some kind of caged beast pacing angrily in its confinement, just waiting for an opportunity to pounce.

Waves knew it would be pointless to try and intervene and attempt to calm the inspector down. He'd tried that once before and had only just survived the encounter. He'd sworn never to interfere with his mentor ever again when he was angry, even if somebody else's life depended on it, he valued his own too highly.

That being the case Daniel settled himself as comfortably as possible on the standard issue institutional plastic waiting room chair with which the room had been furnished, and prepared for a long wait. He had long ago learnt that the more important somebody was, and crucially the larger that persons sense of self-importance, the longer they would keep their appointments waiting. So he sat back, closed his eyes, and relaxed.

The room they were in could really only be described as a waiting room, despite the fact that it contained a desk, a self-evidently busy secretary, and a number of large and very business-like filing cabinets, it still had the aura of a corridor about it. A room with only one function. A room to pass through in order to get to a more important room.

Waves opened his eyes when he heard footsteps approaching the door through which they themselves had walked half an hour earlier. The footsteps slowed, stopped momentarily as the handle was turned, then resumed, bringing into view a large be-suited figure, closing the door surprisingly quietly behind itself.
He watched as Stands turned from his pacing to look coldly at the newcomer who had interrupted him in his mission to wear out the carpet upon which he stood.

The figure was tall and broad, in a bulky kind of way suggesting far too much time spent in a gym for Waves' liking. The cut of the suit was also indicative of far too much disposable income. Waves took an instant dislike to the tall figure that came to a halt before the secretary's desk.

The secretary leapt to her feet. 'The Commissioner has been expecting you Sir. Please go straight in.'

The answering 'Thank you', though brief was enough of a response to be unable to hide the fact that the mysterious suited man was an American. Waves immediately liked him even less.

*

It was around fifteen minutes later that Waves was sat in the Commissioner's office worrying about what was going through Inspector Stands' mind. Waves was aware that Stands suffered a little from the old 'over-dressed, over-paid and over here' syndrome, but he hadn't thought the Inspector would ever let his immediate ill feelings for someone be so obvious. American or not, Waves didn't think the man deserved such an obviously hostile reaction.

Having said that, he was still surprised by the way the Inspector had behaved with the Chief Pathologist, Dr Watkin. Though Waves himself was harbouring doubts as to whether the good Doctor was playing by the rules, what with the odd phone call at the crime scene, and the ambivalent way in which he'd conducted the post mortems. Dragging himself back to the here and now, Daniel was aware that attention was being focused on him by both the Commissioner and the tall American.

'And this is Detective Sergeant Waves, Mr O'Brien.'

'Please just call me O'Brien…everyone else does.'

Stands and Waves exchanged glances.

'So…' Stands interrupted. 'Which Agency is it exactly that you represent?'

O'Brien lifted an eyebrow and looked enquiringly at the Commissioner.

'Mr O'Brien, you can hardly expect the cooperation of my officers if you are not prepared to

125

disclose your authority in this matter.'

'Very well, my unit works under the umbrella of the CIA. We have negotiated with your MI5 and MI6 to gain the authority to take over this investigation. Your superiors feel that our specific experience with cases such as this puts us in a much better position to bring a satisfactory conclusion to the present situation. This can obviously be best achieved with the complete cooperation of those officers already involved in the case.'

O'Brien looked pointedly at Stands and Waves.

Stands was by this point looking a little red in the face. Waves was almost certain that if this continued he would finally really get to see steam issuing from his mentors ears.

The Commissioner caught Stands eyes and held them with his own as he shrugged as if to say *sorry it's out of my hands*.

Waves studied the Commissioner's impassive face. 'So Sir, how exactly is this going to work?'

The Commissioner sat back in his big office chair, the creak of the leather sounding unnaturally loud in the almost silent office.

'You are both to be seconded immediately to O'Brien's unit until further notice. You will consider yourselves to be under his command.'

At this point the Commissioner focused on O'Brien. 'I personally would rather my officers worked from their current stations here at New Scotland Yard, and so keep at least a little contact with the department which they will be returning to in due course.'

The tall American smiled indulgently at the him. 'Of course Commissioner, I understand completely, and I can assure you that it is quite common for officers from other agencies to work with us in just this way. We do it all the time, all over the world in fact.'

Stands had by this point had more than enough. 'So is that it then? I just want to make sure I've got this right. We lose control of our case and have to work in

126

some unexplained capacity for a foreign agency who have just hijacked our case?'

Stands turned pleadingly to his superior. 'Don't we get any say in this Sir? It's only the second day of the case. We can't be expected to produce solid results so quickly. At least give us a few more days before you shut us down.'

The Commissioner shook his head. 'I'm sorry Stands, but this comes down from on high. You are to work with O'Brien's people on this, and cooperate with them in every possible way to bring about a speedy conclusion to this investigation. There are to be no ifs, buts, or whys. Just a fast effective conclusion to the matter using any and all methods and means dictated by O'Brien and his unit. Do you both understand?'

Both Stands and Waves nodded, though both obviously had questions, they kept quite while the Commissioner nodded with satisfaction.

The tall American was all smiles as he addressed Stands and Waves. 'I'm sorry gentlemen, I know this has come as a bit of a surprise, and I do understand and empathise with you regarding your loss of autonomy on this case. But that is all it is, a loss of autonomy, please remember that you are still working on the case, and will be as long as you can be of use to us.'

At this point the smile slipped from O'Brien's face revealing an expression of grim determination. A look which warned both Stands and Waves that he was not a man with whom to fuck. The moment gone, O'Brien was once more all smiles.

'Please believe me, working with me and my team will, I guarantee, put you in a better position to both understand the situation, and bring it to a conclusion.'

Waves was having difficulty taking all this in, there seemed to be a language being spoken here which he didn't understand. Jargon with a political edge to it. Coupled with the fact that his normally composed mentor looked fit to explode left him feeling even more out of the loop. O'Brien raised his hands palm out in a conciliatory gesture. Though to Waves he suddenly looked like a Saturday night evangelist about to launch into his own personal diatribe.

'Well gentlemen, before we go any further there are still a few details I need to go through with the Commissioner here. So if you could excuse us I'll meet you both at the main entrance in around ten minutes.'

With this dismissal still hanging in the air O'Brien turned his back on the two officers and ignored them both as first Waves, then Stands stood and went to the door. The last thing either of them heard as they closed the door behind them was O'Brien's voice addressing the Commissioner.

'You understand the situation here…'

*

When they reached the front doors to the building Stands carried right on out of the building leaving Waves to follow suit.

As soon as they were outside the building, and past the stationary, armed police guards, Stands dipped his hand into his jacket pocket and lifted out the ever present packet of cigarettes. Putting one in his mouth he lit it, all the while scanning the area around the front of the building. Waves watched all this whilst still wondering what the hell was going on. Still watching Stands he was surprised when the Inspector subtly indicated that he should turn his attention to a large black BMW that was parked on Broadway, across the road from the New Scotland Yard building.

Stands turned his back to the vehicle and came to stand in front of Waves. Taking a large drag from his cigarette he blew the smoke out through his nose.

'Can you see the car over my shoulder?'

'Yes Sir.'

'Take a note of the number plate, I have a feeling it might be O'Brien's.'

Waves took out his mobile phone and saved the car's plate number in the phone's messages memory whilst surreptitiously sizing up the driver who looked to be another large American by the size and squareness of his head.

A couple of minutes later, as Stands was just considering lighting another cigarette, Stands noticed O'Brien's large figure approaching the glass doors on the inside of the building.

'Heads up.'

Waves didn't bother looking towards the building. He could tell by the Inspectors sarcastic tone exactly who was approaching.

O'Brien looked very pleased with himself as he walked down the steps from the building towards them. 'Well gentlemen, if you'll just follow me.'

He carried on across the road towards the car Stands had pointed out earlier. O'Brien went round to the front passenger side door and got in without even looking at the two policemen following him.

As they got into the back of the car both of them were beginning to wonder where this was leading. As they sat back in their seats O'Brien leant over the back of the front passenger seat with no trace of a smile as he looked them both up and down.

'Before we start I want you both to know that we have no illusions about you. We've done our homework. Sergeant Waves here has an exemplary military record, though I have to admit to curiosity to the gaps in your official record, gaps that even we couldn't fill, though we do have our suspicions. Followed by some serious undercover work with the metropolitan police. I'm kind of surprised you've ended up here. Though the fact you ended up with Stands is less surprising.'

At this point he shifted his gaze to Stands.

'You must be aware that you are considered by all and sundry to be a loose canon and not a team player, it would appear that the only reason you are tolerated is due to consistently surprising results. This, however, is where your stubborn individualism stops. You will do everything we ask of you, and you will do it in the way we ask you to do it. Despite the fact that you may think of me as a representative of a foreign agency, do please remember that I have the power to end both of your careers whenever and however I should choose to do so.'

With that he sat back in his seat, facing forward with the air of a teacher satisfied by a lesson well taught, he indicated to the driver that he could drive.

Behind his back Waves was surprised to see a smile on his mentor's face. Stands noticed Waves looking at him and instantly schooled his face back into a blank expression, though he did turn his head and quickly wink conspiratorially at Waves. Leaving his subordinate even more confused.

Daniel faced forward and concentrated on trying to follow the route the driver was taking. He wanted to know exactly where they ended up, even though on the inside he was in turmoil.

Why is Stands happy, what with the performance in the Commissioner's office, I thought he'd be livid, especially after that supercilious little speech from this American prick.

Half an hour later they were somewhere in Wapping. The black BMW pulled up outside an office building backing onto the Thames. Fully expecting obedience and without turning and saying a word to the two policemen or the driver, O'Brien opened his door and swung his large frame out of the car.

Stands and Waves had little choice but to follow suit. Waves got out first and then held the door open for Stands as he shuffled across the back seat to get out. Waves looked round and found O'Brien smiling indulgently as he observed this. The sarcastic expression on his face revealing all he needed to of his opinion of Waves' subordination to Stands.

As Stands swung the car door shut behind him he observed O'Brien's sneer and looked at Waves whose face was only a foot from his own. He couldn't help but notice the tightening of the muscles around the Sergeant's eyes and mouth. Stands could guess what was going through the mind of the proud and capable man he had come to depend upon.

In that moment of empathy he put his hand on Waves' arm, out of sight of O'Brien, and squeezed hard. Stepping around the Sergeant and presenting his back to O'Brien, he stared into his subordinate's eyes.

Speaking slowly and softly so as not to be overheard he surprised Waves once more.

'Now is not the time to show any weakness. Do not rise to any baiting, trust me. Stay quiet and follow my lead. Keep your eyes open and just absorb everything you possibly can. Just remember that when the time is right I'll be more than happy to stand back as you choke the life out of him, metaphorically speaking of course.'

With an accompanying wink, Stands smiled briefly before schooling his face once more into an expression of mild irritation, the lines caused by his frown adding years to his appearance. Then he turned back to face the man who thought he held their fates in his hands.

'Shall we get on with it?'

O'Brien didn't respond, but turned and walked up to the building's main doors which were the ubiquitous glass of almost every office building in the country. Again Stands and Waves were left with no choice but to follow. All this time Stands felt he was getting more of a grip on the character of the man they were following. His casual use of intimidation, and the lack of interactive dialogue spoke volumes about his attitude towards those he felt he had power over.

On the way through the first set of doors Waves noticed the standard building legend on the wall to their left, showing the basic floor plan of each floor and a list of all the companies who shared the building and on which floor they could be found. Waves couldn't help thinking that this seemed like an odd place to front the base of operations of a foreign security agency.

O'Brien stood just inside the inner glass doors, holding one open for the two men following him. Both walked through into what appeared to be the main reception area for the building. Waves looked at his boss who seemed quite relaxed, and vowed not to let his mentor down. This in mind he scanned the reception area in more detail, noting that for an office block there appeared to be an inordinate amount of interior security cameras. In fact, from what he was seeing he was reasonably sure that there wasn't an inch of the lobby that wasn't covered by one of the many cameras so discretely dispersed around the room.

O'Brien nodded at the young man behind the large, but not atypical reception desk towards the back of the room. Waves wondered what was hidden behind it besides feeds from the security cameras.

He shook his head, what am I thinking, if I carry on like this I'm going to end up completely paranoid.

Opposite the front doors was a bank of four lift doors, either side of which were fire doors which Waves assumed led to twin staircases. In the right and left hand walls of the room were two more sets of large glass doors separating the office spaces either side of the building from the central reception area. All he could do was follow as O'Brien moved left towards the office space on that side of the building.

As they entered the offices from the reception area Stands thought he detected a change in air pressure, something that one would not normally expect when walking from one room into another, unless of course those two rooms differed hugely in purpose and security. Waves too had noted a change in the quality of the air, as well as the slight sucking sound that accompanied the doors initial opening. He also couldn't help but notice the thickness of the glass doors that separated the agencies fake offices from the reception area behind them. Normal toughened safety glass doors were usually only around a centimetre thick, these must have been at least twenty-five. Waves wondered why he felt like he was walking into a fortress, they were surrounded by security in a building that even featured its own internal bullet-resistant glass doors. Then again this is the secret head-quarters for a foreign powers security agency. He definitely felt he should possibly leave his preconceptions behind. Advice that turned out to be extremely relevant sooner than he would have expected.

O'Brien seemed to be revelling in his role as their guide and ultimate superior.

'Up here we deal with all the mundane communications and admin involved in running our little outpost here in the UK, but downstairs is where all the interesting stuff happens…down in the crypt.'

Stands eyed O'Brien warily. 'The crypt…is this building built over the remains of a church?'

'No, it's just our pet name for where we keep the evidence from our…investigations.'

Stands and Waves exchanged looks, both of them wondering what they'd gotten themselves into.

O'Brien carried on, unaware that his audience was paying more attention to their surroundings than to him. 'So we may as well go straight down to the belly of the beast, and show you two exactly what it is we're dealing with here.'

He looked intently at both of them in turn. 'What you are about to see is of the utmost secrecy. You will not discuss what you see outside of this building.' He laughed softly. 'Though even if you did…no one would believe you.'

As they made their way through the open-plan office space it became apparent that O'Brien was leading them towards the back left-hand corner of the building which appeared to be screened off from the rest of the room. In front of the opening to the screened-off area sat another vigilant young man at a desk that looked as though it too could fulfil a number of functions, not the least of which being to protect whoever was behind it.

O'Brien nodded to the badly disguised security guard, walked through the opening and turned sharply to the right as the screening formed a dogleg leading to a small open area in front of very high-tech looking lift doors that were completely out of place in the corner of what, for all intents and purposes, was a very normal office block.

He led them up to the shiny steel doors of the lift and placed his hand on a glass panel on the wall next to the doors. Waves instantly recognised the panel as a scanner, no doubt scanning O'Brien's hand and fingerprints. Waves glanced at the Inspector, his almost imperceptible nod to go ahead all the answer Waves needed before addressing O'Brien.

'So…we don't get any kind of visitors pass then? I'm kind of surprised considering the obviously high level of security round here.'

O'Brien frowned at Waves's presumption. 'You don't need it. You will be escorted at all times whilst you're in the building. Besides which all our personnel have been briefed of your presence and appearance.'

'So in other words we have no freedom while we're in the building. What would happen if our escort were to leave us on our own? Would your other personnel assume the worst?'

'O'Brien grinned unpleasantly. 'Let's just hope you're never put in a position to find that out.'

Waves nodded to disguise the smile that the American's superciliousness was provoking and looked at Stands. The Inspector raised a hand to his mouth and coughed in order to disguise his grin.

Just then the lift doors opened revealing the lift to be a severe steel box designed solely to fulfil its function, and in so doing to keep its occupants safe from everything but a direct missile strike by the looks of it. O'Brien stepped into the lift without any hesitation leaving Stands and Waves wondering whether there was even room for them as well.

'Please gentlemen, don't dawdle or I may have to draw the conclusion that you're afraid.'

Stands just shook his head in disgust and gestured for Waves to precede him. 'Actually O'Brien it's just a matter of manners, and I'm inclined to believe that you just don't have any.' With that the Inspector stepped in to the lift and turned his back on O'Brien so as to face the closing lift doors.

With the doors closed Stands couldn't think of anywhere he'd rather be less, than stuck in a little metal box with a large American…who stank of cologne, and not even a nice one at that.

Stands only ever wore scent if he knew he might be around women, which is probably why he'd had his current bottle for the last two years, and the way things were going would probably last him the next two as well.

Luckily it was a very short ride to wherever it was they were going. As the doors of the lift opened Stands was not surprised to see another guard stood outside doors leading to what must be 'the crypt'. The area in front of the lift looked to be around twenty feet square, with no furnishings, just another security door, and the guard stood alertly beside it. This time it was obvious that the guard was a spook, he couldn't have looked more stereotypical if he'd tried, being tall and dark, and wearing a suit with an obvious bulge under his arm from his not-so-concealed weapon.

Stands and Waves walked out of the lift and stopped when O'Brien moved in front of them. O'Brien then reached into his jacket and withdrew two neatly folded documents which he then handed to the Inspector and his Sergeant.

'Before we go any further I need you both to sign these documents. Refusal to do so will mean you go no further, and will result in you probably sabotaging your careers.' The smug expression on his face suggested that he would have absolutely no problem with that.

'What is this?' Stands said holding it negligently in one hand and waving it to and fro.

O'Brien studied them both briefly before answering. 'It's very similar to your Official Secrets Act…only more binding.'

Stands unfolded the A4 pages he'd been given and quickly scanned the text before finding where he should sign at the bottom of the last page. Waves raised a questioning eyebrow as Stands took a pen from his own jacket pocket.

It was at that moment that Stands once again realised what a bastard O'Brien was. He'd purposely waited to give them these documents for an opportunity to put them at a disadvantage, to humiliate them, even if it was in only a small way. Stands walked calmly over to the wall and put the paper up against it in order to be able to sign it. As he did so he felt Waves at his shoulder and offered the Sergeant his pen with a resigned expression. After all, what could you do against such petty tactics. The man was obviously an unmitigated prick.

Stands held out the signed and once more neatly folded document to O'Brien who put it back in his inside jacket pocket along with the one he swept from the Sergeant's hand.

'Not going to read it Sergeant?'

Waves didn't bother to respond other than by giving him a bored look before turning away to look around at the room. A dismissive act that was all the more obvious for the fact that there was nothing in the room to look at.

Stands' lips twitched as he suppressed a smile. 'Shall we get on with it.'

O'Brien scowled and turned his attention to the security doors that were this time opened using a finger print scanner. As they opened automatically the air pressure once again seemed to change. Through the doors was a small room with what looked to be an identical set of doors opposite, making it look like some kind of an air-lock.

'What exactly is it you do down here O'Brien? I don't think our government would be too impressed if they were to find out that you're messing about with bio-agents down here.'

'What we do down here is none of your governments concern. However, you need not panic, we are not involved in any bio-hazardous work. We just like to take precautions.'

'Against what?'

'Believe me, when you see what we're dealing with here, you'll understand.'

Stands didn't like the sound of that, but considering the situation there was very little he, or even Waves for that matter, could do about it.

O'Brien carried on seemingly oblivious to any concerns they may have had. 'This is the only way in or out of this part of the facility. There are no windows, and no fire escapes. The basic layout is such that the further you go in to the facility, the more you are exposed to the extremely sensitive nature of our work.'

'Sensitive?'

'Don't worry, you'll see.' With that he led them through the air-lock to the last set of doors leading into 'the crypt'.

Chapter Nine

The room they entered was not quite what they'd come to expect from the high-tech security measures they'd had to go through to get there. They'd entered a huge white painted room roughly fifty feet by forty, which they'd come into from a corner, the basement level obviously reflecting the shape of the building above them. Before them stretched a clear area that led to double doors opposite them leading to what could only be the next part of 'the crypt'.

It would have appeared extremely stark, if it hadn't been for all the books. The room they were in resembled nothing more prosaic than an ultra-modern library. There were desks with computers, filing cabinets, and floor to ceiling white shelves around the walls to their right holding thousands of books.

'You have your own library?'

O'Brien nodded. 'Research is a big part of what we do here. Our adversaries are creatures out of history, therefore we have had to become students of that history.'

Stands was beginning to lose his patience with all the obscure answers they were getting from O'Brien. Just then a not so surprisingly studious looking young man entered the room through the double doors opposite them, giving them a glimpse of more white walls in the next room.

O'Brien turned to them with a look of satisfaction. 'Ahh, perfect timing. This is the head of our research team Dr Ellis. Doctor this is Detective Inspector Stands of the Metropolitan Police, and Sergeant Waves. As you know they're here to help us with the current…situation. Would you care to show our guests around and explain to them what they've got themselves involved in.'

As the Doctor got closer he looked over his glasses at O'Brien. 'Everything?'

O'Brien considered for a moment. 'We'll see, I'm sure these gentlemen understand the need for discretion.'

'Very well, if we could start by you telling me what you already know?'

Waves shrugged and looked at the Inspector. 'Not a hell of a lot Doctor, in fact you may as well assume that we know nothing. The only pertinent information we have so far is that whoever we're dealing with has a penchant for blades.'

Dr Ellis smiled without much humour. 'That sounds like our boys, only it would be more accurate to say *what* we're dealing with rather than who.' He glanced around and gestured towards a number of low padded chairs grouped around a coffee table. 'Please, take a seat and I'll fill you in with some of the background info, then we'll take it from there.'

As Stands sat down he noticed that the books and magazines littering the low table were all reference material; books on metallurgy, weapons, anatomy and a few of the latest scientific journals.

O'Brien seemed a little uncomfortable with the Doctor's informality as he sat opposite them.

Dr Ellis looked at them blankly for a moment. 'Whenever I'm asked to discuss our work here I always worry about where I should start. Oh well, I s'pose the beginning would be how our particular department first came into existence.'

*

'It was the Second World War that brought the whole of America together. It brought us improved communications, better technology and weapons, and the OSS. Before that there had been very little national communication or co-operation on an intelligence level. Before then there had always been rumours and

139

speculation in Academic and Occultist circles, but nothing that was ever openly discussed. We had the FBI, they'd been around since the 1920's, but it was such a small organisation, roughly five hundred Special Agents when Hoover took over the Bureau. It took the creation of the CIA from the ashes of the OSS to make national intelligence work possible. It was then, in the early years of the Agency, that our researchers started noticing a possible pattern of odd events happening all over America with similar MO's. It was then that our particular department was born.'

He paused for a moment to study them both.

'What you have to understand is that in those first years there was overwhelming paranoia concerning Communist infiltration, and a huge lack of governmental control over the Agency, especially after the Central Intelligence Agency Act was passed in 1949. We could do anything we liked, our fiscal and administrative procedures were made confidential and we were exempt from the usual limitations on the use of federal funds. We didn't even have to disclose anything about how the Agency was organised, its function, its funding, organisation, or even the number of personnel it employed. The CIA could do anything without having to answer to anyone, this included the creation of the CS, the Clandestine Service, of which we are an offshoot. At first the Directors thought that the events we were investigating were part of a Communist plot to destabilise the country from within by scaring the public with scandals of Satanism and ritualistic murder. But that view slowly changed as we started to seriously investigate and document what was going on.'

The Doctor looked at them intently. 'You see we started getting reports from our Agents in other countries of similar events, even within the then Soviet Union.'

Stands had to admit that he was finding the history lesson vaguely interesting, but he was still annoyed by the lack of specifics, even though he was beginning to have his suspicions.

'What events? What exactly are you referring to?'

'Events just like the one that you're currently investigating. Events revolving around people being murdered using edged weapons in ways and circumstances that would sometimes seem improbable, if not downright impossible. This being the case, and there continuing to be so little physical evidence, all we could do was continue to document and investigate. It wasn't until the early 60's that the Agency finally admitted that whatever was going on was not in any way related to the Communists. Which in turn worked in our favour as there is nothing the Agency hates more than not being able to explain something. We received more funding and were able to disentangle ourselves from the rest of the CS. We essentially became completely autonomous with our sole purpose being to investigate, document, hunt down and eliminate whoever was behind these events. That's when it started getting really interesting, we had the co-operation of every friendly government around the world. As far as they were concerned we were with the CIA investigating and fighting terrorism. No one knew what we were really doing. We had access to global intelligence gathered by the CIA and any other security service who cared to co-operate, which enabled us to keep the department small and secret. As we travelled from country to country we learned very little other than that the events we were following were happening less and less. At that time it was thought that we were having an effect, that maybe our investigations were making whoever was responsible think twice about doing whatever it was they were doing.'

Stands was curious about the Doctor's tone of voice as he said this, it sounded almost as though he was expressing regret. 'At that time…but not now?'

Dr Ellis shook his head. 'No, with what we know now I have another theory as to why these incidences have been occurring less and less. Anyway we'll come to that later. We did whatever we could to misdirect the media

media and local authorities and collected what evidence we could before moving on. Back home in America there were so few new incidents we decided to continue our search in Europe and the rest of the world in the hope of finding the answers we were looking for. We knew little…but started to suspect so much more. It wasn't until 1985 and Sir Alec Jeffreys perfection of DNA typing that we finally had some proof that what we'd become to suspect was in fact true.'

'Which was what exactly?' Said Stands impatiently. 'Sorry Doctor, but what the fuck are you talking about here. Please be a little more specific.'

Dr Ellis nodded absently before continuing in the same vain. 'You must understand, apart from the odd artefact, we've never gotten near to these people, this group, whoever they are. We've amassed data, but that's it. No photo's, no ID's, no fingerprints worth a damn, or genetic material that made any sense.'

'What do you mean genetic material that made any sense?'

'Well, to be honest the bits and pieces which we have acquired over the years do not exactly conform to the human genome.'

'And what exactly does non-conformity indicate?'

'Without a more legitimate sample I would guess at some kind of mutation.'

'But they are...human, right?'

'In most cases close enough to rule out any far fetched theories of extraterrestrials.'

'In most cases?'

'Yes, there have been some things that we're not so sure about.'

'I'm getting a little tired of repeating you, so can you just tell me exactly what you're talking about. What things?'

Dr Ellis looked round at O'Brien questioningly. Stands followed the Doctor's gaze, and found himself being quite frankly appraised by the Spook sat opposite him.

'If you get any further into this there'll be no going back. We are talking utmost secrecy and security here. You would be joining the ranks of an elite club, those who know so much more about the world we live in than almost every other person on the planet. I'm not joking, this will potentially alter your careers, let alone anything else.'

Stands looked round at expressionlessly at Waves.

Daniel avoided his mentor's gaze by looking down at his feet. He was fighting his own internal battle. Christ, how far do I want to go with this? The old man wants to go all the way, I can tell, just by looking at him. He may appear calm, but he's wound up like a spring, just itching to get on with it. Oh what the hell, what have I got to lose, no kids, no wife to complain. Fuck it!

Stands was watching Daniel closely, he wouldn't admit it, but he was reluctant to take this further without his talented protégé to back him up and keep him grounded. As Waves raised his head Stands couldn't help but grin as soon as he saw the big smile on his Sergeants face. Stands winked at Waves as he turned back to O'Brien.

'OK, were in, but I want full disclosure. I don't want to end up in a puppet show where I can't see the strings. Are we clear?'

'Absolutely Inspector! I'll personally make sure the Wizard shows you all his tricks.' O'Brien said snidely and angrily stood up to lead them deeper into the facility.

Dr Ellis smiled as his boss walked stiffly towards the double doors leading to the rest of that level.

'Maybe it's time we went to the evidence room.' He studied the two policemen for a moment and then smiled warmly. 'Then maybe you'll begin to understand just what the hell I'm talking about.'

With that the Doctor got up from his chair and led them over to the doors O'Brien had just disappeared through. Before opening the door for them the Doctor stopped and looked at them appraisingly. 'Can I assume that neither of you are squeamish? I assume that your line of work has presented you with some unpleasant sights?'

The looks that both of them returned were all the answer he was going to get.

'...because the next room is our medical centre and temporary morgue which leads through to the long term evidence storage room, the heart of the crypt.' He smiled. 'The thing is I've just completed an autopsy on a rather unfortunate young man, and to be honest he's a bit of a mess, and after that the evidence room holds some rather nasty surprises too.'

Waves closed his eyes for a moment. *Just what I need, more blood and guts.*

Stands noticed Daniels moment of hesitation and slapped him good-naturedly on the back as Dr Ellis led the way into the next room.

'Considering some of the things we've seen in the past I still find your sensitivity a little surprising.' Stands whispered as he held the door for Waves.

Waves shook his head and answered quietly. 'Peoples innards are never a pretty sight, they should stay inside where they belong.'

Dr Ellis smiled to himself as he led them into his medical centre. As a Christian he could understand the Sergeants sentiments, but as a scientist he was surprised by the policeman's response. Such a man had surely witnessed death and its aftermath many times in the past. Surely as part of his job he'd have got used to the darker aspects of human existence.

The medical centre was bigger than the research room and was divided into distinct working areas. The first resembled a dispensary with cabinets full of bottles and plastic containers of the type that usually contained drugs. The tables held sensitive measuring equipment, computers and what looked suspiciously to Stands' untrained eye, like an electron microscope, amongst other things.

The middle of the room was obviously where the

144

wet work was done. Two stainless steel autopsy tables, just like the ones in the Royal London Hospital's morgue stood centrally, dominating the space. These in turn were surrounded by smaller stainless steel trolleys holding various pieces of equipment. One of these was draped with a newly blood stained green surgical sheet. What immediately drew the Inspector's eyes was the corpse on the autopsy table next to the trolley. The young man, at least what was left of him had the obvious marks of post mortem incisions, the flaps of skin and flesh created by these had been carefully pushed back into place so that the body could be viewed as it had originally come in. Stands could see that the face had been ravaged, even from the distance he was from it, the gaping wound between the corpse's legs encouraged him not to go any nearer.

Waves could smell the blood, he hated the way the smell of fresh blood always left a tinny, metallic taste in his mouth. It always brought back too many unpleasant memories. He purposely studied the nearer wall to his left as they made there way across the room. Stomach churning he followed the Inspector through the last area of the room which was occupied by the kind of refrigeration units specially designed to store dead bodies. Next to these were further glass fronted units for storing organic samples and temperature sensitive drugs. Next to these was a large, squat stainless steel tube that could only be a liquid nitrogen storage unit. The kind of thing which, in fertility clinics, usually stored innocuous substances such as sperm. In this case Stands didn't even want to guess what might be stored in such a super cold environment.

O'Brien was waiting for them at the final single door which like the initial doors they'd entered were protected by a high-tech fingerprint analyser. He put his hand on the plate as they approached, and then stepped back to enable Dr Ellis access to the panel. Stands didn't comment on the extra level of security, but O'Brien did notice him watching.

'This room contains the entirety of our evidence.

145

As Dr Ellis explained we operate mainly out of Europe now, and the United Kingdom suits our needs as a base of operations. Your government is so eager to help us it would be pointless to be anywhere else.'

Stands scowled at this, he was only one amongst many who deplored the British government's propensity for taking its lead from America, when by rights they should be more European in their approach to foreign policy.

O'Brien continued. 'Because this collection represents decades of work it requires more stringent security. It can only be opened by either myself or Dr Ellis and another member of his team. Only research staff have regular access to the physical evidence.'

As O'Brien was saying this Dr Ellis stepped away from the door as it opened towards them. As it did so Stands could see that it was solid steel almost a foot thick with huge steel bolts which retracted into the frame when it was activated. In reality it looked more like the kind of door that leads into a bank vault than anything you might normally find in a scientific establishment.

'Surely the Vault would be a more appropriate moniker for this place.'

Dr Ellis smiled briefly at the Inspector. 'You haven't seen the contents yet.'

Inside the thick steel door was another small room resembling an airlock just like the last one. This one, however, contained lockers holding white protective jump-suits and surgical masks.

Don't worry, the suits are to protect the evidence...not us.' As Dr Ellis said this the door that they had come through automatically closed with a resounding clunk, accompanied once more by the feeling of a subtle change in air pressure.

Waves was beginning to feel that this whole thing had begun to take on a surreal element that left him wondering if he should be paranoid about psychotic aliens rather than in-human swordsmen obsessed with ritual beheading.

Once they had all donned their protective gear O'Brien and Dr Ellis both stepped up to the last door leading into the evidence room. Stands couldn't help but feel a little apprehensive at this point. He knew that they were finally going to get some concrete answers, but he had a horrible feeling that he really wasn't going to like those answers. Standing behind O'Brien and Dr Ellis as they opened the door Stands felt the presence of his Sergeant beside him and reached up to adjust his mask as he glanced at the man stood next to him. Waves looked just the way Stands felt, tense and on edge. Luckily as soon as the door was open these feelings dropped away from both of them, to be replaced by utter astonishment.

The evidence room was almost twice the size of the medical room behind them. From the looks of it the room definitely continued out from underneath the building, away from the Thames on their left, but out to the right under the street, and underneath the building next to it. Other than that it was similar to the medical room with its white walls, floor and ceiling. But only for a moment, if pushed Waves would have described the room as looking like a futuristic museum.

Obviously a lot of thought had been put into the lighting to create the right atmosphere, but also to accentuate certain pieces dotted around the room. On each wall were a number of very old looking tapestries, most seemed to be medieval, whilst others looked eastern in origin, others he couldn't so easily identify.

The one nearest him showed a mythical theme where armored knights were fighting demons whilst angels looked on from the sky, and mermaids observed from the sea. In the spaces between some of the tapestries, and dotted at regular intervals around the whole room were solid white blocks on which were mounted artifacts of some kind, the nearest of which was some kind of dagger. The weapon was around two feet long from the tip of the blade to the end of the hilt. The hilt itself comprising of six inches of tightly wound leather cording. It was shaped, if he wasn't mistaken, very like a Japanese Sais. There were also a number of computer terminals dotted around the room along with microscopes and other little pieces of research hardware. What drew Waves' gaze, however were over half a dozen large glass tanks, all of which were filled with some kind of liquid and each held something large floating within. Somehow he doubted it was water, and they definitely weren't fish, and somehow he couldn't imagine Damian Hurst being involved with their contents.

O'Brien and the Doctor appeared content to stand back and let the two of them peruse the room at their leisure. Which Stands was more than happy to do, maybe starting with a circuit around the edge of the room to get an overall picture of what the room contained. Or he would have if it hadn't been for the unexpected exclamation from Waves who was stood in front of one of the large glass tanks in front of them.

'What the fuck?'

Stands saw the Sergeant take an involuntary step back as he moved quickly towards him.

'Are you OK? What are you looking…' Stands didn't need to finish the question as he saw what Waves was still staring fixedly at.

Stands looked around in shock at O'Brien and the Doctor. 'What the fuck is that?'

O'Brien smiled indulgently as Dr Ellis hurried over to the two men. He was going to enjoy watching the two over-confident policemen have their delusions torn away. It was always entertaining to watch men realise that everything they'd ever thought about the way their world worked was wrong, and to then realise the truth that there really were monsters out there. Even better than that was the knowledge that with the revelation of the existence of true Evil, came the inevitable, if somewhat grudging admission that if Evil existed, then so must Good, and that America, God's country, would lead the way in search of it.

An hour later, having had the full guided tour of the evidence room, the Inspector found himself once more seated in the library. This time with one of the researchers nondescript mugs before him on the table full of steaming black coffee. He nodded his thanks to Dr Ellis as he watched him hand an identical mug to Waves.

'Don't worry, everyone who goes into the evidence room for the first time comes out displaying some symptoms of shock in one form or another. To be honest when I first saw those things it gave me nightmares for a week. It is always hard to discover that our childhood monsters, myths and legends are based on some kind of truth.'

Stands sobered as he took scalding gulps of his coffee, his initial bewilderment slowly lifted as the caffeine entered his system. 'What kind of freak show are you running here? Those *things* can't be real. As to the natures and traits that you've prescribed them...I hate to tell you this, but I'm not that gullible.'

Dr Ellis shrugged sadly. 'I'm sorry Inspector, you are of course entitled to believe whatever you wish, but I assure you that they are real.
What reason would we have for such an elaborate deception. No, the dissections themselves should be enough to convince you, but there is more. We have done innumerable scientific tests, genetic coding, etc. I can show you the results if you'd like, but the truth will remain...they do exist, and have done since at least the beginning of recorded history. In fact I'm absolutely positive that for every story, myth or legend about a supernatural being or entity there must be a real creature that the story was based around.'

'Does that go for religious stories too?' Waves asked innocently.

'Of course not.' O'Brien snapped angrily.

'Christianity represents an intuitive yearning towards the divine. You cannot think that God could be mistaken for any of the abominations in there. They are the work of Evil.'

Stands looked thoughtfully at O'Brien. 'If that is the case, then is it your charge to kill all such creatures?'

O'Brien sat up straighter in his chair. 'Of course. God created the Earth for Man. All non-human aberrations like these are the work of Satan and should be destroyed.'

Stands glanced at Dr Ellis and thought he could detect a hint of sadness in the man's expression. Maybe Science could be more compassionate than Religion. Hmm.

'So what you're actually doing here is a little like a religious crusade, to free the world from anything non-human.'

'Nonsense.' The Doctor looked irate. 'What we are doing here is trying to protect people. These creatures are dangerous and have been preying on mankind for as long as we have existed. All of the specimens you've seen killed many humans before their own deaths, most still with blood literally on their hands. We've run the tests, the majority were all still digesting human tissue of one kind or another when they died.'

Waves sat up at this. 'So why did you kill them? I would have thought they'd be a lot more useful alive, if for no other reason than research.'

'We didn't kill them.'

Stands flashed to the images still prominent in his mind. The bodies floating in formaldehyde, each bearing the marks of a violent death, and in all those cases the marks looked to be those made by blades of some sort. His mind was racing as O'Brien abruptly stood up.

'That's enough.'

Dr Ellis looked up at O'Brien in confusion. 'What? But I thought you said…'

'No. I think maybe our guests have had enough information for one day. We don't want to overload them.

They have more than enough to digest already, I think we should give them a little time before we go any further.'

'No.' Stands' voice was calm, but there was an edge to it that stopped even O'Brien.

'You promised us everything, and we can't do our jobs unless we know everything there is to know about all this. It may be fantastic, but you'd be surprised what I can accept on…faith.' This last he said directly to O'Brien, his stare challenging him to go back on what he'd said earlier that day.

O'Brien paused, and then shrugged. 'Faith can be a powerful force, and despite what you may think, it does help us with our work.' He sat slowly, gesturing for the Doctor to continue.

The Doctor eyed O'Brien warily before turning back to his audience, and his subject. 'No...we didn't kill them. All these specimens were discovered already dead. We've never been able to track, capture or kill any of these creatures. They have intelligence obviously, otherwise how could they manage to stay hidden from the world, but more importantly they seem to possess abilities unknown to us outside of folklore.'

'What sort of abilities.' Waves interjected whilst exchanging a meaningful look with the Inspector.

Dr Ellis suddenly looked tired and frustrated. 'I use the word abilities because I have no other way to describe it. All of them would have been physically stronger. Their musculature appears to be superior to ours in subtle ways coupled with superior neural and nerve pathways, which altogether would give them much greater dexterity and speed. From the post mortem tests we've done I'd say it's also likely that they heal faster too. The rest of their abilities are speculation, but I can't help thinking that the truth has been with us for millennia, we've just been too blind and sceptical of what our ancestors were trying to tell us. It would seem that there really is some truth to mankind's ancient tales of elves, dwarves and goblins.'

151

Stands shook his head slowly. 'I still don't understand where you think you're trying to take us with this. All I saw in there was a collection of unfortunate mutations and circus freaks.'

Stands bit his tongue in an effort not to take his goading too far.

O'Brien glared at the Inspector. 'Forgive me Inspector, but can you really be so narrow minded, so blind to what we've just shown you to believe that horns and talons for one example can really be the result of natural mutation. You saw that thing. It's huge. There's nothing natural about any of the monstrosities in there. How about the mermaid? You think that's just a case of sirenomelia.'

'No.' He said shaking his head. 'If I might point out the unfortunate souls born with that particular affliction never have gills as well as lungs, and they most certainly never have fins.'

O'Brien sat back and pushed a hand through his hair as Stands stared at him.

Dr Ellis cleared his throat to break the silence. 'And if I may just add, all the unfortunate little ones born with that particular affliction invariably die within just days.'

The Doctor shook his head sadly and sighed. 'Some of them differ from us more than others. The specimens you have seen represent the most divergent, but we do have minor samples from things such as the dagger you saw. It was recovered from the body of one of our specimens when it was first discovered, the one that we've labelled as a vampire, though that is yet of course to be confirmed. It appeared to have gotten lodged between the ribs in a position that made extraction difficult. During the struggle this was obviously inconvenient, meaning the weapon was left in situ. The fact that it was not retrieved at the termination of the action could be contributed to many potential factors, but it has left us with the best piece of evidence we've been able to retrieve so far about this other group. Since the weapon came to us we've been able to carbon date and match weapon residue from wounds and from the scenes of various incidents. This and other trace evidence has given us the few factual pieces of information we have on them. The skin and hair samples we recovered from it would indicate that there are those that would probably appear as nothing more than human if you passed them in the street. It is those that we are most interested in, those who pass themselves off as human. They are the true enemy in our midst.'

'But how could they pass as human, everyone needs an identity, and you can't have one of those without things like birth certificates, passports and driving licenses, how would a group of beings who aren't human manage that. Surely any doctor would notice that they are not what they might originally seem. Plus there's the issue of funding…in fact I can't see any way that they would be able to hide in our midst any more than any other undesirable illegal alien.'

Waves raised his eyebrows at that and Stands had to inwardly concede that there were always ways.

The Doctor shook his head. 'Actually if this group have been operating for even half as long as the little evidence we have on them suggests, then funding really wouldn't be a problem for them.'

'What do you mean, not a problem? Every such organised group in history, whether they be terrorist or religious fundamentalist has always had problems with funding themselves. Just look at the IRA. How can this bunch be any different?'

'Just think of them like the Masons, or the Templers.'

'What? This organisation goes back that far? And you're talking about them like they're some kind of secret society.'

'Well, lets look at the evidence. This particular group based in the UK has been around since at least the crusades. That being the case, and looking at similar incidences, they've been operating in the same way for centuries without detection, without anyone really knowing anything about them, not even rumours. Which if you look at the history of any so-called secret society, is really quite impressive. After all, how many of these secret societies have actually managed to remain secret. This kind of organisation starts out with funds, and husbands them in such a way that no one is aware of the wealth being accumulated, and so they cannot be traced through actively seeking funds elsewhere. Even something as parochial as stealing money to fund whatever it is they do could eventually be traced back and leave them open to detection. They're effectively self-contained, which means they are untraceable.'

This was not the sort of thing that policemen like to hear, though some, especially when such information was coming from these Americans, would take such a statement as a challenge. Stands just wasn't sure which side of the fence he wanted to be on yet.

'So…you still haven't told us who did kill all your specimens.' Waves pointed out.

Dr Ellis blinked slowly. 'We believe it's the work of the group who could pass as human, the ones with the weapons, these others don't seem to carry weapons of any sort. From the DNA samples we've managed to gather from other scenes around the world we've come to the conclusion that there are several such groups of less obviously different beings consistently killing others of their kind.'

'You mean those monsters in there?'

'Well yes, maybe, but they are as near to those monsters, as they are to us in their genetic make-up. Which makes them definitely not human.'

'But if Chimpanzees can be so close to us genetically, and those things, whilst weird and mostly ugly are definitely a lot closer to being human than a chimpanzee, how can they be that different from us genetically?'

'Alas, that is a common misconception flouted by the media. What you have to understand is that every mammal on this planet shares huge similarities in their DNA. Another thing is that there are roughly three billion DNA base pairs that comprise our genetic blueprint and yes the chimp genome has been mapped too, and there is apparently only about a four percent difference between us. But what you have to understand is that each one percent represents literally millions of different mutations that make us different from them, then of course you have a comparable amount that makes them different from us. People just don't understand how different that makes us, they forget that it represents at least four million years of divergent evolution. To put that into perspective these creatures, even the specimens we have in the evidence room are less than one percent different to us on a genetic level.'

O'Brien looked serious as he interjected. 'But we have no way of knowing what that means from a moral or cultural stand point. So yes, there is human and humanoid, but these things are definitely not human, and they are a threat.'

Waves had to interject. 'OK Doctor, going back to what you said earlier, how do you know they've been around since the crusades?'

'Actually I believe they've been around a lot longer, but I have no proof of that. The proof I do have is that the dagger I mentioned earlier was forged around a thousand years ago. Carbon-14 dating is conclusive, and metallurgical tests show that it was made from ore originating in this country. Somewhat unusually it would appear to be a very high grade steel.'

'The Romans had steel.'

'Very good Sergeant, but I mean like surgical grade steel. The sort of metal that can be as sharp as a razor, hence the lack of tissue tearing along the edges of the wounds, and as far as we knew the Japanese were the first to create such metals. Along with that there is the

155

shape of the dagger, similar to the Sais, a Japanese weapon. Frankly it's all very odd. Coupled with that is the fact that this group have been operating in the UK for at least the last fifty years.'

'I thought you just said since the middleages.'

'Sorry, I meant that the same individuals have been hunting and killing their own for the last fifty years.'

Stands looked at the Doctor blankly. 'How could you know that? And even if it's true how could it be possible?'

'Because Inspector we've got DNA samples that date back that far, and they all match. Indicating two non-humans are responsible for killing all the specimens you've seen, apart from the mermaid that is.'

'How old are these people?'

O'Brien twitched.

'Inspector please remember…they are not people.'

Stands shrugged as if to say *whatever*.

'We have no idea, but the tests we've done on these specimens, and the testimony of all the myths and legends which we've all become so fond of here would suggest that they have vastly elongated life spans, much longer than any human. Methuselah was probably one of them. It would appear that the Immortals do exist.'

Stands tilted his head as he looked intently at the Doctor. 'Not jealous are you Doctor?'

He shook his head in response and lost the wistful tone. 'Of course not, they're not human, and though on a medical level we could learn a lot, they are not God's creatures. We have a duty to protect mankind from these aberrations.'

The Doctor sat back in his chair and closed his eyes, he seemed drained by having to explain all this to them. He also seemed reluctant. Stands couldn't put his finger on it, but there was definitely some kind of conflict going on between the Doctor and O'Brien. There was something major they didn't agree about.

O'Brien sat forward and eyed his new recruits. 'So

now you know why we've enlisted your help. We're reasonably sure that they've got a base somewhere in London, but we're restricted in our investigation by lack of manpower and that we don't have complete access to all the information that might help us. You will use all the assets of the police force to help us find them.'

Stands didn't miss the order in that sentence. He didn't like it, he didn't like O'Brien, he wasn't particularly fond of the Doctor either, and he sure as hell didn't like this whole situation. He glanced at Waves and was unsurprised to find him looking back at him. He could read the same kind of instinctive mistrust in his eyes as he was feeling. Something was fundamentally not right about all this, other than the fact that it was all impossible of course, but he couldn't put his finger on it.

'So you basically want us to get on with our jobs, doing what we were doing before you showed up, because you think these guys are the ones responsible for what happened in the cinema.'

'And the hospital morgue, and to that young man in the other room. Though obviously you'll find your job easier now you know what you're up against.'

'Yeah, immortal monsters wielding razor sharp swords. I think we got it.' Waves sarcasm was far from subtle, but the Americans just nodded in response.

Stands knew that they hadn't understood his Sergeant and gave Waves a significant look. He didn't want to antagonise them just now. 'That corpse in the medical room, I couldn't help but notice that his injuries didn't seem consistent with those of the other victims connected with all this.'

The Doctor nodded. 'Yes, besides the blade wounds there are other, post-mortem wounds.'

'They killed him and then did those other things to him?'

'Like I said they do prey on humans.'

'But you said that the more divergent ones don't use weapons.'

'They haven't in the past as far as we're aware, but I'm inclined to think that it was done by the other group. We intercepted the body in Brixton when we got a report of its existence. After what happened this morning at that hospital morgue we didn't think it was safe for it to go through the normal channels. We can't afford to lose any more evidence.'

'How did you know about what happened at the hospital?' Stands asked casually.

'We have our sources.' O'Brien said smugly.

For Stands another piece of the puzzle slid into place.

He could guess who O'Brien's informant was, but why would O'Brien leak details of what happened at the cinema to the media, unless it was to strengthen his own position and force the authorities to let him become involved. That might explain it, but surely the government wouldn't cave in to American pressure just because of a little bit of bad publicity. No, there had to be more to it, something he wasn't aware of yet.

Stands shook his head to clear it of his spiralling speculations. 'How about the other wounds? The ones not caused by blades.'

Dr Ellis looked a little uncomfortable. 'The marks around the wounds are consistent with human nails and teeth.'

Stands cringed. 'I hope you're not telling me that whatever did that ate his eyes and his…genitalia?'

The Doctor shook his head. 'I'd rather not speculate. Like I said, they can pass as human physically, but no human could physically do that.'

Waves laughed humourlessly. 'I don't know, you Americans have bred some rather interesting serial killers in your time.'

O'Brien glared at the Sergeant, obviously less than pleased by that comparison. Stands thought better of fuelling the fire and interrupted with a suitably professional question.

'I don't suppose you've managed to identify him?'

'No, no ID was found on the body, his fingerprints aren't on any database and he doesn't appear to be in your own rather extensive genetic database. Actually from what I understand it's the largest in the world isn't it?'

Stands couldn't believe that this American Special Agent was descending to petty point scoring. Waves was leading him by the nose, earlier in the day he wouldn't of thought it would be possible.

'And no likely missing persons reported?'

'I think I might have mentioned it by now if there was.' The Doctor said in exasperation.

'Oh well, I'm going to need a copy of your autopsy report for our file, if we're going to get anywhere with this we need to continue working with all the pieces of the jigsaw that are available.'

The Doctor looked to O'Brien who nodded once stiffly. 'It goes without saying that anything you get from us is not to be shown to anyone else.'

Stands nodded immediately. 'Of course, this is all top secret. We're aware of our responsibilities. Now if we could have the copy of that report I think we'll be off, it's getting late and we have a lot to think about. In the mean time we'll be in touch as soon as we have anything.'

O'Brien frowned. 'Yes…you will.'

Chapter Ten

It was getting dark by the time they turned off of the B6320 onto the last stretch of road leading to Bower. A tiny place sitting quietly disregarded on the South Western edge of the Northumberland National Park. If you knew where you were going it wasn't difficult to find, though the dead end road which went through it and died an abrupt death at the edge of the forest did tend to deter the casual traveller. The road did reincarnate, the other side of a very large gate, as a rough Forestry Commission track. The type of road that required the potential user to invest either in state of the art four-wheel drive technology, or a horse. Funnily enough the small segment of the local population who did use the track generally went on foot, which just goes to show.

The Forestry Commissions official stance on illegitimate usage of the land was that it didn't happen due to effective security measures. The reality of the situation was another matter entirely. Vast tracts of forest and woodland were generally looked after and patrolled by local people employed by the Forestry Commission, and local people always knew a lot more about what went on locally than did the organisations that they represent.

This couldn't have been truer in and around Bower. Many would have described it more as a hamlet than a village. It had a pub, but no church, and no local doctor. Not that the locals really needed a doctor, they were all surprisingly fit and healthy. Outside of the immediate area many people attributed this to the robust Reiver blood that ran through the veins of many of the old and established families in that part of the world.

In and around Bower they knew better. It wasn't down to a good diet and plenty of exercise, though this was the norm. Nor was it down to the local healers, though they were never that short of work, there were always accidents after all, bones broken that needed setting, cuts and contusions that needed cleaning and closing. None of these were the true secret to such fine and rude health.

No the locals knew better, it was the varying levels of Elemental blood flowing through their veins. A secret which stretched back to before Bower appeared on any map. There had been an Elemental presence in the area even before the Reivers started all the bloodshed centuries ago.

Elarris lived on the very edge of the small community in a large, though easy to defend compound of buildings, all of which were overshadowed by the backdrop of the forest behind them.

As Tris finally pulled the car off the road and into the courtyard in front of Elarris's house the door to the large stone building opened in apparent greeting, spilling light across the smooth cobbles of the courtyard. The light was followed by, and briefly eclipsed by the slight figure of a woman stepping lightly down the front steps from the door as Tris brought the Audi to a stop and crunched the handbrake into place. Only when he'd finally got them there did he visibly slump, the long drive having wearied him more than he would have thought it would. Easing his shoulders back he looked sideways at Garfan who was regarding him with mock concern in his eyes.

'Tired?'

Tris sighed. 'Yes.'

'Big strong boy like you tired after sitting down all day?'

'Fuck off.'

Garfan sniggered. 'Sorry Tris, couldn't resist. But you are OK though, right? Finished brooding over things yet?'

'Yes, and stop bloody tip-toeing around the subject. We both know I'm basically fucked as far as emotional commitment goes, so can we just get past it and enjoy our little road trip.'

Garfan smiled briefly. 'Absolutely.'

Tris smiled tentatively back, looking a hundred times less forlorn than he had when they'd left Avington. Relieved Garfan raised a hand in greeting to the figure waiting patiently for them at the foot of the steps leading up to the house, at the same time he opened the car door, and was about to get out when he felt Tris's hand on his right forearm holding him back in his seat. In turning he was surprised to find a concerned, almost guilty look on his old friends face.

'Garf...we don't have to mention any of this to Elarris do we?'

Garfan pursed his lips and closed his eyes, taking a moment in order to make sure he said what he wanted to say in the way he wanted to say it. 'Tris, you don't have to tell Elarris, or any of the Elders for that matter, anything which you don't want to, and you know perfectly well that I would never divulge anything you asked me not to.'

Tris looked relieved.

'However...'

Tris's face fell.

'If your personal life should in some way infringe on our effectiveness, or effects you in such a way that it is obvious to the Elders, they will ask you awkward questions. Ones which they may employ their telepathy to seek the answers to. You don't want that, I don't want that, we only just managed to keep your little *breakdown* a secret before. So if I were you, which I would like to add I am sincerely grateful I'm not, I would get a grip and bury your feelings while we're here. Just try and be your normal happy-go-lucky self and everything will be fine. OK?'

Tris nodded thoughtfully, and turned away from Garfan as he got out of the car.

Garfan stood up gratefully and stretched, he never liked being cooped up in these metal boxes, it didn't seem natural. Looking round he noticed Tris busying himself getting their bags out of the boot of the car. Sighing with a certain resignation towards the vagaries of life, love and loneliness, he straightened and walked towards the figure waiting for them in front of the house.

He couldn't help but smile broadly as he approached the silhouetted figure before him, calling out in greeting. 'Deelan!'

He had always harboured a crush for Elarris's only child. She had, for him, always represented the epitome of female elemental beauty. With her long straight auburn hair, leaf green eyes and milkmaid complexion, she looked like a Rossini painting come to life. Though he had to admit that the tight jeans and T-shirt, which displayed her athletic figure so well, was a definite improvement on any Pre-Raphaelite mantle.

Deelan held out her arms in welcome as he approached. 'Garfan it is so good to see you, its been far too long since you both graced us with your presence.'

Garfan schooled his features and nodded. 'Far too long, eight or nine years isn't it?'

'Thank god for that!'

Startled they both looked round at Tris who was smiling with genuine warmth at them both. 'I thought for a second Garf was going to say something really cheesy about how gorgeous you look Deelan.'

In response Deelan tilted her head and narrowed her eyes. 'Ever the flatterer Tristellis, and yes, believe it or not, I'm glad to see you too.'

Tris laughed in disbelief. 'So you've finally forgiven me for cutting off your pigtails that time?'

Garfan stifled a snort and coughed as he looked from one to the other, and laughed openly as Tris held out his arms to Deelan.

'Good to see you cousin, it's been too long since I was last home.' Tris stepped forward and swept the woman into a fierce hug, one that was eagerly reciprocated. Stepping back from Deelan, but keeping an arm around her waste he winked at Garfan.

'So my little Celtic throw-back, how is the old man?'

'The old man may be old, but he is far from deaf

163

Tristellis.'

At the sound of Elarris's voice all three turned towards the door standing open behind them. Garfan almost instinctively bowed towards the tall figure silhouetted by the light spilling out from the wide hallway.

'At least one of our Guardians has some manners.'

Tris looked suitably sheepish, nodded once and sketched a hasty bow to his uncle. 'I'm sorry Elarris we were just…'

'I know Tristellis, and do you really think I have lost my sense of humour as well. Come here child and give your uncle a hug too.'

Grinning in relief Tris leapt up the steps to the front door, coming to stand in front of the white haired figure that smiled warmly and opened his arms to him. Pulling him close Elarris whispered in Tris's ear. 'You've been away from home longer than any of us would like.'

The old elemental held Tris away from him so that he could study his face, his expression displaying a hint of sadness. 'I had hoped that you could talk to me about anything. Anyway, just remember that my ears are always open to you Tristellis.'

Garfan studied the two elementals standing in the doorway above him. He had never known Tristellis's father Farell, but he could see the similarities between Tris and Elarris, a certain straightness of the jaw, the curve of the eyebrows. Obviously Tris being half-caste he also had his mother's genes, though to Garfan Tris just looked like a broader, less angular version of Tris's uncle. Coming out of his reverie he realised that Elarris was studying him in turn, and he returned the elemental's smile with genuine warmth.

'Where are my manners, Garfan, welcome old friend, it is good to see you. One would not be the same…without the other.'

Garfan raised an eyebrow at this remark, and glanced at Deelan who was still stood beside him. The look she returned conveyed lightly veiled concern. Garfan shook his head, it was almost impossible for Tristellis's folk to hide anything from each other, after hundreds of years of knowing one another they could read each other too well. Yet another reason why elemental courtship was the minefield of tradition and ceremony that it was.

'Come, you must be weary after your journey. Come and refresh yourselves before dinner.' Elarris turned and moved deeper into the hallway to allow Garfan and Deelan to enter and close the front door behind them.

'Deelan will show you to your rooms. There is plenty of hot water, and when you are done I will have drinks waiting for you.' Elarris nodded to them before turning away to leave the three of them standing at the bottom of the stairs.

Garfan winked at Tris. 'Well...dibs on the bathroom.'

Deelan smiled, she loved having Tris and Garf around, they never ceased to make her feel young again, making her think of the years she and Tris had spent growing-up together. They had both been relatively young when Tris had been picked out by the Fighting Master to be a Guardian. It all seemed like so long ago.

'OK boys, grab your bags and follow me.' Deelan started up the stairs leaving Tris and Garfan to pick up their gear and follow. At the top of the stairs she turned to follow the landing round to the next staircase, Tris and Garfan right behind her.

'Deelan,' Garfan called from the back, 'we're staying in the rooms we always use aren't we?'

Deelan just nodded and carried on up the stairs to the third floor attic rooms. At the top she stopped and waited for Tris and Garfan on the small landing.

As they both reached the top of the stairs they stopped abruptly, neither recognising the new layout.

Tris looked at the three doors, where before there had only been two and looked at Deelan enquiringly.

'So when did this happen?'

'It must have been about five years ago now. I

insisted that we modernise. You didn't even have radiators up here before. Now you have your own little bathroom too.'

Deelan smiled proudly. 'Now I don't have to clean up after you two before I can take a bath. See you in a bit.'

She brushed past them with a smirk as she descended the stairs, leaving Tris and Garf staring at the three doors.

Garf dropped his bag outside the door to what he was assuming was his old room and turned towards the new one. 'Well I did bagsy the bathroom first Tris.' Saying which he opened the door and turned the light on as he stepped inside giving Tris a tantalising glimpse of sparkling white tiles before the door closed behind him.

*

After dinner Deelan cleared the plates and loaded the dishwasher in order to give everyone a little elbowroom at the dining table. The dining room was pleasantly comfortable with its dark green walls and wooden sideboards, the small fire in the fireplace adding warmth as well as mingling its light with the many candles arrayed around the room.

Both Tristellis and Garfan were silent, Tristellis contemplating the wine left in his glass, whilst Garfan studied Elarris expectantly, having been reminded that dinner was a social time and not for discussing business he was hoping that the Elder would at last give some signal that they could begin to discuss that which had spurred them into coming here in the first place.

At last Elarris put down the wine glass that he had been idly toying with as Deelan rejoined them, closing the door to the kitchen behind her.

'Coffee will be ready soon for those that would like it.'

Elarris nodded his thanks to his daughter, glanced at Tristellis who was lost in thought, before then meeting Garfan's eyes with his own.

'So Garfan, what can you tell me about recent events that would explain why you felt the sudden need to speak to me and the other Elders.'

Garfan looked at Tris and raised his eyebrows. Tris acknowledged the look guiltily and spoke up.

'Maybe I should explain Uncle. Firstly it was due to something happening which neither Garfan nor I had experienced before. We had to eliminate a group of, what we thought at the time were Satanists, who had just murdered a little girl. However, the last member of their group left standing I wounded, not fatally, though I was about to deal a death blow, when he…well he…' Tris looked at Garfan who just nodded for him to continue.

'Well he just seemed to instantaneously combust.'

Elarris raised an eyebrow, an expression that required more information.

'He erupted into flame, all over, all at once, and within seconds there was nothing left but ash, and the most alarming thing was he never made a sound, not even a whimper, as though it didn't hurt or something.'

'There was nothing left? Just a pile of ash?'

Garfan nodded whilst studying the old elemental. He could see that Elarris was interested, but not as shocked as Garfan was expecting he'd be. Then he almost thought he caught a sense of eagerness. Was he holding something back?

'Were these men…men? And did they by any chance all wear the same piece of jewellery, a necklace, or a ring perhaps?'

Garfan couldn't help but notice that Tristellis seemed a little startled by this line of questioning too.

'What do you mean by were they men? They were human…they all died like humans, except for the last one that is. They weren't anything we hadn't come up against before, apart from the human torch that is.'

167

Tris's eyes narrowed in thought. 'Actually, now that you mention it I do seem to recall a flash of light on his hand, though I couldn't tell you if they all were wearing rings or not. But even if they were why would that be significant?'

'How many of them were there? Were there five?'

Garfan was becoming increasingly suspicious, he had never had cause to feel this way about Elarris before, he trusted him implicitly, but the Elder was definitely not telling them something. 'Something Tris hasn't mentioned yet, which is what concerns me most, is that I believe the confrontation was engineered firstly as a diversion to stop us following a presence of great power which we had been tracking, and secondly as a trap. I'm sure they knew who, and what we were.'

Elarris's face tightened in alarm, though he still did not appear as shocked as Garfan would have expected at this news. Elarris tilted his head considering something. 'Yet they still thought they could best you?'

Garfan nodded. 'I would assume so otherwise it would have been a pointless suicide. We'd already lost track of the presence we'd been following by that point. We'd stayed to confront the immediate threat, the group we'd assumed to be Satanists.'

'Interesting…' Elarris clasped his hands on the table in front of him, his eyes carrying a far away look.

Garfan and Tris both looked enquiringly at Deelan, who mutely shook her head in response. She didn't know what to make of all this either.

Tristellis cleared his throat. 'Uncle…there is more.'

Elarris slowly turned his head to focus on his nephew's face. 'More?'

'Yes…that night, after the burning man, I went out with Martin…'

Deelan interrupted. 'How is dear Martin?'

Tris looked mortified, his eyes misting. 'He's dead.'

Deelan closed her eyes, a small sound of grief escaping her lips before she bowed her head in sorrow.

Elarris looked from Tristellis to Garfan and back again in disbelief, his face reddening with anger. 'How did this happen Tristellis? Garfan?'

Garfan was about to speak up when Tris interrupted him.

'It was my fault. We went out drinking…it was Martin's Birthday.' Tris coughed a little wetly as he fought back guilty tears. 'We had met some girls, and were going back to their place when I felt something unfamiliar homing in on us. Whoever or whatever they were, they were blatantly malevolent, and closing on us fast. Martin insisted I get the girls to safety.' Tris gulped air, tears welling in his eyes. 'By the time I got back he was already dead, with no trace of who had done it.'

'You could not identify them? How did he die Tristellis?'

'Bravely Uncle.'

Elarris shook his head impatiently. 'That goes without saying Tristellis, Martin was a fine man, he will be missed. No, what I meant was what kind of wounds did he sustain, how did he die?'

Again they were both surprised by the questions Elarris was asking. They seemed very…specific.

Tris was quiet for a moment. The recollection of Martin's battered and bloodied body fuelling his grief. 'He was cut up pretty badly, at a guess the wounds were caused by short swords, rather than the daggers we routinely favour. Also they had opened him up, eviscerated him. They also hacked most of his face away and took his eyes and his…sex.'

Elarris nodded and reached out to briefly squeeze Tristellis's shoulder in sympathy.

Garfan could take it no longer. 'What is going on here Elarris? What do you know about this? And when can we see the other Elders?'

Elarris looked around the table at them all. 'I am

sorry, I do not know anything for sure, but I have my suspicions. As to the rest I must consult with the other Elders alone. Hopefully I will be able to tell you something more tomorrow evening.'

Tristellis sagged. 'Tomorrow! You can't make us wait until then Uncle.'

Elarris's tone was firm. 'I can and I will Tristellis. I may be wrong, but if I am right then I have to talk to the other Elders and get my facts straight before I can tell you anything. I will not discuss any of this until I am sure I'm right. Now I must leave you and alert the others of the immediate need for council tomorrow. Then I must rest. Tomorrow is going to be a very long day. I would suggest you all follow my example. Goodnight.'

Elarris nodded to them each in turn, sparing a swift smile for his daughter as he rose from the table and left the room in silence behind him.

Garfan's sigh reflected all their thoughts as they were left sitting there wondering what was going on.

'Unfortunately our host is as wise as ever, sitting here and speculating won't help. Let's turn in and see what tomorrow brings eh?'

*

When Garfan awoke the next morning all he could hear was the sound of birds singing in the trees around the house coming through the gap of the slightly open window, the fresh air tasting good this far from the capitals polluted streets. Stretching languorously he glanced at the small digital alarm clock on the table next to the bed. Nine in the morning, if he were anywhere else but here he would have felt a mixture of guilt and anxiety at having overslept.

Here he felt safer than anywhere, even than their house in St Mark's Square. Even his family's halls hundreds of miles further north had never felt as safe, even hidden from Man as they were. Besides, he'd never been back, not since he was first called to this place to train with Tristellis under the tutelage of Garanth the Fighting Master.

Garfan exhaled, slowly pushing the air out of his lungs. It seemed like centuries since he'd last thought of his ancestral home, and the family he'd left behind. He knew they must all be fine, if anything untoward were to happen to his parents, or his little sister, he'd be notified immediately, he was after all, one of the Guardians of the Kingdom. *Talking of which, where's that sluggard Tristellis? Better go wake him I s'pose.*

Garfan pushed back the duvet and swung himself out of bed. Soundlessly his feet hit the floor as he pushed himself out of bed. Standing there in his pyjama bottoms he stretched again, reaching his hands up towards the ceiling, the soles of his feet lifting until only his toes remained in contact with the floor. If Tristellis had been there Garfan would have probably felt a little body-conscious. Tris never missed the opportunity to rib him, the fact that he wasn't as hairy as an ape and covered in body hair, despite the luxurious facial growth, always amused his old friend for some reason.

In reality the beard was just an affectation, not all earth elementals grew beards, in fact very few had beards like his. In his more honest moments he knew he used it as a barrier, something to hide behind, to help disguise emotions that would otherwise be far too apparent.

In the mountains of his homeland they lived under ground in an almost perpetual twilight, a shadowed world where ones face was always partially hidden, and where you didn't have to school facial features against betraying what you felt from moment to moment. His people had long ago forsworn all casual contact with men. They were too proud to be looked down on by a short lived race they felt would never understand them, a failing which saddened Garfan, but despite still trading with certain humans for necessities they were set in their ways. The leaders of their people would brook no change in their separatist beliefs. Their only concession being to supply candidates for the Guardianship, which was how he had come to be here, and having to live in the open Garfan had tried to unlearn the openness he had been brought up with, but had had to admit defeat and had hidden himself away behind his beard.

Garfan tried to shrug off such musings as he reached for the robe hanging on the back of the bedroom door. He'd been lucky to be chosen for this life, and would forever be grateful for it. He put on the hooded towelling robe, luxuriating in the soft chocolate brown material he padded quietly out of his room and over to Tristellis's bedroom door. He wanted to surprise his old friend, but as soon as he flung open the door it was Garfan who was surprised. The curtains were open, the bed was made and the entire room looked tidy. He'd been expecting to find the room looking like a tip with Tristellis sound asleep in bed.

'Bugger!' I just know he's going to be a pain arse about this.

Garfan knew Tris would take the piss. Thinking this he drew the robe closer to him and tied the belt around his waist as he made his way down the stairs to the kitchen. As he walked up to the kitchen door he detected the murmur of low voices coming from outside the kitchen's back door. If he wasn't mistaken it was Tris and Deelan.

By the tones of the voices it sounded to Garfan as though Tris was confiding in Deelan. Garfan smiled in relief. That boy always kept things bottled-up too long, he rarely confided in Garfan completely. To hear him talking to Deelan was a relief, although in the back of his mind he couldn't help but be a little peeved that his best and oldest friend couldn't confide in him completely.

He shook his head, just be happy he's getting whatever it is off his chest one way or another. He

172

purposely put on a smile and moved quietly away from the kitchen door before opening it and clumping loudly into the room to let them know he was there. When he walked into the kitchen he was greeted by the heady smell of fresh coffee and toast, the scent of which was still strong despite the back door being open. On the steps leading down into the walled kitchen garden were sat Tristellis and Deelan, both looking back over their shoulders at him and smiling.

The family resemblance was obvious with their faces so close together, though there was a certain element of elvishness that made all forest elementals look slightly similar. Garfan grinned back at the pair.

'So you finally decided to get up then?'

Deelan shushed Tris and got up, wiping her hands on her jeans as she stepped up and into the kitchen. 'Morning Garfan, would you like some coffee? There's toast, and I can fry you up some bacon and eggs if you'd like?'

Garfan pulled out one of the kitchen chairs and sat at the table glancing at the newspapers strewn across it. Tris got up and leant against the back door frame smiling at Garfan.

'You should have woken me.'

Tris's smile widened into a grin.' You obviously needed to sleep, and we don't really have any pressing engagements, so I left you.'

Garfan relaxed, the anticipation of a ribbing had left him a little tense and ready to be defensive. Now he felt it leave him as he smiled gratefully at Tris.

'So?' Deelan said patiently.

He looked back at her in surprise. 'Oh yes, coffee please, and toast would be fine. I don't want you to go to any trouble just for me.'

Deelan smiled warmly and laid a hand on Garfan's shoulder in passing. 'No trouble, the truth is Tris insisted we delay breakfast until you woke up. So now we'll all have breakfast together.'

Garfan sagged ruefully. 'Where's Elarris?'

'He left just after dawn to confer with the other Elders…so it's just the three of us for breakfast.'

Garfan once more felt that he could relax.

'He did leave a message for us though. Apparently Garanth and his apprentice are in residence at the moment, and Elarris thought the old man would appreciate a visit.'

Garfan eyed Tristellis speculatively. 'The Fighting Master is here?' He looked over to where Deelan was busy around the cooker. 'How long has he been here?'

She looked over her shoulder at Garfan before carrying on with what she was doing. 'To be honest I've no idea. You'd know more about it than I would Garfan, you must remember how secretive the training is. He and Keef come and go in the night as they please. I only know that they're here when father tells me.'

Tris pulled out a chair and sat opposite his old friend. 'It was a long time ago, though it sounds as if little has changed…in which case early evening, before dinner, would be the best time to go and see him.'

Garfan nodded in agreement and took a steaming mug of coffee gratefully from Deelan. 'In which case the day is ours.' He put his coffee down and reached for a paper. 'So what are you going to do today Tris?'

Tris leant back in his chair and glanced at Deelan. 'Well Deelan and I thought we might go into the forest for the day. How about you?'

Garfan twitched the corner of the paper he was reading out of the way so that he could look at Tris.

'Going to do some tree hugging?' He said with raised eyebrows.

Tris smirked. 'Something like that…'

Garfan grinned. 'I know, you need to recharge your batteries. Well if I'm going to have plenty of peace and quiet then there are some books in Elarris's personal library that I'd like to take a look at.'

'Don't want to come with us?'

Garfan shook his head before returning to his paper. 'No thanks.'

He smiled to himself. 'Besides, there may well be information in the library that could help us. One of us at least has to keep our head in the game.'

The disgusted snort Garfan heard from behind his paper was all the answer he was going to get. Knowing this he concentrated on the paper and the small story about the murder of a mortuary worker, and the subsequent bizarre theft from said London hospital morgue.

Chapter Eleven

After breakfast Garfan had retreated to their new bathroom to enjoy a long hot shower before he did anything else. When he finally made his way back down stairs it was obvious that Tris and Deelan had already left for the day, leaving the house quiet and empty.

Whenever they came here Garfan always tried to spend some time in the library, but over the centuries he'd still not managed to spend as much time as he would have liked poring through the histories their peoples had written over the millennia. Looking forward to an uninterrupted day of reading Garfan settled himself in an armchair with the first interesting looking book that came to hand.

*

Garfan was startled by Deelan's soft touch on his arm, he'd completely lost track of time.

'Sorry to disturb you Garfan, but Tris said you'd want to accompany him when he goes to see Garanth.'

'Indeed I would.' He said rubbing his eyes. 'Guess I've been reading long enough for one day.'

'Anything interesting?'

Garfan smiled ruefully. 'Frustrating more than anything else. Our forefathers seemed to have assumed that anyone reading these documents would know exactly what they were referring to, which means that there are passing references to unknown events that leave you with more questions than you originally started with. You'd have to be an Elder to make any sense of it.'

Deelan laughed. 'Maybe that's the point.'

'Hmm.' Garfan smiled at Deelan, understanding what she meant, but still not liking the feeling that information was being denied him.

'Where's Tris?'

Deelan gestured to the front of the house. 'Waiting outside for you and enjoying the evening air.'

Garfan nodded and put the book he'd been studying down on the table with the pile of others he'd spent the day trying to decipher.

Outside it was a beautiful evening, the sun was gently colouring everything in deeper shades of red, rose and gold. Tristellis stood at the bottom of the steps leading down from the front door breathing slowly and deeply, his mind obviously focused on the moment.

Garfan padded slowly down the steps to his old friend. 'Shall we go see who he's torturing today then?'

Tris visibly winced and looked round at Garfan with an odd expression on his face.

Garfan laughed, 'You're still scared of him aren't you?'

Tristellis looked down at his feet before stepping slowly forward away from the house. 'Garf, you couldn't understand, you only trained here for around fifty years. The master had me in his clutches for one hundred. Have you any idea what that's like? Tris shook his head. 'No you don't, so don't take the piss.'

He led the way over to a small outbuilding that was built against a small cliff of exposed rough grey rock. The small building huddling up against the rock face blended into the cliff, door, windows, roof and all, rendering the building almost invisible in the dim light of evening.

Tristellis knocked sharply on the door and then stepped back, the banging seeming to echo hollowly, as though there was nothing inside the building. The door opened moments later to reveal…no one.

Tristellis glanced round at Garfan before slowly entering. Garfan hesitated on the doorstep looking around at the large courtyard, the ancient trees leaning over the surrounding walls moved lazily in the light evening breeze. The first stars seemed especially bright above them. He sighed quietly, 'I've always loved this place.'

Then looking at Tristellis' back, he stepped inside, the door closing of its own volition behind him, just as it had opened.

Inside with the door shut behind them the light was subdued, candles providing the only illumination, just as they did everywhere else within the compound. Directly in front of Garfan and Tristellis was the back wall of the building, the solid rock of the cliff face was worked to a minor extent to smooth its surface, but the still rough expanse of seamless rock couldn't be completely disguised.

Neither Tristellis or Garfan had spoken since entering, but now Tris roused himself, a small shudder the only visible evidence as he snapped out of the many reveries that had taken hold since entering the old building.

'Master may we enter?' Tris said aloud, looking at, and speaking to the solid rock wall before them.

The only answer came after a pregnant pause, a period where nothing happened, and they both held their breath. Then with a subtle shift, a shift in what was hard to tell, but suddenly the light was slightly different, along with the texture of the air, and before them where there had been nothing but solid rock, was a rough hewn arched tunnel sloping down away from them into the rock and the earth, illuminated by lone candles at wide intervals.

As with the door to the out-building, as soon as the pair had filed in and were a few paces down the passage, the archway behind them disappeared. Had either of them turned to look back all that would have been visible would have been a curiously flat blackness akin to that present in the doorway leading to the cellar of their safe-house in central London.

Both were familiar with this tunnel though, Tristellis especially so, having paced and occasionally limped its length innumerable times in the hundred years that he had been Garanth's pupil. Tristellis was not alone in this, though few had received the master's full attention, as every forest elemental in the kingdom spent at least a little time as the master's pupil. Even Garfan, as the chosen of the earth elementals had spent time training with the master and Tristellis, so that the two of them would become an even more effective fighting unit. Then even more recently Martin had spent five years under the master, just to learn some of the basics.

After minutes, which easily felt like hours to Tris in the close unchanging confines of the tunnel, they both began to hear the muffled echoes of violence coming up to them from somewhere below. Sharp grunts, noises of substances other than flesh striking each other. In short, the kind of noises which would cause the uninitiated to turn around and head back the way they'd just come with increasing speed.

As the noises became louder and more distinct a door came into view before them at the end of the tunnel. By this time they had been walking for a good few minutes, and had descended roughly fifty feet from the floor level of the building above them.

The door, though taller, was the twin of the one that led to the cellar of the boarding house in London. As Tristellis was leading it was he who once more knocked loudly on this door. Moments later a powerful voice shouted 'Hold!'

Then the door before them slowly dissolved, disappearing from view, and leaving a flat impenetrably black door shape, into which Tristellis and Garfan walked in turn, whilst simultaneously seemingly dragged into the blackness, leaving not a trace of either as the door slowly coalesced back into being behind them.

Moments later, and feeling slightly disoriented, Tristellis and then Garfan stepped forth from an identical patch of flat blackness into an enormous underground chamber. This was the Masters Temple, the Arena. One hundred feet to the far wall, and the vaulted ceiling curving above them forty feet high at its central point. All moodily orange and yellow lit by hundreds of candles in sconce's on the walls, and in huge chandeliers hanging from the ceiling. Around the walls at regular intervals were doorways of a more conventional design than the one through which they'd entered, leading to armouries and medical treatment rooms, the two practices explicably linked by violence.

As Garfan's eyes adjusted to the increased brightness he once more took pleasure in the craft of his forefathers. Gazing around at the walls and vaulting which emulated the boughs of trees, culminating in a domed ceiling that looked like a forest canopy. The feel of the intricately carved floor beneath his feet awoke other memories as he closed his eyes. There were patterns on the floor that seemed random in design until you spent an appreciable amount of time in this room with no candles lit, and soft-soled boots. Then it became clear that if you had the time and sufficient powers of concentration to map it with your toes, whilst eluding other combatants who could see no better in the absolute dark, then you could with time, say ten or more years, tell exactly where you were in the great chamber just by the feel of the stone patterns beneath your feet. All this without a single seam in the rock, all of it carved out, inch by inch, by Garfan's people.

Garfan was drawn from his thoughts by the same powerful voice they had heard before they entered.

'Are you two going to come forward and make greeting? Or do the chosen ones need an invitation these days?'

The short, deep and barking laugh that followed did little to soften the challenge in the words.

Although a little tense Tristellis still managed to grin back at Garfan's huge and happy smile, before striding forward towards the centre of the circular chamber. As they drew closer both were a little surprised to see only two figures, still breathing heavily, stood before them. On the right was the bulky, though still elegant figure of the, behind and slightly to the left was one of the biggest and most human looking elementals Garfan had ever seen. Glancing at Trsitellis beside him, he could see that his friend had recognised the half-caste in front of them.

Halting a little way before the master Tristellis and Garfan bowed in unison.

'Garfan...Tristellis. Always a pleasure, as long as this is a social call. As you can see I am instructing at the moment.'

Tristellis smiled lazily and winked at the figure standing slightly behind the master.

'I must say that from the noise it sounded more like a full pitched battle. I'm surprised to find only the two of you in here...or is Keef testing even your abilities master?'

Garanth eyed Tristellis casually before ignoring him completely and turning his attention to Garfan. 'Sometimes Garfan I don't know how you put up with him.'

Keef leant round the master. 'Always the two of you, never the one without the other!'

The master scowled and idly swatted his pupil standing behind him. 'And that is as it should be...they are a team after all.'

Tristellis was smiling sarcastically at Keef. 'So still in training then?'

Keef groaned. 'Lets face it, the way you two are going, I'm forever going to be in training. You're both too good, and it'll be centuries before either of you even begins to contemplate retiring.'

Tris blinked slowly, considering his reply. 'You never can predict when things are going to go bad. Besides I'm not the retiring type, I'll keep going until someone puts me down.'

'Much as I want your job Tristellis, I would never want it over your dead body.' Keef said seriously.

'Besides, I keep training like this and one day I'll best the master, then I'll become the new Fighting Master and I'll never have to leave the bosom of this wonderful community.'

Garfan and Tristellis laughed at the aggrieved look on the master's face and the improbability of Keefs statement.

Keef groaned once more. 'What am I saying…spend the rest of eternity here in the arena fighting the same battles over and over again, never to travel and see the world. I must be going mad.'

He looked intently at Tristellis. 'Come on old man, can't you just retire, I've been in training for a over a hundred years now…save me!' The last he said in a plaintive, pleading tone.

Garanth shook his head in mock dismay at his apprentice's words. 'So you two, enough of the verbal jousting, how about you both show Garfan and I what you've got. It's about time I had the opportunity to see whether you're still the best Tristellis?'

The master winked at Garfan. 'Come let us repair to the sidelines and take some wine whilst Keef assists Tristellis in girding himself for battle.'

Smirking broadly Garfan backed away from Tristellis in the direction the master had taken, towards a table set against the curved wall of the arena, one laden with various refreshments.

Tristellis looked as though he was about to say something, frowning at the way Garfan was disassociating himself from this. 'You're no bloody help are you!'

Garfan raised his eyebrows, smirked, sketched a quick bow, and turned towards Garanth and the goblet of wine being held out towards him.

The polite cough aimed at gaining his attention brought Tristellis back to the here and now. Looking over his shoulder he saw Keef gesturing to a large wooden rack on the opposing wall from the refreshments, a rack displaying a large variety of weapons and armour.

182

Oh well, s'pose I better get this over with. With that thought in mind Tristellis gestured for Keef to precede him.

*

They both stood, facing each other in the centre of the arena, the main chandelier hanging above them bathing them in the glow of hundreds of candles. Eight feet separated them, little enough room to kill each other almost instantly using a variety of moves or weapons.

Keef stood quietly bouncing slowly and lightly on the balls of his feet, eyes locked on Tristellis' face. Keef could see Tristellis stood, feet planted solidly a shoulders width apart, face calm, impassive, his eyes closed.

From the edge of the arena Garfan could see his friends chest expanding and contracting in a slow steady rhythm. If Garfan hadn't known better he would have guessed that Tris had put himself in a trance state, meditating on god knows what, or even preparing himself for one of his astral wanderings.

Garfan's heart started beating faster with anxiety as nothing continued to happen. He shot a glance at Garanth who stood passively beside him. He looked neither concerned nor surprised by the continued inaction of the combatants. The master's expression spookily mimicked that of Tristellis, calm and untroubled. In a way it was like the expression of a child, innocent of any hint of violence, yet oddly expectant without even meaning to be.

Garfan struggled with this revelation, looking from one to the other, teacher to pupil, pupil to teacher. As he finally let his gaze settle back on his friend Garfan let his focus draw back to once more take in Keef's figure. The hirsute half-caste had stopped bouncing, though his eyes were still locked on Tristellis' face. Keef's expression

183

was slightly quizzical as he tensed in anticipation of action.

The first step Keef took towards Tristellis elicited no response from his opponent. Keef's movements became faster and more fluid as his next two steps took him in a trajectory aimed at Tristellis' torso.

As Garfan watched, Keef moved cat-like, sure and fast. His first swing aiming to decapitate the silent, stationary figure before him. Garfan gasped involuntarily as the blade of Keef's short sword sliced through empty air. Suddenly Tris was no longer there. He was by Keef's side using the momentum of his opponents swing as the impetus for a throw which sent Keef simultaneously flying through the air. Then once again Tris was motionless, his attention on the graceful way in which Keef's headlong flight became an acrobatic tumble. Keef rolled into a defensive crouch, having hardly touched the carven stone floor of the arena.

He grinned at Tristellis and winked. 'Shall we stop fucking around now and get it on?'

Tris smiled mirthlessly and launched himself at a slight tangent to Keef, the long daggers he had chosen seeming to leap out of their sheaths into his hands. The two of them came together in a blur, though there was nothing blurred or diminished about the accompanying thunderclap of sound, steel on steel scraping and clanging continuously. An audible testimony to the frenzied action taking place within the circle of blurred humanoid forms flowing around each other with such speed and precision it was like watching masters of Capavara on fast forward. Thrusts, blocks, ripostes, kicks and punches, all coming so fast that it was almost impossible to distinguish where one figure ended and the other began.

'Christ he's fast.'

The master's eyes did not leave the wheeling figures as he responded. 'Keef's training has lasted longer than Tristellis' did. I had to send you both out before I really wanted to, but with the death of your predecessors I had no choice.'

Garfan glanced up at the Fighting Master stood beside him. 'Actually I was talking about Tris. Since being out there I've not had the opportunity to observe him in action like this. When you're in the thick of it you don't have the luxury of time to appreciate one another's technique.'

The master nodded his head in understanding. 'His abilities are remarkable, and the experience Tristellis has gained in the field has definitely given him an edge.'

A prophetic statement, as just at that moment one of Keef's weapons came spinning out of the melee towards the two spectators, only to be deftly brushed aside at the last moment by the master with a negligent flick of his wrist, sending the blade clattering into the wall behind them.

With only one weapon Keef's moves became that much more defensive, aiming to keep Tristellis off him long enough to at least equalise the fight by relieving him of one of his weapons.

Garfan could see that Tris was having none of it, pressing his attack with the obvious intention of ending it quickly. He hardly had time to register Keef's short sword leaving his hand before he was momentarily deafened by the barked command to 'Hold' that issued from beside him. The two combatants responded equally as fast by swinging away from each other. Each using the momentum of their last move to carry them in safe tangents past each other.

Smiling Garanth looked down at Garfan, 'Shall we?' And swept his arm in a polite, if expansive, gesture for Garfan to precede him towards the centre of the arena.

Both Keef and Tristellis were slowly walking around each other, eyes locked, both breathing heavily, both wet with sweat and steaming gently in the cool atmosphere of the arena.

Garfan could tell there was something wrong as he drew closer to the pair still stalking each other under the

185

main chandelier. Glancing at the master beside him left him in no doubt he was right. The Master's frown etched deep the years in him, making him look older than Garfan could ever think he'd seen him. An almost sacrilegious revelation in its own right, this served to worry Garfan even further as he got nearer to the circling fighters.

Tris had won, he should be pleased, but there was such intensity in his old friends face that Garfan began to wonder if Keef had slighted Tris in some way. Offended him in such a way that merely winning wasn't enough.

In the mean time Keef frowned as he carried on walking around an opponent who had completely disarmed him in a matter of minutes, and yet seemed dissatisfied with his victory.

The master stopped some yards away from the circling pair, planting his feet and crossing his arms, surveying the two half-castes before him. Both possibly the best pupils he had ever had. 'Keef, the combat is over. What are you doing?'

Keef seemed reluctant to tear his eyes away from Tristellis, but decades of obedience to the Fighting Master left him with little choice but to look worriedly at his mentor. 'I'm not sure master, if I didn't know better I'd say Tristellis would still like to kill me despite having already won the contest. I'm following the old adage of discretion being the better part of valour, and staying out of his way.'

These words seemed to have some effect on Tristellis, as he slowed his pace, maybe at last remembering where he was.

Garfan could stand it no longer. It had already been a long day of study for him and he was tired, and pissed off with Tristellis for making him worry, apparently for no good reason. All this he made quite obvious with his tone of voice as well as his words. 'Tris, what the fuck do you think you're doing? Stop this now…you won for god's sake. What's wrong with you?'

At last Tris stopped his pacing, his shoulders

slumping in an attitude of defeat as he turned towards Garfan and Garanth.

What threw Garfan the most was the hopeless look of sheer defeat on his old friends face. 'Tris what's wrong? You won…'

'Only because he didn't want to kill me. If he had he could have won, and I'd be a rapidly cooling corpse lying in a pool of my own blood.'

Keef had stopped moving when Tristellis had ceased stalking him. The look on his face now was one of utter amazement.

Even the Fighting Master looked a little confused. 'What are you saying Tristellis? Explain yourself!'

Tris wearily collapsed onto the floor of the arena, his legs crossing underneath him, leaving him with his forearms resting heavily on his knees. 'The only reason I beat Keef was because of my experience in the field. It allowed me to push my attacks that bit closer, knowing that I could without hurting him. If he had had the same advantage, placing us on equal terms, then Keef would have won.'

He was still looking a little unsure of what Tristellis was saying. 'I do not understand Tristellis. This is a place of battle, blood is regularly spilt here. Yet you say that if Keef had been really trying, then he would have won. I'm sorry Tristellis, but my pupils always give their all within these walls, and if you felt you or Keef had to hold something back, then I'm sorry. But you still won the contest Tristellis.'

Tris looked pained. Garfan suddenly realised that Tris was finding it extremely difficult to say these things to his old mentor. At last Garfan began to understand what was going on here.

Tris sighed. 'Master, how long is it since you were in a position where you had to fight an enemy to the death?'

He looked at Tristellis quizzically as he gave the question some thought. 'It has been many centuries

187

Tristellis. I am an Elder now. I have, after all, seen almost a millennia. Younger, swifter elementals have fought the true battles since I became their teacher hundreds of years ago. But what does that have to do with anything?'

Tris bowed his head, looking into his lap and shaking his head. Keef's expression of surprise had gone, replaced by one of respect and sad understanding. He came forward, squatted by Tristellis' side and silently put his hand on his opponents shoulder.

Tris looked up at Keef, and then once more met the eyes of his old master. 'I am sorry master, but it has been too long since you took an enemies life. You have forgotten the finality of the killing, the difference between mere combat and the wish for your opponent's death. Combat in the arena may be good practise, but that's all it is. Death has never walked in this place.'

Looking once more at Keef, Tris offered his hand, Keef took it, stood and hauled Tistellis up, their hands still clasped. 'Keef I'm sorry, I was unprepared to be bested today, I apologise. If you had a partner such as I do, I would seriously consider retirement, but Garfan and I still have much to do. The thing I thank you for the most is for reminding me of my own fallibility. My thanks Keef, I'm glad to know I have such a worthy successor.'

Keef nodded before stepping back and silently giving way to his mentor.

Garanth, head down, chin on chest, seemed smaller than he had when Garfan and Tristellis had first entered the arena. Garfan's heart went out to the old elemental, he had forgotten how truly old the master had become, always thinking of him as somehow ageless, and invulnerable.

Feeling three pairs of eyes looking at him, the fighting master's head came up from his contemplation of the floor. 'Congratulations Tristellis, you have finally managed to make me feel really old…'

'Master, I'm sorry…'

He waved his hand depreciatively.

'No Tristellis, do not be sorry. You are now truly a warrior, and if the teacher must learn a lesson from a pupil, then who better than you? And what a lesson, it is long since I had the taste of death in my mouth. I have forgotten its flavour, and its teachings. Thank you for reminding me Tristellis. I can assure you in the years to come young Keef here will learn to rue this day. Death may not walk here, so we shall go seek him out, from now on he will be a regular spectator.'

At this Keef's eyebrows rose in alarm. Garfan caught his eye and winked, finding it hard not to laugh at the young half-caste's expression.

'Now masters Tristellis and Garfan, I am sure it is time for you to seek your dinner, as it is mine also, but I would have a few words with my young apprentice here, whilst the memories of tonight's deeds are still fresh in both our minds. Good night, and once more…thank you.'

With that the master turned away from them and put an arm around Keef's shoulders, drawing him into the shadows, and away from the two old friends who now stood facing each other and smiling.

'Your pride will be the death of you Tris. Only you could see defeat in victory.'

'I'm sorry Garf, it was a shock, but it was also the revelation that the master had slipped in his training. I was upset that I was the one who was going to have to tell him.'

Tris turned to go.

'So he could have beaten you then?'

'What?'

'Keef…he could have beaten you in a death match?'

Tris smiled and winked at Garfan. 'What do you think?'

Garfan laughed and dug an elbow in his friend's side as they walked towards the door-shaped blackness in the wall of the arena, and the cool evening air awaiting them above.

*

Garfan went up to his room, trailing slowly behind Tristellis. He needed a moment to think whilst Tris took a shower and cooled off from his ordeal in the arena. He knew Tristellis would recover from what happened reasonably quickly, he always did when it involved violence and death. It was always the emotional conflicts that it took him longer to recover from. Hopefully he may even be able to regain some of the serenity he had achieved by spending the day communing with the forest.

Garfan shook his head and watched his friend disappear into his room and close the door quickly behind him. Such humiliations would be quickly swept aside when action was once more needed. Tristellis was not a deep thinker he relied on his wits, preferring not to delve too deeply into his own obviously wounded psyche. Garfan went to the window in his room and opened it wide to the evening.

The air was cool though far from cold, a little moisture in it suggested that rain was on its way, though Garfan was far too distracted to accurately gauge when it would come.

He often wished that he was more like Tristellis, free of self analysis and over speculation, worry and…he had to admit it, at least to himself, a sense of foreboding about the future.

What made it worse was that he rarely worried about himself. He had come to terms with his own mortality centuries ago. No, what really bothered him was a sadness that he couldn't shake in himself, mostly for those he loved and cared about. None of whom were half as happy as they could be, but who were also seemingly helpless to effect the kind of positive changes which could bring that happiness. Wherever he turned he saw people seemingly trapped by circumstance, and it made him sad…for everyone.

As he stared out of the window at the sky he wondered whether he should take some time when this was all over and go north and spend some time in the wild and barren places that his people cherished so much. He could do with a little calm and serenity himself. Garfan let his mind wander out into the darkening sky and allowed his breathing to slow, his ego slowly letting go of his mind till he was little more than a statue lost in the shadows and darkness around him.

He had no idea how long he had been like this when he heard a polite cough come from the open doorway behind him.

'Are you OK Garf?' Tristellis asked with soft concern in his voice.

Garfan held his breath for a moment as he gathered his senses back into himself. 'How long have you been there Tris? He didn't bother to turn around, he didn't want to see the concern in his old friend's eyes.

'Long enough to wonder when you'd be coming back to us…to me.'

Garfan looked back over his shoulder and raised an eyebrow at Tristellis's posture of little boy lost. 'As if I'd ever leave you Tris. You know I'd never do that.'

'Even when I act like a self-centred arse?'

Garfan's lips twitched wanting to smile. 'Don't you always?'

Tris pouted and shifted his weight where he was leant casually against the door frame. 'I s'pose I deserved that. But I was trying to apologise, I'm sorry about the way I've been behaving recently. I know it hasn't been easy for you, and it must seem as though I take you for granted, and sometimes I suppose I do, but I just want you to know that I would never do so consciously. You're too important to me.'

Garfan breathed in deeply and blew out through his nose. 'Tris…you know we're becoming like an old married couple don't you?'

Tris smiled lopsidedly and stepped into the dark

room towards his friend and held open his arms. 'All I know is that I love you, and I'm sorry.'

Garfan looked at Tris and grinned before stepping into the hug he was being offered. For a long moment neither of them moved as they held each other in an embrace that spoke so eloquently of their mutual friendship, love and respect. The moment was only slightly marred by the loud rumble from Tris's stomach.

Garfan pushed Tris away as they both laughed. 'I think it's time for dinner.'

Tris patted his impatient stomach. 'I wonder what treats Deelan has in store for us tonight?'

Chuckling Garfan moved around his old friend and made his way towards the stairs. As he did so he failed to notice Tris staring out through the south-facing window, Tris's mind momentarily occupied by his own sense of foreboding.

Chapter Twelve

Despite having cleared the air between them earlier, dinner proved to be a subdued affair with the continued absence of Elarris. Deelan had insisted that they eat as her father would not hear of them waiting, and assured them that Elarris obviously had good reasons for missing dinner.

Tristellis seemed lost in thought so Garfan shouldered the burden of conversation and spent the meal catching up with Deelan on the state of the community and the everyday lives of the few forest elementals left in the Kingdom. Many did live in and around the area, but all were well aware that there was a certain amount of safety to be gleaned from scattering themselves throughout the land, living secretly amongst humans and only occasionally seeing their brethren.

It had always been obvious to Garfan that this state of affairs was the cause of a great amount of sadness for them, but having the perspective of a Guardian he knew that, for all that, they were living better lives with many more freedoms than their seperatist cousins. A truth that Garfan had long ago learnt to keep to himself having had many a heated debate with various elementals about the pros and cons of both integration and separatism.

Deelan had as always served a delicious meal of fresh organic home grown vegetables and the game that she and Tristellis had killed that very day whilst out in the forest. Garfan always came away from their visits to Bower with a heartfelt desire to start growing their own vegetables in the more than adequately sized garden they had back at St Mark's Square.

However, as soon as they got back and he started making plans for the garden something else would come up, a witchhunt, or a monster to be tracked and killed. The violence, and the need for it, always destroying Garfan's modest daydreams of living more in harmony with nature. A desire that wasn't helped by Tristellis's apathy, and perverse delight in the iniquities of modern so-called 'fast-food'.

Garfan was considering raising this as Deelan started clearing the kitchen table, he knew she'd back him up and even, possibly, offer to assist in such an endeavour, when he heard the front door being opened and then closed behind whoever had entered. This was followed by the sound of light footsteps in the hallway leading back to the kitchen. He glanced at Tris and knew straight away that he had heard it too, his whole countenance suddenly more alert than it had been throughout dinner. Deelan had cocked her head and listened for a fraction of a second before carrying on with loading the dishwasher. Moments later Elarris walked quietly into the room and motioned for both he and Tris to stay seated.

Elarris was dressed casually in dark blue jeans and a surprisingly stylish dark green jumper that accentuated the piercing blue of his eyes. Despite the casual appearance, white hair and obvious age, he still managed to exude an authority that was obvious to anyone in his presence. Standing before the table he glanced at the debris from their meal.

'So how was dinner?' he said looking at Tris and Garfan. 'I'm sure my daughter excelled herself once more.'

He turned to Deelan and held out his hands to her. 'I'm sorry I had to miss dinner, but there was so much to be discussed. Things which have not been spoken of in centuries.' He could not disguise the weariness in his voice, nor what sounded to Garfan like concern.

'Would you like some coffee father?' Deelan said having taken the offered hands and squeezing them gently.

Elarris smiled gratefully. 'Very much, maybe even a small calvados to accompany it.' He sat down at the kitchen table and studied his two guests.

'It has already been a long day, but we have much

to discuss before...' Elarris stopped abruptly and stared unfocussed into space.

Garfan feeling slightly alarmed glanced at Tris who just shrugged in response to Garfan's questioning look.

'Before what Elarris?'

Coming back to himself Elarris sighed sadly. 'You will find out soon enough my friend. For now let us make ourselves comfortable and I shall tell you what I can, but please give me a moment to compose my thoughts, this is not easy to explain.'

Deelan looked startled for a moment at this admission, but just as her father had done gestured for them not to move, shook her head and carried on preparing coffee before reaching into a low level cupboard for an old dust covered bottle.

Once all the necessary mugs and glasses were on the table Deelan deposited a large caffeteirre in the middle of the table. She then placed the dusty, age darkened bottle she had taken from the cupboard before her father, then sat in the only unoccupied chair next to her father. Elarris studied the bottle for a moment and smiled at his daughter.

'You always know what is required don't you my love. It is a pity that I am usually the only one here to appreciate your gifts.' In saying this he glanced at Tristellis before looking knowingly at his daughter.

Tristellis remained unaware of this exchange as Garfan groaned inwardly at yet another curse of circumstance that he was powerless to do anything about.

Looking once more at Tristellis, Elarris gently took hold of the wax sealed bottle and offered it to him. 'It would seem appropriate that you open this Tristellis. It is the last bottle of the vintage your father and I made before he left us.'

Tris blinked in surprise and looked to Garfan who nodded and smiled sadly.

So much loss, so much pain. Garfan ran a hand over his face and through his beard as he tried to push aside the melancholy that seemed so intent on gripping him. He didn't have the luxury of time for such feelings now. He must concentrate on what was important, the here and now, and the information which Elarris had for them.

Meanwhile Tris had broken the old waxen seal around the end of the bottle's cork and had pulled it free, filling the room with the golden, amber smell of autumn apples that intertwined with the warm rich smell of coffee coming from the cafetierre. As Tris slowly poured four generous measures of the dark gold liquid, Deelan in turn pushed down the plunger of the coffee pot and poured the steaming black brew into the mugs on the table.

Once this was done Elarris raised his glass to Tristellis, Deelan, and Garfan in turn. 'To family and friends…for truly nothing more precious exists.'

The four of them held their glasses aloft before each taking a sip of the fragrant liquid. Each savouring the fiery brandy as its heat slowly filled their mouths and throats before seeming to evaporate before they had the chance to swallow it.

Elarris nodded in idle satisfaction and set his glass down and then picked up his coffee mug and took a quick gulp of hot coffee as he once more looked around the table.

'Much of what I have to tell you relates to the very nature of who and what we are. Much of it is based upon information that, even for us, would seem to be little more than myth. We have unfortunately in our past not been as good record keepers as we could have, so please bear with me and try and save your questions until I have finished. Then I will try and answer them…if I can.'

Elarris took a deep breath and let it out slowly through his nose before continuing.

'Our origins, like those of mankind, are lost in time. We are no more aware of our true beginnings than is the human race, and when I say we I refer not only to the so-called Elves and Dwarves, but to all the races of Elementals. Unfortunately even my old friend John Ronald

Reuel's attempts at making sense of our history came to nothing, though what he made up was probably more poetic.'

Here Garfan and Tristellis both glanced at each other with raised eyebrows whilst Deelan just shrugged non-committally as her father carried on.

'All we can really do is speculate on the evidence provided by human scientists and archaeologists. This being the case I will speculate and give you my theories, though I must hasten to add that much of what I believe is not universally believed by all the Elders. We are not, and never have been in complete agreement about the nature of our own origins, but that is an old argument which is ultimately futile in that it has no bearing on our future. Anyway…our origins would seem to be intertwined with that of mankind, though how we came into being I do not know and cannot guess at, and whether we had any hand in the origins of man I have no idea. Though I am convinced that we have played a role in his development.

Elarris stopped and took a long drink of his cooling coffee before looking around the table at his audience, who, though rapt, had all managed to finish their coffee and were all now idly twirling their brandy glasses whilst listening intently.

'Now I will come back to this I'm sure, but it is my belief that, due to our natures and extended life spans, our varied races are the source of all man's myths and legends, even their religions. For the most part this has been involuntary, but there have been those of our peoples who have openly interfered in the affairs of men. Our races are many, and I'm sure that even we are not aware of all those who could claim some kind of kinship with us. Even those that you commonly term as monsters I am sure are kin to us in one way or another. After all, if you go back far enough are we not all related?'

Garfan nodded at the truth of this, though he was mightily puzzled by Elarris's talk of many races of elementals, and he would only admit to himself that despite the Elders logic being incontrovertible, the thought that he was in some way related to the monsters that he and Tristellis routinely hunted down did leave him feeling more than a little uncomfortable.

'Now, I'll try and leave religion out of this for now, but I believe that our races started as what humans call Spirits, of the earth, of the plants and trees, of water, air and even fire. It would explain our affinities, abilities, and even, to an extent, our varied natures.'

Garfan raised his hand a little way off the table in question, but Elarris interrupted him.

'Please Garfan, wait and let me explain. I know that most, if not all of this is never mentioned in the raising of our children, and as such is news to you all, but there are good reasons for this trust me. I believe we started out as such, and have evolved just as mankind and all other life has. Many forget that human evolution, even just that of Homo Sapiens has covered a period of tens of thousands of years, and that in the distant past each generation of man lived but a fraction of the time that they do today. I think we were the same. Life was so very different then, but I think our lifespans were comparable. Now we may live say fifteen to twenty times longer than a man, but back then a "man" may have lived only fifteen to twenty years, and my guess is that our ancestors may have only lived for around sixty or seventy years, but back then even that short time would have been viewed by mankind as immortality.

As for our races, we know for a fact that we are not alone, the so-called Elves and Dwarves have always associated with each other, though these names themselves have been given us by humanity, our own true identities having been lost in time. But other races do exist, beings of the water, of the air, and of fire, though their natures are not like ours, ours being closest to the nature of man. Sylphs do exist, as do the mer-people, and the true demons. They are beings of their elements, and as you can guess they represent the embodiment of all man's mythologies. Those of the water are as fickle as their element, those of the air as aloof as theirs, and those of fire…as destructive as theirs. Monsters, Mermaids, Angels and Demons, all real, but not as humanity believes them to be.'

Garfan could hold back no longer. Putting his now empty glass down and reaching for the bottle of calvados he interrupted. 'But this is incredible. You expect us to believe this, in Angels and Demons. Mermaids and such perhaps, but Angels and Demons? All the so-called Demons Tris and I have ever fought have been just monsters, none of them ever had any affinity to fire what-so…' Garfan's voice trailed off as Elarris raised an eyebrow in question.

'Ever Garfan? Not until recently perhaps. We have always had very little contact with our other cousins. The only reason Elves and Dwarves have dealt with each other so amicably has been because our natures are so similar, we are creatures of the land.'

'But what about Demons, fire elementals, whatever it is you want to call them. I can't see that fire has an affinity to anything.'

Elarris looked a little exasperated. 'Garfan please, hold your questions, but in answer to that one…heat. Why do you think that Demons and their habitat are so closely linked with fire? Hell is traditionally pictured as a fiery wasteland. Fire elementals are drawn to heat, just as my people are drawn to trees and forests, and yours to mountains and moors. Think logically my old friend, if you do you'll see it all makes sense. After all, where else did the Devil appear to Jesus, but in a desert.'

Tristellis downed what was left of his brandy and gestured for Garfan to pass the bottle.

'I'm sorry to interrupt Uncle, but I'm confused too. I don't understand how any of this can be real when it sounds like religious mumbo jumbo to me.'

Elarris smiled indulgently as his nephew poured himself a large glass of brandy.

'You're taking it all too literally. That's always been Man's biggest mistake. You have to look past the fiction and determine the truths that lie behind it. Our races, as I have already said, are the inspiration for all religions, the source, and that being the case you should be able to see that myths and religions are all stories about our races. We have always known that there has been trouble between our peoples, the most obvious being the enmity between air and fire. The Angels and the Demons, those sorry meddlers who have tried in the past to use Mankind against each other. Spreading rumours and lies that have led to wars and genocide on a massive scale.'

Elarris closed his eyes and took a sip of the home made brandy, letting its smooth heat revitalise him. Deelan reached across the table for the rapidly emptying bottle and topped up her father's glass before getting up to make more coffee.

'OK, to put this in perspective it might be easier if I use the Koran as an example. I don't suppose either of you heathens have ever read it have you?'

'But uncle you know religion is anathema to us. It is one of our oldest tenets, we accept our mortality, and live all the better for it.'

'Absolutely, but I am talking about knowledge Tristellis, a way of understanding perhaps Man's greatest weakness.'

Tristellis and Garfan exchanged a glance before shamefacedly shaking their heads, which both then whipped round in surprise when they heard the quiet confession from Deelan.

'I have father, a little, at least the parts that refer to the Jinn.'

Elarris smiled proudly. 'I would expect nothing less from my daughter.'

Tristellis and Garfan looked up at Deelan in unison and stuck out their tongues like school kids. Deelan made a face in response which made all three of them laugh.

'Now then children, let us get back to the matter in hand shall we.'

He shook his head and held out his mug so that Deelan could refill it. 'Sometimes I wonder about the wisdom of having you two as our protectors.'

Garfan raised an eyebrow at this, but let it pass.

'Anyway, as I was saying, according to the Koran Allah made Man from clay…and the Jinn from fire. Obviously this is referring to the fire elementals. These Jinn were created as mortal, with the power to reproduce just like Man, but they were created to serve Man. This is one of the few religious texts that admits, even in a limited way, to our existence. Not only that, but the observations of the nature of the Jinn are quite accurate. Most other religions view anything non-human purely as an affirmation that Evil exists, and then twists the facts accordingly.'

Garfan chuckled at this as he held out his hand to take the coffee pot Deelan was offering him. Elarris nodded in agreement with Garfan's amusement.

'Yes, short sighted and ignorant. As we well know these concepts of good and evil are little more than that…concepts based on extreme perspectives.
It is only actions that may be judged as such when it is absolutely necessary to do so. No being is one or the other, merely a sum of their experiences and their actions.'

Elarris looked pointedly at both Tristellis and Garfan. 'And you two should know this better than most as our Guardians against those who would carry out evil acts. In every kingdom of Men across the globe this is so, Guardians protecting all, men and our kind alike, from those who would cause harm. But ever in smaller numbers and in secrecy, which is as it should be.'

Elarris watched Deelan pour more coffee for Tristellis before closing his eyes for a moment and inhaling the aroma rising from his nephew's mug before continuing.

'The reason I have spoken of these things is

because of the relevance of what is said in the Koran. It mentions a Jinn who rebelled against Allah. This being's pride would not allow him to help Mankind. This being came to be called Shaitan, which means adversary. It is likely that this is where the name Satan originated, after all, all human religions are related and interlinked, all being evolved from earlier, older concepts. In fact the irony is rife that the so-called Abrahmic religions should all hate each other so much, seeing that they all originate from an older belief system, something that no Christian, Muslim, or Jew would ever care to admit to. That aside it is important to remember what I said earlier about the truth which lies behind these stories.'

'A few of the other Elders and myself believe that such a being did once exist, that the Koran's references to Jinn are references to Elementals. A fire elemental who at that time, and we are talking about the Seventh Century here, openly waged war against Man. He was one of the reasons the Crusades came about. The Guardians of the Western Kingdoms were concerned about rumours and stories coming from the east concerning acts of great evil, and the open subjugation of whole tribes of men.'

'Now I could go into greater historical detail, but I believe that part of the Koran tells a limited, but essentially truthful tale of open rebellion against Mankind by a rogue group of Fire Elementals in Persia. We believed that this group were stopped and eliminated by the combined efforts of the Guardians of the Western Kingdoms who travelled with the Christian Knights expressly to accomplish this. There is a sad irony that the lowly order born of this ambition, and their friendship with and loyalty to us, eventually led to their betrayal by the Christian Church who would like to destroy all evidence of any of our kind if they could.'

Tristellis stopped fiddling with his glass and interrupted once again. 'I'm sorry, this is fascinating, but I still don't understand how any of this is relevant to the here and now?'

Elarris held up a placating hand. 'Please Tristellis, I am getting to that.' He looked at Garfan just in case he to had any questions. Garfan just held out a hand to indicate that he should go on.

'Our records hold details of stories which were brought back to us from those who survived the conflict. Stories of a Brotherhood of Demons who fought for this Shaitan. They all wore an iron ring on their hands as a symbol of their brotherhood, a ring it is said each forged with the heat of their own fire. Not only this, but their were tales that their leader could resurrect their dead human servants to fight for him in battle, undead warriors who could not die twice. But these were not just re-animated corpses like the zombies and such creatures you have encountered in the past. These Revenants were not mindless automatons, but vicious warriors, stronger and faster than they were in life. They were recognisable by certain wounds that were inflicted during the resurrection ceremony, and it is said that they would often inflict the self same wounds upon their enemies as some kind of revenge against those who still lived'

'Fuck!'

Elarris looked shocked at Garfan's abrupt outburst.

'Sorry Elarris, but just earlier today I read a story in one of the newspapers about the bodies from the cinema being stolen from the morgue they'd been taken to. Maybe Martin…'

Tristellis looked at his old friend in alarm before recognising the realisation in his friend's face.

'Oh Shit!'

'Tristellis please!'

Tris looked repentant. 'Sorry uncle…but you can't think that this being still exists do you? This is all too much…'

'I'm sorry Tristellis, but the other Elders and I believe that this group has resurfaced and are here in our kingdom. How and why are bigger questions for another time, but I fear it is true, and if so we are all in great danger. You yourselves said that you were tracking something or someone of great power before the incident at that old cinema. But why would they pose as Satanists? You must see it all fits. I don't know if it is the same being or a descendant who has risen in his stead, but if it is true, and the Brotherhood once more exists, they can only be here for one reason…revenge.'

Chapter Thirteen

Garfan and Tristellis had gone to their beds not long after their discussion with Elarris. Both of them a little shell-shocked by the stories and suspicions that Elarris had shared with them. Both spent the night tossing and turning as a result.

Sometime just after dawn Garfan gave up on the pretense of being able to get any more sleep and tip-toed into Tris's room to see how he fared. On sticking his head round the door he found him sat up awake in bed, arms behind his head as he stared at the ceiling.

'Get much sleep?'

Tris sighed and brought his arms down to hug his knees. 'Not much, but I did realise something laying here in the dark earlier.'

'What's that?'

'Being in the countryside, surrounded by the forest and nature...I realised how much I love the city!'

Garfan chuckled quietly. 'You better not let Elarris hear you say that.' He looked at the window where light was beginning to peek through the curtains. 'Sun's up...shall we?

Tristan sighed and swung his legs out of the bed. 'Why not, no time like the present.'

*

'It's good to be back home!'

'Tris we're not staying.'

'What do you mean we're not staying?'

'Sometimes I really worry about you. Were you not listening to what Elarris said? We've got to take the fight to them, which means we can't use the house as our base, at least not until we've disposed of whatever sort of hit-squad was sent after you and Martin. They've obviously got the ability to track us somehow. I don't know who or what they are, or even if they're Revenants, but I don't think we want to bring their attention to our home, do you?'

'No, I s'pose not. OK, how long have we got?'

'Ten minutes, then we need to leave all this behind for a while and hit the streets.'

'What about the car?'

Garfan gave Tris a look. 'What do you think?'

Tris blinked and then shrugged. 'I'm not helping much am I?'

Garfan just laughed and shook his head, 'Just give Avis a ring and tell them we'll drop it in at the nearest office, wherever that is. We can't hang around here any longer than we have too just in case they get a lock on us somehow.'

'OK, do you need anything before we leave?'

'No just make the call then we're out of here, unless you need anything of course?'

Tris looked out through the windscreen at the house he'd come to love so dearly over the last couple of centuries. 'Fuck it! No, I'll call them on the way there, I think they've got an office in York Road next to Waterloo Station.'

*

The traffic was slow leaving Tris plenty of time in the twenty minutes it took them to get to Waterloo to make arrangements for the car with the people at Avis. Once they'd got there the same young man who'd delivered the car took a cursory and somewhat nervous look over the Audi. Standing, clipboard in hand, he was obviously trying not to look at his clients and hastily got Tris to sign off on the rental before handing the keys to one of their mechanics and bidding Mr Forest and Mr Stone a good afternoon. That done he scuttled off as fast as he could.

As they were both walking out of the Avis centre Garfan couldn't help but comment. 'You seem to make that young man a little nervous Tris.'

Tristellis ignored it and carried on walking. Once they were out on the street Tris turned and looked down at his friend. 'OK Einstein, where to now?'

'The Bank…eventually.'

'What do you mean eventually?'

'Well clever-clogs, we don't know how they're tracking us do we? And like you said before it could be electronically. So we're going to try and rule that out before we do anything else. This being the case I have a cunning plan.'

'How cunning?'

Garfan just looked at Tris blankly.

'Garf, there are times I wish you'd spend more time with humans, get your head into some popular culture.'

'What do you mean? I read the papers, and we go to galleries. What the hell are you talking about?'

'Nothing, I just think we could laugh together a lot more if…'

Garfan quite blatantly did not have a clue what he was talking about.

'Never mind. So what's the plan?'

'OK You're going to give me your mobile phone, and I'm going to take both our phones for a casual stroll for a couple of hours whilst you go to the safe house and pick up our street gear. Then we're going to meet at the Bank and put our phones in the safety deposit box.'

'And what's that going to accomplish?'

'Don't worry I've thought this through. I organised with Elarris before we left for him to organise surveillance on the bank around the clock whilst we disappear onto the streets and try and find them, before they find us.'

'OK, softly, softly, catchy monkey, I get that, but what if they are tracking us through our mobiles? They'll know we're not staying in the Bank, besides which even if they were there's no way they could get any signal from the Bank's vault. As far as they're concerned we'd just drop off the map'

'Well that's what we want.'

'Yeah, and what if they do show up at the Bank? We don't know who they are, so how the hell is Elarris's surveillance going to know what to look out for?'

Garfan frowned.

Tris shook his head. 'Thought this through my arse. This plan stinks, it's so full of holes you could catch fish with it!'

Garfan stopped walking and looked up at Tris, the corners of his mouth twitching, 'Could catch fish with it?'

Tris had stopped a pace or two in front of Garfan, but didn't turn to look at his old friend.

Garfan repeated himself a little louder, 'Could catch fish with it?'

Tris pursed his lips, and turned slowly to look down at Garfan. 'OK, OK…I admit it was the first thing that popped into my head.'

'Could catch fish with it!' Garfan's face seemed to dissolve into a mass of lines and hair and hugged himself as the laughter bubbled out of him uncontrollably.

Tris could only stand there and watch as Garfan slowly bent over at the waste, tears streaming down his cheeks and into his beard. He could vaguely hear Garf repeating, '…fish with it!' and grinned, finally letting his own laughter free.

The pair of them both ended up bent over, leaning on each other, and unable to move in paroxysm's of laughter. Their mirth helping to relieve a lot of the tensions that had been building between the two of them over the last couple of days.

Eventually Garfan pulled himself together enough

to wipe his eyes and slap Tris on the back. 'We'd better keep moving, when we get a little more central we'll split up. You can go and get our gear, and I'll lose myself in the crowds. I'll meet you later at the Bank, and we'll discuss the plan again there, OK?'

Tris was now in control of himself despite the moisture left in the corners of his eyes. 'Fine. So how long are we gonna be homeless?'

'Who knows?'

'So we'll need plenty of cash then.' Tris smiled and started to walk in the direction they'd been heading before they'd been ambushed by the giggles, Garfan in step beside him.

Garfan sneaked a peek up at his friend's profile and said very softly, '...couldn't catch fish with it!'

The two friends turned the corner of the road onto Westminster Bridge, heading across the Thames towards Westminster Tube Station, both chuckling quietly.

*

The journey to Canary Wharf was not one that Garfan took very often. Their safety deposit boxes at Coutts & Co held any number of valuable, irreplaceable items that the pair had collected over the centuries, but for all their intrinsic value neither Garfan or Tristellis found much pleasure in the mere accumulation of wealth. Those that Man called Elves were less mercantile in their thinking than the Dwarves, valuing land more than anything else.

Despite this Tristellis and Garfan's kin were rich beyond measure, owning huge tracts of land across Britain through the families of those they had helped over the millennia, also through the more base accumulation of money and artefacts. Hence the fact that the pair had access to fortunes squirreled away in various trusts and old, established private banks, such as Coutts & Co. As ever familiarity with such wealth left very little respect for it or any true appreciation of the value of money.

Garfan got on the circle line at Westminster. It was the usual nightmare of heat and the smells of sweat and unwashed bodies, Garfan's height putting him in uncomfortable proximity to too many armpits. Garfan hated the tube, which was why he had got onto the Circle Line heading for Tower Hill, rather than taking the quicker and more direct route using the Jubilee Line. The thought of spending a moment longer than was absolutely necessary underground made Garfan shudder. This way he could take the over-ground Docklands Light Railway from Tower Hill to Canary Wharf.

Tristellis often commented on the apparent dichotomy of a Dwarf not liking being underground. To which Garfan always replied that, racial stereotypes not withstanding, he just didn't trust modern man to construct anything that would outlive a single generation of Dwarves. Which meant, when considering the average lifespan of any Dwarf not involved in Garfan's line of work, he probably had a point.

The Docklands train took Garfan through the traditionally poor area of Shadwell. Garfan could remember back to when Shadwell had been the site of a Sailors Refuge, housing many of the 'Lascars', indentured Indian sailors abandoned by the British merchants of the East India Company, in the late eighteenth century. It had always astonished him how these men seemed to deal so easily with being marooned half way round the world from there homes in an alien land with an alien language.
He and Tris had often made friends with such refugees and had done everything they could to help them settle in their new home.

Then the train went past the marina in the Limehouse Basin, and past the present site of the Billingsgate Fish market, it having moved from the Blackfriars area around thirty-five years ago, a move that

Garfan had never approved of. The original site had been so steeped in history, it had been a great place to wander and listen to the gossip. Garfan sighed and tried to let go of his reminiscences as the train pulled up to the elevated platform at Canary Wharf.

As soon as Garfan got off of the train at Canary Wharf, breathing in the air of the West India Docks, he started to surreptitiously look around himself, trying desperately to shake the feeling that he was being watched.

Despite being uncomfortably aware of an indefinable presence watching him from somewhere nearby, Garfan couldn't help but once again be amazed by what had become of the Isle of Dogs. Once upon a time it had been a haven for thieves, beggars and prostitutes. All attracted to the bustling docks, and the constant flow of money between innumerable pairs of hands.

It seemed like an age ago, even more so for what Canary Wharf had become; a concrete, glass and steel landscape, tastefully decorated with formal plantings of trees and shrubs. There was even the odd patch of open grass in the standard square or rectangular motif, which just managed to echo the prevalent themes around them.

Without having actually planned a meeting place Garfan made the assumption that Tris would head for Smolensky's Bar and Grill in Reuters Place, just around the corner from No.1 Canada Square, the home of Coutts & Co's Head Office. They could meet at the Slug and Lettuce opposite, but Garfan knew how Tristellis felt about these things.

Besides, on a sunny day like this it was preferable to pay vastly inflated prices in order to sit outside and receive superlative service, rather than paying less and having to wait an age only to be the recipient of sloppy service. More importantly they had met there before, and if Garfan slipped the waiter something extra, and warned him that he was expecting rather disreputable company, he was sure that they would pass a blind eye over the substandard attire which Garfan was sure Tristellis would be turning up in.

Still he was bothered by some unconscious instinct that was wary of danger somewhere in the vicinity, a feeling that prompted Garfan to make his way straight to Reuters Place and the comfort of an open public place.

Walking across the large concrete space outside the station Garfan kept a close watch on the area immediately around him, as well as taking in an overall impression of the landscape. The buildings were almost blinding in the bright afternoon sun. The huge glass and steel constructions around him glinted evilly in the sun, patches of reflected light momentarily stunning the unwary into snatching for their sunglasses.

The expense and opulence of the whole area raised a smile on Garfan's face every time he came here. The ostentation was supposedly subtle in its inference of wealth, power and prestige housed within these skyscrapers. In these times of renewed violence between the Christian and Muslim faiths Garfan felt uneasy in such a place. Besides the indefinable presence that intermittently made itself felt, there was the nervousness of being only too aware of what the fanatical were capable of. The twin towers were gone, and if any terrorist wanted to make a similar statement in Britain and murder as many rich people and damage as many financial institutions as possible in one strike, then this was the place to do it. Besides Coutts & Co, the immediate area played host to Citigroup, Credit Suisse, not to mention the Bank of America. Not a comforting thought as he finally sat down outside Smollensky's to wait for Tris.

*

Garfan was drinking his second cup of tea when he couldn't help but notice a beautiful young woman walking past the bistro. She was dressed in a smart grey business suit and carrying a slim briefcase. Her hair was long and golden with deeper tones of copper that glinted as her hair moved in the sunlight

It was just as Garfan was pulling his gaze away from this sight, that he became aware of someone behind him...uncomfortably close behind him. The whirling defensive move which carried Garfan out of his chair, and away from the table at which he'd been sitting, dissolved into a rather expansive greeting as soon as his eyes recognized the tall tramp stood quietly with his arms folded and a sly grin on his face, a grin which just got bigger as Tristellis recognised the discomfort his old friend was displaying at being caught out in more ways than one.

'She was very beautiful Garf...can't blame you for looking.' One of his eyebrows arched knowingly as he said this.

Garf couldn't quite decide whether to be embarrassed, angry, or amused. Lumping for amusement he snorted and threw an already out-flung arm around Tris's back in greeting.

'If you hadn't taken so long I wouldn't have had to resort to people watching to keep myself amused. What took you so long?'

'What took me so long! Do you know how far I've had to come carrying all this lot?' At which point Tristellis un-slung the bulky, cheap looking backpack he was carrying and dumped it with a dull thunk next to Garfan's recently vacated chair.

'Besides which I decided that if this was to be an exercise in discretion then I'd be much harder to track if I used public transport. In the last couple of hours I've seen more bus stops and tube stations than I even want to think about. But I wasn't followed by anyone, and I'm pretty sure that long range tracking would have been impossible.'

It was only when Tris stopped talking that Garfan had a chance to fully take in his friends attire.

'So did you get any funny looks, or comments, or did the general public just give you a wide berth? What should I call you...Aqualung?'

Tris scowled momentarily at Garfan. 'Well I wasn't going to slog all the way here carrying both sets of clothes and battle gear in bags was I.'

Garfan smiled and raised a questioning eyebrow. 'So you're all tooled up then?'

Tris looked a little shocked, but laughed throatily. 'My god Garf, an Americanism! Whatever next…a spot of stand-up? Though it might help if you clawed your way out of the Seventies first.'

Garfan laughed too. 'I thought you might appreciate that particular use of patois. So are you…'

'Yep. All ready to rock and roll. So what's the plan now? Do you want to change first, or go straight to the bank?'

Garfan thought for a moment, considering whether he should mention the presence he'd felt as soon as he'd arrived. Looking at Tris he was puzzled that his old friend didn't seem to have detected anything strange, though neither did he at the moment. Better to wait and see maybe.

'Well lets think that through shall we. How welcome do you think two tramps would be in the main offices of a private bank? Think about it Tris! I'll go in with the phones, leave them in the safety deposit box, and come straight back out while you stay out here and keep an eye out for anything strange.'

Tris thought he detected a slight emphasis on the "anything strange", but declined to comment.

*

As Garfan made his way back across the extensive lobby of No.1 Canada Square he couldn't help but notice that the weather had taken a turn for the worst whilst he'd been inside. The huge expanse of glass which fronted the lobby had earlier let in a dazzling amount of light, and now displayed a sky hidden behind a dull grey ceiling of cloud.

Garfan's business inside had taken only a short amount of time as soon as the staff of Coutts & Co had realised whom the diminutive businessman represented. The families of Forest and Stone held considerable wealth within this bank, and as such the company fawned around Garfan in a most irritating way, though he was glad it expedited his mission to deposit their mobile phones.

As he approached the glass plate doors ahead of him they swung open automatically as he tripped one of the many electronic sensors in the door's frame. The doors opening let in a gust of still warm afternoon air, slightly heavy with humidity…and something else.

Garfan was on guard as he stepped out from the relative safety of the huge air-conditioned building into the increasingly humid afternoon. Looking up at the clouds Garfan knew they could look forward to rain before the day was out. Sleeping rough was so much more…fun in the rain.

He looked around for Tristellis only to spot him lounging against the corner of the building trying to look nonchalant, a clever trick considering he was dressed as a homeless person in the one part of London where there were none. Garfan turned and walked towards him.

As he walked he experienced the same sensation he had when he'd first got off the train, only this time he was sure the presence was somewhere behind him. At the same moment he saw Tris stiffen in front of him, a look of disbelief and then anger flitting across his face.

'What is it Tris? Do you recognise it?'

Tris nodded slowly whilst staring over Garfan's head. 'It feels the same as when Martin was killed. It's them…I don't know how they did it, but they've found us.

'Where are they Tris?'

Tris walked to the edge of the pavement and stopped, apparently looking intently at his feet as he pushed his senses to their limit in an attempt to pinpoint whatever it was that was out there. Garfan had followed him, and now stood next to Tris peering in concern at his old friend, then upwards and around at the tall buildings surrounding them. His nostrils flared as he sniffed the air. Slowly he turned looking southwards towards the less developed part of the Isle of Dogs. His feet seemed to move of their own volition as he moved towards the far corner of the building.

Tris sighed and lifted his head to follow Garfan's movement. 'I can't get a lock, but they're definitely south of here.'

Garfan ignored him as he continued to move his head slowly from side to side, his face held up to what little breeze there was.

Tristellis folded his arms and tapped his foot impatiently as Garfan wandered away from him, sniffing the air. Before Garfan got as far as the corner of the building he stopped, lowering his head and looking straight ahead. Then he looked over his shoulder at Tris twitching his head to beckon him over. Tris held his head tilted to one side in question as he walked up to Garfan.

'What is it?'

Garfan held up his arm and pointed due south. 'That way…they're somewhere close over the water.'

Tris looked down at Garfan before following his gaze. 'So, the Isle of Dogs, or maybe Heron Quay…'

He was just about to continue when Garfan raised the hand he'd been pointing in warning. 'Tris there's more.'

'More?'

Garfan turned to Tris and looked up into his face, his expression grave. 'I smell death.'

Tristellis returned his look blankly, trying to figure out what Garf meant. 'Is this some kind of premonition? Because if anyone's going to die it's gonna be them.'

Garfan smiled, but there was absolutely no warmth in it. 'Actually I think they may already be dead.'

*

Do you think they're Revenants?'

Garfan grimaced. 'The stench of death is in my nostrils Tris, and in this day and age you don't find many human corpses just lying around. Maybe a couple of hundred years ago, but not now. I'm pretty sure they're undead, which means Elarris may have been right.'

Tristellis shrugged non-committally. 'The only problem is we've dealt with the so-called undead before, only what kind of undead are these? They're not Vampires, and they're definitely not Zombies, Martin would have had no problem with Zombies, they move slower than old people with zimmer frames. Besides if it were any of those we'd have identified them straight away. These things are something else entirely, and if they are Revenants then we could be in trouble.'

Garfan shrugged. 'I've not got a clue, but they're somewhere near, and we've got to take them out.'

He looked up at the steel and glass towers surrounding them. 'And I'd rather not do it with an audience.'

Tristellis tried to ignore the worried frown on Garfan's face as he thought about their options. 'Only place round here where there is any open ground without tall buildings round it is on the Isle of Dogs. The only problem is going to be making sure there aren't any casual bystanders who could get hurt.'

'I don't think we need to worry too much about that. They're definitely after us, but I would prefer to have no witnesses. I'd rather not get any innocent humans involved, besides, I have an aversion to answering questions raised by the police.'

Tris looked thoughtful. 'How long do you think we have?'

'A few hours until it gets really dark, then they'll try and surround us wherever we are.'

217

They both knew that who or whatever they were wouldn't dare showing themselves during daylight. Such creatures of the night were aptly named, no self-respecting monster of any description would venture out during the day. Half the magic...half the terror, was in the shadows, in the very fact of being disguised by the darkness. Man would always be afraid of the dark...and what his imagination populated it with.

Tris blew out his cheeks with a sigh. 'In that case if we want to do anything on the Isle of Dogs we better go and talk to the lord of the manor.'

Garfan didn't look any the wiser.

'The Huguenot...we have to go and talk to the Huguenot'

*

'From what I hear if we want to find him we'll have to go to 'The Ship' on Westferry Road after dark, apparently that's where he holds court these days. That's the other side of the Isle from here, but it should only take about thirty minutes to walk there from here, we want to be sure that they follow us, right?'

'Unfortunately yes. But between now and then I could really do with something to eat...I'm starving.'

'Well if we've got time to kill lets go to 'The Gun', it's not far from here and it's probably the best pub in the area.'

'Is that the one we used to go to where they kept saying Nelson was upstairs with Lady Hamilton, but we never saw them?'

'That's the one, though I'm sure it looks a lot different now. More importantly I've heard the foods pretty good these days, Martin mentioned it once...' Tris stopped. Mentioning Martin had suddenly killed his appetite.

Garfan gently took hold of Tris's arm and squeezed. 'I liked it when it was full of smugglers, they never quite knew what to make of us did they.'

Tris smiled wanly back. 'Come on, lets go eat. We may as well have a decent meal if it's to be our last.'

Garfan raised an eyebrow. 'I suppose that if we're going to walk into a trap of our own making tonight we may as well enjoy our last hours…and a pint would go down nicely right about now.'

Tris nodded back at his friend. 'First round's on you then.'

'My pleasure.' Garfan sadly quipped as he flourished an arm at Tris. 'Would you care to lead the way.'

As their eye's met the two friends shared a moment of perfect communication; so many things said, and at the same time not said.

Both of them over the centuries had said everything that ever needed to be said between them, but this could never equal the feelings they had for each other, feelings that went too deep to ever be easily expressed.

They both knew that death was their constant companion, and had come to terms with that hundreds of years ago, but it didn't mean that either of them found it any easier to picture each others death, the look of it, the smell of it, the very texture of such physical loss.

With a tight-lipped smile Tristellis started walking again. 'I s'pose you're right. May as well have a decent meal if it's to be our last.'

*

They made their way through Churchill Place to Trafalgar Way, choosing the most direct route they could walking North East towards Blackwall, then south down Preston's Road to Coldharbour and 'The Gun' pub.

When they got there it was already busy with the usual mix of after work suits and the other young professionals who'd infested all the new exclusive housing developments around the waterside edges of the once squalid Isle of Dogs. Tris felt a little under dressed in his street gear, but he was with Garfan who had the suit, and the money. He doubted there'd be any fuss, a few raised eyebrows no doubt, but they wouldn't turn away paying customers.

Tris was of course right, as soon as he followed Garfan in heads began to turn, and whilst the barman's expression wasn't openly hostile, he didn't look too happy. When Garfan got to the bar he stepped aside so that Tris could join him at the bar.

Garfan gestured expansively at the bar and said to Tris in a posh voice. 'So Tristan, I feel nailing that role deserves a little celebration don't you. I thought you were marvellous. So…what would you like?'

Taking Garfan's lead Tris smiled winningly at the barman and in his usual cultured tones ordered a large Gin and Tonic, and a pint of Guinness for his 'Agent'. Upon hearing this the barman visibly relaxed and smiled warmly at his theatrical customers before turning to the back of the bar to get their drinks.

Garfan winked at Tris and got out his wallet to pay for the drinks. This accomplished, drinks in hand they both made their way through the crowded bar outside onto the terrace where it was reasonably quiet due to the unsettled weather. In fact the breeze was picking up, and it was perceptibly more overcast than it had been.

They sat at a vacant table with a view over the Thames to Greenwich and the Millennium Dome; that testimony to complete human idiocy and the power of the few over the many. Tristellis gazed blankly out over the choppy grey water to the stupidly huge white dome, completely lost in his own thoughts.

Garfan could see that he'd lost Tris for a while, any mention of Martin was likely to do this until he put it

220

behind him. So he left him to it and looked at the menu on the table as he got stuck into his pint. Tris didn't even notice when a few minutes later he got up to go and order two rare roast beef sandwiches with creamed horseradish and side orders of fries with aioli from the bar.

The next thing Tris was aware of was the welcome smell of chips, and low and behold sat next to his untouched G & T was a bowl of golden brown chips, next to which sat a large white plate with a very large sandwich in the middle of it. He looked up at Garfan and smiled shyly.

'I knew you'd get your appetite back when you saw it.' Garfan smiled. 'And I ordered the same so there wouldn't be any argument over who had what.'

Tris's smile faded for a moment. 'I'm not a child Garfan.'

'Then don't behave like one.'

That was all the rebuke he was going to get from Garfan, but it was enough to remind him who they were, where they were and what they were up against. He looked up from his plate at Garfan who had a mouthful of beef, which he hastily swallowed.

'And don't even think about saying sorry. Just eat your sandwich before it gets cold. The chips are pretty good too…'

Chapter Fourteen

After they'd finished their almost silent meal neither of them felt any huge desire to linger for another drink. They could sense their pursuers were close, not a feeling conducive to sitting down and relaxing with a glass of your favourite tipple.

The sun was almost down behind the clouds, the gathering darkness oppressive and expectant. Despite this there were only a few scattered drops of rain as they made their way across the Isle of Dogs, past Cubitt Town and into Millwall, and at last Westferry Road.

As they stood outside 'The Ship' Garfan looked up at the dark sky. It looked as though the heavens were ready to open, the clouds black and heavy with rain waiting to fall, waiting for what he didn't know, but he could appreciate the feeling. Garfan lowered his eyes from the sky and found Tris looking at him.

Garfan spoke, to break the silence as much as anything else. 'OK, so how come you know so much about the current Huguenot? We haven't had any dealings with the family since his grandfather died.'

'You know me, I like to keep tabs on old contacts and their descendants, especially the shadier ones. You never know when their particular talents may come in handy, and as it turns out I was right. If anyone round here knows a discreet place in the vicinity where we can spring this trap without witnesses or unnecessary casualties, then Jack's the man.'

'I thought his name was Jacques?'

Tris laughed quietly. 'I tell you what, why don't you let me do all the talking.'

'Very funny Tris, but you know you'd better handle security. You're better at reading humans than I am, besides he must be old by now and I'm sure he'd respond better to my maturity.'

222

'Maturity…'

'Don't even think about it.' Garfan snapped pointing a finger at him. 'Just point him out when we get in there…and watch my back.'

*

As they entered the pub what little conversation there had been ceased immediately. Luckily for them it wasn't a busy night, just four customers and the landlord. Two were big looking bruisers sat near the door who eyed them warily as they walked past their table towards an old man sat on his own with his back to a wall facing the door. A third man was sat at the bar talking quietly with the landlord. Garfan didn't even have to guess which one was the Huguenot.

Jack sat there quietly as Tristellis and Garfan approached his table. They did so quietly and as slowly as they could without seeming hesitant, to come forward faster would have seemed brash and impolite, to be slow and overly cautious would have suggested weakness or fear. Jack knew the differences, and as he studied the unlikely pair moving purposely towards him he could see that they did too.

He raised an eyebrow in silent enquiry as they stopped before his table, each without a drink, but each making sure that their hands were in plain sight.

'May we intrude for a few moments Jacques De Beaufort?' Garfan asked politely extending a hand to the two empty chairs before them.

Jack was surprised by the use of his old family name, the one his father had given him at birth but had not been entered on his birth certificate, though he managed not to show it in any other way than a slight tightening of the muscles around his mouth. He inclined his head in assent.

223

In speaking Garfan kept the old man's focus, leaving Tris free to observe the ageing crook, and keep an eye on their surroundings. Both of them were aware that all it would take was a word from the old man and they'd have at least three large men coming at them with weapons, one of which was a handgun of some description, Tris could smell the distinct scent of gun oil and burnt cordite from where he now sat, though with his back to it, it was a little difficult to pinpoint where the smell was coming from.

Jack was curious about the odd pair sitting before him. They held themselves with the authority of the law, but they weren't coppers. They moved like soldiers, but they weren't military, and they didn't display the obvious arrogance of mercenaries. The air of calm and patience they exuded reminded him of something, something from his youth.

Yes, that was it. The old men who had taught him to fish when he was a boy, when they had sat by the side of the river, they had displayed that same aura of quiet watchful alertness, the patience of the hunter. Looking at the pair more intently he inclined his head in silent greeting once more and took hold of his empty pint glass, holding it up a little and waggling it at the barman. As he did so he watched the taller of the two, the younger looking one, noticing that though his half open eyes seemed to follow his every move he also gave the impression of listening intently to whatever was going on behind him in the rest of the room.

Placing the empty glass back on the table before him he glanced at the young man's hands that were relaxed before him on the edge of the table. They looked like smooth, well cared for hands, the nails clean and shiny, having received their fair share of manicures he'd wager. Then he spotted a small, well-defined callus on the ball of one of the thumbs, a callus that looked out of place on such a hand. Definitely not a workman's hands, but hands that handled something regularly enough to leave a

Callus. He just couldn't think what that something might be.

Smiling slowly he brought his attention back to the stocky bearded one who had spoken in rough gravely tones. He had nice hands too.

'So what can I do for you gentlemen?'

Garfan had not missed the scrutiny they had both had from the old man and smiled as he replied. 'As tradition dictates we are here to extend our greetings to 'the Huguenot' and to offer a gift before proceeding with our business in your territory.'

Now Jack really was nonplussed. First they'd addressed him by a name that very few outside his closest circle of family and friends knew, and now they referred to a title and tradition which had all but disappeared in his father's day.

'Who are you two to offer tithe to a title that died along with my father?'

Garfan shrugged casually. 'The world is poorer for the loss of such titles and traditions, especially as they held sway here for over two hundred years. For all that time there was always a Huguenot, a member of your family running the shadier side of the Isle of Dogs and Cubitt town. We should know...' He leaned forward slightly eclipsing the old man's view of the rest of the pub. 'We've known them all.'

The Huguenot's eyes widened in surprise and disbelief. His grandfather had told him stories when he was a child, stories which as he'd grown up he'd discarded as myth and fairy tale, old smuggler's stories meant to frighten and intimidate, stories that had always held two consistent elements, the guardian warriors, always a tall young man and an older dwarf. He shook his head in disbelief.

'Is this some kind of joke? Who are you? Did my sons put you up to this, or are you just interested in local history or something?'

'I'm sorry, this is a little rash of us to do this, but

225

we don't have much time, and obviously your father died without having told you about us.'

'What has my father got to do with this?' The old man said suspiciously .

'We knew your father. Did he die suddenly?'

The old man regarded the hairy little man sat opposite him. 'Yes, in an accident when I was still a young man, so you can see how I would be sceptical that you could have known him, you're too young.' His voice got louder as he went on causing the man by the bar to stand up and take a step towards them.

'I don't know what you think you're doing here, but unless you get to the point very quickly I'm going to have to ask you to leave an old man in peace.'

Garfan leant forward in his seat, his arms reaching across the table towards the old man. 'I'm sorry about William, he was a good man, but the truth is we need to ask you a favour, one that your family would never have questioned in the past.'

'What?' Jack exclaimed loudly whilst nodding to his men behind the two strangers. 'I'm sorry, but I think it's time you two left.'

Garfan looked round at Tris and nodded once before turning back to look pointedly at the old man. 'Well Huguenot, we don't like public displays, but it would appear you leave us little choice.'

As Garfan spoke Tris pushed his chair back and in the same movement stood and stepped into the reach of the first man who'd come from the bar. He was big and balding, and by the state of his nose was an ex-boxer and still in pretty good shape by the looks of it. He went down without a sound like a sack of potatoes, and without any discernible movement from Tristellis.

The other two men saw this and tried to rush him together…only to find him grabbing their necks from behind and literally banging their heads together. The accompanying thud was enough to make the landlord wince and reach for the phone on the bar in front of him.

Garfan was still looking the old man in the eye as he raised an eyebrow in silent question. The landlord looked at the Huguenot as he raised the receiver to his ear. The old man shook his head and the landlord put the phone down. Seeing Tris grin at him the landlord stayed exactly where he was, as still as a statue, as Tris made his way back to his seat.

Jack studied them both for a moment and then smiled thinly. 'So…this favour?'

Garfan held up a hand to make him stop. 'First to keep faith, the gift we bring as tithe. The gift is two pieces of information, the first you should find enlightening. The second you probably won't believe, but it is this which brings us here.'

Jack snorted. 'Just because I've agreed to listen doesn't mean I want to feel myself getting older whilst you tell me.'

Garfan nodded politely. 'To the point then…do you still live in the terrace house in Lawn House Close near the drawbridge?'

Jack was beginning to get a bad feeling about this, they knew far too much about him, and he had no idea how the younger one had managed to take out his muscle like that.

'Yes I do, but how do you know? Have you been following me?'

It was Garfan's turn to snort in disgust. 'No my dear Jacques, we have much more important things to do than tail small time crime lords. We know where you live because we bought that house for your grandfather and his family.'

Jack shook his head sadly.

'I don't know what you two are trying to pull, but how can you possibly expect me to believe that?'

'Because we have proof. Does the house still have an open fireplace in the front room, because if it does you'll find that just up inside the chimney there are two loose bricks on the right hand side. Pull them out and inside you should find a small strongbox that contains all the proof you'll need.'

Garfan nodded slowly. 'We bought that house for your grandfather Hubert as a gift in return for a difficult service he did for us. We have always helped your family, the Huguenot De Beaufort clan who settled on the Isle of Dogs and made it their own.'

Jack looked at them both in utter disbelief, but managed to stop himself from saying anything that might provoke these madmen. Having said that, the old stories were trying to make themselves heard above the rest of the clamour in his mind, along with the mystery of his grandfathers outright ownership of a brand new house, at least it had been when Victoria still ruled.

Garfan continued. 'The second piece of information is that there are creatures abroad, in your manor, who want blood. Specifically ours, but anyone who gets in their way won't live to tell the tale.'

'Creatures?'

'Yes, they are evil and only we can stop them. Here is where we ask our favour, and it's not even a big one. We need an open space preferably with a descent line of sight where there won't be any danger of innocent bystanders getting hurt.'

Tris could see that the old man was really having trouble with all this. 'OK, we can see you think we're crazy. If so fine, just tell us where the best place would be and we'll lead them there. Then you can call the police, though that would probably be a novelty for you. But do one thing before you do call the police…find the strongbox, and once you've seen what it contains do as your conscience dictates.'

Tris stood slowly so as to not startle the old man, Garfan followed suit.

Jack shook his head as if coming out of a dream. 'Who are you? I don't even know your names.'

'Forest and Stone. After tonight I hope you will remember us as all your family have over the centuries.

Now…tell us where to go.'

Jack nodded. 'Behind the West Ferry Printing Works by Millwall Outer Dock, it's just up the road on your right beyond the sailing centre.'

Garfan smiled warmly at the aged Huguenot. 'Au revoir Monsieur, merci.' Then he walked out behind Tristellis.

With the words of the old language still in his ears the old man got slowly to his feet. 'I must be mad, that or going senile…' He nodded to the landlord as he made his way to the door. Leaving behind him three unconscious heavies and a very confused landlord.

*

They made their way up the road to the old West Ferry Printing Works as quickly as they could. Both of them could feel their enemies moving in from different directions, once more trying to surround them. Knowing this they didn't let the chain link fencing around the industrial sight slow them down. The sooner they were out on open ground the better.

There turned out to be a fair bit of open space behind the printing works making Garfan silently thank the old man, rough scrubland for the most part with no access to speak of apart from the water that surrounded them on two sides.

Most people in the same situation would have backed into the corner of land thinking that the water would protect their backs and leave them with less open ground to defend. Which is of course true, but the problem with this is that they'd also be trapped in a corner with no escape. Knowing this they opted for the middle of the open ground, leaving them more space to defend, but leaving them inherently more options.

The beauty of knowing that you're walking into a

trap is that you're ready, on edge, and anticipating the moment when your adversary is going to spring it. Not being sure whether it is a trap or not in the first place is infinitely different, it can cause you to jump at shadows and over-react. Not something to be laughed off when over-reacting could easily end with a dagger in someone's throat.

They wouldn't have admitted it, but this was the situation that they now found themselves in, and it was actually something new to them. Not knowing either way was making them both nervous, and nervous is not a good way to be when handling scalpel sharp eighteen inch long daggers. In waving them around you could easily lose a lot more than just an ear.

The two daggers were Tristellis's personal favourites, but he also had about his person around a dozen flat, leaf shaped throwing knives, an elemental designed elaboration on the medieval Bodkin, and a hunting knife. Defensive items included hardened leather braces on his forearms and shins, and a minimal breastplate made of the same material, all effectively concealed by his street clothes.

Garfan was also heavily armed, though his weapons were somewhat different. A pair of small double headed hand axes were his weapons of choice, though he also favoured a couple of small throwing hatchets similar in design to the traditional Indian tomahawk. He also possessed the obligatory razor sharp hunting knife. After all, if you're going to slit someone's throat, even he would find it difficult to do it quietly with an axe.

*

Across the river in Brixton Waves was not in a good mood. The car was beginning to smell of stale coffee and even staler food. In a situation like this the options for sustenance were decidedly limited. Luckily, if you wanted to look at it that way, there was a kebab shop just around the corner from the entrance to the club. It wasn't bad, but it wasn't good either. Besides which kebabs two nights in a row were leaving their mark on the Sergeant's digestive system.

After last night he'd decided to give the chilli sauce a permanent miss. The next morning had been bad enough, but Lebanese inspired indigestion had begun to leave a heady funk inside the car. One which Waves, even though being a bachelor, was sure was far from attractive to the opposite sex. Also Daniel's taste in coffee was, for a copper, surprisingly refined, and the stewed, badly made offering from the kebab shop was beginning to pall in his opinion.

All in all Daniel was thoroughly pissed off. For one thing he was putting in a full days work with the Inspector. Including briefings from their new 'friends' at the Agency, which left both he and Stands a little wound up due to the equal amounts of unlikely information and badly executed attempts at indoctrination into 'their way of thinking'. Add to this Daniel's unofficial stakeout of the club in Brixton, and he'd only managed to grab around seven hours sleep in the last fifty odd hours.

Thank God for Amphetamines thought Waves as he put the takeaway coffee cup between his legs and reached inside his jacket for one of the wraps of Speed that the Inspector had somehow procured for him the day before in an effort to help when he couldn't physically be there. After all, one of them had to be on their game. They wouldn't survive if they were both strung out from sleep deprivation and stress.

*

'They're getting closer…I can feel them. They're circling like they did before.'

Garfan looked at Tristellis, his voice had almost cracked. 'Are you OK?'

'Yeah, just eager to find out who we're really up against…and maybe get some payback.'

Garfan winced. 'Look Tris, we need to be focused right now. We've no idea what we're up against. This isn't about revenge…it's about protecting the innocent...'

The pause caught Tris' attention.

'Just try and remember what Elarris said, *complacency and over-confidence can be just as dangerous as ignorance*, and going into this blind just makes it even easier for things to go wrong.'

'Garf you worry too much.'

'Yeah, 'cos I have to worry for both of us.'

Tris grinned and slipped the long, ragged leather coat he was wearing off, then flung it aside into the darkness. The harness that looped his chest held his daggers against his back. Blades pointing up and crossed in the centre of his back. With practised ease Tris reached behind him, gripped the twin hilts, and drew the blades free, spinning them in his hands, the blades a blur as he brought them round before him.

Garfan shook his head. 'Stop showing off Tris, who is there to impress?'

Tris shrugged as Garfan followed suit, loosing the long flowing leather coat which concealed so much, but would only be a hindrance in a fight. Garfan's nose twitched. 'Can you smell that?'

Tris sniffed deeply, grimaced, and looked back at Garfan, his face a picture of distaste. 'Yep, mortal decay, like you said, the smell of Death. I don't like this…'

Garfan closed his eyes and concentrated on his other senses. 'There's three of them, circling but closing fast. They know the wind has picked up, they know we've got their scent. The trap is sprung…'

Out in the shadows, where the little starlight and light pollution from the surrounding civilisation couldn't reach, there was definite movement. Black forms, human sized but unrecognisable were moving closer, spiralling in towards them.

'Tris, I know you don't like doing it, but until we've got a better idea of what these things are I think it might be wise to fight back to back.'

Tristellis was busy biting his lip and straining his eyes staring into the darkness around them. 'Yeah, they move fast and fluid. I think you're right…but what the fuck is that smell all about? No ones breath is that bad.' He said this loud enough to carry as he backed towards Garfan. Garfan did likewise, backing up until there was only a couple of feet between them, enough room to manoeuvre, but not enough for anyone to get in behind either of them.

The black forms were even closer now, still circling, each of them reeking of fleshy decay, the evil kind of smell that draws carrion eaters from miles around, out here on this wasteland with the lights of Canary Wharf winking in the background, it seemed even more pungent because it had no place here. Tristellis had not smelt this odour so strongly in centuries, not since the great plague.

It was as though someone had reopened the mass graves on Blackheath only to find thousands of corpses still rotting. Tris almost smiled, if that had been the case and the wind was in the right direction it would be possible to smell it. You could almost see Blackheath from here, but the memory of those graves were all too real for Tris. He'd been there. Such images did nothing but strengthen his resolve not to end up the same way himself.

A gust of fresher air brought him back to the present. He and Garfan had unconsciously started circling in response to the movements of their adversaries, trying to keep at least two of their opponents in sight at any one time as the three figures got steadily closer.

As the three shapes closed in on them, both Garfan and Tristellis could make out that they were definitely human shaped, draped in black robes and hoods which hid any other detail from them.

At this point the gravely laugh from behind him caught Tris by surprise, almost making him flinch in response. Risking a quick glance over his shoulder he could see Garfan's shoulders twitching as his laugh dissolved into a softer chuckle.

'Garf, would you care to share the joke, because right now I fail to see what there is to laugh about.'

Garf sniffed and wiped his nose on his sleeve. 'Sorry Tris, just had a flash back to one of those films you insisted we watched, 'The Lord of the Rings'. I suddenly thought what all this would look like to an observer…like some low budget remake. It just made me laugh, especially after what Elarris said.'

Tristellis couldn't help but smile, though it was very unlike Garfan to find his sense of humour at a time like this. That thought wiped the smile from his face. Now he was really worried.

The black robed figures stopped moving towards them, but continued to circle them from around thirty feet away. Luckily the wind had picked up and was doing a good job of dispersing the terrible smell of rotting meat.

Tris's adrenaline was running high, making him anxious to get on with it. 'OK, lets stop fucking around and get this over with.' He snapped at the nearest figure. He could just hear Garfan's breathing quickening behind him.

Quite suddenly all three figures stopped moving in unison, each one halting equidistantly from each other and their prey. The figure which had stopped directly in front of Tristellis reached up to its head and slowly drew back the hood from its face.

'Oh shit!'

'Tris what's wrong?' Garfan couldn't risk taking his eyes off of the other two, so couldn't see what Tris was seeing.

'Garf you were right.'

'About what?'

'About them already being dead.'

'What? They're Revenants? Are you sure?'

'Yeah I sent this one to the morgue a couple of days ago.'

Garfan didn't have to wait long to confirm this, as the other two figures drew back their hoods, and then opened their robes, slowly letting them slip to the ground around their feet.

'Shit.'

'My sentiments entirely.'

'Fuck!'

'Actually that's not very helpful Garf. Just tell me how we kill something that's already dead?'

Garfan was trying not to panic. This was not good, he'd never heard of anything with enough power to do this, that was until Elarris had mentioned Shaitan, or Satan as he was more commonly known, other than that old myth, raising the dead in this form was unheard of.

The Revenant in front of Tristellis opened its mouth, the voice that issued forth was gurgling with rattling phlegm, sounding like disease personified.

'You can only kill me once Elf, and having done that…I'd say you're fucked.'

The other two gurgled in response, Garfan could only assume they were laughing.

'Tris I shouldn't worry, if that's the best put down it can come up with then its brain has obviously started to rot along with the rest of it.'

The creature in front of Tristellis snarled at this. 'Our master will put us in the ground, but only once you are already there Dwarf.'

'And who might your master be slave?'

'My master names you Al-Qusitun…and you must die.' With that all three of the undead Revenants started to circle them once more, getting slowly nearer.

'Bollocks!'

'Garf that really doesn't help. Think! How do we kill these fuckers?'

'That's just it…I don't know.'

Tris frowned. 'OK, if in doubt cut them into little pieces and then see what happens.'

'Yes! Tris that's it!'

'I know…I'm a genius...sorry but what the fuck are you talking about?'

'No really. If they're decaying then they obviously can't regenerate. They're only able to survive through the power of their master, so if we literally dismember them it should dissipate their master's magic.'

Chapter Fifteen

It had been two days ago, a few hours after O'Brien had said good-bye in the reception area of the fake office above their facility that Stands had called and asked to meet with him.

'Daniel…'

'Hello Inspector, I wasn't expecting to hear from you this evening. I thought we'd agreed not to discuss what happened today until we'd both had a chance to sleep on it?'

'Yes…but this is something else. Do you remember that case we were involved in when we first started working together, the one involving that politician and the dead prostitute?'

'Of course, the one in…'

'Daniel just meet me at the coffee shop on the corner. Do you remember?

'Yeah. What's this all about Sir?'

'Just meet me there as soon as you can.' And with that Stands had hung up.

Waves had had little choice but to go and meet him, even though it had taken around forty minutes to get there. The tone of the Inspectors voice had been cautious, and butting in to avoid naming the area had made Daniel at least a little paranoid about what was going on, and more importantly, who might be listening in. That being the case he'd gone with the paranoia, letting his experience in undercover police work guide his actions.

He drove cautiously at first to try and detect anyone tailing him, and then drove erratically even though he couldn't. He'd parked five minutes away from the café Stands had specified, again in an attempt to ascertain whether he was being followed, and so that he would have the leeway to lose anyone who was following him before he got too near to the meeting point.

When he got there he scanned the place and didn't see Inspector Stands anywhere, so he ordered a cappuccino and sat down at an empty table with his back to the wall and a good view of the front door and the back of the café where there was a fire escape. He and Stands had been here a couple of times during the course of the previous investigation which Stands had alluded to on the phone earlier, and during that time he'd had reason to check the fire escape. It led onto a little alley that ran behind the row of shops that the café was on the end of, making a good escape route if you needed one.

Five minutes later, his coffee cup already half empty, Daniel had looked up from the discarded newspaper he'd been idly scanning, to see Inspector Stands walk in, his eyes searching out Daniel's as soon as he'd walked through the door. The Inspector's expression was guarded, wary, a look that made Daniel look away, and take a renewed interest in the paper in front of him.

Stands went to the back of the coffee shop and ordered, leaving Daniel to fuss with his paper whilst waiting and wondering whether his boss was going to join him or not. The Inspector glided past him, his peripheral vision taking in tiny details, such as the fact that the Inspector was carrying a surprisingly small cup and saucer, both of which made a delicate tinkling china sound as they were gently placed on the table in front of the chair opposite him.

The Inspector was wearing a charcoal grey wool polo neck jumper, and a long black raincoat. The entire scene put Waves in mind of all the old spy thrillers he had loved as a teenager. Stories of clandestine meetings between colleagues in places like Berlin before the end of the cold war, long before the wall came down.

As he sat down Stands raised an eyebrow at his Sergeant's smile. 'Something amusing you Waves?'

Daniel shook his head wearily and concentrated on controlling his features.

'Sorry Sir, just a stray memory.' He looked down

at the tiny cup the Inspector was raising to his lips. 'A little late to be drinking espresso Sir?'

Stands sipped his coffee and sighed. 'I've got too much thinking to do to indulge in much sleep tonight. Talking of which I have a rather onerous duty for you Daniel. One which will be depriving you of sleep too I'm afraid.'

Stands brought his free hand up to his face and massaged the bridge of his nose. 'What did you make of our new friends from the Agency? I know some of their revelations were eye opening, and the factual information was startling, but what did you make of them…O'Brien for example?'

Without missing a beat Waves answered. 'I wouldn't trust him as far as I could throw him, and as for all that talk about their little crusade…well, I've unfortunately had some experience with fanaticism in the past, and all his preaching reeked of it. To be honest being involved with them and their shady sphere of operations makes me feel decidedly uncomfortable.'

Stands sat back and smiled. 'Yet again Daniel you have demonstrated why I was wise to take you on. Not a few of our supposed superiors questioned my decision, your military background scared them, as did your success in undercover operations. That and your *usual* verbal reticence.'

Waves frowned. 'Trust is a two way street Sir.'

'Exactly, and I would like to think you trust me, as I have grown to trust you Daniel.'

Waves smiled in response.

'I'll take that as an affirmative. So I'll get to the point…I don't trust them either. They are working to an agenda all their own, and I don't think it has anything to do with law and order, let alone the pursuit of justice.'

Stands downed what was left of his coffee, and continued.

'Since we left O'Brien I've been doing some digging. I made a few calls to old friends connected with the Security Services, and received some interesting answers to the rather cagey questions I was asking. It seems our new friends are almost completely autonomous, their funding originating, as it does, in America. Their exact remit is unknown, as is their speciality in what many would refer to as the occult. What is maybe not so surprising is that the majority of their funding seems to originate from organisations such as the Discovery Institute, and the Christian Coalition in America, as well as other Christian Fundamentalist organisations.'

Waves held up his hand, palm out, halting the Inspector immediately. 'Hold on, are you telling me that a supposed American Governmental agency, which operates in a clandestine capacity abroad, and has security clearances and the clout to interfere with domestic British Police investigations is funded by, and probably answerable to a bunch of American Christian fundamentalists?'

'Is that so hard to believe Daniel? I'm not saying that any of this is fact. I've had to piece my conclusions together from various scraps of information I've gleaned from sources, who if they were ever confronted on this issue would deny everything and probably retort with some rather awkward questions of their own. This is why I had to resort to this rather cloak and dagger method of meeting. It suddenly came home to me that we're among the big boys now, and I'm not sure how they like to play, or how rough. Our phones could be bugged, we could be under surveillance. Just contacting some of the people I did could cause questions to be asked about what we're involved with here.'

For the first time since the Inspector had sat down Waves noticed the tight lines around the corners of his eyes and mouth, sure give-aways to the stress under which the Inspector was operating.

'It got to me so much I got here and hid myself across the street in order to watch you arrive and make sure you weren't being tailed.'

'Sir you don't have to worry about that. I've been well trained in surveillance techniques, and I know how to avoid it too, I wasn't followed. In fact I think maybe you're worrying a little too much about this situation. A little paranoia can be a good thing, it can in fact keep you alive longer than you might survive without it, but take it too far and it'll kill you quicker than not caring.'

Stands nodded, obviously tired, but looking slightly calmer. 'Wisdom Waves? One day we are going to have to sit down and have a chat about what exactly it was you used to do for Queen and Country.'

Waves snorted, suppressing a mirthless laugh. 'I would tell you…but then I'd have to kill you.'

Stands smiled. 'Touché!'

'OK Sir. What now? We both agree we don't particularly like this Agency, let alone trust them. Where does that leave us? And you mentioned a task which was going to deprive me of sleep?'

'Yes I'm afraid so.' Stands passed one of the photo's he'd got from Dr Ellis across the table. 'I want you to do some unofficial official detective work. I want you to get in touch with the local authorities in Lambeth and have a look at the CCTV footage from around the area in Brixton where that unfortunate young man was found early this morning, the one that they've got locked away in their 'crypt'. I'm almost certain that with the Agency holding the body our boys won't be investigating the incident. In fact the Met may know almost nothing about it, they sure as hell won't know that there's a connection with the Forrester Street Cinema incident. That being the case, and our Mr O'Brien not being the detective type, in fact their whole set-up seemed far from pro-active, we may be able to get away with it. They seem to have very little experience in, or inclination, to do any practical detecting.'

'So we're going to stage our own investigation?'
'Absolutely.'
'But…'

'But what…'

'Well Sir, what's the objective? If we should find these guys, well whatever they are, they've been, in my opinion, doing us a favour over the years by eliminating the weirdest kind of shit I've ever seen, well what then? I'm personally inclined to shake their hands rather than arrest them.' Waves looked intently at his superior. 'What is it you want to achieve here Sir?'

Stands shook his head. 'I'm sorry Daniel, you've got me there, I'm not really sure. I've got to think all this through, and do some more digging. Maybe then I'll be able to figure all this out, but in the mean time I'm sure that the only way we'll get to the bottom of all this is to try and stay at least one step ahead of everyone else.'

It was at this point that Stands had reached into the inside pocket of his raincoat and produced a slim metal tube, the kind used to package large cigars.

'We need to act quickly, and as secretly as possible. We can't involve the rest of our department, or any other department for that matter. We're going to have to work around the clock on this.'

Stands looked at Waves guiltily. 'I know this is at the very least a little unethical, but I felt the situation warranted it.' As he said this, the Inspector pushed the cigar tube across the table to Waves.

'What are you talking about Sir?'

'Take a look.'

Waves looked up from his scrutiny of the tube in front of him to see the Inspector nod reassuringly, so he took hold of it and unscrewed the cap on the end. Glancing around to make sure that he wasn't being observed by any of the cafés other patrons, he tipped the contents of the tube into his palm.

To his complete surprise out slid four small folded up pieces of paper, looking for all the world like the kind of wraps that traditionally held the kind of drugs you could only buy illegally. Waves funnelled his hand and tipped the wraps back into the tube before looking up at Stands enquiringly.

'I took the liberty of acquiring, through a very reliable source I might add, some very pure Speed.'

'What…'

'I know it sounds a little drastic, but we're going to need all the help we can get, and if that includes chemical stimulants, then so be it.' Stands sighed. 'Look, you don't have to use it, but at least you'll have it if you need it. Better to be prepared huh?'

Waves could hardly believe his ears, but he had to admit that it followed his mentor's usual adherence to logical conclusions, even if it was taking it a bit far. He covered the tube with his hand before sliding it off the table and putting it in the pocket of his coat.

'I'm sorry if I've in any way disappointed you Daniel. It just seemed that it might be necessary…'

'No Sir,' he smiled broadly, 'just surprised me a little.'

'OK Now go as far as you can on your own with whatever you can get from the CCTV of the streets around the area. Contact me only when you feel you have to, and be careful about what you say in and around the office. If we need to we can meet here again if you manage to find anything useful.'

'What will you be doing Sir?'

'Digging.'

*

Jack had done exactly as the two strangers had asked and gone straight home from the pub. As soon as he'd got there he locked himself in the front room and went straight to the open fireplace. Pausing only to shake his head in wonder at what he was doing Jack had reached up inside the chimney to feel along the brickwork on the right hand side.

He had, despite his disbelief, found the loose bricks and had carefully extracted them, treating them almost as though they might bite, he put them gently aside and reached inside the hole which he'd just created. Only when his hand had closed on a small metal box had his thoughts really started to spiral out of control. What the hell was going on?

Five long minutes later he unlocked the door to the front room and called for his three sons to join him. His wife Fay had wanted to know what all the fuss was about, but Jack had shaken his head slowly and gently kissed her on the forehead before locking her out and his sons in. A further five minutes later Jack once more unlocked the door. He had a grim but determined expression on his face that confused his wife, her expression mirroring that of her three sons who silently followed their father out of the house.

Despite the warnings of both Garfan and Tristellis, Jack could not leave these newfound benefactors to whatever lone fate they had assigned themselves. He and his sons could never let something like this happen without being present, even if it was only as distant, hidden observers and as such they'd be in a position to make sure that they were the only observers. After all you never knew what you might learn, and as Jack knew very well, knowledge often equalled power.

So it was that he and his sons, watching through binoculars, were witness to something that very few mortal men had ever seen, the Guardians of the Kingdom fighting for their lives against three opponents who just wouldn't die.

Jack could not take his eyes from what he was seeing, his sons equally glued to the spectacle unfolding before them. All his sons had seen freshly dead men, but only Jack had seen them in a similar state to the corpses attacking the figures before him. He's seen a lot of bad things during his time, some of which he'd been responsible for, so he recognised the slightly bloated look of the limbs and trunk, the puffy discoloured edges of the old wounds. What made him nauseous were the new wounds, not bleeding, but still displaying moist flesh beneath.

He really hadn't believed them. Their story had been too far fetched, even though they had radiated an aura of strength and authority. But now he believed. He'd seen the old black and white photo of his grandfather standing with these two same men, his grandfather's, and father's signature had both been on the back of the photo, along with the deeds to the house which had the names Forest and Stone as the signatories. If that wasn't enough, what he was witnessing now dispelled any doubt in his mind that they'd been telling the truth, dead men do not attack the living, especially with archaic weapons like short swords and daggers.

The fighting figures were almost a blur at times, the ring of steel on steel, blade against blade was loud, even at this distance. It would be deafening in the midst of it. Then as he watched he saw a dismembered hand fly out of the melee, a hand still gripping a dagger. He heard a retching sound from somewhere beside him. Which of his sons was losing his dinner he didn't know, but nothing could drag his eyes away from what was deteriorating from battle into butchery. Even he paled as suddenly limbs were being severed, weapons still held by dismembered hands flying into the mud at the combatants feet amongst other, less identifiable gobs of flesh. The whirlwind of steel at the centre of the battle expanded until he could once more discern two separate figures standing over their fallen dead again opponents.

More retching ensued around him as the two distant figures continued to hack at the corpses until every limb was severed, and each head detached from its neck. With this job finished Jack saw the two figures drop their weapons and rub their faces, wiping the blood from their eyes and running their hands through their hair, their fatigue obvious in their expressions.

At last Jack pulled the binoculars away from his eyes and looked around at his sons. Surprisingly it had been his two eldest sons who had been sick, both still pale, shaky and breathing hard. His youngest son, Paul, was a little pale, but he returned his father's look with a determination that made Jack smile.

Looking at the other two he shook his head. 'You two go back to the car and grab the jerry cans from the trunk and meet us over there.' He said pointing to the figures still stood in the midst of the carnage they had wrought.

'And pull yourselves together. You will not embarrass me.' With that he clapped a hand on Paul's shoulder and propelled him forwards, towards the two figures still breathing hard amidst the remains of their enemies.

*

Waves had done as the Inspector had asked first thing that following morning, and had used his police credentials to gain access to the Lambeth central CCTV unit. He'd been left alone with a junior technician who had asked what the Sergeant wanted, and from what time period. The tech had then proceeded to call up hours worth of footage from all over the Brixton area Waves had specified.

Who would have thought there would be so many cameras around Brixton, but as the Tech pointed out the average Londoner could expect to be caught on CCTV hundreds of times a day. Not only that, but the quality of the images was a lot better than Waves had been expecting, apparently this was due to advances in video technology meaning that many CCTV cameras now had night vision and motion detection modes which deliver pictures of incredible clarity. The Tech told him that some of the cameras even have bullet-resistant casings. Daniel had known that he was looking for a needle in a haystack, now the haystack wasn't quite so big, but there had to be a way of reducing it even further.

What was it they had said at the Agency Headquarters? They'd picked up the body as soon as they'd been informed of the incident by one of their friends in the police. They had been informed of the M.O. and requested jurisdiction immediately. Their own forensic team had gone to the scene headed by Dr Ellis, who had requested that the Met guard the area against public contamination. They'd completed their inspection of the scene and then transferred the body back to the lab at their headquarters, which is where they had ascertained that the man had been killed at around 3am. In which case he only had to study the footage from the hour preceding this. The man who had been so hideously mutilated had to pop up on at least one of the cameras in the surrounding area during that period.

And he had, along with another man and a group of three girls. It was at this point that the Technician finally had something relevant to tell him, having seen which cameras the footage had come from he'd mentioned in passing that the camera in question had randomly shown just static a little while later before clearing up as though nothing had happened.

Waves nodded his thanks and squirreled away that little tidbit to share with the Inspector later.

Then rather than waste time going through the rest of the available footage in the hope of finding more images Waves got the technician to copy the appropriate piece of footage for him. The resultant disc leaving him with a new problem, where to get the images enlarged, enhanced and printed. He couldn't use the police computer labs, the technicians would require authorisation, and if he tried to circumvent standard practise there'd be too many questions.

Not knowing what else to do Waves had called the

Inspector at the office and asked him if he'd had breakfast yet. The Inspector had immediately ascertained that Waves was looking for an excuse for the two of them to meet away from the office, and had agreed to meet at the little greasy spoon where they invariably ended up having breakfast if they went out for it. As soon as they'd settled down to their bacon and eggs he'd brought the Inspector up to speed on his progress and admitted to the stumbling block which had necessitated their meeting.

The Inspector had looked pleased despite the fact that without technical assistance the disc Waves was carrying was useless to them. He's then asked Waves for the disc, winked and assured him that he'd have hard-copies of the enlarged and enhanced images by the end of the day. They'd finished their breakfast and the Inspector had bustled off before Waves could get anything else out of him.

An hour before Waves had been due to leave the office he got a call from Marcus Benning at the pathologists lab. Apparently he'd had a visit from an Agent O'Brien, asking questions about the incident involving the stolen cadavers. It had been while he was listening to Marcus that the Inspector had walked in with a newspaper under his arm. Stands had walked up to his desk and dropped the paper on the desk in front of him.

'I noticed that you hadn't got a copy of today's issue yet, so I got you one while I was out.' With which the Inspector had about turned and walked out the way he came.

As soon as he'd finished reassuring Marcus that he would find out what he could about the mysterious Agency who had the authority to just stroll in and interrogate him, Waves had grabbed his coat and headed for the door. He couldn't wait until he got home to rifle through the paper, and had driven to the nearest coffee shop he could find.

Paper securely tucked under his arm, he'd ordered a coffee and taken it to a table in a corner where he could not be easily observed by anyone. Sitting down he'd opened the paper gingerly, half expecting something to just fall out in front of him. But there was nothing…until he'd reached the fifth to last page, where an A5 brown envelope had been taped to the lower half of the page. Inside he found three black and white images on photographic quality paper held together with a paper clip. The paper clip also held in place a scrap of paper with the Inspectors handwriting on it.

'Daniel, remember the Agency's lab report, the man had a large amount of alcohol in his blood stream when he was killed. Late bars and nightclubs, doormen and bartenders, that's where you start!'

Waves unclipped the note and stuffed it in a pocket before taking a closer look at the pictures. The first was an image of a group of five people, three girls walking a couple of meters ahead of two men. The second picture was a blow up of the first image showing just the faces and shoulders of the two men. It was an odd sensation to get a good look at the face of the man who was now little more than a badly mutilated corpse lying on an autopsy table in 'the crypt', especially as what was left of his face gave no real hint as to what he had looked like in life.

Looking more closely at the shaggy haired man walking next to the unidentified victim Waves felt a tremor of recognition. Somehow he recognised him, he was sure he'd seen him somewhere before, but he had no idea where.

The second picture was a close-up of the three girls faces, again head and shoulders included, if only because the obviously male technician had appreciated the fine looking cleavage belonging to the girl in the front of the picture. Finally he had what he needed to take this forward. Finishing his coffee he contemplated buying some food to take out before realising that where he was now headed there would more than likely be plenty of places he could get something more appealing than a day old sandwich and a piece of carrot cake.

As he headed South East over Vauxhall Bridge,

passing the MI6 building at Vauxhall Cross Waves couldn't help but wonder if they were watching him. He tried to dismiss his paranoia as he continued into Stockwell before passing into the streets of Brixton.

*

Both Garfan and Tristellis looked up as they were approached by the Huguenot and his youngest son. Glancing at each other they both slowly picked up the weapons they had dropped and wiped the blades clean before sheathing them.

'We told you not to be here old man, no witnesses. This was not meant to be entertainment.'

Jack nodded. 'And neither was it. Though it was an education.'

He looked at his son intently.

'Mark my words boy. Remember this place and what you've seen here. There is evil in this world, real evil that must be recognised, and must be fought. Most of all remember these men, our debt to them is already old, and now I would say un-repayable. As such should they ever ask anything of this family it will be given, unhesitatingly and without question. You understand me boy?'

The young man glanced at both Garfan and then Tristellis, a look that, though it contained fear, was one of respect. He nodded at each in turn and then turned away to give his father a moment alone with these two superhuman beings.

Jack studied the two figures stood before him, each covered in sweat and spatters of blood, flesh and filth, here and there accompanied by unhealthy smears of what looked like pus.

'I would offer you hospitality, but I have the feeling you wouldn't accept it.'

Garfan nodded once and then caught Tristellis'

250

eye. 'Thanks for the offer, but we should be going. Besides, if you are seen with us there could be questions…and possibly more.'

'I understand, though I would recommend a quick swim in the river before you do anything else.'

Tris grinned at this. 'Yes, we will. Goodbye old man, we needed no thanks, but we thank you for it all the same.'

Jack nodded. 'And don't worry about all of this, my sons and I will burn it all. Better that there are no questions.'

'Thank you, this is a little more public than we would like.'

Garfan looked around at the charnal house mess they had created and kicked at a solitary hand laying at his feet. It flopped over, fingers seeming to grasp at the ground beneath it, the ring on one of its fingers still shiny despite the filth around it. Garfan squatted down to take a closer look.

Tristellis raised an eyebrow at his comrade's actions. 'Garf, it's time to go.'

Garfan looked up, lines furrowing his forehead. 'What was it Elarris said about a ring?'

Tris looked down at Garfan's feet, at the hand and the ring on its finger. 'Something about them forging rings with their own fire. Why?'

Garfan lifted the severed hand. Where it had been sliced off at the wrist the whiteness of the bone looked strange against the discoloured flesh around it. Taking a firm hold on the wrist Garfan separated the fingers in order to get a good grip on the ring. Pulling seemed to have little effect, the dead flesh was puffy around the ring, swollen and red. Garfan spat on it, rubbing his saliva around it and tried again. Again to no avail.

Tris shook his head. 'Stop fucking around Garf, just cut the damned thing off, we need to get out of here.'

Both Jack and his son turned away as Garf pulled his hunting knife from his belt sheath and deftly sliced through the flesh around the finger, then sliced the length of the finger, before peeling skin and flesh from the bone in much the same way as you would remove the plastic covering from electrical flex. Giving it a tug the ring slipped easily over the remaining bloody finger bones.

Just then the Huguenot's two eldest sons appeared out of the darkness, each carrying old green jerry cans that sloshed noisily as they walked. Jack looked over his shoulder to see if Garfan had finished his grisly task, only there was no one there. Both he and Tristellis had vanished, leaving behind only blood, guts and body parts.

Chapter Sixteen

Around three hours later Waves was parked around fifty feet away from the entrance of the 'Fridge', in Brixton. A nightclub that had very recently become of particular interest to Waves. The doormen having been surprisingly helpful once he'd shown them his badge. Even more helpful was the fact that they had recognised the girls in the pictures and told Waves that they were in fact quite regular in their attendance of the club, and were bound to show up again sooner rather than later. One of them, a large athletic looking black guy called Kevin, even remembered the two men featured in the images.

'Yeah, I was here the other night when those two came in. Plenty of money by the looks of them. Very well dressed, but looked like they could handle themselves too if you get me. You know what it's like, you're a cop, you kinda get to recognise the ones who aren't afraid of anybody.' He looked again at the photo Waves was holding. 'Yeah, those two had the look. The guy with the longish hair specially, even though he maybe doesn't look the type, the way he moved, and the confidence he had, you know. The other one seemed a little edgy, maybe he just wasn't up for it, that night there weren't a lot of white guys ya know. Anyway, I would've thought twice before taking them on. I just waved them through, never seen them before, but the girls…yeah, they'll be back.'

That had been last night. He'd stayed till the club closed without seeing any sign of the girls from the photos. He'd even given the doormen copies of the picture of the girls and asked them to give him the nod if they turned up. The management were of course only too happy to help with an on-going police investigation. Of course they didn't know it was an unofficial investigation, but it was never a good idea to piss off plainclothes cops.

So here he was again, sat in the car, the cold

congealing remains of a kebab wrapped in paper on the passenger seat next to him, a Styrofoam cup of lukewarm, badly made coffee in his hand.

As he watched the queue that had started to form outside the club at around 10.30, he noticed a group of three girls attach themselves to the end of it. Waves reached under his seat for his binoculars and gingerly placed the Styrofoam cup between his thighs as he tried to get the binoculars up so he could get a better look at the end of the queue. From his vantage point Waves could only see one of the girls clearly, he glanced at the picture he'd taped onto the dashboard. She was one of the three, he just hoped that the other two were the ones with her now.

He balanced the cup on the dashboard and grabbed the envelope containing the original pictures and his micro-cassette recorder from the glove compartment before getting out of the car. When he was around fifteen feet away from the club's doors Kevin, the doorman he'd talked to last night, looked round and saw him coming. He stepped over the low rope around the doorway and smiled at Waves.

'Good evening Sergeant, seen something you like?'

'Yes, there's at least one of those girls in the queue. She appears to be with two other girls, hopefully the ones in the picture. Talking of which, have you still got the copy I gave you?'

'Yeah, you want me to single them out and bring them into the club, or you wanna do it out here?'

'No, insides better, the manager said I could use his office for the interview if they ever turned up. Can you maybe offer them free entry on the condition of a quick chat with a copper. Then bring them in and escort us all to the office.'

'OK. Sounds good, but what if they don't go for it?'

'Then tell them that they don't have any choice, if

they don't co-operate I'll nick them for obstructing the course of justice. Just get them inside OK'

Kevin nodded soberly, then winked at Waves and motioned for his colleagues to let the Sergeant through. Taking the folded copy of the picture he'd been given out of his pocket, Kevin ambled off towards the end of the queue.

Waves stepped over the rope and nodded at the huge guy who was blocking the doorway. You could never tell with club security guys whether they were going to be friendly to the police or not, some of them moved in some very dodgy circles. This one actually smiled before stepping out of his way.

A couple of minutes later all three of the girls in the picture were ushered into the reception area of the club by a grinning Kevin. 'Right, this is the man, so if you'll all just follow me.'

Waves stepped in beside Kevin as he led them through a door marked 'Staff Only' next to the club's cloakroom, and down a short, badly lit corridor, past a couple of side doors to one at the end of the corridor. Kevin knocked twice before trying the handle and opening the door. The room proved to be small, with only enough room for the standard office furniture and a rather battered looking brown leather sofa pushed back against the far wall of the room.

The doorman stood aside to let the three girls brush past him into the office. He looked enquiringly at Waves, eyebrows raised.

'Sorry Kevin, could you stand outside and make sure no one comes in. This shouldn't take more than ten minutes.' This said Waves slowly closed the door in the bouncers face before turning to face his newly acquired audience who'd already settled themselves on the sofa.

'Well, firstly let's deal with introductions. My name is Detective Sergeant Waves, I'm with the Metropolitan CID, though I'm based with the SCD.' As he said this he took out the little leather wallet from his back pocket which held his badge and identity card and held it up so that the girls could see it clearly.

'The reason I need to speak to you girls is that three nights ago you were seen in the company of a couple of men who you then left this club with. For reasons which are central to an on-going police investigation we need to identify these men, and so far you are the only link we have to them.'

Waves held out the envelope containing the three pictures from the CCTV footage. 'Hopefully these will help jog your memories a little. Take a look and then tell me what you can remember from that night.'

The brunette took the envelope, held it open and peered inside before slipping in a couple of fingers with which she withdrew the three pictures.

'While you're looking at those I need to take your details. If it's OK with you I'd like to record this interview so that it won't take so long, and so that I can quote it accurately later. The tape will then of course be held as evidence so that there will be a permanent record of this interview, which will also protect you all from being misquoted at any point in the future. Is that OK with you?'

All three of the girls looked a little nervous but nodded their assent.

Waves took his micro-cassette recorder out of his jacket and placed it on the edge of the desk, the condenser mike pointing towards the three girls. 'Now if you could start by individually giving your names and addresses, and then stating for the record that you have no objections to this interview being recorded.'

Theresa, Sandra and Kylie dutifully did as they had been asked whilst Waves silently hoped that he'd be able to understand their London drawls when he came to play the tape back.

*

The two friends were taking off the wet clothes in which they had just taken a swim, the blood and muck had proven harder to get off than they'd thought, when a faint 'Whooomph' and a burst of light signalled the lighting of a rather unusual bonfire in the near distance.

Standing naked in the starlight the two friends looked straight up at the stars in the now clear sky above them. Even with their unusually good eyesight it was difficult to see more than just a few of the brightest stars due to all the light pollution.

Garfan found his gaze drawn back to Canary Wharf and the blinking light atop No. 1 Canada Square. Now that the Revenants were gone Garfan found himself sensing the other presence he'd detected earlier that day.

He frowned as he turned to Tris. 'I have a feeling we're going to be coming back here sooner than we'd like.'

*

An hour and a half later, Waves was once more sat in the little late night café waiting for the Inspector to join him.

It had been an interesting interview. The girls had been helpfully garrulous, and had obviously had no idea what had happened to the man that they referred to as Martin. The other man had introduced himself to them as Tristan, and was the more dominant of the two men, and therefore obviously the one with all the money.

They'd been convinced that Tristan was some kind of gangster, and that Martin was his bodyguard or something.

The three girls had not used the term 'dynamic', but from what they'd said Waves' own interpretation was that although the two men were friends the dynamic of their relationship was such that strangers came to the conclusion that Tristan was in charge. From everything he had learnt Waves could not imagine that any member of the group he was looking for would need a bodyguard, especially if what O'Brien had said was true, in which case with the man called Martin being human, the other calling himself Tristan may or may not be one of the not so human group they were looking for.

The most interesting information for Waves had been comments that the girls had probably considered unimportant. These related to the fact that both men had moved with an unusual grace, and that Tristan had proved to be surprisingly strong when he'd dragged the girls away from his friend after leaving the club. The reference to 'unpleasant enemies' had also peaked his interest, though by far the most useful information the girls had given him was that they had talked about the men's usual haunts and had received references to establishments in Camden and the West End. With the photo's and an educated guess as to where to start their search Waves was now convinced it was only a matter of time before he and the Inspector tracked down their quarry.

He was mentally running through the interview once more when the Inspector arrived. Once again Stands ignored his subordinate until he'd got his coffee and sat down in front of the Sergeant.

Stands sipped his coffee before sitting back in his chair. 'Can I take it from the tone of your message that you've got some good news for me?'

'I found the girls form the pictures tonight and interviewed them in the club where they met the unidentified victim and his associate.'

Stands grimaced. 'I don't think you need to report this quite so formerly Daniel, especially considering the nature of what we're doing.'

Waves nodded. 'Sorry Sir, I taped the interview so that you could listen to it and draw your own conclusions.'

'Excellent, but I'd like to hear what conclusions you've made from what they said first.'

Waves grinned in response and took a moment to organise his thoughts. 'Well, I think we've got them Sir! Apparently this Tristan's usual drinking holes are in Camden Town and the West End, and human or not I'm willing to bet that his base of operations is located somewhere between those two areas, somewhere around Marylebone and Regents Park. From what we've learnt about them so far they're well funded, and I would guess that they would own the property they are based in, it would give them more privacy and security, and the fact that property in that area is reasonably pricey would not be a problem, in fact it would probably be an advantage to be honest. Neighbours in such expensive areas tend to know very little about each other.'

'So our only problem now is locating them,' said Stands. 'The biggest problem is how we proceed from here. Do we wander the streets hoping for a random sighting of our target, or do we actively canvas the area using the photos we have. Possibly risking alerting them to the fact that we've got a picture of one of them which we're using in order to hunt them down, especially dodgy when we don't know how many of them there are or how they're going to react.'

Waves considered this, there were a lot of potential dangers in an unofficial investigation like this, especially when they were operating alone without the aid of armed response units, or any other kind of back-up.

'Of course you're right, but where does that leave us Sir? If we limit our exposure we may be able to ascertain exactly where they're based and hopefully that would enable us to estimate their numbers. But in a city like London, and the size of the potential search area we could be wandering the streets indefinitely.'

Stands had sat back in his chair and now looked thoughtful as he steepled his fingers in front of him. How to proceed? 'You're absolutely right Daniel, both choices have their pro's and con's, but it boils down to two things. Either we're very careful and this takes forever…or we take a risk which will have unknown consequences.'

'If you put it that way Sir, I'm tempted to take the risk. It could go bad either way, and to be honest I'm not entirely sure who the bad guys really are in this scenario.'

Stands grinned. 'I thought you might see it like that, and I'm inclined to agree. So we'll take the risk, and the Devil take the hindmost.'

Waves wore a thoughtful expression, obviously working something out in his head before voicing his thoughts. Stands let him be, and silently finished his coffee, taking the time to get straight in his own mind the sequence of events which it would take for the two of them to track down the elusive Tristan.

'Sir…'

'Mmm…'

Daniel had been contemplating their position in terms of defensive and offensive actions against them should they actually locate the people they were looking for, and had spoken without really focusing on the Inspector.

Stands brought his hands up to his face and massaged his eyes tiredly. 'Sorry Daniel, what was it you wanted to say?'

'Sorry Sir, but I was just thinking that we're on the verge of really going out on a limb here. No one can know what we're doing, and because of that we're entirely on our own. In a way we'll be operating outside the law.'

Stands gestured for Waves to continue.

'So we'll be on our own with no back-up, and we'll have to deal with any repercussions on our own too.' Waves was looking very serious as he voiced his concerns.

Stands frowned. 'What are you driving at Daniel? Speak freely.'

'Well I'd feel a lot happier if we possessed the means to at least defend ourselves should we need to. I doubt very much that if it goes south we'll be in a position to retreat to the nearest police station. I think we should acquire some weaponry of our own.'

'Ah, I had a feeling you might. The problem is that although I have the contacts to get us drugs, I'm not in a position to acquire firearms without there being a lot of awkward questions involved.'

Daniel smothered a laugh, then looked a little sheepish as the Inspector gave him an enquiring look, one eyebrow raised sardonically.

'Sorry Sir, you just brought to mind that conversation we had when you expressed an interest in what I got up to before joining you. The thing is I can get what we'll need quite easily, but it will require cash. Even though I'll be calling in some favours in order to track down the items, we'll still have to pay for them.'

The Inspectors face was registering mild surprise at what his Sergeant had just revealed, but he didn't feel inclined to ask any questions. Plenty of time for that if they managed to make it through all this in one piece.

'So, how much?'

'That depends on what we want. You've had experience with small arms Sir?'

'I've done the training, but I've been fortunate enough to never have to use one in the field.'

'Standard issue semi-automatic?'

'Yes.'

'OK, so a semi, and something with a bit more 'oomph' for me. Then there's rounds on top of that. I reckon we'll be looking at around three grand all in. Would you like to go Dutch Sir?'

Stands laughed and shook his head. 'You're quite a piece of work Sergeant, but I wouldn't do this without you.'

Stands rarely expressed such sentiment, and as such Daniel appreciated it all the more.

'So how soon can you dig these items up?'

Waves shrugged non-committally, I'll make the calls tonight, but I'll have to wait until the banks open in the morning to get the cash. But as soon as I've got it we should be good to go.'

'So we start tomorrow then. As soon as you've got the guns.'

*

The next morning dawned dark and dirty. It was a dismal, grey, wet morning, the kind of morning that makes you not want to get up.

From outside of the car any passers-by would probably have assumed that the two men sat in the front seats of the car were just waiting for the rain to let up before making a dash for whatever destination they were headed for. This being the case the fact that the two men were in fact discussing the firearms hidden in the boot of the car would probably have come as an even greater shock.

'So Waves, how much did you have to part with? Were these dodgy friends of yours reasonable, or did they enjoy the chance to fleece a copper?'

Waves smiled. 'They don't know I'm a copper, and actually we did rather well. Talking of which I'm afraid you owe me thirteen hundred pounds Sir.'

'Less than you thought. Have we ended up with World War Two army surplus, or am I going to be pleasantly surprised?'

'Like I said Sir, a semi-automatic for you, though it turned out to be a rather nice Glock 17, you should be familiar with it as it's the same model our own armed response units use, probably the same model you trained with. As for me, I would have been happy with a Mac-10, but I've ended up with a rather cute Uzi.'

'Cute? Please don't refer to such a thing as cute Waves, otherwise you'll start to make me nervous.'

'But Sir, it's an Uzi! It's a design classic.'

Stands shook his head slowly. 'Well I'm very happy for you Waves, I'm sure you'll make a very happy couple, but lets concentrate on the job in hand shall we, with any luck we won't need the guns. I sure as shit would rather not end up in a situation where we have to use them.'

Having said that the Inspector reached round onto the back seat to recover a large print A to Z. Stands opened the book and leafed through it looking for the pages he wanted.

'OK, so we're here,' said Stands pointing to a small square on the map.

'Manchester Square off of Wigmore Street. For today I think we should just try and cover as much ground as possible of the area around Regents Park.'

Stands again gestured at the map.

'You go right and head up and around the Western side of the park around the Euston Station area and into Camden Town, and I'll go East covering Edgware Road, St John's Wood and round into Primrose Hill. The only thing we can do is show the photos in bars, cafés and restaurants, and just hope that someone's seen them recently. Take notes, and if either of us dredges up any significant intel then inform the other by phone, and we'll adjust our strategy accordingly. If, however, we don't have any luck we'll rendezvous at Chalk Farm Tube station, make our way back here, and think again.'

Stands glanced towards the back of the car. 'For the moment I think we should leave our new friends in the boot. I don't relish the thought of walking around London with a concealed handgun.' Turning to Waves he went on, 'and to be honest the thought of you wandering the streets with an Uzi under your coat gives me the willies.'

Waves laughed. 'Thank you Sir, I appreciate your confidence in me, though I was going to suggest the same thing. We don't know if these people can somehow sense the presence of firearms. If they can it might explain why we haven't come across any in connection with them. I wasn't planning on carrying the Uzi until we're in a position where we know we're going to confront them.'

Stands nodded. 'Great minds think alike, my feelings exactly. In which case why don't we get on with it! He reached for the door handle.

'One moment Sir, we haven't agreed on any regular contacts.'

'What?'

'Regular contacts Sir, Standard Operational Procedure when in the field. We agree specific times, or intervals of time between contacts. That way we know where each other are, and if one of us misses the schedule, then the other knows that there's a problem.'

Stands grimaced. 'Is this really necessary Daniel?'

'I think so, we're still operating in the dark here Sir. We don't know what we're really up against, and we don't know if we're being watched. I'd feel a lot happier if we used every resource available to us. Sticking to SOPs would be sensible at this time Sir.'

'Is this something they taught you in the Army Waves?'

'Sort of.'

Stands tilted his head. 'Ah…why do I get the feeling you're not going to tell me where you picked this up. OK, you've sold me, so how do we do this?'

'Well we're both wearing wrist watches, talking of which, what time do you make it Sir?'

'8.37am.'

'Good, mine's at 8.40. We have to remember that I'm three minutes ahead of you. Now we synchronise the clocks on our mobile phones. We'll make them five minutes ahead of my watch.'

They both took out their mobiles and prepared to change the time on the internal clocks.

'On my mark we start them at 8.46am. Ready…mark.'

Stands nodded. 'Done…but can you please explain all the time differences.'

'OK, I reckon it'll take us three to four hours to cover the ground we've set ourselves as a target, what with stopping at cafés, restaurants, and any bars and pubs that are open during the time we're out. Obviously we'll have to come back at another time to check out those we miss because they're closed. In the time we're out we'll call each other in turn every forty-five minutes. I'll call first at 9.45am. I'll be taking that time from the clock on my phone, so it'll be exactly 9.45 according to your phone, or 9.37 by your watch.'

'This still isn't making a lot of sense Waves.'

'Sir, let me explain. All the variables allow us a lot of ways of informing each other if something is wrong. For instance, because we take it in turns to call, if one of us calls when it's the others turn then there's a problem. If you were to call me exactly eight minutes early then I'd know that you were taking the time from your watch, which would indicate to me that you were under the duress of someone who understands SOPs, but doesn't know the details of ours.'

'That's actually quite clever.'

'I'd like to take the credit, but it's all stuff I was taught. The various different connotations enable us to make educated guesses about the others situation. We should also agree on our call signs Sir. For instance if I should refer to you as anything but 'Sir', and you refer to me as anything other than Sergeant, then we'll know that someone else is there.'

'Now you're just making this complicated. Do I really have to remember all this?'

'Yes Sir, also try not to react to anything indicating that there is a problem. Just act as though everything's fine, and then react accordingly. Just remember our SOPs and we'll be fine, besides, if things continue like this we may have to carry on using them for a while. In fact it would probably be best if we carry on using these until this is all over. Every time we call each other we should stick to these rules.'

Stands studied his Sergeants face. Waves was deadly serious, his face intense, and to be honest a little scary with a look of dogged determination that he rarely displayed. Stands closed his eyes and once again thanked the lord that he had chosen this man as his subordinate.

Opening his eyes he smiled at Waves. 'It's going to become a little impersonal Daniel.'

'Only over the phone Sir, and if I can handle it, then I'm sure you can.' Waves smiled, 'besides, it kind of takes me back.'

Stands shook his head. 'Daniel, if I didn't know better I'd say you were enjoying this. OK, you've convinced me. As of now we'll stick to these phone procedures. Lets just hope they are completely unnecessary.'

Waves nodded in agreement. 'At least its stopped raining. Now let's see if we can track down this mysterious Tristan character.'

Stands opened the passenger door and got out. Closing the door he leant his arms on the roof of the car and watched Waves get out.

'So you'll call me first?'

'Yes Sir.'

'OK…well, see you at Chalk Farm then.' With that parting shot Stands pushed himself away from the car, turned his back on Waves, and strolled off down Fitzhardinge Street towards Portman Square.

Waves watched his boss's back for a moment before turning in the opposite direction towards Hinde Street for the first leg of his search for their strange quarry.

Chapter Seventeen

Around forty-five minutes later Stands was stood looking up at the façade of Marylebone Train Station when his mobile started to ring. Slipping the small plastic oblong out of his pocket he glanced at the time display on its small screen before answering it. Spot on, he pressed the little green button and glanced at his watch as he held the phone up to his ear.

'Hello Sergeant, can I take it all is well?'

'Yes Sir, I'm fine, but I've got nothing concerning the hunt. No leads at all so far. How about you?'

'Nothing yet, though I have discovered a little restaurant that looks very good. First chance I get I'm going to give it a try.'

'That's wonderful Sir.' Try as he might Waves couldn't disguise the sarcasm in his voice.

'I was going to ask you to join me Sergeant, but if you're going to be like that about it…'

'Sorry, just a little frustrated by the lack of results Sir.'

'Chin up Sergeant, it's early days yet. I'm sure someone will have seen this person at some point, he's not a ghost after all. In fact he's rather striking, I'm sure we'll find a young lady somewhere who's fallen under his spell and notices his every passing. Don't worry we'll find him...eventually.'

'Yes Sir. Oh, and don't forget it's your turn to call next.' Waves grinned as the Inspector abruptly hung up on him. He hates being told what to do.

*

A couple of hours later Stands was beginning to

regret his promise of success to Waves. He'd walked literally miles in the roundabout route it took to cover the mercantile areas where all the cafés and restaurants could be found. Now he wasn't far from Chalk Farm Tube Station, and all he had to show for his efforts were a couple of phone numbers for promising looking little restaurants he'd discovered, and feet that felt two sizes larger than normal, and ached like a son-of-a-bitch.

He'd skirted Regent's Park and had finished with St John's Wood, which had in turn led him to Primrose Hill Park. Not wanting to walk up the hill yet Stands made his way along Prince Albert Road, the park on his left, and London Zoo concealed on his right.

As he had innumerable times already that morning Stands reached into his pocket for his miniature A-Z of London, and flicked through t, wondering which left-hand turn he should take.

'Hmm…Albert Terrace or St Mark's Square,' he said talking to himself.

The latter seemed more appropriate as Stands made his way past the park. In half an hour he'd be at Chalk Farm, and be able to sit on a nice comfortable tube train all the way back to the car.

In turning left into St Mark's Square Stands could see he'd made the right choice. Looking ahead he could see a nice looking pub and an expensive looking beauty clinic. He could almost smell the affluence, and if what O'Brien's boy had said was true, then maybe the people they were looking for were hiding behind the casual anonymity of wealth in this kind of area where as long as you looked the part no one asked too many questions.

Leaving the parish church of St Mark behind him, Stands crossed Kingstown Road towards the entrance of the 'Albert' pub on the corner. Wishing he had the time to stop for a pint, the Inspector pushed open the door to the pub and went in.

Inside it was as tastefully decorated as any of the pubs in the Primrose Hill area, all of them locals to the wealthy, if not the famous. Sat at one of the many stripped wooden tables were a pair of suited businessmen, but other than them, and the bartender sat on a barstool reading a paper, the pub was empty.

As Stands approached the bar the barman glanced up and put down his paper smiling. 'Hi there, what can I get you?'

The obvious Australian accent wasn't lost on Stands as he reached into his jacket pocket to retrieve his ID. 'Actually I'm just after some information,' he said as he held out his open identification to the barman who seemed unperturbed by being approached by a Detective Inspector.

'Oh, nothing too serious I hope?'

'No, I was just wondering whether you've seen either of these men recently?' He said holding out a copy of the photo of the two men Waves had acquired from the CCTV, one of whom was now dead. 'We're hoping that they may be able to help us with some routine enquiries.'

The barman gave the photo his full attention before he looked up at the Inspector and smiled. 'Actually I have. Not in any trouble are they?'

Stands was momentarily taken aback. At last, a result. 'No, like I said, we're just hoping they can help us identify someone else. They're not in any trouble, just routine questions. They just happened to be in the wrong place at the wrong time.' Stands smiled slowly, trying to be as casual as possible, he didn't want the barman to clam up.

'In that case I'm sure Tris won't mind me telling you…he's a local, and the other guy in the picture is a friend of his, though I haven't seen him around here for a while, and I can't remember his name. Tristan lives just around the corner…' he said pointing back towards the church, 'with a friend of his, Garfield I think his name is. In one of the big houses on St Mark's Square.'

'You don't know which one?'

'No sorry.' The barman leant in closer to Stands,

his voice lower. 'The natives are friendly…but not that friendly.'

Stands straightened and smiled his thanks. 'Never mind, we'll find him. In the mean time if you do see him could you give me a call.'

The barman looked at him suspiciously as Stands reached once more into a pocket for one of his cards.

'Or when you see him give him my card, and ask him to give me a call. Though we'll probably have talked to him by then.

The barman studied the card before looking up and shrugging. 'Sure, no worries.'

Stands looked intently at the barman for a moment longer. Satisfied that the guy was genuine he smiled, nodded, and made his way out of the pub, all the while musing on why you couldn't walk into a pub in London these days without being greeted by an Australian or Eastern European accent. Outside the pub he looked back down Princess Road towards St Mark's Square, then about faced and strode off purposely towards Chalk Farm, and his rendezvous with Waves.

*

As Stands approached the tube station at Chalk Farm he could see Waves waiting for him, his large athletic frame leant casually against the wall outside the station. Hands deep in his pockets, it was obvious to Stands that he had been waiting a while, and was trying to be inconspicuous. Stands somehow knew that Waves had spotted him long before he had seen him waiting for him. Waves had an annoying ability of being aware of his surroundings without seeming to spend any time studying them.

Thus it was with surprise that Stands watched Waves push himself lazily away from the wall and walk into the station before he had got anywhere near him. As he watched the Sergeant disappeared inside without even looking back, immediately triggering a small rush of adrenaline in Stands' chest. They had not discussed anything like this as part of their SOPs, but there had to be a good reason for Waves to avoid openly meeting him outside the tube station.

Stands had to force himself to slow his pace and not go rushing in after the Sergeant. As he moved into the relative gloom of the station he looked ahead for Waves just in case he'd felt that inside would be a better place to meet and was waiting for him beyond the ticket barriers. As his eyes adjusted he spotted the Sergeants back heading towards the escalators leading down to the train platforms.

Something was definitely wrong, but he was at a loss as to what could cause Waves to behave like this. After all he was a Detective Sergeant, the Law was behind him, what could spook the man into behaving so furtively? Suddenly Stands thought he might have the answer...Spook. Maybe he'd spotted a tail and didn't want whoever it was following him to know that he was meeting Stands. But if that was the case then why wait for him outside the tube station at all? Why not just take off and explain the situation later?

Stands' head was full of questions as he stepped onto the escalator going down into the bowels of the station. For the time being all he could do was hang back and follow Waves as he was obviously intended to and see if he could spot who was tailing the Sergeant.

*

Meanwhile Waves was just walking onto the southbound platform of the Edgeware branch of the Northern Line wondering what he was going to do next. It had started in the last hour as he'd been working his way through Camden with the increasingly uncomfortable feeling that he was being watched. The thing was, try as he might, he'd been unable to identify anyone following him. At first it had just been a feeling that something wasn't quite right. The sort of feeling you get when you randomly make eye contact with a complete stranger in passing, but the look they return is somehow wrong. Waves liked to think that he was intelligent enough and resourceful enough to take care of himself in almost any situation. But he was having trouble rationalising the disturbing sense of disquiet that was beginning to verge on open paranoia. He was familiar with covert work, but in all that time he'd never experienced in himself such blatant irrationality.

*

He'd had to stop walking. To cover his actions, just in case he was being observed, he stopped in front of a Newsagent's window and pretended to study the small handwritten notices in the window advertising the services of local handymen, secretaries and middle aged escorts. In actuality he was using the window's reflection to study what and who was behind him in the street. He tried to relax as he took in his surroundings. No one around him seemed to be paying any attention to him, but still he couldn't shake the feeling that he was being shadowed by some kind of presence. As he thought about it he latched onto that word…presence. Maybe that was it, after all they knew that they were dealing with people who weren't exactly human, and some of the things they'd learned recently definitely indicated that there may be something to all this 'occult' stuff after all.

But if that was it, then what was going on right now? Waves had no experience with this kind of thing. What if someone had put a 'Hex' on him or something? And if so what the hell did that actually mean? What would happen to him?

Fuck this! Waves knew he'd just be chasing ghosts and going round in circles if he continued with that train of thought. Stick with what you know, and what you can deal with. For now all he could do was carry on with the search for the mysterious Tristan, and meet the Inspector at the tube station as planned.

As he'd walked up Chalk Farm Road towards the station Waves had slowly relaxed. He was reasonably sure he wasn't being followed by a person in any conventional sense, and if someone was employing some other method of observation, occult or not, then there was nothing he could do about it. This being the case Waves squared his shoulders and settled into a steady rhythm, a stride that his mother had always said was more of a lope and reminded her of her father. Waves had long ago resigned himself to the fact that worrying about things that were beyond his control was not only pointless, but potentially damaging. An act of will which had left Waves free to deal with the present and respond from moment to moment in a way which had led to his being noticed by his superiors, and to training in fields of operation that were beyond the abilities of the majority.

It had been this ability to size up a situation and react immediately, and apparently without thought that had led Waves to move away from the Inspector before he got too close. He'd been waiting patiently for about fifteen minutes or so, and was secretly relieved when he'd seen Inspector Stands approaching from down the street. The inactivity of waiting had begun to make him feel suspicious and slightly paranoid again. Which was when he'd spotted the man around twenty feet behind the Inspector walking purposely with his eyes on the Inspector's back.

It had taken Waves only the briefest moment to act, and without looking at the Inspector's tail again he'd ducked into the station, mind racing as he tried to decide what to do.

As he'd walked out onto the southbound platform it had come to him. Even if he was being followed, though he didn't really think he was, he knew the Inspector was, he just knew it. In which case the best thing he could do would be to try and find out whom it was doing the following. At least then they may be able to determine the state of play. Without information they could only guess, and that wouldn't get them anywhere.

He had to assume that whoever they were they were tailing Stands and not him, probably because Stands was less likely to spot it. Working on that assumption Waves ducked into the tunnel leading off of the platform and waited for the Inspector and his tail to arrive.

*

As Stands walked out on to the platform he scanned the crowd of people scattered along the platform waiting for the next train. He couldn't see Waves anywhere. He hadn't gone past him, and he couldn't have got on a train as there was one just about to arrive. On this branch of the Northern Line the trains weren't as frequent as they were at the central London stations. So where the hell was he? Stands shook his head as he decided the only thing he could do would be to get back to the car and wait for his wayward Sergeant to turn up. He glanced at the line map opposite him on the curved platform wall. The quickest way back would be to get off at Tottenham Court Road and take the Central Line to Bond Street Station, just five minutes walk from Manchester Square.

Stands looked towards the black hole of the tunnel mouth as he felt the first stirrings in the air and heard the rails in front of him start to hum. Here comes the train. As the air moved faster it was accompanied by the usual clattering and screeching which heralded the arrival of any underground train in London.

As it slowly squealed to a halt and a crowd gathered around the doors waiting for them to open, Waves ducked his head out from the entrance passage in which he'd concealed himself just in time to see that the man that he suspected was following the Inspector was stood almost directly behind him in the crowd waiting to board. Obviously the target was completely oblivious to the close observation he himself was under.

Waves stepped out of the passage and went to the next carriage along from the one the Inspector was getting on and jumped on board just before the doors closed automatically behind him. There weren't enough people on the train for Waves to be able to get as close to the Inspector's tail as he wanted. He needed more of a crowd in order to mask his intentions. Stands would, knowing him, take the most direct route back to the car, which had to mean Bond Street. Waves looked up at the line map above his head on the wall of the carriage. Hmm, Tottenham Court Road…perfect.

*

Waves made sure he wasn't the first person out of the doors when they opened at Tottenham Court Road station. By this point the trains passengers had swelled in numbers, and Waves found it easy to be swept along in the crowd. His height made it easy for him to spot Stands ahead of him heading towards the Central Line platforms, and just behind the Inspector he could see the back of the man's head who was tailing his boss. Waves slowly gained ground on the man until they were squeezed into the final stretch of tunnel leading on to the westbound platform.

It was an easy matter to jostle the man as the crowd spilled out onto the platform. As it was the man was so intent on not losing sight of Stands that he had no idea who it was who'd bumped into him.

Waves just hunched his shoulders and disappeared into the throng of people pushing towards the doors of the train which had just arrived. It was easy for Waves to join the flow of people heading towards the exits. He never thought he'd be so grateful for the rush hour as he entered the passage leading away from the departing train. All he had to do now was get back to the car before Stands. Waves picked up his pace as he headed straight up and out towards Oxford Street. If he could hail a cab going the right way he just might do it.

*

Stands was relieved, though he wasn't all that surprised when he got back to the car to find Waves sat inside patiently waiting for him. As he walked around to the passenger side Waves leant across and pushed the door open for the Inspector. He swung himself inside and closed the door before sitting back with a sigh. Looking round at his subordinate he found Waves staring straight ahead through the windscreen.

'I don't suppose you'd like to tell me why you took off like that would you? Did you think you were being followed or something? Because if you were I didn't spot anyone.'

It was with immense satisfaction that Waves turned to his boss and smiled. 'I wasn't followed, you were…' he held out something in his hand for the Inspector to take, '…by MI5.'

Stands took the wallet Waves was holding out for him and flipped open the ID inside. This was not what he'd been expecting. If anything he'd have thought that any kind of tail would have originated with the Americans. To have yet another agency involved just complicated matters even more. But then again, in for penny…he chuckled quietly before handing it back to Waves with a nod.

'You do realise Daniel that picking the pocket of a Security Services Agent is probably a treasonable offence.'

Waves grinned in response. 'Do you think it would help in my defence that I didn't know who he was when I did it?'

'Probably not.' Stands said, his chuckle dissolving into a full-on laugh. 'Shall we go, it would appear we both have some stories to tell. Though mine is going to lead us somewhere interesting.'

Waves turned the key in the ignition and checked the mirrors. He wasn't surprised to see the face of the man whose ID now resided in his pocket talking into a mobile phone on the corner behind them. He smiled as he pulled the car out into the road, sometime soon the poor man was in for a bit of a shock.

Chapter Eighteen

At roughly the same time that the two policemen were playing hide and seek with MI5, Garfan and Tristellis were once more paying a visit to their bank in Canary Wharf.

That morning they'd both decided that not only did they need to get their mobile phones back, but both of them were beginning to think that it was far too convenient that those creatures had just happened to catch up with them on the Isle of Dogs. That and the fact that Garfan had told Tris about the presence he had felt before they had dispatched the Revenants, had convinced them both that they should go back sooner rather than later.

This time they both sensed it as soon as they stepped off the train at Canary Wharf.

Tris stopped abruptly and turned his face up to the air. 'It's here.'

Garfan closed his eyes and concentrated on his senses. 'It feels different to me.'

'No, it's the same. The one we were tracking before…only this time I think it knows we're here.'

Garfan smiled grimly. 'Do you think you can get a lock on it?'

Tris nodded slowly. 'It's high up in a building somewhere across the water from here.' Tris pointed past Canada Square towards Heron Quay. 'I think it's watching us.'

Garfan shook his head uneasily. 'I don't like this. Lets get the phones and get out of here. We can come back when it's dark, when we've got all our gear.' That said he stomped off towards the bank.

*

As they turned their phones back on Garfan's was the first to beep, then it beeped again, the little icon for a missed call appearing in the top right hand corner of its little screen. Tris's followed suit straight after. Garfan glanced at Tris before calling his voice mail.

'You have two missed calls…first missed call…'

Suddenly Garfan could hear Christine Wessex's voice sounding more than a little scared.

'Garfan…Garfan, please…where are you? David's disappeared! I need your help…please call me!'

'…second missed call…'

'Garfan, it's Christine again, where the hell are you two? I'm going crazy here, I can't locate David and no one else seems to know where he is. Some of his friends seem to have dropped off the map as well. Call me please!'

'Tris you better check your voice mail, that was Christine, David's missing!'

Tris wasted no time and punched the right buttons to call his answer phone before he held his phone to his ear. 'Tris, I don't know what's going on. I hope to Christ you and Garfan are OK, I hope this hasn't got anything to do with you two? Please call me Tris, James and I really need you right now!'

Tris was frowning as he handed the phone to Garfan so that he could listen to the message. Garfan reciprocated and held his out to Tris.

A minute later they were both worried. Christine had sounded frantic towards the end of the last message.

Garfan handed Tris his phone back and raised his eyebrows. 'This doesn't sound good Tris, but if David's friends are missing too then it's unlikely to have anything to do with our activities.'

'Garf we've got to call her, those messages are from yesterday. We've got to help her if we can.'

Garfan wasn't looking too comfortable, biting his lip he looked at Tris' face. He could see he was upset and wanted to drop everything and go to Christine straight away.

'Tris, all we can do is call her and give her the best advice we can. In case you've forgotten we're kind of in the middle of something here. We can't abandon the hunt and let who ever's behind all this get away, besides, you wouldn't want Christine to get dragged into this too. If we go running to her aid now we could be putting her and James in danger just by association!'

Tris's face hardened. 'No way Garf, she needs me…she needs us, we've got to go to her.'

Garfan wasn't about to let Tris get away with not thinking it through. 'Listen to yourself! She needs the Police, not us. They'll be able to help her more than we can, just calm the fuck down and think it through!'

Tris didn't look mollified in the slightest, but he didn't look as tense, as though he was about to sprint off at any moment.

'Look Tris, let me call Christine and we'll see what the state of play is. Like you said the messages are from yesterday, anything could have happened since last night. Hell, David could have been partying with his pals. He could have turned up by now. Let's just wait and see…OK?'

Tris's face relaxed a little as he slowly calmed down, though he still thrust his hands angrily into his pockets and stared up at the sky, looking anywhere but at his old friend.

Garfan shook his head and studied his phone once more, concentrating on finding Christine's mobile phone number. Having found it he pressed the call button and put the phone to his ear.

After what seemed like minutes to Tris, Garfan's face relaxed, indicating to Tris that someone had answered. All he had to contend with now was hearing only one side of the conversation.

'Hello Arthur, it's me Garfield, is Lady Christine there?' He nodded at something Arthur said on the other end. 'Thanks.'

'Hi Christine, yes it's me, and yes, Tris is here too…we're fine, we've just been unobtainable for a while. So have you heard anything from David?'

Garfan glanced up at Tris as Christine was obviously giving him details of what was going on.

'No, OK it's going to be fine…what have the Police said?'

This time Garfan looked rather alarmed, and Tris wished he could hear what Christine was saying.

'What do you mean you haven't reported this to the Police? He's been missing for what...two days now! What...since we were there?'

Garfan slowly began to pace backwards and forwards, only taking a few steps before swinging round and repeating the same movement, to Tris this usually indicated rapid and intensive thought on Garfan's part.

'Yes I realise that Christine, but I really don't think you should worry about the Iranian thing, it's more important that you locate your husband, and to be honest the Police can be more help on that front than we can. They have the manpower and the resources, we're not private investigators Christine, we're hunters, and believe me they're very different disciplines. Besides which we're still in the middle of this thing here, and the way things are looking it could be dangerous for anyone to be around us at the moment.'

At last Garfan stopped pacing, though he was facing away from Tristellis, and as if he had become aware of this he slowly turned to face him.

'Yes, just call the Police…explain who you are and that sometimes David does go off without telling you where he's going, but that its been two days and you can't seem to locate the friends he normally spends time with either and that you're worried.'

Despite the fact that Tris was desperate to talk to her he had to smile when Garfan pulled the kind of face that men everywhere make when they're beginning to become exasperated by a woman on the other end of a phone.

'I know...but for fucks sake Christine, he's Lord Wessex, he's a Lord of the Realm, I'm sure they'll put their best men on it. If a Lord goes missing they'll probably pull the country apart to find him.'

Garfan looked up at Tris again, 'Yes Tris is right next to me.'

Garfan took the phone away from his ear and held it out to Tristellis. 'She wants to talk to you.'

Tris took the phone and stepped away from Garfan as he lifted the phone to his ear.

'Hi Chris, how's James doing? Is he OK?'

At last he heard Christine's voice. 'He's fine Tris, I told him that his Daddy had to go away for a few days and was sorry that he didn't have a chance to say goodbye before he left.'

'OK...how about you?'

'I'm worried Tris, David may do a lot of things that I don't particularly like, but he always told me where he'd be and who he'd be with, but the last few weeks he's been so secretive.'

'You think this is definitely linked to this trip to Iran he'd been planning with his friends?'

'Tris I can't think what else it could be. He's a lousy liar, and he'd never have an affair...he wouldn't be able to hide it from me, and the only thing that he's been evasive about has been this damn adventure to Iran. Besides his friends that also seem to be missing just happen to be the one's he gets all Indiana Jones with.'

'Yeah I see what you mean. Look, just do what Garf told you, tell the Police he's missing, you don't have to tell them much of anything else. They'll find him...but keep us informed.'

Tris was just about to say something else when he had a sudden thought. 'Look, Chris, this may be a long shot, but can you get hold of any of his fathers old friends, you know the ones who had links with the security services...if you can they may be able to pull some strings and get things moving for you. In the mean time why don't you get Arthur to bring you and James to your flat here in London. It might be safer than being alone in that big old house, you could even catch up with some of your old friends here, and I know I'd definitely feel better knowing that you're close.'

There was a silent pause on the phone. '…thanks Tris, that's a good idea, I think I'd feel a bit better having more people around me right now. Look I'd better go, I'll get Arthur to prepare for a stay in town. Thank you Tris…I won't forget this.'

Tris pulled the phone away from his ear, looked at the screen and pressed the button to end the call only to find his old friend looking at him intently.

'What?'

'Are you OK?'

'Yeah I'm fine…just worried about Chris.'

'Don't be, she'll be fine, and I'm sure David will turn up somewhere. That was a good idea by the way, Davids father's old friends will make sure the Police take it a lot more seriously than they might, and having her come down to London will help take her mind off it a bit.'

Tris held out the phone to Garfan. 'Thanks.'

Garfan shrugged. 'Now that's dealt with I think it's time we got the hell out of here.'

Tris was just about to agree with his old friend when something occurred to him. 'Garf what did Elarris say about whatever it was David wanted to know about?'

Garfan suddenly found he'd held his breath. 'Shit...what with everything else that was going on it completely slipped my mind, though it's hardly important now.' He shook his head in annoyance. 'Don't worry, when he turns up I'll arrange for him to speak to Elarris himself.'

*

Arthur was descending the stairs carrying Lady Christine's bags down to the hallway, ready for their departure when the phone on the console table in the hall started to ring. Speeding his pace Arthur got to the bottom of the stairs before dropping the bags he was carrying and scuttling over to the telephone. On reaching it he mentally took a moment to compose himself before lifting the handset to his ear.

'Good afternoon, this is the Wessex residence, may I be of service?'

An elderly voice with a clipped upper-class accent answered. 'Hello, is that Arthur?'

'Yes Sir, I'm afraid you have the advantage of me. How may I be of help?'

'I'm sorry Arthur, this is Lord Murray, I was hoping to speak to Lady Wessex, is Christine there?'

'Yes my Lord, please forgive me for not recognizing your voice, Lady Wessex is in residence at this time. If you would kindly wait one moment I'll put you through to her immediately.'

Arthur pressed the internal transfer button on the phones base unit, and then chose the third extension. The phone in the main lounge, where Arthur had last seen Lady Christine, began to ring. By the fourth ring Arthur was about to try a different extension when the ringing cut out and was replaced by Lady Christine's voice.

'Hello Arthur, is it for me? Is it David?'

'No my Lady, I'm sorry it's not Lord Wessex, it's Lord Murray, an old friend of Lord Wessex's Father.'

'Oh yes, Lord Christopher Murray isn't it? He's come to a few of the functions we've held here at the house a few times in the past hasn't he?'

'Yes, I believe so my Lady, shall I put him through?'

'Of course Arthur, he may have news about David.'

'Very well my Lady…'

Arthur put the phone handset down on its cradle,

transferring Lord Murray through to the other phone.

'Hello, Lord Murray?'

'Christine, how are you my dear?

'I'm well Lord Murray.'

'Christine please…just Christopher to my friends.'

'Of course Christopher, I just didn't want to seem too familiar.'

'Nonsense my girl, I've known the Wessex family all my life, and David's father thought the world of you…even though he knew you such a short time.'

'Thank you, anyway, how can I help you Christopher? If you were after David then I'm afraid I can't help you, he's not here.'

'Ah, actually that's why I was calling, do you know where he is? I've been trying to contact him so I could pass on some information he requested.'

'I'm sorry, but actually I have no idea where he is, he left here rather abruptly without telling me where he was going, and that was two days ago. I was rather hoping it was him when you called.'

'Right…I'm afraid what I can tell you isn't going to help much. He called me the other day from Heathrow Airport to ask me if I could help him obtain some information on that rather nasty business at that old cinema in South London, you know…the Satanist thing.'

'Yes I saw the news coverage…'

'Anyway, I agreed to find out what I could for him, I thought it was a rather odd request, but I asked him where I could contact him. Well he gave me the name and number of a hotel in Anchorage, in Turkey.'

'Pardon?'

'Yes, I thought it sounded a bit odd too. David admitted that he was just about to board a flight for Anchorage, something to do with a trip he'd organised that had to suddenly be moved forward. Do you know anything about this trip of his Christine?'

'Yes, well…a little. He'd mentioned it to me, but was a little sketchy about the details.'

'OK, well I asked him how long he'd be at the hotel, and he said two days at the most. So I tried to contact him at the hotel he'd mentioned once I had the information he wanted. The problem is that according to the hotel he never checked in.'

'Oh my god, where is he Christopher?'

'I don't know Christine. I checked with Heathrow, and David wasn't on the flight he said he was getting, so he could be anywhere. Now I don't want you to worry Christine, the reason I rang was to find out what you knew and if he'd contacted you.'

'No, not a word. Christ, where is he? You don't think someone's kidnapped him do you?'

'Christine…please try and stay calm. I very much doubt there's anything underhand about all this. David said he was meeting friends at the airport who he'd be travelling with. I'm sure it's just some kind of mix-up, or misunderstanding. In the mean time, if you don't mind Christine, I'd like to contact the British Embassy in Anchorage, and get there help in locating David just in case he made it out there after all.'

'Of course Christopher, it would be wonderful if you could, I was going to ask some other family friends to help with some enquiries. Could you let me know as soon as you hear anything?'

'My dear, the moment I do you shall be the first to know. In the mean time I don't want you to worry, David is a very resourceful young man, he can look after himself. He's very like his father was you know, a natural adventurer.'

'Yes, I know. Thank you Lord Murray, you're very kind. I'm taking James to the flat in London for a few days, but I'll look forward to hearing from you.'

'Of course. I tell you what, when David's back safe and sound I'll have to come down to Avington for dinner, it would be lovely to see you both again.'

'It would, I'll look forward to it, and again, thank you.'

As Christine put down the phone her frown deepened, deeper and much more pronounced than the one she'd been wearing earlier. She looked up and started with surprise when she saw Arthur regarding her from across the room by the door, sporting the self-same expression of deep concern.

*

Stands had had a gut full of listening to those American clowns with their badly hidden agenda. How hard could it be to move forward with all the information they'd accumulated. They were scared, simple as that. They'd gone as far as they could without confronting the beings that they'd demonised, and were too damn scared to face up to what they didn't understand. And now they had MI5 watching them. He and Waves were rapidly running out of options.

They knew where they were, just not what they were. As a policeman you could never let fear get in the way of doing the job, no matter how hard. That *was* the job. He was nervous yes, he wouldn't admit it to anyone but Waves, but yes...he was a little scared, but that wasn't going to stop him moving this thing forward. There was no other way of bringing this case to some kind of conclusion, and he wasn't about to baulk at the first major hurdle, but he had to be careful, and he wasn't about to involve the Agency in this.

He had a grudging respect for his adversaries, and a badly concealed disdain for his allies, and one thing he'd learnt to trust in all his years on the job was his gut. If he couldn't trust his so called friends, then maybe he should go and meet those who his so-called friends had labelled enemies.

With this in mind he picked up the phone, he trusted the Sergeant implicitly. They'd been through too

287

much together not to. Besides which, Waves had never let him down, and Stands didn't think he was going to this time.

He hardly looked at his mobile as he pressed the buttons on the phone. Waves answered on the second ring.

'Hi Daniel, where are you?'

'At home Sir, are you OK, you sound a little…'

'Weird? Well Daniel, I think it's time we found out just what the fuck is going on here. And between you and me I think the only way we're going to get any meaningful answers is if we go to the horse's mouth. What do you think?

'You're asking me?'

'Well it would certainly appear so wouldn't it. So how about it? I think you'd agree that we can't trust these American Nazi's we've rather inadvisedly hooked up with. How about we give the underdog a chance to explain their side in all this. We know where they are, even if we don't know exactly who or what they are.'

Waves was hesitant in his answer. 'I agree but…'

'But what Sergeant?'

'Do you think it's safe Sir?'

Stands put his hand to his face, scratched his cheek and sighed. 'If you ask me then truthfully no, I don't think it's safe. But I think they probably have more to lose than anyone else we're dealing with at the moment, and if we go in there holding a white flag I think we'll be in a good position to negotiate.

These guys wouldn't like the publicity of an incident on their home turf, and I think we'll be safe enough as long as we make it plain that should anything untoward happen there'll be repercussions.'

Stands held the phone tighter as he listened to silence from the other end. 'Waves…Daniel, are you still there?'

'Sorry Sir, I was just thinking.'

'Look Daniel, there's no way I'm going to do this without you. You're the only one I trust to watch my back right now. What do you say?'

'Fuck it, lets do it. When?'

'Well seeing as we're both not doing anything else right now...'

'No time like the present huh?'

' Well you know what they say Waves…'

'No, what's that Sir?'

'Tempus fugit.'

'Time flies?'

'It does indeed Waves…it does indeed.'

Chapter Nineteen

When they got to St Marks Square they arrived just in time for Waves to see something that almost made him crash the car. Just as he was pulling into the curb behind a parked BMW he looked in his wing mirror and saw the two homeless guys from the cinema incident on Forrester Street, only this time they weren't dressed as tramps.

'Oh my god…it's them.'

'What?' Stands started to turn in his seat.

'Don't move they're going to walk past the car, just try not to attract their attention.' As he was saying this he could see that they'd just come level with the back of the car. Oddly enough both policemen found that their reaction was to hold their breath, there didn't seem to be much else they could do as the odd pair walked past the car and into a driveway a dozen metres further along the road.

Waves let out his breath in a small explosive sigh. Stands sat back heavily in the passenger seat and looked over at the Sergeant.

'So that was Tristan…but who was the short bearded guy? You said 'it's them', what did you mean?'

Waves shook his head angrily and slammed his open palms against the steering wheel in front of him. 'I knew I recognised him from somewhere.' He looked over and met the Inspectors eyes.

'Sorry Sir, I've been an idiot.'

Stands snorted. 'Daniel, if I had any idea what the hell you were talking about I might feel inclined to accept that apology, but as things stand I'd rather you just explained yourself.'

Waves took a deep breath before answering. 'They were outside the cinema that day.' He took the photos from inside his pocket and pointed at the man they were calling Tristan.

'He was outside the cinema…with that other man you just saw.'

Stands still didn't look as though he understood. He shook his head.

'How could you not have recognised him?'

'They were the two tramps you sent me to talk to. I thought there was something a little odd about them at the time, but I didn't get the chance to mention it to you because the forensic team turned up. It must have been them…and I'd bet it was this Tristan character who phoned it in from that call box.'

Waves closed his eyes and slowly shook his head. 'They must have laughed their arses off when I just let them walk away.'

Stands reached over and put his hand on Waves' shoulder. 'Daniel I very much doubt it, I don't think these people do this stuff for kicks. Try and remember what we're dealing with here, these are not your average murdering psychos. These people have some kind of agenda, they're more like soldiers. What we need to do is find out who they work for or with, and why they do it. We're not here to arrest them, at least not yet. We're here to try and find out what the fuck is going on.'

Stands could feel the tension slowly leaving Waves' body as the Sergeants shoulder relaxed under his hand.

'Sorry Sir. To be honest I'm more angry at myself for not seeing it. I should have recognised him. It was only when I saw him with the other one that I remembered.'

'Well…don't worry about it now Waves. Even if you had recognised him I doubt we would have found them any sooner. The question is what do we do now?'

*

As Garfan and Tristellis turned into their driveway Tris glanced over at Garfan. 'I suppose you recognised the car?'

'Hmmm.' Garfan didn't look pleased.

'And I suppose you recognised the Sergeant we spoke to at the cinema sat in the drivers seat?'

'Couldn't miss him.'

'So we can safely assume that the man in the passenger seat was the Inspector.'

'I should think so.'

Tris paused at the bottom of the steps up to their front door. 'You think they know what's going on?'

Garfan stomped up the steps angrily. 'I don't know, but I think we're about to find out.'

*

After a tense five minutes, during which time neither Tristellis or Garfan could do more than pace around the lounge, the door bell announced that someone was at their door.

Tris, both excited and a little panicked, looked at Garfan. 'How do you want to play this?'

Garfan ran his fingers through his beard. 'Lets play it dumb and see what they know. With any luck they won't know anything for sure, and I doubt very much they have proof of anything.'

The doorbell chimed again. Tris shrugged non-committally before walking into the hall and opening the front door. He couldn't help but smile when he saw the two policemen stood on their doorstep. They both looked very tense, which was when it suddenly occurred to Tris that if they didn't know anything neither of them would have any reason to look so tense.

Stands noticed the smile slip from the face of the young 'Man' stood before them and wondered why the loss of the welcoming smile worried him so much. 'Good afternoon Sir, we're policemen and we'd like to ask you and your friend a few questions. May we come in?'

'My friend?'

'Yes Sir, the gentleman you just entered this building with.'

'Ahh, may I see some identification first?'

'Of course Sir.' Stands held out his ID so that it could be clearly seen. 'I'm Detective Inspector Stands, and this is Detective Sergeant Waves. May we come in?'

'Of course.' Tris stood aside as the two men entered. It was as they moved past him that he caught the familiar scent of guns, cordite providing a tang similar to that found in the air every 5th of November. He could even tell that one of the two weapons was some kind of larger automatic by the stronger, more intense scent.

'Could I take your coats gentlemen?' Tris offered courteously. His smile returned when he noticed the slight discomfort his offer made them both unconsciously express.

'That won't be necessary Sir.' Stands glanced at Waves. 'We won't be keeping you very long.'

Tris nodded. 'Of course, if you'll come with me, the lounge is through here.' As Tris entered ahead of the two policemen he looked intently at Garfan and, using his body to hide the gesture, made a pistol shape with one hand, and then winked.

Garfan's eyes widened slightly, but he didn't move from where he was stood with his back to the open fireplace, the fire irons conveniently within reach of his right hand.

Tris gestured towards one of the two sofas facing each other in the centre of the room, before seating himself on the other. Stands and Waves glanced at each other and each of their hosts in turn before sitting down. In doing so both were careful to keep their coats in place.

'So how can we help you Inspector?' Tris said purposely not introducing Garfan, making them keep their attention on him rather than on Garfan.

Waves took out his notebook and a pen. 'Could we start with your names?'

Tris smiled once more. 'Of course, my name is Tristan Forest, and my friend here is Garfield Stone.' Tris looked over at Garfan. 'Garfield, this is Detective Inspector Stands and Detective Sergeant Waves. They'd like to ask us some questions.'

Garfan nodded and studied the two policemen. 'Very well, fire away.'

Stands raised an eyebrow. 'You haven't asked us what this is about, or even what this enquiry is connected with.'

Garfan shrugged. 'I assumed that you'd get around to telling us.'

Stands put his hands on his knees and stood up, his face angry. Waves almost jumped as the Inspector got up. He really wasn't liking this situation.

Tris and Garfan declined to react to the Inspector's movements, showing no surprise as he walked around behind the sofa he'd been sitting on. He was looking curiously at them, the frown on his face making him look older.

Tris couldn't help but goad him further. 'Something on your mind Inspector?'

Stands stopped moving abruptly and put his hands on the high back of the sofa, gripping it hard enough for his knuckles to whiten. 'I'm sure we could keep this up for quite a while, but why don't we just dispense with the bullshit. We know who you are, the question is are you going to co-operate?'

Garfan tensed and his fingers twitched as he glanced down to his right at the poker that seemed to be calling to him. He forced himself to relax.

'If we knew what you were referring to Inspector we'd be more than happy to co-operate. As lawabiding citizens we are more than happy to help you with you're enquiries.'

Stands seemed to be on the verge of apoplexy, his face was quickly becoming suffused with blood, his hands gripping the back of the sofa so hard that the tendons were clearly visible. Then suddenly he reached inside his coat and produced the Glock and aimed it shakily at Garfan.

'Lets just stop fucking around shall we. We can make you co-operate.'

Waves was shocked by the Inspectors behaviour, he really wasn't sure that being confrontational with these people was a good idea, but he'd back the Inspector up if he needed to.

Tris smiled gently at the Sergeant. 'If this was poker Sergeant I'd be anticipating you raising the Inspectors semi-automatic with your sub-machine gun. Besides, it must be a little uncomfortable underneath that coat.'

Now Waves knew they were in trouble, their hosts were far too relaxed. They couldn't be faking it, Waves knew bravado when he saw it, and this wasn't it. They knew they were completely in control of the situation, and now so did Waves.

Stands glanced down at Waves as he slowly withdrew the Uzi from deep inside his coat. He couldn't believe it when Waves quietly placed the sub-machine gun on the coffee table in front of him.

Waves looked up at the Inspector. 'Sorry Sir, but I think it might be a good idea for you to put the gun down.'

Stands glanced from Waves to Tristellis who smiled lazily back, and then finally at Garfan.

'You should listen to your Sergeant Inspector. He has a wise head on his young shoulders. You really don't want to carry on pointing that at me…I might take offence.'

That said Stands saw Garfan's stationary figure seem to blur. The next thing he knew Garfan was stood in front of him casually holding the gun that he'd been pointing at him only a moment before. Stands could only stare at him mutely.

Garfan looked down at Waves who looked equally stunned.

'Could you put this on the coffee table for me Sergeant?' Garfan asked politely as he held out the Glock to the Sergeant.

Waves took it then slowly leant forward and placed it with a quiet thunk next to the Uzi.

Stands shook his head in amazement as he carried on staring at Garfan. 'How did you do that?'

Garfan shrugged before moving to join Tristellis on the other sofa facing them. 'It's what we do Inspector, it's who we are.'

Tris gestured that the Inspector should sit down. 'Please Inspector take a seat. It would appear that you know something about us after all. Our question is…what do you want? If you're here to try and arrest us then we may have a problem.'

Stands moved around to the front of the sofa and slowly sat down next to his Sergeant. He was still shaking from the huge adrenaline rush that had provoked him to act so rashly.

He shook his head. 'No, we're not here for that. In fact we just came for some answers. One of which you have just demonstrated, the problem is it just raises more questions, like…what are you?'

'What are we?'

Stands nodded. 'Yes, we know you're not exactly human.'

'Ahh.' Garfan and Tristellis exchanged a look. Neither of them wanted to admit how surprised they were to hear that.

'Maybe you should tell us what you think you know about us, and we'll tell you if you're right.'

Stands was having real trouble with this. First he'd lost it and drawn a weapon on an unarmed suspect, then he'd gone on to lose control of the conversation. In fact he didn't feel in control of anything at that moment. This really wasn't going too well.

'OK, you are both at least seventy years old, you share some DNA with humanity, but you are not Homo Sapiens, and you spend your time hunting down and killing things which are even less human than you are. On top of this you are well funded, and at this moment in time being hunted by a top-secret wing of the CIA.'

Both Garfan and Tristellis raised their eyebrows at that bombshell. They turned to each other, their faces unreadable despite the fact that they were obviously sharing some form of silent communication.

'I'm sorry to have to lay that on you, but we're involved in this too. We need some answers if we're going to do anything to stop this from blowing up in all our faces.'

'Shit! If it's not one thing it's another.' Tris slumped back into the sofa. 'So...can we trust you?'

Waves didn't smile as he leant forward. 'Trust is a two way street.'

'Indeed it is.' Garfan frowned. 'OK, let us start with introductions.' He smiled ruefully. 'I really didn't think I'd have to do this again so soon with strangers. My name is Garfan, though inaccurate I am what many would refer to as a Dwarf...in the mythical sense, and I am five hundred and three years old. My handsome friend here is called Tristellis. His people are what were once commonly called Elves, though again that is completely inaccurate. He's five hundred and two.'

Garfan smiled at Tris before looking back at the two policemen. 'We are the chosen Guardians of this Kingdom.'

Waves' mouth hung open as he looked at the figures from legend sat opposite him.

Stands noticed the Sergeants response and felt it might be a good time to start again. 'I'd like to apologise for my behaviour just now, this whole situation has been rather stressful for us. We're usually a lot more polite.'

'That's OK Inspector, believe me we've experienced much worse in our time.'

'Please just call me Stands, and the Sergeant here responds equally well to Waves.'

Tristellis laughed happily. 'Well now we all know who we are, why don't we go down to the kitchen where we can have a drink and find out who wants what in this little scenario.'

*

When their guests were settled in the much more homely and relaxed environment of the kitchen, each sat at the table with a mug of coffee, Garfan finally sat. There was an awkward silence as they all sat looking at each other over their coffee mugs. Tris, as ever being the most relaxed, broke the silence.

'You do realise that when you say your names together it sounds a bit like...Stands With Fist? Don't people laugh?'

Stands looked back at Tristellis blankly. 'Sorry?'

Tris shook his head. 'OK, obviously that's just me being weird and making odd connections. I meant like in the film 'Dances with Wolves' the white girl brought up by the Sioux is called Stands With Fist.' Tris looked around at the other three, all of whom seemed somewhat bemused. 'Well I thought it was funny.'

The two policemen smiled and shook their heads. Stands studied Tristellis for a moment before answering him.

'Generally when we introduce ourselves to people the situation is such that people tend to overlook the potential humour in our combined names. Though I think the humour is just in the sound of it and not any cultural connection'

'Sorry Inspector I didn't mean any offence.'

'None taken.'

Garfan took a swig of coffee before straightening

himself in his chair. 'Lets get down to business shall we. You mentioned earlier that the CIA are hunting us. I don't suppose you'd tell us how you know that?'

Stands too took a gulp of his coffee before responding, pausing to make some sense of all this. 'The short answer is our investigation into what happened at the derelict cinema on Forrester Street has been taken over by a group who are part of the CIA, who seconded us in the hope that we'd help track you down.'

'So how come you two are alone? Or can we expect them to try and break down our front door sometime soon?'

'No we're here alone...working alone. They see you as abominations, enemies of God and servants of the Devil. As far as they're concerned if you're not human you are by definition evil and must die.'

'Well, it's always nice to know that the Americans are living up to their stereotypes.'

Waves laughed out loud, the first natural response he'd allowed himself since pressing their doorbell about a lifetime ago. 'I'm sorry...but this is too fucking weird. I'm sat here having coffee with an Elf and a Dwarf, who are both over five hundred years old, making jokes about the CIA.'

Waves looked at the Inspector sat next to him. 'I'm sorry Sir, but at this point in time I'm seriously considering retiring and walking away from all this.'

Stands smiled in sympathy.

'If it's any help I know exactly what you mean, but I for one am far too curious to walk away from all this without some answers.' He looked at Garfan and Tristellis. 'That is if you'd both be kind enough to supply some.'

Tristellis grinned. 'If it's any consolation this situation is a new one for us too, but I think I'll leave it to Garfan to explain. He's better at this kind of thing than I am.'

*

An hour later they had all just about finished bringing each other up to speed on what had happened in the last few days, during which time Tristellis had seen fit to find a bottle of Calvados to fortify their coffee, an addition that had been gratefully received by all concerned.

'So what you're saying is there's a demon, or Fire Elemental, based in a high rise in Canary Wharf who may or may not be Satan?'

Tristellis shook his head. 'Inspector, please don't try and oversimplify this. Like we said, we don't know for sure who or what it is, but we do know it's responsible for the death of that little girl, Sam Goodwin at the hospital, and our friend Martin. Whatever it is it's powerful enough to raise the dead in a way we've never seen before. Our Elder called them Revenants, but we've never seen anything like them before. All in all there is an evil at work that must be stopped for all our sakes.'

'Can't you just use magic or something?'

'Who exactly do you think we are?'

'Well…look I don't know. Some of the things we've seen recently have put me in a position I'm completely unfamiliar with. I'm a policeman, and essentially we operate in a manner very similar to scientists. We work with evidence, with facts. Then when all the evidence points to someone being guilty of a crime we arrest them. But here we are, and what are you guilty of, being a myth made real? As far as I'm aware there's no law against being an Elf,' Stands glanced at Garfan, 'or a Dwarf for that matter.'

Tris laughed, 'I'm sure we'll sleep better knowing that. But can I just correct you before we go on. We aren't the fairytale stereotypes you keep referring to. We are Elementals, unfortunately man often over simplifys things. We do not refer to ourselves in the way that mankind does.

As to magic, well it's difficult to explain, but it's not anything like what you've seen in Hollywood films, or read about in books. Real magic is in things, in individuals, even in places, it enables an individual to do things that would not otherwise be possible. And when it is in an object, then that object when used has the ability to influence things around it. That's magic.'

Garfan could see that the two detectives still looked none the wiser. 'What Tris is trying to say is that magic is the practice of influencing the elements in the world around us. That influence can take many forms. I suppose the closest use of real magic to what you obviously think of as magic would be moving things without touching them, or making fire or air behave in unnatural ways.'

'But isn't moving things without touching them just a form of telekinesis?'

'That's what your scientists call it, yes, but…well it's difficult to explain. The scientific explanation is fuzzy, but suggests that certain minds have the ability to move objects just through the power of the mind, they don't actually know what that power is. The reality is that it is the use of magic, magic is essentially a mental discipline, but there is more to it than that. Everything is connected, there are magnetic fields, electro magnetic fields, all sorts of power fields that surround and infuse everything.
Animate and inanimate, magic gives the practitioner the ability to influence these to his own ends, even to be able to store energy in objects. It would be a lot easier to explain it if it was scientifically studied, but the closest thing that our peoples have to scientists are what you would call magicians, or wizards. Most important though is to remember that before science came along anything that couldn't be easily explained was referred to by the ignorant as magic.'

'OK, so what you're essentially saying is that mind over matter abilities like psychokinesis, telepathy, E.S.P, etc., are all the result of using magic?'

'Yes.' Garfan looked pleased to be able to at last give an unequivocal answer.

It was Daniel's turn to look confused. 'But how can that be? All the proof that we have of stuff like that comes from scientific experiments on humans. Humans that have nothing to do with magic.'

'I see where you're going with this Sergeant, but humans can use magic too. Like I said it's a mental discipline which gives you the ability to manipulate your environment. Basically magic gives you the power to look at the world in a way that makes that manipulation seem reasonably simple. This ability is potentially in all of us, and when someone stumbles on to a way of making things happen like that we call it wild magic. When such abilities become manifest they are untrained and weak. We have in the past trained humans who have shown this power, and some of them have become great magicians, though to be honest it's not something we really do any more.'

Stands was intrigued by all this talk, he liked the idea that magic was a discipline rather than some weird kind of supernatural gift. 'So why don't you teach humans magic any more?'

Garfan was startled by the question at first. 'Well Inspector, with the kind of power that can become manifest in an individual, it can be dangerous.
To give a human such power we would have to be able to trust that individual implicitly, and though we have many human allies, few could be trusted with that much power.'

'So does that mean that you two can't *do* magic?'

'*Do* magic?'

Tris and Garfan laughed.

'Please forgive us Inspector, it just sounds funny you saying it like that. One thing you should always try and remember is that as far as magic is concerned there is never a simple answer. There are always too many variables for magic to ever be explained simply.'

Tris was watching the Inspector carefully, he seemed genuinely interested. 'Sorry Inspector, Garfan can be a little impenetrable at times. The answer to your question is that we can use objects that are magical, as long as we know how to access the power within the object, and that we ourselves are magical. Our very essences are infused with magic, but before you scratch your heads, let me put it another way. Our races are often referred to as magical, and that is accurate, our very bodies are infused by a power which enables us to do things which you can't, and that power is a direct result of our origins and our intimacy with magic and its uses. Does that answer your question?'

Stands and Waves exchanged a look as their hosts looked on hoping that they were making a connection with these two men.

Stands picked up his coffee mug, and grimaced as he swallowed what turned out to be lukewarm coffee. Tris gestured for the Inspector to pass him his mug, which he did with a shrug. Daniel looked round at Garfan who nodded in understanding of what Tristellis intended.

'Inspector, this is probably the most magical thing which I am capable of in the extent that I am consciously changing the state of elements around me. Our other abilities are so much more mundane.' Tris passed back the mug to the Inspector.

Even before Stands put the edge of the mug to his lips, he could feel the heat from inside it. The coffee was hot as he slowly drank from it. As he put the mug down he raised an eyebrow questioningly.

'I simply excited the molecules within the liquid to create heat. You could compare the process to the way a microwave works. I just did it using my mind. Like I said our other abilities are much more mundane. Being faster, stronger, moving unseen, even healing faster and not being easily killed, these are as much a result of what we are, as they are the result of the magic which is within us.'

Waves was obviously impressed by this display. Suddenly he smiled.

'Sir, it's a bit like the Force in Star Wars, only

magic is the discipline which gives the individual the ability to manipulate that Force.'

Now it was Garfan's turn to look confused. Tristellis couldn't help himself and burst out laughing at the look on his old friends face. Meanwhile Daniel looked a little offended that he might be the source of the hilarity.

Tris struggled to control his mirth. 'I'm sorry Sergeant, I'm not laughing at you. Garfan here always has trouble remembering films.' He looked at Garfan, 'You know Star Wars!' He raised an eyebrow, 'Darth Vader?'

Garfan snorted in recognition, 'Oh yes, 'may the force be with you!' I remember.' He smiled, 'actually Sergeant you're spot on, in a very simplified kind of way, but yes, magic is what gives us the ability to utilise the energy fields around us.'

'So what about raising spirits, and summoning demons? How does that fit with your theories about magic?'

'Hmmm…' Tris looked at Garfan and then back to the Inspector. 'We're really not the best people to ask about such esoteric arts.'

'Esoteric arts? That sounds mysterious, especially after your explanation of magic as being a discipline.'

Garfan coughed, clearing his throat. 'OK, I'll try and explain to the best of my abilities. I could say that you should ask practitioners of such arts for an explanation, but the problem with that is that you would probably get a different answer from each one you asked.'

Stands put down his coffee mug, settled back in his chair and folded his arms. Tris watched this classic piece of body language and smiled at Garfan.

Garfan meanwhile looked from Tris to Waves, and back at Stands. 'OK…I'll try to make some kind of sense out of this. The kind of magic that we're talking about here is always referred to as an art because that's what it is compared to normal magic, it's more art than science, and it takes a talent to master it that has nothing to do with intellect or strength, it is the kind of talent that in humans creates great artists.'

'The oldest lore we have cannot explain it all. Our races, the elementals, the jinn, whatever you want to call us, were once referred to as spirits or demons, depending upon our abilities, appearance and attitudes. It was our peoples that first introduced mankind to magic. One unfortunate result of which was that we also ended up being the inspiration for your religions.'

Tris could see this rapidly descending into a theological debate about divinity and it's origins. Garfan liked nothing better than to bemoan the fate of mankind weighed down by the burden of blind faith, the emphasis being on *blind*. 'Let's just stick to what's relevant Garf.'

Garfan caught the hint of exasperation in Tris's voice and smiled knowingly. 'Yes...anyway, when Man first started practising magic the angels of the air started to take an interest, as it was interfering with them in some way.'

At the mention of angels both Stands and Waves had raised their eyebrows and turned to look at each other as though they were unsure of whether they were being wound up or not.

Stands shook his head and turned back to Garfan. 'Hold on...angels? What are you talking about? You're not suggesting that God sent down his angels to stop men playing about with magic?'

'No, sorry, slight confusion there, I'm not talking about imaginary, Divine angels here, no the real angels are air elementals, spirits of the air. In just the same way that Fire Elementals are classically described by christian scholars as demons, because of their infernal nature.'

'We know very little about air alementals, or Angels, as they are usually invisible to the naked eye. Some now think that they are pure energy, some that they are pure spirit, whatever that means. No one really knows. Whatever they are, they're a law unto themselves, they manifest only at their own whim, and are suspected to be the source of tales of ghosts and poltergeists, and of spirits and demons being conjured from thin air. More obviously they are thought to be the source of tales of heavenly angels too.'

Daniel didn't look too convinced. 'You're saying that ghosts, poltergeists, people being possessed, etc., is all down to these angels, these air elementals?'

'Some believe so, and would say that that was the case…yes.'

'Do you believe that?'

'Actually no…I don't. There are too many things out there that cannot be so glibly explained away like that. I think it's a lot more complicated, and to be honest I don't think you would be given that explanation by a practitioner of such magic. No…that is the answer you would get from many of our lore keepers, though I'm not sure that all of them would necessarily believe it wholeheartedly either.' Garfan sighed, it was interesting seeing the reaction of these men to such revelations, but he was weary of his own voice. Looking at Tris he motioned for him to continue with the subject.

Tris smiled in understanding before turning back to the two policemen, shuffling forward on his seat as he did, so that he could lean towards them. 'We've experienced all kinds of things which would require a much more complex explanation. Ghosts for example, personally I think that ghosts are just echoes from the past, created by the energy fields which surround and imbue everything, being influenced, or damaged in some way, by a person, or an event in the past; merely the shadow of something or someone who's no longer there.'

'So what about spirits for example?'

'Spirits are a different matter entirely. They can display evidence of intelligence, purpose, even what could be considered personality. Though I'm inclined to believe that poltergeists are just bored angels mucking about, maybe jealous of mankind's corporeality…'

Waves looked confused. Stands chuckled. 'Daniel, remind me to buy you a dictionary for Christmas.

Corporeality; having a physical, tangible body. You know…flesh and blood.'

Tris grinned at the two policemen, strangely enough their relationship reminded him of his and Garf's. He glanced over at Garfan, meeting his eyes he could tell that Garfan was thinking much the same thing.

'Anyway, as you mentioned possessions, they could have the same cause, but there are plenty of less easily explained phenomena, things like lycanthropes, and vampires. There are also innumerable other creatures which cannot be so easily explained or categorised, some of our Elders believe them to be elementals too. There are many mysteries out there that Man will never be aware of, and those that he is aware of he may never be able to explain. I for one am glad of this fact, life needs a little mystery, mankind is far too keen to define and pigeon hole life and experience. The world would be a much better place if we could all be a little more fluid in our thinking.'

Tris sucked his bottom lip for a moment before continuing. 'Please forgive the little rant there, normally I try not to impose my opinions on others, it makes for very tiresome conversations. But getting back to the subject of esoteric arts, it has long been an accepted myth that the Adepts, those who truly become masters of magic, never truly died. Some think that their wills, their spirits if you like, are so imbued with power that they live on in some way, and that these spirits are the source of the tales and myths that surround such mysteries. I don't know…it sounds kind of plausible to me…but hey, what do I know, I'm just a simple warrior.'

Chapter Twenty

Having come away from their encounter with the two Guardians with their heads full of amazing ideas, and yet more questions, the two policemen decided to go for coffee at the little café they'd met at just the other day. There was much to talk about. As Stands sat down opposite Waves with his back to the door he heard it open behind him.

As usual Waves tilted his head so that he could get a look at who was coming in past the Inspectors head. Waves relaxed when he saw it was a couple, a young woman and an older man, obviously coming in to round off their evening with a late coffee, or maybe it was the end of a date and neither of them wanted to go home yet. Daniel came back to reality to find Stands observing him closely. Waves followed the couple with his eyes as he smiled ruefully at the Inspector.'Sorry Sir. Sometimes when I see people together I imagine little scenarios around them.'

Stands nodded. 'That sounds like a symptom of being alone for too long. I often wonder why a good looking, capable man like you is still single. Maybe you should go out and find yourself a wife.'

'As if it were that easy.' Daniel shook his head. 'Besides, I could well say the same thing to you Sir.'

'I hate to interrupt, but could we join you?'

Startled Stands looked up and Waves swivelled round in his seat to find the couple who had just come in now stood there clutching large coffee mugs. The man and woman were both looking at them expectantly.

Stands frowned up at the man who had just addressed them, and curtly replied. 'There appear to be plenty of free tables available, I'd suggest you go and sit at one of them instead.'

'But then we wouldn't be able to talk to you…

Inspector.'

Hearing that both men sagged in their seats. Stands sighed heavily and indicated with his hand that they should both sit down.

'In that case be my guests.'

'Thank you Inspector, I believe we will.'

Again it was the man who spoke, and then pulled out the chair next to Inspector Stands. The young woman with him drew out the chair from next to Waves, making sure that it was slightly away from the table, with an angle that would give her a clear view of the door to the café when she sat down.

She turned briefly once she had sat down and smiled at Waves before focusing her attention once more on the door. In that moment Daniel realised how incredibly attractive the woman was. He'd acquired, over the years, the ability to ignore women who were with other men. Not in a rude or boorish way, but in a way that meant that he never really registered whether they were attractive or not, even if it was just a couple on the street. It was a self-defence against coveting that which he could never have.

So as soon as he registered that the woman was not 'with' the man sat diagonally across the table from him, he unconsciously allowed himself to look at the woman sat next to him with open eyes. Unfortunately though he had to pay attention to the man sat next to Stands.

'So Inspector Stands, what were you and Sergeant Waves here discussing before we so rudely interrupted?'

Waves could see that Stands was in no mood to be cooperative. The lines in his forehead had deepened along with his frown.

'Actually we were discussing the state of my love life.' Waves said to fill the silence.

'How very intimate.'

'OK, who the hell are you, and what do you want.' Stands snapped.

The man reached inside his jacket and withdrew an ID wallet very much like the ones that Stands and Waves both carried. The man offered it to Stands, who took it impatiently and flipped it open. After studying its contents for a second he held it out to Waves.

Daniel didn't need to take the wallet in order to be able to see the ID card within, he could see it clear as day from where he sat, and what he saw spelled trouble. He looked up at Stands and raised his eyebrows.

Stands shifted in his seat so that he could look more easily at the man sat next to him and handed back his identification.

'So what can we do for MI5?' Stands said quietly.

The MI5 Agent smiled back at Stands and glanced at Waves before focusing once again on the Inspector.

'At the risk of sounding clichéd, I think it's more a case of what we can do for you.'

Stands nodded thoughtfully. 'If I had any idea what you were talking about I'm sure I'd be grateful for your offer, but unless you can explain what you're doing here this isn't going to get any of us very far.'

The Agent's smile faded. 'So we're going to play it like that are we?'

'Look, you could be here for any number of reasons. Unless you're prepared to be a little more frank I'm afraid the Sergeant and I will have to say goodnight.'

Stands glanced at the Agent before looking over at Waves and sliding his chair back.

'Very well.' The Agent reached out and touched the Inspector's arm. 'Don't leave just yet. We're here because of your involvement with a certain Agent O'Brien formerly of the CIA.'

'That's a shame, because neither the Sergeant or myself are at liberty to discuss such a matter with you, or anyone else for that matter.'

'Yes, we are aware that you've both had to sign the Official Secrets Act, and what passes for a non-disclosure agreement with a foreign agency. The thing is that despite what you may think, or may have been told, we have been aware of Agent O'Brien's operation for some time now, that's how the two of you came to our attention, and believe me when I say that having come to our attention we are not going to accept non-cooperation concerning a matter that may threaten National Security.'

Waves didn't like the sound of this, what had they gotten themselves into now? Maybe this had something to do with the MI5 ID he'd pick-pocketed. Both he and the Inspector were rapidly running out of friends, as well as room to manoeuvre.

The government Spook continued. 'As such we've also become aware of your own investigations, which for some reason you seem to be keeping from your new friends, as well as from your own department. We'd like to know why?'

Stands looked at Waves. Waves stared back blankly and shrugged, obviously at a loss as to what to think about their current predicament. Stands pursed his lips and blew air out slowly before rubbing his nose and looking from the woman sat next to Waves to the man sat next to him.

'You said you were here to help in some way?'

'Yes.'

'Who can I trust?'

'It would be easy for me to say that you can trust us, but from what I've learnt about you, and from what you've been up to recently, I would suggest that you should trust your own instincts.'

'Hmmm…what do you know about O'Brien's operation?'

'I suppose at this point I'm hardly going to be revealing anything you don't already know. Right?'

'Right.'

'OK They are mainly involved in research that most people in our positions would consider crazy if they heard about it. Research into a group which he and his superiors would like to see eliminated. We're not sure why, but considering the attitudes and beliefs of those who give him his orders it's not really that surprising. This group has been in existence for a long time, and would be considered by most within the scientific community to be non-human.' He stopped and looked pointedly at Stands. 'Correct?'

'So far so good.'

'This group were involved in the incident at the cinema on Forrester Street, which is how you initially became involved in all this. Then there was the incident at the hospital morgue. It was after this that O'Brien sequestered you and the Sergeant here. O'Brien believes that the same group is responsible for both incidents.'

Stands tilted his head slightly as he studied the man sat next to him.

'But you don't?'

The agent smiled. 'Very good Inspector, no we don't...it's not their style.'

'Not whose style?' Waves said trying to bluff. 'What is going on here?'

The agent looked over at the Sergeant. 'Don't worry, I'm sure it will all become clear in time. Until then just bear with me.'

He turned once more to Stands.

'So you're both taken under O'Brien's wing, and you learn a little of the truth behind some rather startling events, which until then, can't have made an awful lot of sense. Now you know that the world isn't quite the place you always thought it was. You know that there are people out there who appear, to all extents and purposes, to be human, but are as close to being human as your average primate. Now instead of cooperating fully, as you'd been ordered to do by your own superiors, you go out of your way to mount your own investigation into who these people are. Now before we go any further we need to know why? Why are you acting independently? What is your objective? Are you acting on behalf of O'Brien or not?'

The Spook sat back in his chair and glanced at the woman sat opposite him, then at both of the policemen in turn.

'Personally I don't think you are, but if that is the case it just raises more questions. Questions to which we need answers.'

'OK...'

'Sir?' Waves wasn't sure what was going on, but to admit to anything at this point could only weaken their position.

'It's OK Daniel, I don't think we really have any choice left at this point.'

'But Inspector...'

'Trust me Daniel.' Stands turned back to the agent. 'Firstly, how do you know all this?'

'We've been aware of this group for a very long time, but it has always been a closely guarded secret. As to O'Brien's operation, well his group are actually a sub-group of a sub-group of a sub-group of the CIA. They're more secret than the ones responsible for all the stuff that the CIA does abroad, the kind of things that have to have plausible deniability by the American Government. You know...all the black bag stuff, assassinations, smuggling captured terrorist subjects between secret prison facilities around Europe and the rest of the world.'

The Agent grimaced at the two of them before continuing.

'But this lot get up to some really ugly things. Anyway, to be honest the only reason we stumbled on to O'Brien and his people is because of their interest in the group they are currently hunting. If it wasn't for our own active interest in these people I doubt he would have popped up on our radar. Though I'm not altogether sure whether or not MI6 know what he's up to. We're hoping not for their sake. We normally keep tabs on all foreign Agencies operating within the United Kingdom, as well as keeping an eye on our own brethren. Which, for example, is why we haven't just pulled you two in and taken you down to Thames House for questioning. If we had MI6 would know about it, and very likely CIA as well. We'd like this meeting to remain our little secret, after all the Americans are not the only ones who need to maintain deniability.'

'And how did you follow us?' Stands asked quietly.

Waves perked up at this point. He'd been positive that he hadn't been tailed, and was certain that they'd given the agent following the Inspector earlier the slip.

The Agent noticed Waves' reaction to the question and addressed his response to the Sergeant. 'I'm afraid we cheated a little there. We've put radio transponders in both your cars. We can track you from almost anywhere, and mark your position down to a few feet. From there it was just a matter of finding the meeting point. Nice café by the way…the coffee's not bad.'

Waves shrugged sulkily. 'Yeah, we like it.'

The Spook grinned and directed his next words to the Inspector. 'So my turn to ask the questions, why are you carrying out your own investigation behind O'Brien's back?'

'Funnily enough I'm not really sure…it's difficult to explain.'

'Come on Stands, don't play games with me, this is far too important. Try and explain.'

Stands looked at Waves. He could see that the Sergeant was surprised and disappointed by his decision to play ball. It was a shame that Daniel couldn't for the moment see past his own feelings of selling out, and realise that they were in a position where, not only could they learn something, but if they played their cards right, they might end up with an ally, even if it was an ally with its own agenda.

'OK look, you have to understand that this started out as our case. The old cinema is where it started for us, and we were working it, working the scene, and studying the evidence. It may have all been a little strange, but it was our case. Then with what happened at the hospital morgue it all got a little stranger, but we were hooked, we were going to get to the bottom of it no matter what.'

Stands looked over at Waves again, he seemed a little fidgety.

'Daniel would you get me another coffee.' He looked at the two Agents. 'Would either of you like anything?'

The man sat beside him shook his head. 'Just the information Stands.'

Waves pushed his chair back and squeezed past the woman sat next to him, inadvertently catching a waft of female scent, that warm comforting scent that women's hair so often has, the kind of smell that Daniel associated with nuzzling a woman's neck. Distracted, he went to the counter and ordered two coffees.

Back at the table Stands was wondering why Waves had suddenly appeared so thoughtful as he had got up. The look on his face had suggested to Stands that he was miles away, and Stands wanted to know where. He couldn't help but notice that the female Agent sat opposite him was watching him. Looking at her he smiled thinly as he realised that she was really rather attractive.

'Sorry where was I?'

'At the morgue.'

'Oh yes. Well that was when we were recalled by the Superintendent and introduced to this O'Brien character. Suddenly it was his show, and we had to follow his orders. I know you're probably thinking this is all about ego, but that's not it. When we went to O'Brien's base of operations we learnt some things that just made us more curious than we already were. The thing was we didn't like O'Brien, his team, or his attitude. We don't trust them, and couple that with their moralistic preaching about their crusade…'

'Is that how he put it? His crusade?'

'Yes.' Stands shook his head. 'From what we'd seen we weren't convinced that the same people were responsible for both incidents, and if that was the case, then the ones that took out that little girl's killers were doing everyone a favour.'

Waves came back to the table carrying two white coffees. As he sat down he pushed one across the table to the Inspector.

'Thanks.'

Waves nodded and sipped at his coffee, his chair now slightly skewed towards the woman sat next to him. His eyes focused on her over the rim of his coffee mug.

'Anyway, we were in a position we didn't like. Not only that, but despite all O'Brien's posturing about cleansing the Earth of these abominations, their outfit is hardly pro-active. They seem quite content to just sit there and react to whatever happens around them, rather than taking the initiative themselves. So Daniel and I discussed it and came to the conclusion that the only way to better our situation would be to try and stay one step ahead of everyone else.' He looked intently at the man sat next to him. 'Looks like you beat us on that one.'

'Yes, but all that still doesn't explain your intentions, and that's what I'm really interested in.'

'Our intentions?'

'Yes. What were you going to do when you found them? Procuring weaponry would suggest that you intended to try and eliminate them as O'Brien is intending.'

Both Stands and Waves looked startled. As far as Waves knew his underground connections were good. No one should have known about their little 'transaction'.

'No. No you've got it all wrong. Look we're operating on our own here, and we still know very little about these people except that they can obviously be extremely dangerous. The guns are for self-defence only. I don't know how you operate at MI5, but in the Met we know it makes sense to be as prepared as possible.'

'Fair enough, though it seems only fair to warn you that if you were to go up against these people, the guns wouldn't do you any good.'

As he said this his female companion glanced away from the door towards the Sergeant sat next to her, she could feel his eyes on her.

Daniel had to look away as their eyes met, finding an MI5 operative attractive was just asking for trouble, besides he was intrigued by what the Spook was saying, he wanted to know more.

'So who are these people, more to the point, what are they, and how do you know so much about them?'

'I'm afraid I'm not at liberty to share that information, though I can tell you that as far as we're concerned they're the good guys. Anything else you'll just have to ask them yourselves. Though...' and here he glanced at his companion before smiling at the two Policemen, 'I was told to tell you something, something which may help you gain their trust should they consider you a threat, but you should only share this with them if you have to. We're not sure if they're aware of how much we know about them, and if at all possible we'd like to keep it that way. However, they are under threat, and we intend to do what we can to help them. Hence...'

He nodded towards the woman sat across the table. 'My colleague here is to be your contact. Should you need us you can contact me through her.'

The young woman reached into her jacket and produced a business card, which she casually handed to Waves with an accompanying smile.

Stands raised his eyebrows at Waves, looking at him slyly as he suddenly realised that the Sergeant was distracted by the attractive young woman who had just given him her phone number. He knew he shouldn't, but he couldn't resist teasing him a little. 'That number is for emergencies only Sergeant.'

Daniels mouth tightened, though he did notice the woman blush slightly, which went a long way to curbing his annoyance at his boss.

Stands looked back to the Agent sat next to him.

'So…what was it you were told to tell us?'

*

Five minutes later they were alone once more. The Agents had delivered their information and left with some of the answers they'd wanted.

'So they know about them, and they know about us, surely they know we found them today? They've been tracking our every move for fucks sake. Why not just come out and say so? Christ I've still got that agents ID I pilfered, why didn't they ask for it back?'

'Daniel please, just because they know, and we know they know doesn't mean they're going to come out and admit to anything. Remember they're Spooks, they're advanced game players, and in their line of work knowledge is power. That being the case how can you ever expect them to admit to anything?'

Waves swore under his breath in exasperation.

'They knew damn well we'd been there. They just wanted to find out why we're still alive. I'm sure they thought we'd never survive such an encounter, but having done so they've had to reassess their attitude towards us. Before we were just an annoyance that they had to keep tabs on just in case. Now as far as they're concerned we may be allies with a secret they've been keeping for God knows how many years, which puts us in a much better position. In fact, if we play our cards right we may survive this and even walk away with our careers intact.'

'What do you mean Sir?'

'Well, they've got a problem which is potentially a problem for all of us, and we've got a problem which is potentially a problem for them. If we help them with theirs maybe they'll help us with ours. Perhaps we could truly kill two birds with one stone.'

Waves looked over at the Inspector and raised an

eyebrow at his use of the old adage. 'I don't see how they can help us with O'Brien and his little band of loonies...unless they go in there and kill them all that is, and tempting though that may be I don't think Garfan and Tristellis would go for it.'

The Inspector looked sharply at Waves, at his use of their new acquaintances real names. 'I think unless we're in their company we should refrain from using those names and stick to the cover names they've given themselves, just to be on the safe side. We don't want to draw any more attention to Garfield and Tristan than we have to.'

Waves nodded, understanding immediately that the Inspector was right to be circumspect when it came to anything to do with those two.

Stands glanced at their coffee cups. 'Let's get out of here, it's getting on.'

Waves nodded and stood up nodding to the woman behind the counter who had served them before making his way to the door. He and the Inspector hustled out into the now rainy night and hurried over to the Jag.

'Any chance of a lift back to my car Sir?'

The Inspector just nodded quickly and got in. Once they were under way Stands continued. 'I think our first priority should be to find out as much as we can about their so-called Adversary.'

Waves glanced over at the Inspector as he drove. 'You want me to do some recon for them?'

Stands smiled. 'That was my first thought, yes. I'm sure you're more than capable of scouting out the terrain and coming up with all the necessary information needed when a targets location is already known. Especially now we have a face and an area to look at with CCTV you should be able to trace them after you've got the pictures of that supposed Satanist from Marcus. Just make sure his boss finds out, but only tell Marcus what we want Dr Watkin to hear.'

Waves laughed quietly at the Inspector's

implication. 'It should work, it'll confirm your suspicions if it does.'

'Excellent. Whilst you're playing Jason Bourne I need to come up with a way to make MI5's involvement in this work for us.'

Waves looked at the Inspector questioningly. 'Do you want me to ditch the car and the surveillance for this?'

Stands stared out through the wet windscreen, past the moving windscreen wipers at the lights of the passing traffic. 'No, I think not. In fact it could be to our benefit if our Spook friends are aware of your efforts, especially if we need their help later on.'

Chapter Twenty-One

The following evening Stands and Waves found themselves ensconced in their new friends basement kitchen once more, only this time it was they who were doing all the talking.

'I paid a visit to the CCTV centre in Tower Hamlets and used the times you gave me for the activities of that group you took out at the cinema and managed to track the car going in and out of the car park of a highrise in Heron Quay.' Waves stopped and glanced at his audience, not for the first time thinking how odd the whole situation was.

'According to our sources the building is owned by a corporation which is in turn owned by another corporation, basically a series of dummy corporations which, when you reach the end of the line, is owned by three of the most powerful independent companies in Europe. Funnily enough the CEO's of these companies each owns a flat located in this building. Each one located on one of the top three floors below what appears to be a penthouse apartment, the other ten floors are supposedly office space. The owner of the penthouse is a mystery though. We tried tracking ownership the way we did with the building, but the only name we could come up with is Iblis Holdings Inc. However, the impression I got is that the owner is linked to all of the other corporations, in what way I'm not sure.'

Stands nodded at Waves, indicating that he should continue.

'From what we've been able to dig up it would appear that the building has a state of the art security system, and is guarded around the clock by a detail of security guards supplied by one of the subsidiary companies. I thought it might be a good idea to check them out too, and it seems that they specialise in high level private security, and tend to hire exclusively ex-military types.'

Stands looked around at their hosts and shook his head. 'It would seem that these people are rather serious about not being disturbed. The only access to the building is either through the main entrance or the roof. So unless you two can fly you'll have to go through at least ten men before you can get off the ground floor, and I wouldn't be surprised if they have their own armoury in there.'

Garfan was busy stroking his beard, his eyes unfocused as he processed all the bad news.

Tris made a more immediate response. 'Shit!'

Waves smiled. 'That was my thought exactly.'

He looked enquiringly at Stands, who nodded that he should continue.

'I have to admit that it did all seem a bit too easy to me.'

Garfan stopped stroking his beard. 'What? What's too easy?'

'Well lets consider the scenario; we have a group of men to whom money is no object. They are infamous, within their personal spheres of operation, probably wielding more immediate power than most politicians. This being the case, how come it was so easy for us to find out almost every detail about the building where they have their London residences? Even the security systems and guards, it just seemed a little too easy to me.'

Tris nodded his understanding. 'You've got a suspicious soul sergeant. So where are you going with this?'

'Actually it's more a case of where I went.'

'What?'

'I thought I'd better do some eyes on recon and see for myself, so I turned delivery boy and delivered a package to one of the CEO's.'

Garfan frowned. 'Surely they didn't fall for that old one did they? No offence Sergeant, but you're a little old to be a courier.'

Waves smiled back. 'No offence taken, and actually it was reasonably obvious. I knew they knew, and it's possible they knew that I knew. But what could they do, they couldn't just refuse me access to the building for no good reason. So I managed to get as far as the front desk and hand over the box.'

'And what did that achieve exactly?'

'I found out that all the official information we have on the building is…garbage. Complete fiction.'

'What? How can that be?'

'Like I said, very rich, very powerful men. Though it shouldn't really surprise you that much. Look around you, believe me, I did my homework on this place before we came anywhere near it, and I've already spotted one or two little inconsistencies.'

Tris glanced over at Garfan and grinned. 'He's good!'

He inclined his head in recognition of the compliment.

'Anyway, back to our little problem. I studied the blueprints before going down there, including the records of the security system installation, and there were some pretty obvious differences. Doors where there shouldn't be, and CCTV cameras where they weren't supposed to be either.'

Tris slapped his palms down on his knees in frustration, 'So where the hell does that leave us? I was thinking it was going to be difficult before. Now it just sounds impossible. We can't go in there blind, not with the amount of potential personnel and arms they may have in there. Not forgetting that we have no idea what goes on upstairs. We could be walking into anything.'

Waves nodded, but still held his smile.

'That's what I thought. Which got me thinking…how could you take a building like that? How would I do it if there were no limitations?'

Garfan snorted. 'OK, I bite, how would you do it?'

Waves laughed. 'Ah, now that's the clever bit, I

wouldn't…I'd get Special Forces to do it for me.'

'What…like the SAS or something?'

'Exactly, a couple of squads of SAS going in from the roof and the ground at the same time could clear the entire building in around five minutes. Job done.'

Garfan and Tris exchanged looks before Tris spoke up.

'OK, I don't understand how you plan to involve UKSF, but that's beside the point. The problem is that we don't know what they'd be walking into. If it was just a case of human guards, then yes, I agree the boys in the beige berets would be in and out in a matter of minutes. But lets, for arguments sake, assume that not only are there human guards but maybe some beings with the same kind of abilities as Garfan and myself. Do you really think they'd survive such an encounter on unfamiliar ground, and in such close quarters?'

Stands frowned. 'I'm afraid you have the advantage of us. To be perfectly honest we have absolutely no idea what you two are really capable of. All we can do is trust your judgement, and hope that you don't overestimate your own abilities.'

At this Garfan laughed, causing Tris to frown in response.

'That's not funny Garf.'

'Are we missing something here?'

'Sorry Inspector, Garfan was just laughing at my expense. I very recently had good reason to re-evaluate my faith in my own abilities. But that is neither here nor there. In that kind of situation, in a building, at close quarters, probably with the power out. And everything dark and confused, I'd have to say that we wouldn't have too much of a problem. Especially if we were defending ground we were familiar with.'

Stands raised his eyebrows. 'So you're saying that if you were part of their security, then in that situation you'd have no problem taking out a couple of squads of SAS, possibly the best Special Forces Regiment in the world?'

'Yes.'

Stands looked over at Garfan, who nodded slowly in agreement.

'I'm afraid he's right Inspector. I know it sounds a little unlikely, maybe even arrogant, but you have to remember what we are. Also the fact that we've been doing this sort of thing for centuries. We're warriors. It's what we do…it's what we're best at.'

In an uncharacteristic gesture of frustration Stands slapped his hands loudly onto his thighs and propelled himself out of his seat and stormed over to the fireplace, looking down at the empty grate and presenting his back to the rest of the room.

'Well that really fucks that plan doesn't it!'

Garfan studied the Inspector's back before turning back to Waves. 'What exactly was your plan?' I have to admit to being a little confused here.'

Waves glanced at his boss's back and took a deep breath while collecting his thoughts. 'OK, the way I see it is that everyone seems to be after you two at the moment. On one hand we have some mysterious, and you think, powerful figure holed up in his fortress sending out assassins to kill you in order to leave the way open for this person to do God knows what, but whatever it is we've got to figure that it can't be good…right?'

Tris nodded. 'So far so good.'

'On the other hand we have a branch of America's Spook Squad, which is being funded and guided by what appears to be Christian Fundamentalists to an agenda we can only guess at.

This agency for some reason also seems intent on taking you, and anything like you, out of the picture. Whether it's because you represent some kind of an affront to their religious beliefs, or whether, as Guardians of this Kingdom you stand in the way of some other objective, we don't know. But either way we don't like it, so as far as the Inspector and I are concerned you're the good guys.'

325

At this point Stands turned around to face the room, his eyes roving over his subordinate and the two beings with whom he unaccountably already felt he shared some connection.

'And so are we, which means that as fellow good guys we should be working together against all the bad guys, who in this scenario are represented by your mysterious adversary, and the Americans. So we thought what could be more appropriate than pitting the two against each other.'

Stands raised his eyebrows questioningly, tilting his head to look from Garfan to Tristellis in turn, waiting for a response to his statement. Both were once again looking at each other with expressions that the Inspector found to be unreadable until smiles slowly spread across both their faces.

Tristellis laughed and shook his head, looking first at Waves and then up at Stands.

'If you don't mind me saying so…that is fucking genius!'

Garfan interrupted. 'But how do you see this working? And how did you plan to get the SAS involved in all this?'

Waves grinned. 'Well O'Brien has already informed us that his people at the CIA have already approached UKSF about the possibility of an operation against you. Apparently you have been identified by him and his people as undesirable internal terrorists working to an unknown agenda.

Your strengths and whereabouts have not yet been determined, but it is known that you are well funded and well armed, and therefore represent a clear and present danger to the Government and the people of the United Kingdom.'

'Christ…and the Security Services and UKSF swallowed all this without any intel of their own?' Tris shook his head in disgust. 'And we…Guardians of this Kingdom, get branded as traitors and terrorists.'

Now it was Stands and Wave's turn to laugh.

'Actually…this is where it all starts to become a bit Machiavellian. We hadn't got around to telling you this yet, but it would appear that your existence is not as big a secret as you may think, or like for that matter.'

Garfan was by this point feeling a little bewildered by all this. He and Tris had been doing this for centuries, and in all that time it had been just the two of them. Admittedly there had been occasions when other members of their races had aided them both against particularly difficult, entrenched, or too numerous opponents. And of course there were the operations they had carried out in both World Wars, aiding their mortal allies against greater threats to the Kingdom. But they had always somehow managed to keep themselves to themselves. Now it seemed that on all sides were groups and individuals who were aware of their existence.

Tris studied his friend's face, he could see a sadness in Garfan's eyes. 'Garf, how many times has the world changed around us? It happens…and we adapt. Change is inevitable, and necessary, and if we can't deal with it then we shouldn't be here.'

Garfan looked at Tris's face and nodded. 'I seem to remember saying that very thing to you…'

'You did…and you were right.' Tris looked up at Stands. 'So who else is aware of our existence?'

Stands had to admit that he felt a little uncomfortable with all this.

He couldn't shake the feeling that they were all pawns in a much bigger game, one in which he had no way of ascertaining the rules, or even the objectives.

'MI5 approached us. It seems that they are very much aware of O'Briens operation, and of your existence. In fact I think they've known about you a lot longer than O'Brien has. It would also seem that you are, in some way, approved of. In fact I got the distinct impression that certain high-ups in the Security Services feel that the country in some way owes you a debt of gratitude.'

Waves could not help but grin at the utterly shocked expressions on the faces of the beings sat opposite him.

Tris frowned at the grinning Policeman. 'This better not be a wind-up Stands. If I find out you've been informing on us I will be more than a little displeased.'

Waves stopped grinning and looked to his boss for support.

Stands looked from Waves to Tristellis and cleared his throat. 'Like I said, you're the good guys. You've chosen to trust us, as we have you, and neither Daniel, or myself, would do anything to betray that trust.'

He shook his head before continuing. 'I was actually given certain information…I was told that if such an eventuality arose, and you should be worried about just such a breach of trust, then I was to tell you what they told me.'

'And that was?' said Tris, raising an eyebrow.

'That your country had never truly been able to acknowledge its secret soldiers, and that your country was grateful to those individuals who had fought in both World Wars, and would always be viewed as valued citizens. I'm not entirely sure what they're referring to, but I was told that you would understand.'

Both Tristellis and Garfan visibly relaxed at these words. Garfan who'd just been thinking about the Wars was particularly surprised.

'Well, well, well…and there I was all these years thinking that our involvement in those operations had been a big secret known only to our immediate friends.'

Tris smiled. 'Yeah, but just think what happened to those friends. Where did they end up? And where are they now?'

Waves couldn't help but ask. 'Did you two fight in both the World Wars?'

Garfan looked intently at the young man sat before him. 'We offered our services to human friends of ours who were involved in topsecret covert operations. We never got involved in pitched battles, that's not where our skills lie, but we did take part in various operations involving Guardians from other Kingdoms too. Most memorable for me were trips we made to Scandinavia in the Second World War. I have to admit that one day I'd like to go back there and see the mountains and fjords again without having to worry about getting my head shot off.'

Waves sat back and looked from Garfan to Tristellis and back again, viewing their new friends with a new, and profound feeling of respect. He knew what it was to be a soldier, and being under fire changed your perspective on the world immensely. Something he now knew he shared with the two beings sat in front of him.

Garfan studied the Sergeant and nodded his understanding before continuing. 'It would appear we have very old friends in very high places.' He grinned. 'How very gratifying.'

'For all of us,' Stands chipped in. 'Because of you both Daniel and myself are going to be able to walk away from this with our careers intact. It was one of my major worries that in acting against O'Brien and his Agency we were either going to end up dead, or disgraced. Now we have allies we can act without that hanging over us.'

Stands suddenly grinned and looked at Waves as he remembered something else. 'And you're finally going to be able to use that number.'

Waves shook his head but smiled all the same, meanwhile both Garfan and Tristellis grinned at the two Policemen.

'So…tell us again what you had in mind?'

Chapter Twenty-Two

The following evening, having had a full day of waiting for confirmation from the two policemen, both Garfan and Tristellis were beginning to feel a little jumpy. So much so that when the telephone did eventually ring the two friends looked blankly at it before Tris picked it up on the third ring.

'Hello?'

'Hi, it's Stands.'

'Hello Inspector, it's Tris, what can I do for you?'

'It's all set…the arrangements have been made, and the team will meet you at the appointed place at sunset today. When you get there just ask for Mr Wolf.'

'Mr Wolf?'

Stands chuckled quietly on his end. 'Yes, it would seem that their anonymity is as precious to them as it is to you. In fact I think you'll probably get on like a house on fire.'

Tris laughed. 'Well I've never really understood that particular expression, or known where the hell it came from, but I'll take your word for it Inspector. I take it O'Brien took the bait then?'

'Hook, line and sinker!'

Despite the Inspector not being able to see it Tris smiled in appreciation. 'Well, good luck with your end.'

'Thanks, though Waves and I aren't the ones going in, so I think we'll just keep our fingers crossed for you two OK!'

'Thanks. Well, goodbye Inspector, please don't take this the wrong way, but we're kind of hoping we won't see you or the Sergeant again.'

'Understood, to be honest we're of the same mind. Goodbye Tristellis.'

The Inspector put the phone down, leaving Tris holding the phone lightly with nothing but a low hum coming from the earpiece.

*

By the time they'd geared themselves up for what lay ahead the weather had decided to play along too. It had started out overcast, but as they shut the door of the house behind them the clouds were getting darker, threatening rain in the not too distant future. With the wind picking up in a playful, blustery way, it all promised one hell of a storm if all the elements managed to get their act together.

Looking up both of them stood, feet planted firmly apart as if they were sailors on a rolling deck. Breathing deeply each of them grinned into the wind, the promise of violence once again sending a warm feeling of truly being alive through the two of them, the kind of appreciation of the moment that only comes when facing a very real and very possible death.

It was an easy walk from St Mark's Square to Paddington Green. Right, down Prince Albert Road, along St John's Wood Road, and then left onto the Edgeware Road. As they neared the Marylebone fly-over the skyline began to take on a more foreboding aspect as the concrete tower of Paddington Green Police Station loomed to their right. As the light was just beginning to disappear the huge tower of concrete looked even more like a huge castle keep.

Dressed in their long leather coats, both buttoned up against the wind and to conceal the full battle gear they were wearing underneath, they looked a little like a pair of Goths on their way to a gig. As they approached the Police Station Tris looked round and down at Garfan trying to gauge his mood.

'Well, this should be interesting.'

Neither of them really liked the idea of exposing themselves to humans like this. Such close scrutiny went against everything they'd been taught, but there didn't seem to be any other option.

'At least there is a precedent for this.' Tris said, trying to make Garfan look at it in an optimistic light.

Garfan's brow furrowed as he walked beside Tristellis. 'That was around seventy years ago Tris and we set it, and back then we never needed to worry about computers and CCTV. We're risking complete exposure, not only for us but for all our people.'

'But you heard what Inspector Stands said, he's arranged for all the electronic surveillance to be suspended whilst we're in the building, and he promised that any footage taken of us before the system is stopped will be removed as soon as we've left the building.'

Garfan snorted derisively. 'I know what he said Tris, but I just don't believe it.'

He shook his head in disgust. 'So why the fuck are we about to do this?'

Garfan's shoulders sagged. 'What choice do we have? There's no other way.'

Paddington Green loomed over them menacingly as they got nearer to the entrance. The tall grey tower block structure lacked any comforting human detailing, looking instead like a vast monument to the solidity of steel and concrete.

Having crossed the road to get there they halted in unison as they contemplated the future that might await them inside one of the most secure police stations in the country. It was no coincidence that the most dangerous criminals and terrorists were brought here, the place was a modern day fortress.

Looking at each other Tris smiled, treating Garfan to a broad wink before he took the first step towards whatever awaited them inside.

*

As they got to the door it took all of their self control to walk calmly in and not turn tail and run. They had become aware of being watched as soon as they'd gotten within twenty feet of the doors. The pair let the doors swing quietly shut behind them as they went forward towards the reception point and the Desk Sergeant sat behind it who was looking at them both with open curiosity.

Garfan's mood was not in any way improved by the indignity of having to eye the policeman over the edge of the built in reception desk which came up almost to his nose. Tristellis glanced sideways at his friend and laid a gently restraining hand on his shoulder.

The policeman's curiosity soured as he regarded the top half of the heavily bearded face scowling at him.

'We're here to see Mr Wolf.'

The policeman's face went strangely blank at these words. Taking a breath the suddenly pale policeman nodded before reaching under his desk and audibly flicking some kind of switch. Tristellis stiffened in alarm until he noticed a slight drop in the surrounding background hum of electronics. Garfan had felt the tension in Tris's hand on his shoulder and was ready to move at the slightest provocation until he too noticed that the red lights on the visible surveillance cameras had all gone off. Then he noticed the almost inaudible change, inaudible at least to humans, of the background hum. Then he noticed that the tension had left Tris's hand, a physical indication that all was well.

Maybe Stands really was someone they could trust after all. Tris gave Garfan's shoulder a quick squeeze before taking his hand away. The Desk Sergeant picked up a phone and tapped in a few digits then waited for someone to answer what was obviously an internal call.

Both of them could hear the tinny ringing coming from the receiver the policeman held, which was quickly replaced by a man's voice.

'Yes?'

The policeman glanced at them as he replied.

'They're here.' With that he put the phone down and looked at the strange pair standing in front of the desk. He didn't have a clue who they were, but he had a fairly good idea who they were about to be associating with.

'Someone will escort you through the door over there,' he said pointing to a very secure looking door at the back of the room that opened just as he indicated.

Standing in the doorway was a tall athletic looking man dressed in a black T-shirt, black combat trousers and black boots, but he didn't look like a policeman. Though if he were regular army there would have been something to show it, insignia, or some indication of rank or regiment. The lack of it left them in no doubt that he was Special Forces.

He beckoned them forward. 'This way gentlemen, if you'd both like to follow me.'

With no other options the two of them stepped forward and followed the soldier through the doorway into a stereotypically institutional corridor, replete with strip lighting and shiny linoleum flooring. The soldier walked quickly, and surprisingly quietly, keeping himself about a metre ahead of Garfan and Tristellis.

The unidentified soldier turned his head slightly in there direction when he spoke. 'We've been given a ground floor briefing room next to the garage at the back of the building. It's from there that we'll be taken to the target.'

Tris was impressed, though he wasn't sure what he'd been expecting, it was a good start that their escort seemed completely unfazed by the odd couple who would be joining them on this little adventure.

Coming towards the end of the corridor the soldier came to a halt before a door on their right that he indicated they should enter first. The glass panel in the door was covered so Tris didn't know what he was walking into. Glancing at Garfan he shrugged, reached for the handle and pushed the door open.

As he and Garfan stepped into the large room they both scanned the area out of habit, both of them on the alert for anything that didn't feel right. As they did so the assembled men, all similarly dressed in black, all snapped to attention. One figure stood in front of the men, a brawny older man with a dark beard turned towards them and smiled before coming to attention himself and saluting them.

Stunned, Tristellis and Garfan stood there not knowing what to do, or how to react until the bearded man tilted his head to the side slightly and offered them some advice. 'It is still customary for a fellow officer to return a salute.'

Both feeling a little foolish they returned the salute, both of them feeling confused by what was going on. They had been made officers in Her Majesties Armed Forces as a thank you for their service during the First World War. Then they had both been promoted when they had presented themselves for action in the Second World War, but it had never been officially recorded as far as they were aware, neither of them knew how the hell this Special Forces Officer would know anything about it.

Grinning the officer offered them his hand. 'I'm Major Wolf, and welcome to SAS 21st Battalion. I realise you must have many questions, but I'm hoping they can wait for a more opportune moment. We don't have much time before our American friends get here so I'll keep this as brief as possible. The salute by the way was a courtesy, we received a top secret briefing regarding you both and have been told that you still rate the rank of Captains, and that you are just to be referred to as Forest and Stone.'

The Major nodded to each in turn. 'We were also told that you would be able to shed some more light on what we're about to go up against…and that we should take your word as gospel, no matter how far fetched it may sound.'

The Major raised his eyebrows as Tristellis nodded in response to his words.

335

'Good, we also have extra kit for the pair of you. We'll obviously be wearing balaclavas during the briefing we expect to get from the Americans, as our anonymity is fundamental to our work, and in this case will serve to help keep your presence a secret. We know we're going into a multi-levelled building from the ground, unfortunately going in from the air as well is out of the question due to the impression we're trying to give to the Americans. If you could take it from there, fill in the gaps as it were...'

Major Wolf stepped back leaving the open area before the group of soldiers for Tristellis and Garfan. Tris stepped forward uncertainly, he'd not come prepared to give a briefing, this wasn't really his thing. Garfan could sense Tris's nervousness, and though it was tempting to just step back and watch him sweat, this really wasn't the time to appear as though they didn't know what they were doing.

Garfan stepped forward to stand beside Tris. 'As the Major rightly said the target is a fourteen storey building in Heron Quay, in the Borough of Tower Hamlets. We will be entering through the one ground floor access point. On the ground floor is a large reception area which is guarded by ex-military security guards who we believe will have access to weaponry, probably semi and fully automatic, probably HK's. It is in fact likely that the whole building is guarded by men with guns, luckily it's beginning to get late, and by the time we get there it will be around eleven o'clock, just when their energies will begin to flag. Our major problem is that we have no idea about the true layout of the building, the official building plans are wrong, so it will be a case of taking the building room by room if necessary. Sweep and secure, I believe this is something you're familiar with.'

The men in the room all stayed silent, though their expressions were all that more sombre having learned how little reliable intel they had on the op.

Tristellis was quietly impressed by Garfan's

professional sounding assessment of the situation. Garfan stood still and let the soldiers take in what he'd said before continuing.

'However, that is not the worst of it.' He looked at the Major. 'How much time do we have before they get here?'

'Half an hour, maybe more. But we will have warning of their arrival in the building.'

'Good. Now Major, exactly what were you told about us?'

The Major raised his eyebrows. 'Not as much as I would like. In fact it's what they didn't tell us that worried me, I know that you are both decorated Captains who have seen action with Special Forces, and that you had specialist information specific to this mission. Though I've never seen or heard of either of you before.' At this point he looked a little embarrassed. 'I was also told, as I mentioned earlier, that you may share information that we would have trouble believing, and that should it come to it any orders you give in the field are to be followed without question. Orders such as this I will point out right now I am far from happy about.'

Garfan looked at Tris who just shrugged. 'Well thank you for your candour Major. We'll try to refrain from giving you any orders, but there are some things you need to know. The worst part of this situation is that we have reason to believe that the building is also guarded by people like us.' Garfan glanced up at Tris and nodded.

Smiling Tristellis undid his long leather coat, slipped it off his shoulders and let it fall to the floor behind him. The shuffling of feet and chorus of indrawn breaths was the only response. Both Garfan and Tristellis were pleased and relieved, maybe this would work after all.

Tris stood before the men dressed from neck down in what could only be described as armour. His arms and legs were protected by bracers and greaves made of hardened leather, as was the breast plate that was moulded to fit his well muscled torso. The leather itself was mottled in tones of brown and grey, lending it an almost camouflaged effect. There was no detailing of any kind on the armour, unlike historic steel plate armour which generally was decorative as well as functional. Under the hardened leather armour appeared to be a mixture of dark cloth and various scraps of what could only be described as chain mail. Dotted around his person were also various sheaths displaying the hilts of knives and daggers strapped securely to calves and forearms. As he slowly turned to allow the men to see the full extent of his armour his two favourite long daggers strapped to his back became apparent with their downward pointing hilts. If this wasn't enough Garfan followed suit, shedding his own coat to reveal identical body armour moulded to his smaller, though heavier build, and displaying on his back not sheathed daggers, but his favourite hand axes.

Standing there before this group of elite soldiers, the SAS, probably the finest Special Forces Unit in the world, Garfan had expected to feel naked and exposed. But now it came to it he felt curiously elated, empowered even. The initially shocked expressions on the faces of the soldiers had turned to curiosity.

'As you can see we've come prepared for a different kind of opponent. One who uses blades rather than guns. An opponent who fights hand to hand. One for which the confined areas of our target site are ideal. They will not be afraid of you or your weapons, in fact they will consider them a weakness. During this operation your objective will be to suppress or eliminate anyone carrying a gun and secure the building, leaving those like ourselves to us.' Garfan smiled at his audience. 'Any questions?'

All eyes immediately went to the Major who was frowning at the amount of confusion in the room around him. 'There is obviously something we're missing here, as I don't understand how someone equipped as you are is going to beat a bullet, or the man firing it?'

Tristellis tilted his head whilst studying the Major.

'I think a demonstration is called for. Could

338

everyone pick up their chairs and take them to the sides of the room and stay there so that we've got some room.'

The soldiers did as they were asked at a nod from the Major, leaving a space around ten square metres in the centre of the room. Tristellis hadn't moved from where he was facing the Major.

'I noticed that you have your sidearm with you. Could you move towards the back of the room, leaving enough space between us for me to be unable to prevent you firing your weapon.'

The Major looked at him questioningly, but obliged him by following his request, putting about eight metres between them.

'Now could you draw your weapon and make sure that the safety is off.'

'What?'

'I'm going to ask you to try and shoot me Major…and you can't do that with the safety on.'

'You can't be serious. Besides I have no wish to be skewered by one of your knives, thrown, or otherwise.'

Tris laughed briefly, it died in his throat when he saw the expression on the Major's face. 'Sorry Major, please take no offence. I promise you I will not be throwing any of my knives at you.'

Garfan felt it was time to get on with it.

'Please Major, this is necessary and I can assure you he knows what he's doing. When I say 'now' take aim on my companion and try and shoot him.'

'This is madness.'

'Consider it an order Major, your men will all vouch for it being given as such.'

Making a dubious face at Garfan, Major Wolf nodded before checking his gun and clicking the safety off.

'Ready…now!'

Before the Major had his gun at eye level he felt himself pushed and held in place backwards, off-balance with his back wrapped around Tristellis's torso and with a blade at his throat. Tris smiled down at him.

'It's OK Major, don't be alarmed. I'm going to take the blade away from your neck and release you slowly. Please refrain from trying to shoot me.'

The Major took a deep breath as Tristellis levered him back up and around him so that he wouldn't fall backwards. 'I don't think I could if I tried.'

He looked around at the stunned faces of his men. Focusing on the man who'd escorted Garfan and Tristellis to the room he raised his eyebrows and just got a shrug in response.

'Sergeant, what just happened?'

The soldier shook his head. 'I'm sorry Sir, I have no fucking idea,' he said incredulously. 'He moved so fast he was just a blur. I've never seen anything like it, not in real life anyway.'

Garfan stepped back into the centre of the room so that he was stood at Tris's side. 'Major I'm sorry if you found that in any way embarrassing, but please believe me when I say that if we had to we could take out your entire unit here and now before any of you could do anything about it.'

The immediate tensing of his men was all the warning the Major needed for him to take action. 'Stand down!'

The shouted order sounded even louder in the confined space of the briefing room. The sudden silence following it seeming all the more distinct as the Major scanned his men's faces.

'These…gentlemen are here to lead this unit into what would appear to be a rather unusual situation. I would recommend that you all listen very carefully to anything they have to say, and do whatever the fuck they tell you to without question. Are we clear?'

An immediate and resounding 'Yes Sir' left little doubt that iron hard discipline was second nature to these professional soldiers. The Major turned to look at the armoured figures stood almost casually in the centre of the

340

room.

'So what should we do if we come across someone like you in there?'

Tris spoke up, turning his head to look at them all as he answered. 'Back up slowly and do not engage unless you have to. Leave them to us.'

*

Fifteen minutes later both Tristellis and Garfan were sat, incognito, at the back of the briefing room. Both were sat in the far left-hand corner of the room, their armour hidden from view underneath black army fatigues. Their faces hidden behind black balaclavas just like all the other seated figures in the room. The Major was standing at the front of the room waiting for his second batch of 'guests' to arrive. The squad had been warned only moments earlier that O'Brien had entered the building along with Inspector Stands, and were being escorted to the briefing room.

Luckily Tris and Garfan had finished their 'disclosure' and were just putting the room back together when they were informed of the Americans arrival.
A few short, barked commands from the Major had seen surplus black army gear shoved in their hands by various edgy, but grinning soldiers. Now here they were, sat at the back of the room trying to look inconspicuous.

Moments later there was a knock on the briefing room door quickly followed by it opening inward to reveal the tall muscular form of the American Agent O'Brien. Tris couldn't help but sneer slightly underneath his balaclava. So this was the American bullyboy Stands and Waves had described, he certainly fit the description. Tris had no problem attributing such behaviour to such a one as this, talk about stereotypes. Tris managed to replace his scowl with a smile as the burly American was followed

followed into the room by the more diminutive Inspector. An unlikely ally, but one to which he had quickly warmed.

Stands, for his part, knew that Tristellis and Garfan were supposed to be in the room, at least that was how they had planned it to be. He was sincerely hoping that nothing had gone wrong. In glancing around the room he was reassured by how calm the atmosphere in the room appeared to be. Then he noticed what he thought was the give-away, in the far left-hand corner of the room there appeared to be a soldier a good head shorter than any of the other figures in the room, it could only be Garfan. He could only guess that the taller figure sat next to him must be Tristellis. Stands let out a small sigh, oddly enough, knowing that the two warriors were in the room actually made him feel more relaxed. It was only now that he realised how tense he'd been since he had been picked up by O'Brien and his driver. As it was he was trying to tune O'Brien out.

'...you'll be split evenly into three teams, point, back-up and mop-up. Your objective gentlemen is to enter and secure the building, subdue any resistance, using lethal force if necessary, and to make sure that internal systems, both electrical and mechanical are not compromised or sabotaged.

Then hand over any prisoners to my team who will arrive once we have received the all clear from the Major. At that point we will require your assistance in loading the prisoners for transportation to a secure facility.'

It was at this point that Stands stopped listening. He was amazed by the bullshit the brawny American was churning out. How in all good conscience could he knowingly send soldiers in against beings like Garfan and Tristellis and not warn them what they were going up against. Had they really been attacking the two Guardians Stands had no doubt that it would have been a suicide mission.

The Inspector had already overheard O'Brien alluding to this when talking to one of his lackeys at their base in Wapping. Stands was well aware that he intended to use the SAS as a battering ram and a diversion, only to be followed by a team of his own agents deployed with high-tech weapons and some kind of nerve agent in gas form. The lying bastard had no intention of taking any prisoners. He wanted them dead, and anyone who aided or abetted them. There was no room for compromise in the fantasy world of O'Brien and his Christian fundamentalist buddies.

Stands was still vaguely aware that O'Brien was talking to the group of men in front of them as he studied the group of men in the room. He twisted his wrist and glanced down at his watch, and felt his body slowly un-knotting itself, he had very little to do from here on in apart from keeping tabs on O'Brien in case he decided to do anything unexpected. Tristellis and Garfan were exactly where they were supposed to be, and according to his watch Waves would be with MI5 just about now.

As he slowly tuned back in to what O'Brien was saying he realised that the American was preaching again, only this time it sounded more like something a coach might say in a locker room before a big Monday night American football game.

Only he wasn't telling them the truth. Appalled, Stands looked around at the soldiers sat attentively before them. Now he was looking more closely he saw that the balaclavas didn't hide everything. He could see a slight tightening around the eyes of most, accentuating existing laughter lines, as well as those caused by very real pain and hardship. Stands unconsciously shook his head slightly and glanced at the Major stood next to him.

The Major was standing at ease, but there was a steady strength, an impression of a spring, coiled and inactive, but full of potential energy. The Major must have felt Stands eye's on him as his impassive face turned to look at him, his gaze swept over the American as he looked towards the Inspector, and winked before facing front again as if nothing had happened. Slightly taken aback his mouth twitched upwards towards a smile before he managed to attain control once more, keeping his face poker blank.

As O'Brien wound down he was half expecting him to say he 'loved the smell of napalm in the morning', a quote which would have been the icing on the cake for Stands. No wonder Americans had such a hard time when abroad with walking stereotypes like O'Brien mouthing off left right and centre.

Stands couldn't wait to see his face when MI5 turned up. As soon as the Major entered the building with his SAS team following behind Garfan and Tristellis Waves would signal MI5 and a rather large number of armed response units would descend on O'Brien and his team from adjoining side roads in time to catch the Americans toting illegal firearms and some incredibly illegal nerve gas. Stands silently cursed the civilised society that he helped to protect. Permanent expulsion was too good for the likes of O'Brien and his cadre of bloodthirsty bigots.

If he had his way he'd take the lot of them, guns and all and lock them in a room with the shadowy Adversary Garfan and Tristellis were after, maybe then O'Brien and his like might attain some perspective as to who the bad guys really were.

*

The last words out of O'Briens mouth were a further request for speed and stealth before signing off with an arrogant, '...thank you men, I know you'll do your duty.'

Stands was amazed the Major didn't just put a bullet in him right where he stood, patronising twat, hell he'd do it himself if he thought he could get away with it. Major Wolf had just stepped forward and thanked O'Brien for his rousing words and excellent strategic planning, he was impressed that the Major managed to keep a straight face as he said it.

O'Brien seemed not to have noticed the sarcasm, taking the comments at face value as he moved towards the door, tilting his head at the Inspector to indicate that he should follow.

Stands ignored him and offered his hand to the Major. 'Thank you for your assistance Major.'

Major Wolf took his hand and pumped it once, a stifled smile crinkling the corners of his mouth before he turned back to the room. 'Attention!'

As one the men seated in the room came to their feet and saluted. Stands grinned, the facetiousness of the gesture wasn't lost on him.

'Time to get going I suppose.'

Chapter Twenty-Three

By the time the SAS team drove past Canary Wharf, and on to Heron Quay the weather had definitely turned. The wind seemed to howl from every direction at once, bringing with it an almost solid wall of rain. Looking around them as they got out of the van both Garfan and Tristellis were reminded of the storm they'd endured when they'd confronted the unknown assassins in the old cinema in South London. Thinking this they both exchanged a troubled look as the coincidence in circumstances finally came home to them.

Tris opened his mouth to say something, but Garfan beat him to it. 'Don't bother.' He shook his head and shouted into the wind, 'Lets not start reading anything into this.'

Tris nodded before running his hand through his already wet hair and hastily throwing a salute at the balaclava clad men behind them as he sprinted off into the howling dark.

*

Tristellis got to the corner of the building first, his longer legs yet again frustrating Garfan's attempts to keep up. But that wasn't the only reason, Garfan was well aware that Tris had a tendency to try to protect him in battle. As he caught up Tris turned his head towards him and grinned.

'Nice of you to join me.''

'Nice of you to wait! So…you ready for this?'

'You lead, I'll be right behind you.'

Garfan nodded and took off round the corner, his short legs pumping. Tris just a step behind him, his own feet moving at speed as he raced up the wet steps to the doors of the building only moments behind Garfan. When Tristellis slapped his palms against the glass of the doors Garfan was already knelt at the side of the door, both hands pressed to the area where the lowest hinge was behind the bulk of the frame. As soon as his palms hit the glass Tristellis gathered his will, his thoughts focusing on the excitation of the molecules within the glass, all thought focused on rupturing the integrity of its construction.

Tris was somewhat startled when the glass almost instantly exploded inwards, shattering into tiny almost cubic pieces. Garfan almost fell backwards at the sudden noise, his attempts to soften the metal of the hinges suddenly superfluous. He watched as Tristellis threw himself through the jagged glass bordered opening towards the security guards who were rapidly closing in on the doors. Rolling sideways he braced himself and leapt through right behind Tristellis, discarding his coat as he went just as Tris had done.

He found himself slightly behind Tris as he rolled to his feet, all six of the reception area guards had come to a halt in a rough semi-circle before Tristellis, weapons seemingly materialiusing from nowhere into their hands and raised in their direction, moments away from mowing the pair of them down where they stood.

Tris rolled right, Garfan knowing instantly to go left, both moving with preternatural speed towards the opposing ends of the guard's semi-circle with weapons in hand, arms sweeping in apparent unity, opening throats and dancing on to the next. The only shot fired was the dying reflex of the last guard as Garfan yanked one of his hand axes free from the unfortunate man's chest.

Looking down at the bodies Garfan noticed that one of them had a large bunch of keys attached to his belt. Leaning down he unclipped the bunch of keys and shook them at Tristellis.

'Time to go, though with any luck we shouldn't have to worry about any more locked doors.'

Tris nodded grim faced as he knelt and wiped the blood from his two long daggers on the chest of the man he'd just killed. 'We need to go up now. Throw the flash-bang out the door and let's get this done before we have time to think through what we're really doing here.'

Garfan reached inside his moulded leather cuirass and withdrew one of the small black puck shaped stun grenades that the Major had given them in order to signal that they were in and that the entrance was clear. Thumbing the arming switch he negligently threw it behind him through the shattered doorway behind them.

The ear-shattering bang, and momentarily blinding flash that accompanied it illuminated nothing other than the still bleeding bodies of the dead guards. Tristellis and Garfan had already moved on.

*

Just minutes later they found themselves at the top of the building with apparently nowhere else to go but forward.

'Tris stop! This is it, behind this door is where this has to end…one way or another.'

Tristellis grimaced as he wiped blood off his hands. 'Ever the optimist Garf.' Tris shook his head. 'Well standing here isn't going to do us any good. Outclassed or not we still have to try.'

Garfan and Tristellis pushed the double doors before them open. Having expected them to be locked, both were a little surprised to see that there appeared to be no locking mechanism of any kind on the doors, or as part of the frame.

Inside the doors was a single huge room devoid of decoration, though the walls themselves seemed to suggest patterns, possibly writing, or maybe geometric diagrams, with the low level of light in the room it was hard to tell.

Besides which there attention as they stepped into the room was suddenly taken by the figure sat in an old, well worn leather armchair which unaccountably neither had noticed until they were fully inside the room.

It was only then that the double doors behind them seemed to close of their own volition, sealing themselves with a suggestively audible click. It was only then that another figure seemed to swim into focus directly behind the seated figure they'd initially seen, though both were so heavily shadowed no discernible detail of either could be seen.

Tristellis glanced at Garfan whispering, 'I don't like this.'

Both were startled by the reply that they both heard in their heads, but which didn't seem to get there by way of their ears.

'What is there to like Tristellis? You break into my house, kill my servants, and then have the temerity to enter my inner sanctum with the intention of murdering me. Tell me Tristellis, do they pay you well for your unthinking loyalty?'

'What?' Garfan snarled. 'You started this with the murder of that little girl. We've just come here to make sure that no more innocent blood is spilt.'

'Innocent blood? And even then, innocent of what?'

'Word play won't save you, whoever you are.'

'Yes, you bested my guards, but do you think you could beat their Captain?' He gestured weakly with his hand to the large shadowy figure looming behind him.

This signal was all the figure needed by way of order to step forward around the chair behind which he had stood so patiently. As he passed it his hand briefly stretched out and touched his master's shoulder before he came to a halt in front of the armchair. As he did this he pushed back the hood of his cloak and undid the clasp at his throat before slipping it off his shoulders and letting it fall to the floor behind him.

Without the cloak they could finally see what they were up against, and neither of them liked what they saw. He was beautiful in a way, if beauty could be attributed to such a being. His long black hair was swept back into a ponytail making his pointed ears plainly visible, as were the many scars that could be seen wherever his tanned skin was exposed. He wore little other than leather trousers over which he wore a leather battle harness, cuirass and greaves very similar in design to those that were worn by Tristellis and Garfan, only his were black and charred looking as though they were regularly exposed to flame.

His arms reached around to his back grasping for the weapons he kept strapped there in exactly the same way as Tristellis and Garfan's. Seeing this they reached for their own. When the huge warrior's hands whipped round from his back he had a short sword in his right hand, the blade roughly two foot long, and in the other a large dagger similar in design to Tristellis's. He smiled as he brought these weapons on guard, then winked just before his entire body suddenly burst into flame. His figure became slightly hazy within its shield of yellow and orange flame, the obvious heat distorting everything immediately around it.

Tris and Garfan knew instantly that it was not just an illusion employed to frighten the ignorant, they could both feel the heat from where they stood. How could a being stand such heat, even a demon, for that is obviously what this creature must be, a fire elemental, a true demon, just as Elarris had said.

Almost without thinking Garfan and Tristellis started circling away from each other, around the blazing creature, both knowing that to split the elemental's attention would give them the best chance of taking him quickly. In fact Garfan's mind was working overtime, he had already noticed that when he and Tristellis started moving the huge elemental made no move to protect it's master, even as they continued moving and getting closer to the ancient being in the armchair. Maybe confronting the demon captain would be unnecessary.

'Tut, tut Garfan, do you really think I need his protection from the likes of you?'

The voice in his mind was scathing, and drew his eyes to where the being sat calmly returning his gaze. Garfan shook his head in disgust, what had he always told Tris, never take an enemy at his word. Swiftly switching both his hand axes to one hand he quickly drew a small, flat, leaf shaped throwing knife from his belt, the blade seeming to fly from his hand almost as soon as he held it. He switched his weapons back to both hands just as he watched the blade he'd thrown come to an abrupt halt in mid-air before the face of the ancient being. The blade hung there suspended for a moment longer before it almost casually fell to the floor with a soft clang.

'I suppose you had to try, though now you know better my earth cousin.'

Meanwhile Tristellis had seen the failure of his friend's blade, and knew that the only way to defeat the Adversary would be to confront him together using what little magic they possessed in conjunction with a physical attack. Which meant that first they would have to put this hulking great demon down.

Tris lunged, his blades wheeling before him, the captain's short sword swept through the point Tris's head had occupied just moments before.

Tris pushed the attack wanting to get within the boundary caused by the demons wickedly fast sword, knowing that the demon would trust the defence of his flame to stop anyone getting close enough to plunge a blade into him, and that he would be wary of Garfan attacking whilst he was engaged so intimately with Tris.

Garfan watched as Tris pushed forward his attack, waiting for the perfect moment to launch his own attack against an undefended flank or back. He knew that they were in trouble, this warrior was at least as fast as they were, with a longer reach and with the flames it meant certain suicide to get too close to him. Suddenly seeing an opening Garfan sprang forward into the melee, his axes sweeping in blurred patterns before him as he went for the demon's back.

Watching from his armchair the ancient elemental's eyes were bright, it had been hundreds of years since he had seen such a spectacle. His captain was all but unbeatable, and had been for centuries, but these two were good. Fast, evasive, and fierce. True warriors, and with two of them the captains superiority was being sorely tested. The combat was difficult to follow, but it looked as though the winner would be the last one to make a mistake.

Both Tris and Garfan had come to the same conclusion. No matter how they feigned an attack to give the other an opening the demon was too damned fast, not to mention the flames which created such an excellent defence, not only with the heat, but with the light. Also the way the flames swept around with the demons movement leaving vivid trails of flame, it was very...off-putting.

Tris circled slowly back towards Garfan, their defence being easier with two pairs of arms in closer proximity. He could see from his friend's expression that Garfan was as stumped as he was. Getting closer Tris mouthed a couple of words at Garfan, hoping he'd read his intent.

'Back off!'

Garfan nodded and they both stepped quickly back out of range of the demon's sword and dagger and kept going until they were almost back to the door through which they'd originally entered. As they back-peddled their flaming opponent made no move to follow them and press an attack, choosing rather to stand his ground and relax his stance.

Both felt the relief of the relatively cool air around them, what with the exertion of battle and the demon's flames it was like being in a room with a bonfire. Both were sweating profusely, the moisture leaving streaks in the sooty smudges they were both covered with.

352

Garfan's shoulders slumped as he took a moment to relax. 'This is ridiculous, with this kind of stalemate it's nothing more than a test of stamina.'

Tris nodded in agreement, though he grinned as he saw the demon captain extinguish his flame. He stood in almost the exact same spot he had started, his shoulders heaving as he panted quietly. His eye's were on the two friends, and his expression which had once been haughty, now displayed a grudging respect.

Garfan and Tris straightened and nodded to the demon captain, acknowledging a fellow warrior. In the silence of the moment the weak laughter that intruded from behind the demon captain seemed very out of place.

'Bravo Guardians. Never has my captain met his equal in battle, yet you two together would seem to have managed to do just that. I declare this contest a draw.'

The demon captain looked displeased for a moment before he schooled his expression to blankness and turned back to his master and returned to his position behind the armchair where he once more became little more than a looming presence in the background.

Garfan clenched his hands tightly around the smooth wooden hafts of his hand axes. 'Contest? We came here to kill you and you speak of contests as if this were a game. Who are you? Are you truly Shaitan, the one spoken of in the Muslim's Holy book?'

'I have had many names, however, you may call me Iblis, but surely you are not here because of those old rivalries?'

'Old rivalries? I don't know what you're referring to, but you yourself hailed us as Guardians, so you know who and what we are, and therefore why we are here. You cannot be allowed to do as you please without any thought for the beings around you. We protect the people of this kingdom, and you are an enemy of those people.'

The ancient being uncurled himself from his seat and leant forward towards Garfan and Tristellis. Only now could they see any of the beings face, though both wished that they couldn't. It was black as if burnt into a mask with dry deep lines in it making the skin look like bark. But what was worse was the expression, a look of arrogance and malignant hatred that could not be hidden.

'I am no ones enemy. It is true that once I fought for my people's freedom, but I was betrayed by those you answer to, not mankind. Despite this betrayal I hold no grudge. All the Elders of the races of Jinn were probably right. It does seem best that we elementals should exist in secret...but that does not mean that we cannot seek power for our kind in other places and in other ways.'

'Power...you speak of power, but why would our peoples desire power? Can it feed us? Clothe us? No. We serve ourselves and guide those who need it. We do not want power.'

'Noble words Garfan, and I would expect little else from a representative of your kind. Your people have always hidden themselves away, though you have had more contact with Man than our cousins of the Water and the Air, you have managed to avoid Man's taste for blood and conquest. Even you Tristellis would agree with your friend. Those that Men once called Elves were often regarded as the friends of Man. But us, so called demons and evil spirits, Man has always feared our flames, and as such has always persecuted us, even from the beginning when we wished nothing more than to guide in the same way as your people. But no, what Man fears and does not understand...he hates. We have been despised and hunted for millennia. We once tried to rebel, and we were put down by our own kin. Now you wish to stop us conducting legitimate business too? Can we have no freedom? We are not devils, we are the same...'

Garfan and Tristellis were taken aback by the suddenly beseeching look in the eyes of what must be one of Man's oldest enemies and experienced doubt. Tristellis slowly sheathed his daggers and then ran his hands through his damp shaggy hair as he leant closer to Garfan.

'What do we do now? We don't seem to have any

way of completing our mission, I don't think we could eliminate him even if we wanted to, and right now I'm beginning to wonder what we're doing here?'

Garfan looked up at Tris in surprise. 'Just think of that little girl Tris and you'll remember why we're here. But you're right, I see no way forward from here. We were not prepared for this.'

From outside the room the muted sound of semi-automatic gunfire could just be heard, and was slowly getting nearer. By the sound of it the SAS were on the floor just below them.

'Sounds like the cavalry's here.'

Garfan nodded as he turned back to their adversary. 'Why are you here? If you wished for us to be at peace why did you not approach our Elders? Why all the deception, the hiding and the needless bloodshed?'

'Need you ask the hunted why they hide? The pursued and persecuted why they fight? Your Elders would like nothing more than to finally see my head on a spike, but I won't be giving them that satisfaction.'

The being shook his head sadly, as if the weight of the world were his could they but see it. Then once more he pierced them with his attention.

'You have ruined my position here, but my people will prevail. Remember that Guardians, and consider the gift I give you...of your lives, and consider why the Devil would let you live?'

With that the ancient elemental made a complicated gesture with one hand and darkness bloomed inside both their minds.

*

The next thing they knew both were being shaken by Major Wolf whilst two of his men stood over them, the torches on their weapons casting the only light in the pitch black room.

'Are you OK? I have to admit I was a little worried when we came in through those doors and saw you two lying there. I had a horrible feeling we'd just walked into something we couldn't handle.'

Tris groaned as he sat up. 'No Major, it would appear that it was us that did that.'

Garfan struggled to stand as quickly as he could. 'Did you see anyone? An old being garbed in black, and a huge warrior dressed like us?'

The Major looked at him blankly then shook his head. 'No. No one. Though there does appear to be another exit from this room, and possibly from the building, one that we were not aware of. At the back of the room there is what appears to be a small service lift. My men are checking it out now. I'd guess whoever left you here must have gone that way.'

Tristellis stood in one graceful motion as he helped Garfan to his feet. 'So Major how did you find us?'

The Major forced a smile. 'This is the last room in the building, though we did follow a trail of bodies to get here...there wasn't a lot left of some of them.' He raised an eyebrow. 'Some of them seem to have combusted in some way?'

'The less you know about these things the easier it will be for all of us Major. How about your men? Were there any casualties?''

The Major grimaced. 'One dead, two wounded though they'll both live. It appears your insertion created major confusion. You must have moved through them so fast they didn't know what was going on. Then by the time we got here they were expecting the worst and didn't want to go down without a fight. Strange really, almost as though they were too afraid to just surrender.' He shrugged. 'I'm just glad you took out those others, I hadn't thought they'd be so many of them. I'd hate to think what would have happened if we'd come up against the likes of you two as well as the human mercs.'

Tris grinned, then frowned as he remembered, 'and the American, O'Brien?'

The Major visibly relaxed and smiled broadly.

'MI5 descended on them as soon as we came in after you. Apparently they went surprisingly quietly. I've had reports back that they were totting some rather nasty looking hardware. Shame really...I can't imagine who could of tipped them off.'

Garfan's scowl at the mention of the American softened slightly. 'I still think it's a shame we couldn't contrive a meeting between that bigot and the monster we found here. If only he wasn't such a coward.' He looked at the Major intently. 'You know what he had planned for you and your men.'

The Major shook his head. 'Yes, but he wasn't aware of the kinds of friends we have.' He winked in a comradely fashion then looked back towards the end of the room where two of his men were returning from checking out the lift.

'By the way, I noticed that all the others were wearing one of these.' He handed Garfan an iron ring.

'Some kind of emblem?'

Garfan reached into a small pouch on his belt and withdrew the ring he'd taken from the hand of the Revenant. They were a match. 'Something like that.'

The two black clad soldiers came to a halt a few feet away. 'Sir, the lift opens at the basement level at the back of the building into a small room with two very secure camouflaged doors. One would appear to lead back into the building while the other one opens out onto the river. It looks as though there may have been a boat moored there till very recently, there was oil on the water, as well as water splashed up the lower half of the outside of the door and the surrounding wall, I'd guess where some kind of speedboat had turned in a hurry and kicked up the water behind it.'

'Thank you Sergeant, that sounds more than likely, though I doubt the boat was moored there, it would have been too obvious a target, and would have given away the presence of the door. No it's more likely that the boat was summoned from nearby.'

Tristellis nodded. 'That would make sense, and I doubt he would even have needed to use a phone to make that call.'

The major looked at him with puzzlement, wanting to ask him what he meant, but thinking better of it. 'We could call the river police and inform the Coastguard.'

Garfan shook his head wearily. 'No, there's no point. It would be far to dangerous for anyone to try and stop them from going wherever the hell it is they are going. Lets just hope they don't come back.'

Tris grinned. 'Amen to that.'

The Major gestured to his men who immediately moved quickly out of the room towards where the rest of the unit were tidying up. 'Well gentlemen, the building is secure, so it's time for us to disappear. I suggest that you take the opportunity to slip out behind us.' He turned to follow his men. 'I know it's not my place to ask, but one of my men died tonight, and I'd like to know it was for a good reason…was the operation a success?'

Garfan and Tristellis regarded each other. Both of them were buzzing with questions, rather than the answers which usually accompanied the end of something. Garfan turned away, unable to answer, leaving it to Tris to make some sense of it all.

'I wish I could say yes without hesitation Major, but the truth is…I really don't know.'

Epilogue

In the pre-dawn light the post-storm Thames had a feeling of newness, cleanness that wasn't lost on the dark being sat in the prow of the small speedboat. It was cold, but his inner fire warmed him still. Behind him sat his most trusted disciple, the captain of his personal guard. His smile was grim as he bespoke the huge captain.

'Make sure that the right ones find the body, their association with our cousins can be used to our advantage, those meddlers must be made to suffer for their interference. Yet even more importantly they must be led to uncover the traitors for us. Let them lead us to the vipers within our midst.'

The captain nodded to himself, smiling in anticipation of his next meeting with the two Guardians, a meeting which he hoped would see both of them die.

*

To be continued in...'The Brotherhood', the sequel and final chapter in the tale of the Guardians. In which we find Garfan and Tristellis still stunned by the sudden disappearance of their Adversary, and the questions which their confrontation with the ancient being has left them asking. Detective Inspector Stands and his Sergeant Daniel Waves once more become entangled in the Guardians lives when they discover the dead body of an old friend which sparks such a need for vengeance that they may even have to leave the Kingdom in search of the their newest, yet oldest foe.

Made in the USA
Charleston, SC
20 March 2015